PENGUIN BOOKS
FINAL THINGS

John Sligo was born in New Zealand in 1944. After completing his university education at St. John's College, Cambridge, he worked for a time at FAO, United Nations, in Rome, and later as a film and television journalist. His articles and criticisms have appeared in magazines in both Italy and New Zealand.

John Sligo has published two other novels, *The Cave*, which won the New Zealand PEN Award for best first novel, and *The Concert Masters*. He is now a full-time writer with a love of Italian food, Jungian psycho-analysis and gurus.

FINAL THINGS

John Sligo

PENGUIN BOOKS

PENGUIN BOOKS

assisted by the Literature Board of the Australia Council

Penguin Books Australia Ltd,
487 Maroondah Highway, P.O. Box 257
Ringwood, Victoria 3134, Australia
Penguin Books Ltd,
Harmondsworth, Middlesex, England
Viking Penguin Inc.,
40 West 23rd Street, New York, N.Y. 10010, U.S.A.
Penguin Books Canada Limited,
2801 John Street, Markham, Ontario, Canada L3R 1B4
Penguin Books (N.Z.) Ltd,
182-190 Wairau Road, Auckland 10, New Zealand

First published by Penguin Books Australia, 1987

Copyright © John Sligo, 1987

Typeset in Sabon Roman by Meredith Typesetters, Melbourne
Made and printed in Australia by Australian Print Group, Maryborough, Victoria

CIP

Sligo, John, 1944-
Final Things
ISBN 014 009880 1

I. Title

A823'3

Creative writing program assisted by the Literature Board of the Australia
Council, the Federal Government's arts funding and advisory body.

For Annabel Ross
       Hayat Mathews de Madariaga
       Rose Creswell

— a circle closed

A u t h o r ' s   N o t e

The pages of experience are scattered, as Dante noted,
yet joined into a coherence which creates a sense of
trilogy. Characters come and go, interwoven in intention
but not by plot.

There are places in New Zealand called Milton, Dunedin
and Burnham Camp but unfortunately none of these
characters lived there, nor anywhere else, for that matter.

Nel suo profondo vidi che s'interna,
legato con amore in un volume,
cio che per l'universo si squaderna.

La forma universal di questo nodo
credo ch'io vidi, perchè più-di largo
dicendo questo, mi sento ch'io godo

Dante — Paradiso XXXIII

CONTENTS

A New Eden?   1
Going Home   145
Burnham Camp   244

A NEW EDEN?

A NEW EDEN?

1

The world was in a frenzy of mating. Cows in an agony of lust climbed on each other for lack of a bull, birds fought in the air and the Toko River ran in a spate of pure mud as cloudburst followed rainbow. There was a canopy of light that drove the most blind to comment that spring must be on its way, except, in that hemisphere, January was the middle of summer.

In that temperate climate that morning, everything had the appearance of being opened to the weather which unexpectedly arrived from the South Pole and swept through to harass the more important settlement of Dunedin, thirty miles up the road.

True, the houses were solid, yet the only townfolk who came to grips with the current reality were the dead at Tokoiti cemetery who knew, too late, that the main street, the fish-and-chips papers blowing along and wedging around the horse trough, wouldn't survive the reality of a good gale.

But that day Natalia Dashkov woke up feeling more-or-less successfully nationalized.

Why she'd arrived there she didn't know, except it was a place on the map that any refugee, in ignorance and with some means, might have put her finger on. So in 1938 and fresh from Rome

she bought the house in Tokoiti that looked down on Milton
from a small dun hill. She had met Pearse when walking down
the main street for shopping one night. She had worn her Viennese
blouse and silk stockings with a smart gaberdine skirt. There had
been a rebellion at life in Michael Pearse which attracted Natalia
and for which she had a feeling.

When he was off to war, one of the first to enlist and see the
world, she knitted him a balaclava, remembering her mother
telling her this was the thing to do. Mama had knitted for several
of the young men who were staff officers of General Brusilov in
the Austrian Campaign, World War I.

Of course, Pearse was engaged to a distant cousin, Margaret
McClean, and her act was purely friendly. But then it was discovered Margaret had a tubercular spine and post-operation was
left with a hump. Margaret did not visit her acquaintances after
that, or had tried to but found people unused to deformity unless
of the growing, invisible kind. So she had retreated and left the
town wondering how Pearse would feel, if spared, to be saddled
with diseased goods.

Margaret saved him the trouble and wrote a letter in 1940.

Since he was a farmer and would not have mated a prize ram
with a sick ewe (Pearse still felt that way before his own wound),
he accepted with rage and guilt that this was how it must be.
And wondered what love meant anyway.

It was during a spell in Cairo, when he was given his decoration
and promotion, that he remembered the balaclava meant for
some other front and wrote to Natalia and later telegrammed
in mid-1942 that he loved her, after quite a few of his mates had
gone up in smoke and him now a bloody lieutenant.

Natalia, caught in the prison of the town with her father buried
at Tokoiti, knew she could not escape. So, she had driven into
Milton in her 1935 Morris.

The street had been empty at two, the photographer's studio
part of the chemist shop: a room at the back with lights and an
ancient camera on a tripod pointing towards the painted back-
drop of ferns and flowers, that represented the rural gardens and
gracious parks of the Olde World, into which the sitter had
strayed, almost by accident.

Natalia, who knew them as more than a chocolate-box reality, had no time to sneer as she adjusted her large picture hat with the fresh red rose pinned to the ribbon and sat facing the eye. She knew what she would get when Pearse came home and so her lower lip was tremulous, but she carried in her soul so rich a humus that any rose would bloom, so she knew.

'Smile,' said the chemist's assistant as she adjusted the lights to the sitter's best advantage. 'Think of something happy, like the death of Hitler.'

Afterwards, Natalia had parked her car in front of the railway station and walked along the tracks to the Mill Stream. Ahead was a large wooden bridge spanning the Toko River and beyond that on her right the Pearse homestead with its two small, secure gables white in the sun.

Over the rolling hills the gorse bloomed with the wild certainty of victory over the tidier plain. Even the blind must comment on the season and its gold. Not of course 'the golden age', which was arriving with socialist legislation and everyone protected from almost everything except love and death.

She stood with the dust on her good Italian shoes and a train roared past, hooting madly, to the crossing ahead.

She was still standing there, in some part of her mind, when the news came of Pearse's wound and his return with some other men. For them the war had ended and the photo not yet sent, and she peering at the crossing ahead where Mr Pearse's car had been mangled to pulp by another train, along with Mr and Mrs Pearse, just two months before.

The morning of Pearse's return Natalia lay in bed late, reading again a potted biography of Stalin and catching up on the war news from the Geneva and Zurich papers cousin Ariadne had sent her. Then she ran her bath and added some essence of rosemary and considered again the Jewish refugee Ruth Schenkle and her husband.

Ruth had wished her to write to cousin Ariadne in Switzerland; the International Red Cross, she had suggested, could find out about her cousin, the concert pianist Rebecca Weiss. She was the only relative for whom the Schenkles held out much hope. Natalia had written, but not to the International Red Cross. She lolled back and stared down at her twenty-seven-year-old body with its full curves and pleasing softness.

Ruth would be at the station, too, almost due with her first.

Natalia stood up and reached for her towel. Outside the window the Morris Minor was in the drive, brightly polished although she wished it was not black.

She concentrated on the day and its seasonableness and dressed in her silk floral with a picture hat and sunglasses. She used little make-up, unlike Mama, who had had the Russian habit of over-kill in every department.

She kept the windows open to enjoy the warmth.

'It's an exciting day,' she suggested to Dionysius as she free-wheeled down the hill to save her petrol ration.

She parked the car and Dionysius took her arm for the steps. She could feel through the material his thin old bones and this too added to her determination.

In the waiting room, flowers had been arranged and out on the platform some stewed tea stood in an urn.

Someone had painted the weatherboards a fresh buttercup yellow.

Natalia basked and nodded to acquaintances. She looked down to the goods shed where a train was shunting and on to the roundabout where the trains were turned. The line was flat on its way south while north . . . she could see the smoke in the distance.

The Home Guard in their khaki picked up their instruments and breathed deep to give the men a good, rousing tune. The Mayor, podgy and important in his captain's uniform, adjusted his chain of office. Some collies whined and yelped or lolled their tongues; in quick short pants of breath they caught the rhythm of the dun-looking ladies. And had a compensatory scratch.

How small the ladies felt with this train diving into their sight with one easy thrust of power.

Natalia's foreignness rocked, shivered and almost broke through her Miltonian persona. Her eyes unfocused as she saw the cowcatcher and wheels and she held tight to Ruth Schenkle's arm. Both, after all, knew a different dispensation and a different journey to this town. Then, with a belch of steam, an iron crash of wheels, the train came to a stop.

'They look strained,' whispered one lady of the lads looking out of the windows.

Ruth Schenkle and Natalia looked at each other and felt it was the shock of returning.

But the other ladies decided with a collective gush of pity it was their wounds. And Michael Pearse with his Military Cross for some heroic but no-doubt foolish act, although thought the ladies, led by Magga Trout, now with his parents dead he might grow up and stop being a larrikin.

Natalia could not reflect further for the boys, all ten of them, were clambering down from the troop carriages with their kitbags over their shoulders. Only Michael Pearse and a couple of others were from the town, or the next best thing. The others would be dispersed further inland to places much like this, Natalia supposed.

Other travellers ran for the conveniences, having seen all this up the line at Dunedin, where a proper band had played. A few helped themselves to a cup of tea. The train spurted steam and the guard walked along with his iron rod to tap and check the wheels, carriage by carriage.

As Michael Pearse, the ranking officer, dressed the men, the Mayor adjusted his notes, glued on a smile and promised the returning boys a fair deal when it was all over, and a white stone Memorial, already in place, for those who would not return to their dear ones. The Glorious Fallen!

Mrs Fergusson dug him in the ribs. The Mayor got the message and concentrated on King, Country and Hitler and avoided the Japanese who didn't enter much into anybody's calculations, since they hadn't bombed 'Home'.

Looking along the men the Mayor wondered who *had* fallen. There were still too many away and there was too much bunting — not victory bunting, but with a promise of better things to come.

The Presbyterian minister, Bible in hand to remind *them* who *he* was, prayed, close to the ranks. It was also fitting the Anglican vicar should speak, though less fitting, as Magga Trout considered, that the Doolan priest who was always hanging around the convent, as everyone knew, should address the souls of the departed.

The furnace door opened, coal was shovelled in, the fiery sparks belched and whirled; a smoky orange light glared before the door crashed shut again.

Then, from the hospital carriage behind, a stretcher was lowered to the ground, accompanied by a Red Cross nurse, all in wedding white like a nun making her final marriage vows. The nurse had bronze hair which was carefully done up in a bun so that regulations, Natalia supposed, were adhered to. She had mild white skin which had been burned by the sun, or perhaps, thought Natalia, a fire. For a moment as she stood there, the collective eye of the town took her in and remembered.

'It's Alison Black,' whispered Magga Trout, 'that woman who left to nurse the soldiers in Noumea.'

The one who protected the Schenkles and found money to get their business started. The one who was progressive and probably radical. The one who had come from somewhere else and must have been rejected by her family. The one who stood now staring down at the mangled body on the stretcher with a look of angry compassion.

'She's been seconded to the hospital,' whispered Ruth Schenkle, 'to nurse there. She didn't want to return from Noumea. She was bombed out.'

Dionysius observed the nurse and the soldiers staring at her. With their bronze skin and virile glances he could detect no particular mutation produced by their pain. He did not mind their out-thrust jaws waiting for a blow on the chin, nor their beer-swilling and goodwill. He knew fear when he saw it but did not think their decency would save them from themselves.

But he saw them with a backward glance, only nodding at their faces and sweat smell, which blended with the cheap perfume the mill girls wore.

The mill girls, let off early from the morning shift, had arrived for the spectacle, and also, as it turned out, for Pearse, drunk on whisky.

This one warranted attention. Natalia was tensed for flight but Dionysius already knew Pearce was the link in the chain the Russian Revolution had broken. Now it must be repaired in a different way by Natalia.

He took in the tight body standing to attention: the sandy-coloured hair, the Irish blue eyes, the sullen mouth with lines of temper and paradoxical good humour with now a mean cynical look that would become as trusting as a little boy before the wisdom of authority, when he couldn't get around it.

Dionysius looked at his niece, an overblown Georgian rose that any day might turn to fat. She needed the tension he could feel in that thin body of Michael Pearse.

Pearse hardly noticed his future uncle, bloody old crow! He was swimming in a fume of whisky and his throat raw with Park Drive roll-your-owns he'd been smoking solidly since the port of Lyttleton. He was buggered and he knew it. Three deaths were hanging around him on the platform, not to mention Natalia. First his parents, really dead; then Margaret with her golden hair, more red really, blue eyes and shortness of breath when they ran across the home paddock to the river. Sitting looking at the water in her blue wool swimming suit, seeing something he sure as hell didn't see. Panting with the sun and drying her hair and now humpbacked, they said, so dead.

Pearse sniffed and saw old Davie her father bent over his walking stick, a new Harris-tweed jacket on and a pair of old pants that flopped around him with one fly button undone. He'd taken a pee before coming down and Margaret hadn't seen him off; she always checked the old bugger over. Pearse felt a wave of love around him, then pushed it away into the past. He concentrated instead on the memory of that snake in a jar they had on the mantlepiece, with its brown coils and yellow eyes . . . Old Davie had brought it back after a trip to Fiji and used to put it on the table for Sunday dinner – to look at.

Old Davie was pulling himself straight and waving and smiling, trying not to lean too much, holding onto a white pressed handkerchief. That was the only sign of Margaret; she would have slaved over that, having first found the one which would be white and stainless and bare – so he would know she was alive, if not for him.

Jesus! His head was beginning to split open again like an overripe melon. He focussed on Natalia, then weaved on to the imported mill girls who turned their tails up easier than the local talent; spotty faces, white handbags, as if off to a wedding with Father O'Fee giving him the once-over. Hadn't been near the bloody church in years and anyway Margaret was a Presbyterian. And Natalia Orthodox. Made him lapsed or damned. Bugger the lot of them.

He could smell Margaret and her steamy skin odour when she ironed, and the wound on his forehead, red and flowering, grew redder until, with the final clash of 'God Save the King', he toppled over.

The mill girls, who longed for romance and wall-to-wall carpets, shrieked in unison and hoped, for a romantic moment, that he might be dead. They'd not had anything except one Jap submarine sighting over at Crystal's Beach and a couple of abortions. They grouped themselves in a chorus, throats taut, and clutched at their accessories.

Then Natalia made her decision and ran. Alison Black made hers and ran too. Both women met over Michael, face white and breath uneven. They looked at each other as Natalia, remembering the smelling salts, a relic from Mama's regime, fished them out of her handbag. Alison took the soldier's pulse and Natalia held the bottle under his nose.

'Bloody whisky,' one of the soldiers catcalled from the train, but was silenced when it became obvious that Pearse, like a heroine of love stories, was sniffing the smelling salts and reviving.

While he snorted and coughed the train pulled out.

'You are staying?' asked Natalia.

Alison nodded. 'I'm stationed at the war veterans' hospital. More are coming down by ambulance.'

'My name is Natalia Dashkov.'

Alison smiled. 'You're the Russian woman, the friend of Ruth Schenkle. I thought you'd have left by now.'

She glanced at Pearse as the men broke ranks.

The mill girls, damp-eyed and ignored, drifted away like so many hens that had hoped to be pecked towards the altar.

Pearse coughed and stood up.

Outside the station the cars were starting to pull away and the urn was being emptied over the platform.

The national flag hung limp.

Nothing much else stirred either, until some dust blew towards them. Pearse looked at an engine shunting, the shunter jumping onto the cowcatcher and waving the driver on. 'Nothing's changed.'

'Margaret sends her affectionate regards,' called out old Davie and left with Magga Trout.

Natalia and Alison watched while Pearse shut his eyes. He could smell Natalia now, which was better, and could feel in her breath and placid blue eyes strange schemes and unknown re-actions, different from his own straight view of life.

'I've got the phone in,' said Natalia, accepting the inevitable.

Pearse looked down the railway line. 'Come after shopping.'

Natalia remembered it was Friday night and late closing.

Pearse picked up his kitbag and jumped down to the tracks, straddled them for a moment, daring any bloody train, then set out to walk. He didn't look back, just watched the cinders grinding into dust under his boots.

Everything was small – the mill and the Mill Stream smaller after three years; the Toko bridge with its wooden struts, small.

He could look over his land, well enough kept what with a manager and then – Jesus! – the homestead! He climbed over the boundary fence.

'My property now,' he thought, but didn't feel any ownership.

The front gate was off its hinges and the hens had got in.

Down in the orchard some sheep were grazing.

The flowers grew with proprietary assurance around and over the wooden front verandah.

The door was open.

The linoleum floor smelt of polish.

The clock was going on the mantelpiece.

He looked at the phone. They had a new number – 45D, party line.

Time to eat. He reached into his bag for the half-empty bottle of Johnny Walker. Took a swig. Sat down on the old sofa under the orchard window, felt at the covers which were the same, the same cushions. A few tears came, but more snorts and sobs for all the emptiness he could feel soaking into every last nook and cranny. Not even whisky could stop this so he rolled a fag. Then he heard a tap tap on the linoleum and wondered who the hell it was while he wiped at his eyes.

'Hello, Gran,' he said, hiding the bottle under a cushion.

She was dressed up in her best black dress and some brown beads. Her face, thick and heavy, was falling into sags. She nodded to him and came and sat beside him, too old herself to know what grief she could release.

'I'm sorry, sonny boy. I'm sorry.' She heaved herself around to kiss him and hold him in some vaguely remembered embrace of a mother for her son. He smelled her old skin and rubbed against her.

'It's too lonely since they went.' She started to cry in little shallow gasps. 'Why them? Why not me?'

He strained into her, his rangy frame as taut as hers was loose, and the combination comforted them.

'Until you find a wife I'll cook for you.'

She lived just across the line. She must have seen it happen.

'Let's forget,' he said. He helped her up and together they left.

It was still twilight with the moths battering round when he stood close to the mirror over the mantelpiece. 'To you, mate.' Outside a peculiar orange light changed to a violet limpid nothing as night readied itself for the takeover. It played tricks with his head wound so that he seemed to have grown a rare fungus.

He lifted the window sash and an open tin of Dad's tobacco fell onto the flowerbed below. In the paddock beyond some mushrooms had come up with the heavy dew last night.

The air cooled his face while he waited for the eight o'clock express to come along, its light to cut swathes and catch for a moment the brass bedstead and the dark varnished wood of his father's violin.

On the back path the moths were still busy. Over in the home paddock the windbreak of pines he'd planted stood a good ten feet tall, some fourteen by the look of it. His cigarette burned down to his lip and he spat it onto a clump of cow-pad green grass.

He shambled back through the fallen logs, rotten full of hu-hu grubs, and then he was where he had intended to be . . . but could only be if he arrived without thinking of it.

The rubber tyres had perished and the front-left side buckled in, rusting in gashes and cracks. He approached timidly, touching the crushed steel, the dust, the dried blotches on the seats which were all he had left of them. The windows were broken, the windshield smashed, the steering wheel just a mess of spokes with the shaft crooked. It had driven through Dad and smashed his heart to pulp. He leaned over and tried the horn, knowing it couldn't work. He sat on the running board and rubbed his cheek against a hank of canvas. Weeds grew around the wheels but everything was going to be allowed to do what it liked. The birds could nest or the chooks lay eggs here. Maybe a tree would seed and grow and, Pearse, the energy building tighter and tighter, picked himself up in a rage, kicked the chassis, and stumbled back along to the verandah where she used to sit on the top step doing some knitting.

'Natalia's different,' he said to the shade of his mother on the step — click, clickity click. Mum was wearing a brown cardie to keep off the damp. 'She's not like us, she's Russian. Natalia says she hasn't got any home but here. She's just got Milton. She wrote that her father's buried here so she'll stay. "Milton," she says, "must have been totally worthy of his speechless last days." I suppose when you have a stroke you don't feel obliged to be interested in anyone.'

He went to the bathroom and peed. The talk had made him as clear as a bell. The bathroom was just the same as you were always in it by yourself anyway with the glass window that was Victorian, deep blues and browns and someone on a horse with night and the delineating lead holding the pieces together. He stood where he was, his dick hanging out, and dreamed, then washed his feet in the basin. Mum had hated smelly feet.

Natalia would be coming at nine. Pearse was outside again, clear as a bell, when he saw her lights on the road, her car kicking up dust past Sanders', so she was on him almost, now moving slow as he had hoped she would do. Stopping at the crossing. He could see her blonde head peering up the line in case there was another goods train with a light failure. Nothing to south, nothing to north. The car mounted the tracks up and down like a boat breasting waves and across onto the track that stopped at Pearse's farm.

He knew he must run towards her, even though he'd taken off his shoes and socks to feel the grass between his toes under the first apple tree of the orchard. But the long grass round him was a sea with the sharp smell of a hemlock that he'd have to root out. So he lay where he was. She saw him as she turned the car and switched off the lights. She came over, stopping to take off her high heels and put them into her shopping bag. As he waited a strange desolation spread from his loins to his heart. Natalia was wearing a hat of velvet and straw with a rose and a smart dress of silk, full of the moon, the lights of the town over there past the mill, the perfume she was anointed with. They sat together and held hands, the fronds touching her nose and the seeds catching on her hair.

'Natalia?' Pearse asked.

She nodded and sighed to herself, took off her hat and then

threw it away from them so it wouldn't get crushed by what now must happen.

He lowered her into the grass, into the smell of it, while she could look at the small hard green apples that hadn't ripened yet. She hoped this was destiny. Why otherwise throw away your hat? She welcomed it anyway whether it was or not as she welcomed his attentions which would put a final shape to her life.

He fumbled with her underclothes but she wouldn't help him: the moon was golden and too delicious a fruit to give up eating.

'We will be husband and wife,' he assured her when she gasped with the pain he caused. He stopped then to kiss her breasts which he had freed and ran his hands around them to get their shape, muddled up with the dress as her hands were muddled up in his pants and shirt. He was part of her centre and how she had been left unattended for twenty-seven years surprised her.

She could no longer see him because his lips were over her eyes and she felt the division between them which she had not known before. She was alive in her isolation and her fear that this moment could not last. The space must be crossed.

Pearse came into her like an artery suddenly cut.

He felt her sighing under him and her lungs filled.

Later he put on his underpants and went to the house for a glass so that she could drink whisky with him.

She lay, her long blonde hair freed of pins and spread across the grass, her dress grass-stained, she smiling. As they toasted their love a star fell across the drapery of sky and disappeared.

Natalia opened her weak blue eyes wider. 'It got burned up on the way to our planet, like people. So many burned up, Dionysius says.'

Her voice was soft and confiding and Pearse was pleased, although suspecting that such softness might provoke in him the wish to kick.

They went to the homestead where she could look through the rooms which were now hers to arrange. She went with him to the car his parents had been killed in and she shuddered. Then she sat at the wheel of her own car while he cranked it for her. 'I knew,' he said, panting with the effort, 'that you'd have me.'

'We'll make a good garden,' she promised. 'Gooseberries, blackcurrants, redcurrants. I'll make wine. I have a recipe book.'

Her eyes were vague with future plans as she drove off, hardly giving him a second glance. She must ring Alison Black, at once, and offer friendship. Both she and Pearse, sensed Natalia, would need Alison in the years ahead.

2

The wedding, thought Alison to the new day, was almost on them.

Like two girlfriends, she and Natalia had talked late after getting to bed.

Natalia had heard yesterday from her cousin Ariadne in Geneva, who had discovered where Rebecca Weiss was. Perhaps, thought Alison, a camp like those the British had set up in the Boer War.

Natalia had been dithering over a pleat and her bouquet.

'Do you think hyacinths will do with rose silk? Or roses, pink and red from the garden?' She had examined the pleats again. 'I will ring Ruth Schenkle after the fitting.'

'What does Ariadne say?'

'Ariadne? That the place is Ravensbruck and the Germans insist she is there for her own protection.'

'Then it can't be so bad.' Alison adjusted the recalcitrant pleat.

'Who do you protect a great artist from?'

Alison sat back on her haunches and rocked for a moment. The air for some reason felt cold.

'Who would *we* be protected from,' continued Natalia, 'if that happened – here?'

Alison picked at a freckle on her leg. 'I don't know.'

Natalia exhaled some air. 'They might learn new habits here as the Germans have. It would be a way of fencing off their own minds.'

'Could human beings do that here?' asked Alison.

'Why not?'

'In a camp?'

'Apparently,' said Natalia giving up, 'the SS are quite acceptable.'

'SS?'

'The Hitler storm troopers. The SS run the camps, or some of them. Now they are sending vast quantities of gold to Zurich.'

'It must be stolen.' Alison noted a spot on her uniform and was irritated.

'Most likely extracted from people in the camps, blackmailed, I suppose, into giving up their wealth. Ariadne knows since her lover is a Swiss banker. Mama always said that Ariadne would incline towards unfortunate liaisons.'

'How could they take . . . the gold?'

'Neutral!' Natalia pirouetted on the Persian carpet and let the fashionable ankle-length dress swirl around her in a cloud of pure joy. 'The only enemies for the Swiss are lack of hygiene and of money. The SS gives joy to whatever takes the place of the heart in the Swiss national breast. They have even invented numbered accounts so that no one will know which sturmbahnführer has taken advantage.'

'That's capitalism for you,' said Alison.

Natalia stripped to her bra and girdle and Alison carefully draped the dress on a clothes horse. Wrapping herself in her dressing gown, Natalia seized Alison's arm and together they executed a smart enough gavotte.

'I've written to a German, Alison,' said Natalia, catching her breath, 'a beau from my Rome days. Hans von Leinon, a great friend of Adam von Trott und Zu. Ariadne will post it on. I have said that he must help Rebecca and ease her confinement. God knows, both Adam and Hans adored Rebecca. They played her all the time. And Hans was inspired to write me a love poem after listening to her Chopin.'

'Germans?' Alison was aghast.

'Yesterday's friends, tomorrow's friends. Neither were Nazis,' said Natalia. 'Like myself and Russia, we keep up our acquaintance.'

Alison sniffed.

'What would you do, Alison, if you found your country agreeing to war and plunder? Did your ancestors disagree when New Zealand was, after all, taken by force from the Maoris? Or did the Australians disagree when they massacred the Aboriginal people? Of course not. And now Germany is doing the same and the only offence to the Europeans is that they want European land. Which is not allowed since, against the rest, they *all* see themselves as the Master Race. In just the same way, I have read, as the early New Zealanders talked about Aryan destiny in the prospectuses they put out to attract new colonists.'

Alison considered the problem, grim-lipped.

'The only just cause,' added Natalia, remembering her biography of Stalin, 'is the class struggle. The workers of the world, who will end all exploitation.' Natalia grimaced slightly at the prospect.

'I have read quite a lot,' said Alison, 'but don't understand this yet.'

'It comes from isolation, not understanding.' Natalia pecked her friend on the cheek. 'Not seeing history and races at work with each other.

'And,' added Natalia, outdoing herself, 'I am pregnant. Michael and I became lovers the night he returned from war. It was like Tolstoy – like – André, under an apple tree.'

Alison melted with the news and the two women held each other.

'You, of course, must be godmother. And if a girl we will give her your name.'

'My second name,' said Alison unexpectedly, 'Charlotte! I never liked Alison.' She licked her finger and lifted off an eyelash from Natalia's eye. 'I've always felt Charlotte was my real self.'

'It is a war of empires,' added Natalia. 'And it is only accident that one represents freedom and the other tyranny. Except, Ariadne suspects the Germans have been possessed!'

'The Americans,' said Alison, 'know it's about empires. It is all sort of straight with them. The intelligent ones, I mean. They believe in money. Some of them talk already of how Japan will be when they take it over, for their markets.'

'Carl Jung,' pontificated Natalia to make her second point clear, 'who has analysed Ariadne, says the Germans have resurrected their pagan past and are living again in the woods of Wotan. He says they are no longer European men.'

'That seems ridiculous,' said Alison, as Dionysius wandered in. 'What do you think, Father?'

Natalia had suggested plain Dionysius, but Alison was not one to push too far.

Dionysius sat down on the sofa and rocked for a moment in thought. 'It will bring its fruits elsewhere. When madness is acceptable, men lock themselves into a room and do what they want to one another. Whole countries or a small town can become a locked room. And it will spread. In Russia, Alison, the pogroms were much loved. Blood lust only needs a theology for men to agree to it. It is, I imagine, exciting for them. And, drinking blood, I dare say they then become something new.'

Alison laughed her high laugh that sounded as if it might shatter crystal. 'Yesterday we had to amputate the leg of the boy I brought down by train just a month ago.' She looked at Natalia's wedding dress with a kind of yearning, as if, like a relic, it offered some saint's protection. 'Anyway, we're all safe here and progress will look after us all.'

'Perhaps.' Dionysius picked up Natalia's kitten, a present from Pearse. He said nothing else and it was rather disconcerting.

In the silence, Alison busily picked up pins and suggested a cup of tea. The next morning she still found that silence disconcerting as she leaned over and studied Natalia's face, so unlike her own yet so close to her in spirit.

At least Ruth would be relieved to know her cousin was in some privileged capacity in the camp. Presumably not comfortable, but safe.

Alison gently shook Natalia into wakefulness and got out of bed to make the breakfast which Natalia would have in bed, as a special treat.

The news of the wedding had been gossip for days and the large Austin moving slowly along the main street, searching for the turn-off to Tokoiti, was confirmation that the foreign woman and Michael Pearse were the first of the war weddings.

Muriel Fieschi had brought her twins with her. George was being amorous with his twin brother Nicholas, who giggled at the sloppy kisses he was receiving.

'It seems,' said Bertie, 'that Alison will settle here, with her new friends. And open a dress shop.'

'I wonder,' asked Mu, 'whether your cousin has told them about, well, you know what.'

Bertie scratched at his moustache, 'Alison has probably matured with the war.'

'I consider,' said Mu, 'that her mother was to blame with her suffragette activities. All of those things affect a girl and leave her with unsuitable thoughts. Not to mention Henry, always into whisky.'

'She will probably settle down,' said Bertie.

Mu was mollified. 'There was something, well, threatening, about Alison, from what I remember. One felt she was always *judging* people.'

'Alison did not have an easy childhood.'

'But has made good with the war,' Mu decided, to be positive. 'The experience has no doubt changed her for the better.' She glanced around. 'But why would she want to settle here?'

'Perhaps it is the challenge?'

Mu snapped open her powder compact and checked her face.

Pearse was properly in love, there was no doubt of it, decided Alison. Dressed in his father's best suit and the McCloud tartan tie, he looked as scared as a new boy at school. Natalia, in rose with pearl earrings and a large lace picture hat, stood beside him.

For reasons of the war there were no attendants and the informal gathering of twenty had chatted while Bertie Fieschi fixed up the necessary forms to be signed.

With the long drapes swelling in the breeze, and perfume of roses from the verandah, it did have, thought Mu Fieschi, a refreshing strangeness about it. Perhaps Chekhovian. She decided to remember the remark when congratulating the bride and groom.

Pearse had had a bachelor's night down at the farm and was slightly worn and had lost no time, as Magga Trout noted, in deserting poor Margaret McClean, her neighbour. Maybe it had been him lurking late last night outside, in the garden, but not knocking on the window, thus probably one of those mill workers. A Peeping Tom at the wrong house, since Margaret would be no feast for the eyes, in or out of her underwear.

Alison sat down at the piano and began playing some incidental music.

Bertie Fieschi cleared his throat and Pearse fished for Natalia's wedding ring.

The door was open into the kitchen where Ruth and Chaim stood.

The service was short, the papers signed.

Alison wound up the gramophone and Dionysius returned, dressed in his golden robes. The two candles were lit. Dionysius placed an ancient leather book on the table, and opened it while Natalia and Pearse knelt.

Alison placed the steel needle on the record and found her eyes prickling with tears as the deep voices of the Paris Orthodox Cathedral wound through the polyphony of the wedding anthem. Hurriedly, she turned the record over.

Natalia held Pearse's hand tightly and he, coached in the few words he had to say, replied when Natalia gave him the look. The blessing was offered and Natalia crossed herself from left to right, with Pearse after a startled glance – they hadn't told him about that – trying the same himself.

'Let us pray,' said Dionysius in English, 'for the happiness of the married couple before us and for the peace of the world here and in the countries where war has come.'

As if they had been deprived of some experience which the old man, Alison and Pearse, not to mention Natalia, knew about.

But it all put Natalia Pearse into a category by herself; a refugee with some money, and titled. The magistrate's wife was wetting her lips, prior to discourse with a social equal.

Alison Black stood tight and straight, talking with the lawyer, both straining towards a temporary truce, Alison's long white fingers playing nervously with the stem of the glass.

'Isn't it good,' said Natalia to them both. 'The Mayor is tipping Pearse for a seat in parliament. His being a hero I expect.'

Mr Fieschi made some classical allusions and mentioned that both Russia and New Zealand had the greatest *levée en masse*.

Outside, the placid landscape accepted the tribute while Natalia's grey kitten washed itself and enjoyed the peace of the late morning.

'A charming occasion,' said Mu Fieschi, who'd done a season in London and had noted the signed photograph of Tsar Nicholas as well as a silver samovar she had her eye on. She favoured Alison with a bright glance and went to talk with the old woman, Pearse's grandmother, sagging in brown silk.

'Well,' said Ruth Schenkle in the kitchen, over the crayfish mornay, 'Rebecca is safe.'

'Safe?' Chaim mocked her with his eyes. 'Safe? In Germany?'

'Perhaps we exaggerate, Chaim?'

'Exaggerate?'

Ruth sat down suddenly, her face white. 'It's started, Chaim. This time!'

'That's no exaggeration!' Chaim smiled in triumph.

'The fish mornay,' said Ruth, being helped through the door by Alison and Natalia, 'will be ready in ten minutes.'

3

Natalia had a strong pelvis with broad hips and both were now in use as the pains grew more frequent. So frequent that nurse had given up timing the space between them as she and Natalia prepared for the child. Which must be coming, with Natalia's nightdress pulled over her stomach.

Alison, dressed in her uniform, held her friend's hand.

Natalia was not put off by her nakedness. She gripped the bed frame and looked as if she'd crush the brass as she rocked it in her storm. The doctor had turned out the kero lamp nurse had lit – on mother's insistence, as if, thought nurse, electric light wasn't good enough for this lady. Natalia's startled blue eyes pierced for a moment the mist around the crucifix she'd hung up near the painting of her mother.

The doctor grasped the forceps.

The bag had long burst so the baby must come.

The grey light of the early dawn was penetrating, the radio on, down in the kitchen:

'Blue Moon, Wha! Wha!
Now I'm no longer alone, Wha! Wha!

Without a dream in my heart, Whaaaaa!
Without a love of my own.'

Nurse called from the door to turn it off while mother dilated larger and larger into this morning. Today would be her child's birthday. Her son's birthday. Oh, she knew that, she told Alison, as she tossed around on the sheets.

Pearse, waiting in the kitchen with Gran and Uncle Dionysius, had put on pots of boiling water until the midwife had laughed at him and said that only happened in the films. Pearse surreptitiously picked his nose and with red-rimmed eyes glared out at the new day; nervy too, what with all the screams and moans that Natalia made. 'A real one for letting go,' the nurse had said when she phoned the doctor since this was a first birth and the mother not as young as some.

Pearse shivered. It was worse than being shelled. He'd had a few whiskies and Dionysius had had one with him before withdrawing into his meditations, his old eyes opening and shutting placidly while he roamed with his prayers through the night.

At least the kitchen stove was on and the fire lit in their bedroom. She'd wanted flames, not the old kero heater, and he'd obliged, as he had with the other little things she'd taken a fancy to: raspberries out of season, no less.

Dionysius stopped praying as he saw the dawn-capped clouds reflected onto the oak table still covered with Mrs Pearse senior's oilcloth. The child would be born in the light. He peered at Michael Pearse with his best suit on.

'Whata you think he'll be?' said Pearse. Gran got on with snoozing.

Dawn grew heavier. The dew, thick against the windowpane, forced its way into light and water with the heavy reds of the day. Wet weather. He stood up to get closer to his land, found the old man had joined him, and, in a rare comradely action, supported himself with his arm around his nephew's shoulders. 'You are a good man,' said Dionysius with that thick Russian accent. Pearse sized up the potato patch. 'One good frost and they'll be ready to dig,' he said and jumped. Natalia was making a last effort through the pain, and they heard in the kitchen, muffled by the new green velvet drapes in the hall, a thin high cry followed by a lustier bellow.

'It is a boy,' said the old man. 'Our family go first to men.'

Pearse made for the open door, blundered up the hall with the old wallpaper they'd not got around to changing. Their bedroom door was ajar. And he saw her. Legs still high apart, her white thighs bloody that he liked to bite, the veins on her legs pushed out, her stomach floppy.

The child was in the arms of Alison while doctor cut the cord. The kid wriggled and bellowed again. Covered in hair!

'Jesus,' said Pearse, the whisky reasserting itself. 'It's like a bloody monkey.'

'Put wood on the fire, Michael,' Natalia said. 'It may get cold, the snow on the ground.' She was dazed and flying over foreign territory.

'And Mama's Requiem!' moaned Natalia. She came back to herself. Familiar objects were reasserting their place but she held out her arms, limp like a heroine from Tolstoy, and pulled the child slimy and messy against her breasts. She, with her hair drenched in sweat.

Alison looked as if she'd been through it herself.

Then midwife Taylor told him to leave so that she and Alison could tidy up mother and wash baby in some warm water. So the water on the stove was some use after all. He'd kept a couple of pots on despite the old bag.

Nurse Taylor caught on to his thoughts. 'We'll use *your* water now, Mr Pearse,' she said and gave a bright professional Plunkett Nurse smile.

And pop goes the weasel, thought Pearse sourly.

'You are a father,' she called down the hall to him, as consolation prize for not being a mother.

He let her voice drown in the soft green velvet drapes.

The child sucked. And started to grow.

Alison, face pouched with the effort she and Natalia had put in, came down for a cup of tea. On her white uniform were some spots of blood from Natalia's afterbirth.

Pearse turned on the radio and caught the early news. It seemed the allies had invaded Italy.

The old priest baptized the male baby naked in a tub of water, according to the Orthodox rite.

Alison was godmother along with two cousins in Europe for whom Chaim and Ruth Schenkle stood in as surrogates.

The Miltonians were part scandalized by the garish rite and the chanting as well as incense and candles. What was worse, it took place in the kitchen with that haphazard elegance for which Mrs Pearse junior was becoming noted. What with the Russian-New Zealand Friendship Society which she and Alison Black had started, and blackmailing the mill manager into getting together clothing to be sent off from Wellington to Moscow! But with Churchill in cahoots with the Russians, nothing could be said for the moment.

The child was lowered into the iron washing tub and christened, after oil, salt and other elements were sprinkled over him, Benedict Alexander David Nicholas Dashkov Pearse.

The town gaped when told of the number of names, which had about them an anti-democratic ring, and of Mrs Natalia Pearse rattling off the responses to the prayers in Russian. It was peculiar and boded ill for the child who would not be content with his place which they were already determined to show him.

They gazed grim-lipped at the jewelled cross on Dionysius' chest as well as the new magistrate and his wife Mu from Dunedin. Not to mention the Schenkles with their baby Karl.

4

'"Brighter than a Thousand Suns," so they say. First exploded at Alamogordo on 16 July. And dropped on Hiroshima, 6 August, and Nagasaki, 9 August. And yesterday Japan surrendered. August the 15. The war is over. Over with Germany, 7 May,' chanted Pearse in triumph. 'And now we can get on with things.'

'Michael,' said Natalia. 'Even if you contest the conservative seat, Alison and I will not support you. Nor Ruth.'

'Well, bugger you lot!' Pearse kicked off his gumboots. 'And it's not conservative, it's National.'

'Same thing.' Natalia glanced at Benedict, her future ally, exactly two years old and walking.

'I expect, Natalia, support,' said Michael, picking up his cup of tea, his hands dirty from the sheep's dags shorn off their bums for easier birthing.

Natalia's hand went to her belly. The new child was three months on the way.

'One will support, Michael, but one must be true to one's beliefs.'

'The trouble is, with this war, you women think you more

than run the place.' Pearse was feeling belligerent. 'But what about me?'

'It will help civilization,' decided Natalia, 'to know your wife is independent. Not of the pavlova and cream-puff brigade.'

'And Alison, addressing meetings of those mill girls for your society. Next she'll be turning them towards strikes and demands?'

'Why not, Michael?' asked Natalia. 'The Russian Revolution depended on women like the mill girls.'

'Oh, yeah? What did they do? Wave their bloomers at the Tsar?'

Natalia tried for a bit of pre-revolution dignity. 'They fought at the barricades and were part of the "spirit" of things. And, Pearse, don't forget Lenin's wife.'

'And you ran away?' Pearse slurped on his tea to annoy, 'since you lot would have been executed. They didn't want you, Natalia, nor Dionysius.'

Dionysius glanced at the paper to confirm what he knew already.

'"Brighter than a thousand suns". A travesty,' he murmured a moment later.

'Of what?' asked Pearse, who found trouble in concealing his intelligence with the old man.

'It refers, Michael, to the light of God. The quotation comes from the Vedas or perhaps the *Bhagavadgita*.'

'Oh, yeah,' said Pearse.

'Yes, Michael,' said the old man, tranquil in his knowledge. 'It is even symbolic, this atomic bomb. The energies, Michael, have been known by the saints and mystics. This energy, now unleashed, is like an anti-illumination. It appears as vision and reality to those bound in matter. It is their Christ, their truth.'

'Truth,' said Michael sourly but feeling depressed, as Pilate had.

'Simple things, child,' said Dionysius, not in the least put off by the façade which Pearse felt he needed. 'This energy was always inherent in the human mind as is the other, from which this newspaper quotation from Indian scripture comes.'

'Well,' said Pearse, 'today we dedicate the RSA club.'

'What?' asked Dionysius, less versed in temporal matters.

'The Returned Servicemen's Association.'

'I am not going,' said Natalia. 'There has already been a war to end all wars. The First World War. I refuse to attend the negation of that sentiment. It is simply encouraging fools to try again.'

'Get off me back,' said Pearse, understanding perfectly. 'I'm only a human being. Anyway, with all your dialectic and talk of the proletariat, you don't seem to have found the answer. It's more like you and Alison are simply in rebellion. Maybe from being women.'

Nellie, the year-old bitch, batted her tail in agreement, already convinced of her powers.

Pearse lit a roll-your-own.

Natalia was half convinced.

'Tell me, Michael, would the electorate not wish for a thinking woman?'

'Dunno,' said Pearse, and got on to important news. 'Five of the ewes have got problems with their private parts. I had to tie them up. Otherwise, they'd been trailing them. Dunno either if they'll make lambing – like that.'

Natalia was not to be intimidated. 'After what has happened in Germany, as I have *translated* for you from the Geneva and Zurich papers! Even if we are at the end of the world, surely what has happened must connect,' she said in triumph, 'like the private exposed parts of your ewes with their wombs?'

'I've gotta get ready for the ceremonies,' said Pearse. 'We've got to remember five local boys who didn't make it back.'

'As well as the Rugby Club,' added Natalia, 'who will take off with the peace. How many goals, Pearse, will be scored today?'

'Dunno,' said Pearse with that flat Miltonian accent, 'but they've arranged a good lunch and then we'll just amuse ourselves.'

'So be it,' said Natalia, picking up Benedict, 'but remember your responsibilities.'

'Okay,' said Pearse, amiable. And bent over to kiss his son. 'I'll do me best, by my lady wife.'

'Merde!' said Natalia.

'What?' asked Pearse.

'And so,' orated Alison, her flaming red hair in a permanent wave, 'we have a duty, as women, to the peace. War, girls, has always begun with men. No woman has ever declared war.'

'Must have been some,' objected one of her audience.

'Perhaps a queen or two,' agreed Alison.

'And how do you think we'll get the money for the Working Girls' Club?'

'We can apply for grants,' said Alison, 'to the government. Equally, now that the war is over, business is as usual and you women are essential to the smooth running of the mill, I am sure your union will be prepared to support you. And I'm sure the management will take the point.'

In the distance they could hear the band playing.

Alison glanced around the mill tearoom. The tables were stained with cup rings. Some old biscuits had been left on a plate. On the walls were a few paintings done at the evening class Natalia ran.

'We may not be many,' Alison told her audience of fifteen, 'but in the mill there are two hundred women, and most like us are single. Together we can accomplish reform.'

The girls ground out their cigarettes and picked up their coats. Their faces were white and some had spots. Alison decided the next talk would be on diet and exercise. The local proletariat seemed to lack the essential conditions that Lenin had listed: class-consciousness, anger, revolutionary awareness.

'We like the dresses in your shop, Alison,' one mentioned. 'The girls reckon its the best fashion in town.'

They walked out together to the new tarseal.

Ahead, on the main street, was the temporary wooden dais. The buffet lunch had already taken place and Alison could see

Pearse in his best suit, wearing his war ribbons and medals, sitting next to the Mayor.

Alison shepherded the girls together.

The Mayor was finishing his short speech on the heroism of the men. 'And,' he said, 'we'll make sure that the boys get the attention they deserve.'

'And,' called out Alison, flaming angry, 'what about the women? I don't notice the women who fought on the platform. I don't notice an invitation for the nurses to join the RSA.'

'War is mainly men's work.'

But no one dared to heckle Alison, since she too had won a medal for her gallantry. 'Anyway,' said the Mayor, 'there is only one of you here who has actually seen service.'

The mill girls, confused, clapped.

Alison pushed her way out and left them to it.

The warring was over, so Pearse knew, following her proud back. He thought then of his parents through the beer fumes and looked at the Rugby banner waving in the breeze beside the flags of Great Britain, Australia and New Zealand. By now the wood would have rotted away and they would have subsided into each other, bone on bone, flesh on flesh, together at last, as he and Natalia would be one day.

Pearse blew his nose sentimentally.

His own flesh, he admitted, was showing its cracks earlier than expected. It might be that the head wound had affected his lungs – or Natalia.

At least the atomic bombs had ended the Yellow Peril for the time being, as the Mayor had pointed out.

Who knew? When he saw a really beautiful sunset flooding into the plain, with the ice-cold air building kingdoms and palaces of clouds above his ploughed paddocks, he thought that had caused his cynicism, since he didn't hate anyone that much.

The ceremony ended. Pearse and the boys piled back into the half-finished clubroom and had a drink or two with the Mayor and councillors. They were driven out at three by the painters, their balls tight with the memories of Egyptian whores, Roman and Neopolitan girls and matrons only too willing for a few cigarettes or a bar of chocolate.

Tired by the war more than the town, they wandered up the road. They scuffled paper in the gutter and stood at the gate by the Rugby Club.

No markets with stink and bustle, bright trays with colours, cooking smells, roasting goat and couscous.

Young Angus and Terry, both Rugby hopefuls, were along, and Angus, catching the mood, farted.

Pearse grinned.

They stopped at Maxwell's corner to light up fags.

Angus and Terry discussed Rugby prospects. Pearse went blank. Not even sand or a burned out tank, he thought. Too much bloody green grass, too much water!

They grew moody and shuffled slower past the Anglican Church, dedicated by Bishop Selwyn on his way to the gold rush back in 1866. Pretty though, with the daffs that would be out in Spring.

They sat down in Chaim Schenkle's new milk bar; six partitions, plastic tablecloths which were the new thing, Worcester sauce, salt and pepper for the pie eaters, a glass rack with sandwiches, and Chaim.

The kids had thrown stones on the roof, so Pearse had heard. They'd taunted him: 'German Sausage, Sauerkraut. What are ya gettin' up to with the radio set. Signalling old Hitla!' So had yelled the boys and girls, much relieved to be part of the war effort, while some of the more mature ladies and gentlemen had looked suspicious ... until Natalia Dashkov had written her letter, Alison seen clergymen, and both threatened a scene.

Chaim Schenkle could hardly believe they didn't know what a Jew was. His happiness had been tempered by caution, and when he found out what the camps had finally done ...

Pearse knew about them and told the boys: 'Those bloody abbatoirs!' And Ravensbruck not a restful place for Rebecca Weiss.

Chaim tried to smile at them all, after Pearse had finished his recital and they all brought an extra sandwich to show support. As he was to do for many years, Chaim said Kaddish under his breath to keep his balance, for all the Schenkles and Rosenbaums and Weisses.

'Blessed be His Holy Name.

'*Agata*, blessed be His Holy name.

'*Emmanuel*, blessed be His Holy name.

'*Franz*, blessed be His Holy name.

'*David*, who had won military decorations for fighting in the first war, as a true German.

'*Rebecca*, the star of the firmament, who must have perished in the flames. *Rebecca . . .*'

He wandered around chatting with the boys, mixing at times the prayers with sandwich fillings, with his heart and his wounds.

'Didn't you know what *they* did to *them*?' asked Pearse to young Angus and Terry. 'Don't they teach you kids anything at school these days. It wasn't just petrol rationing for them!'

So they left, looking respectful, and arrived at the Chinese fruiterers: Mr Wong and Mr Ling were relics of the gold rush, or their honoured ancestors were.

Young Angus sang mockingly, with a swagger and threat of peace to be disturbed:

'My name Sing Sing,
Come from a China,
In a velly big ship
Come along here,
Wind flow velly high
Kick up a bubbely,
Make poor Chinaman feel velly Queer!'

In the days of the Rush Mr Wong Senior had worked over the leavings at Gabriel's Gulley and had found enough gold for a local Mrs Wong and another Mrs Wong who was number-one wife in Canton.

The Chinese fruiterers stood out in the sun, canvas aprons over their portly bellies, grinning amiably and chopping their fine sets of porcelain teeth at the light.

The boys stood while Pearse poked at the cabbages, tested the turnips, looked inside at the fruit and a wind thing that tinkled crystal chimes, the dark interior beyond which no one penetrated, hidden by a red brocade curtain with vegetable stains and mud on the bottom.

But beyond? He craned his neck to see as the wind lifted an edge of the curtain and passed through, for back there he heard another tinkle of glass leaves. Pearse waited, suddenly hot, for the Chinese fruiterers.

The boys walked on, rooting about in their private memories of smells and feelings and colours they had built up through the war; remembering the most intimate habits, the most peculiar desires that whores and bazaars brought out, which could become part of the compost of their friendships – had there been no Chinamen with their yellow faces. What did they get up to behind the brocade curtain?

Magga Trout, weighty and full of the town gossip, which under the needs of her customers was maturing into town wisdom, took a squint, touched at her brown and yellow-streaked hair and felt a saying cracking open. She hopped around the oak counter, dragging the ball of white wool behind her on the floor, needles in front of her belly – divining. She sniffed to herself and dragged the wool up to her bosom and speared the ball with the needles; decided on judgement. That Michael Pearse with the foreign Russian girl from Europe. Not to mention Alison Black he was reputed to see – in private.

The saying was in place: 'Happy in war, unlucky in love.'

The boys were down at the horse trough and looking towards the hotel and the days that were ahead. All they wanted was fun, something to do as the time sped by and they started work, what with weddings coming and going, in and out, hoping that dose of clap never came back, though they said it didn't with the penicillin drug; with hard heads pressing into, pushing and thrashing, forgetting scented houris in the hurry to spear this piece of Miltonian flesh, too bloody compact, and these small hotel bedrooms dripping confetti like manna on the Luxed carpets with some blood on the sheets – sometimes.

Then because it was hot, someone fetched a peter of home-brew and they walked along the narrow track between the north-bound and the southbound lines. Two trains hurtling at them; it was enough to make Pearse feel five again, almost peeing his pants with excitement as the trains bore down, then the wheels, the rush of wind, the passage, steam spouting and the faces of people going somewhere.

They sunbathed by the river. High up. A pretty little spot with a willow.

One ex-soldier crouched, spear-in-hand in the rushes, waiting for an eel. The others drank the home-brew and snoozed, tan half gone except on their faces, scratching at themselves and belching, dreaming of the clouds in the desert. The melon tits of Araby, the musk and cedar!

Pearse lay shading his eyes and looking across the water to his river paddock, then slipped into the shallows to cool off, in what was, after all, water flowing through his land — one bank his, anyway.

The water gushed by him as he walked upstream, picking up the thick streaming weed and covering his head and loins with it; out into the grass patch, belly thrust out, head thrust into the sun, arms tensed like a windmill.

While his friends gaped at him his lungs caught the sun's breath, and in easy long strides he capered about, his balls bouncing.

'Remember the brass trays,' he chanted, 'all them bloody colours, those designs!' Through which the eye itself was caught into a vanishing point.

He danced for that and the morning when he was still a good runner in the desert near Gaza where the sky gripped like a scarab at the earth. Night was pumping from one element to another, a subtle bloodstream, and old men told stories in an incomprehensible glottal singsong, and yet he understood as the hands of the night pumped, the heart pumped against the body while the flush of veins around the horizon extended up until he himself shot out of the night and became a ball of fire with the camp a mile behind.

The others watched with a single face while Pearse came to and belched loudly with embarrassment, looking at his half erect cock throbbing with the desert life. He slunk back and lit a roll-your-own.

It was over, except for the trials for the first fifteen.

Pearse leaned over, coughed and spat out a glob of phlegm into the green grass, and something closed over in him. He could feel it like a knife in his chest cutting out something. He didn't resist for how could he? But he opened his eyes and saw things. 'Silly lot of buggers!' He roared and grabbed for the peter of home-brew, glugged and belched and lay back.

And each year he'd go to the service they'd hold for the Victories: 1914-18; 1939-45. The white obelisk was already holding in one embrace the living and dead on the same stone. It being white and veinless, the Miltonian ladies could safely swoon over it. While Pearse could swagger and march in his medals.

Pearse wandered about in his interior house. There it was twilight, with moths battering round, cobwebs needed dusting off in the bedroom they slept in. Outside it was a peculiar orange light, like whisky or pee, changing to a grey-violet limpid nothing as night readied itself for the takeover. In the front room he stood close to the mirror which was over the mantlepiece. 'To you, mate,' he said. The smell here was of his parents: his mother was lavender still dried in a vase; his father a tin of tobacco. He picked up the dirk with the cairngorms studded along the hilt and the shoe buckles used by a Davie Pearse at the Battle of Culloden. There was a view of Loch Lomond and a miniature of Bonnie Prince Charlie that Gran had painted while a little girl. The bulb had gone in the light, so he had to stay in the dark with the two brass candlesticks.

Pearce came back to himself.

'I'm not bloody standing for parliament. Who wants all those old *farts*.'

The boys all cheered and Pearse lit up another ciggie.

He'd leave all that sort of thing to Natalia and Alison and

Ruth. Not to mention Benedict, with his blond hair and blue eyes. They could all work it out themselves along with old Dionysius.

Natalia had managed to retrieve from storage some stuff the Germans hadn't looted, and then cousin Ariadne had sent more from Switzerland. It seemed as if all the memories were going to end up on her back.

Natalia baked, and tried to make the garden she'd promised herself. True, there was now a creeper growing over the front porch, and a small pond with goldfish in it, but it did not drain properly and bred mosquitoes. And Pearse could not stop himself punching at Natalia.

To escape them, Benedict often went to see the old man who told stories and might be seeing into the future. The boy liked the pictures on the wall, called ikons. The old man had made him learn their meaning and then bribed him to begin learning Russian. He liked the wooden cross, with the Christ in agony painted on it, like his parents fighting, and Benedict in his deep romance defending Natalia and thrown against a wall . . . By mistake, it was obvious, from Pearse's white face; it was just that he didn't like competition.

The mother had picked up the son and knew when she had blackmail material. She sailed from the room, diamonds glittering in her hair, a long poplin dress that sailed about her, billowing with nobility, and poor Pearse in his dungarees – he'd never have managed the ermine – looking a bit sick.

'I must get away,' said the mother, 'to Geneva. Now that cousin Natasha in Paris is dead we own a Swiss bank account and also a house in Rome. Practically a palace I expect.'

'Palace?' said the boy opening his mouth, he felt, for the first time. 'Can *we* live in a place like that?'

'Of course,' she answered, 'you can. One day you will escape all this! You will escape and come back and tell Mother all about it. No, *we* will escape.'

The diamonds were falling from her hair and glittering around her pompom slippers. 'He throws at me the disease of his cousin Margaret. How could I know that he loves her, that I am the rebound?'

Natalia's English in moments of stress inclined to slither. She heaved herself around and focused her pale-blue eyes on the window. 'I must find out.'

'In the palace,' suggested the son, 'with Charlotte and Dad.'

'You don't understand,' she insisted and then Charlotte came in, Pearse close behind her.

Natalia pushed her children in front of her to act as a shield between herself and her mistakes. Both parents hammered at each other through them, for children, after all, could bear the brunt of their pain.

It was then that she bought a piano. Not just any old piano, but a boudoir-sized grand. It took up the front room which they extended.

When they screamed and shouted Benedict slipped out of bed under the battery of the guns, creeping up the hall, then skirting into the front room where the piano stood, black and shining. He would lift the lid, take off the green baize cloth, and would sound one note. Then he would play another.

Natalia decided this gift for music would be developed. He would learn theory and compose something for Mother for her birthday, as her cousin Dmitri had done for her in Geneva.

The escape route was laid.

'I'm gunna leave one day,' Benedict told his sister.

'Why?' she asked.

Time passed.

Benedict grew used to seeing sheep killed, knife into the neck and a quick slit deep and around, taking in the windpipe.

Pearse didn't like the stink of still-warm guts.

Time passed.

Benedict didn't roast blowies any more over a candle. Though one day at Karl Schenkle's he'd threaded them up on a needle and Karl had done the same. Then they'd had chariot races with the blowflies harnessed to steel, groggily walking along the floor and batting their wings which would never carry them again to the front window where the Schenkle pies and sandwiches were displayed, along with some foreign dishes that were sold to travellers euphoric with passing through.

'Up to "Für Elise" already,' said Miss Crabtree with pride, 'and some easy Mozart. All in one year. Phenomenal! Soon, "Rondo Alla Turca".'

While Pearse and Natalia were again content with some memory – perhaps just one, the eye in the storm – and would reflect on it for an evening, going to bed early, hardly noticing the children as they bathed in a night under the apple tree.

That much Benedict knew, because Natalia had said, drunk on the moon when the blossom was out, 'Once I knew heaven, just under that Granny Smith'.

Later the son had gone and sat there, but it seemed that heaven had moved on.

The old priest hardly talked now; his skin had become fine as paper. The boy went and sat with him and watched him with his old golden eyes, like a bird of prey, the eyelids raised and lowered onto his thought.

'Why were you born?' asked Benedict of his great-uncle. The other might have been weary with youth simply because it existed, or he may not have known how to put things. He thought for a moment. 'Let me tell you a story,' he suggested finally. 'Something – about Russia.'

'Yes,' said the boy, easily diverted. 'Tell me about the monastery you lived in.'

'It was close to Kiev. It was founded in the twelfth century by Saint Vladimir.'

The boy never tired of the story which took him through passages which smelled of damp, through stone rooms covered in tapestries, into the church with the Royal Gates open before him on the Mass of the Easter. His grandmother wearing a sable coat and high boots and served the Holy Communion by her brother whom she loved.

There was also an estate out of Petersburg, in the middle of a pine forest where the bees swam through the green light. Trees stretching all the way to heaven. The boy smiled and his skin reflected the green light while he walked with his great uncle, hand in hand, through the trees, as far as the lake where they had a boat and there they stopped to watch the water.

'We exist as part of a pattern, as part of everything. We come from silence and we eventually return to it. Now we are pilgrims in time. But I have thought,' he said, laying his hand on Benedict's head, 'that we have also arrived at a point where time does not exist. Why? Because our civilization is vanishing into a small point and will vanish altogether. Perhaps with their atomic bomb. So we are buzzing about like flies in a bottle, waiting for the day.'

The boy half slept, mouth open, drifting away on the words and washing up again in the silence.

Later, the old man came swimming with them, walking with the shepherd's crook Pearse had presented to him. Natalia carried the afternoon tea — fresh girdle scones, a pot of strawberry jam, cream, a thermos of tea, and some meatloaf.

They plunged through the high grass until they were on the bank. On the other side Ruth Schenkle and Alison were already sitting with their knitting and Karl was in the water, bony and white.

Benedict stared snootily at his friend, trying out the butterfly stroke to impress them all. Flop flop; chest puffed out of the water, lips drawn into a death-like rictus. Flop flop flop. Again around the pool.

Natalia looked at Ruth Schenkle and Alison and they giggled.

So were those summer days. Who could believe, then, that evil men existed anywhere? Or that men had persecuted members of the Schenkle family in Germany and sent them to the gas chamber.

'Personally,' said Karl Schenkle, Benedict's friend, 'I kind of find it difficult. It's so mad, isn't it?'

'It is, isn't it?' asked Karl again, suddenly frightened by what his friend's silence might mean. 'I am a Jew, but so what? I mean, it's not normal to kill people, is it?'

There were moments when the boy Benedict knelt down as the old priest had taught him, and prayed, for Karl and his family – in case. And for his parents. And he had to escape their love that darkened him, forced him deeper. Not always. Months would go by without the darkness singing to him like a live thing. Months would go by and he would forge ahead in their world, and then the cracks were there again in the ground, just under his feet.

5

Natalia went early to the hut and heard the Russian mass which brought down to them the body of Christ. Her two children came with her, but for the visit to Margaret McClean she needed only her son, as proof of her fecundity and as an arm to lean on.

She left the woolshed and Charlotte stayed to help the old man out of his rich vestments.

Natalia wore her new light-blue suit. She could also claim to visit Margaret as a mark of respect. For old Davie McClean, Margaret's father, had died two weeks ago. Natalia's Pearse had gone to the funeral but could not go in, for even to see Margaret – or Davie in his open coffin – was too much. He clung to the wheel of his new Chevrolet (fat lambs had fetched outstanding prices) and had averted his eyes from the hearse although he had followed in the cortège to the cemetery.

The two pilgrims ploughed on across the railway paddock, Natalia avoiding sheep dung as best she could.

Pearse was still asleep, wheezing in their double bed. He'd given up on church except for weddings or the funerals of people he didn't care about one way or another, and for the Church Parade of the Returned Servicemen where he wore his medals and strutted a bit, having flattened down what was left of his hair.

Natalia and Benedict walked in the centre between the north and south tracks, Natalia balancing on her thick-blocked high heels and with her fading blonde hair blowing out from under a small, pert velvet hat.

They stopped to observe the peace of the water and the flowing green weeds like the hair of the river.

Benedict was suddenly hot with what he'd seen once of his mother's blonde bush when she stepped out of the bath.

He and Karl had watched Mum, and then Dad with his dong. 'Pretty big,' said Karl, 'bigger than us even flat like that.' They peered at Pearse with his white flanks, sunburned face and neck, small buttocks and hair on his chest and a lot around his dong. 'Circumcised!' said Karl, triumphant. Pearse had lowered himself into the water. 'Just like a Jew. Why aren't you?' 'I dunno,' Benedict answered. 'They didn't do it to me. I dunno.'

What impressed Benedict was the intimacy of things. For Dad hadn't bothered running another bath, he'd just got into Mum's and wallowed in it, playing with a bit of Mum's hair he'd found stranded on the enamel side. His thing floating on the water. The son had stared with fascination and fear at it, bigger than his own.

Karl, not being the son, could afford to be more judicial.

'I'd think', he whispered, 'that it'd be about eight inches when it's up.'

Then they'd made a noise and panicked and escaped. Dad would think there were a couple of possums on the roof. Skylights had their uses.

The trout were hiding in the shallows, warming themselves with the battery of weed and sun. Natalia sighed and adjusted her hat and looked at her son's legs, scratched by the cutty-grass down at the river paddock where he'd been sent to round up a bunch of ewes at seven in the morning.

She could ignore the evidence of matter and materialism – the factory and the stink ahead from the mill stream. She could watch the water flowing down to Toko Mouth and thence to the sea. The railway track with the cinders! Oh, they would surely be superseded. She held her son's hand and stared with him into the depths. The thick red mill with the red chimney belching smoke even on Sunday.

But she sang to herself:

'Down by the old mill stream,
Where I first met you,
With your eyes of blue.'

They trailed past the stationmaster's house, canopied by a large oak, and then out to Grey Street with the mill cafeteria closed in by a low concrete-block fence. The manager lived in the adjacent bakelite house – a monument to socialist functionalism.

Natalia, still caught in the morning with the sun warm and the day seasonably sharp, hardly glanced at it. Her feet were firmly on the dust road, where the second turn to the left and a longish haul would bring her to Margaret McClean's house.

Mr Smelt leaned against a post, amiable in his white apron, smoking a roll-your-own and flicking out bits of tobacco. Mrs Smelt, head in a scarf with rollers and butterfly clips glinting metallically through the chiffon, poked her head out the window. A halo of fatty smoke was around her as her large brown eyes assumed a mannish firmness and a Capstan plain appeared in her mouth. She was not one to let a human being by without comment.

'Nice day,' said Mrs Smelt. 'On your way to Church?' Which she knew she wasn't since the bells had stopped their bloody racket half an hour ago and Mrs Pearse was Russian and therefore not catered for. 'Could try the bloody Salvation Army though,' sniggered Mrs Smelt to herself.

'No, just walking, Mrs Smelt.'

'Bloody foreigners!' said Mr Smelt with a benevolent wink.

Natalia simpered and walked on, unable to meet the occasion with anything but her back.

They turned into Spencer Street, its footpath as pebbly and hard on the feet as the road. Benedict waded through the uncut grass verges.

Natalia stopped at number seventy-seven. A wooden house set back on the land with a high macrocarpa hedge that was running itself as it saw fit – large fronds weighed down with nuts and older ones consolidating into branches. The gate was wooden, with some fungus growing under the bottom strut and a gauzy blue lichen creeping over the supporting stones. The hinges were rusted into a pleasing brown. They pushed it open and walked into the domain over which Margaret McClean presided.

The house had a colonial verandah supported by three wooden pillars, and behind these three sets of windows. There was a flower bed in front, which Natalia paused to admire – Michaelmas daisies and phlox as well as a border of nasturtiums. The brass doorknocker was a dull green but functional.

Benedict wandered around. The house had taken on the colour of dull lupin pods. The side hedge by now quite blocked out Magga Trout's kitchen window, but with a sudden gust of wind he saw through the green reflection to her plastic-bright kitchen.

He turned to his mother.

'Who's house is it?' He knew it belonged to a humped back woman the kids said was a witch.

'This is the house of a distant cousin of your father's,' Natalia said, and knocked for the second time. Surely she would not be denied admittance?

Benedict saw a curtain move and a moment later the door opened.

In front of them stood a woman with a large face, her hair pulled back by clips and a shawl around her shoulders knitted of wool of many colours. It covered her hump, which rose as high as her head, and over it a cascade of tawny hair streamed down to her waist.

She smiled.

It was the sweetest smile Benedict had seen, and to his mother . . . it seemed to break open something in her. She started to cry with great gulping sobs, not at all as ladies were wont to cry.

'Come in,' said Margaret, in a low voice, still with a Scottish burr in it. 'I don't want the neighbourhood to see your grief, my dear.'

They followed her down the hall of dark linoleum and on through a door into her room. There sun streamed and a canary trilled while briskly scattering seed to the floor. An orange tom dozed in front of the fire. Benedict lifted it onto his knees, where it purred and lazily dug its claws. Natalia collapsed in a chair and her wails subsided into long, drawn-out shudders of breath. This distant cousin sat quietly, looking at them both and the prints on the walls.

'They are Italian, a painter called Botticelli and another called Piero della Francesca, but I do not know how they are pronounced,' she said.

Natalia dried her eyes and gave the right intonation.

'I found them in a magazine,' said Margaret. 'Along with an article about a tomb just found in Paestum in southern Italy. It is of a diver.' She handed Benedict the magazine. 'I have sent for the book to discover what it is about. The magazine says the dive is the leap into eternity and true knowledge while still in the body. It is apparently archetypal.'

She patted the boy, who still looked a bit strained even though the cat did its best, what with washing his hand. 'I've made some toffee. I must have guessed that you would be coming. Take some and go out to the sheds. They're full of comics and the *Boy's Own* your father read, Benedict, when he was your age.'

He would have liked to sit enjoying her burry voice.

Natalia had stopped collapsing and was busily viewing the damage and repairing it with lipstick and powder puff. And telling Margaret about that part of Italy around Paestum, much further south than Monte Cassino, the only place Margaret had heard about.

Margaret left the kitchen door open, so Benedict wouldn't feel left out.

'I'm your cousin,' she called to him.

*   *   *

It was evening before he walked home with his mother.

On the way back Natalia was feverish with the pleasure of this new relationship. 'My first real friend in the town apart from Alison Black, and Ruth who is too busy. Margaret studies life. Not in a popular way, Benedict, but as a serious concern. Your Uncle Dionysius should meet her.'

They passed by the mill. There was fresh ash from the furnaces in an open bin. 'I could jump in there,' she said, pointing to the red centre. 'That would fix Pearse.'

'Fix you, too,' said Benedict.

They reached the stationmaster's house.

'What did you talk about to the lady?' asked Benedict.

His mother shut her eyes as she leaned against the oak trunk to gain strength.

'About this town. Myself. Herself. Her life, her house. About many things. About the diver of Paestum. That is important for Margaret. To know that such a thing as truth exists inside her. That she may find the means to dive out of this world – or see it as it is, if she throws herself off the diving board.

'And I've laddered my stocking.' She shrugged and started towards the Toko bridge. Ahead was the homestead, the porch light on. Someone was standing in the doorway.

'I must tell you,' she said, 'about Dionysius. He also is what is called a mystic. Of course in the Russian way. Margaret is more into nature, which suits her well.'

The words faded as she smelt roast lamb.

She smiled deeply into the distant red of the sky. 'Look,' she pointed. 'The sun's going for the night.'

They companionably strolled across the two bridges.

Ahead was the white wicket paddock gate. On either side the gorse had been cut back ruthlessly, exposing the nest of a thrush or blackbird. But now, in this season, the mud cup was empty of all but the pale hard droppings of the yunkers who had grown towards flight, poised entangled in the gorse flowers, buffing and cheeping and had flown – or had fallen on too-weak wings.

Beyond was the garden his mother was still making; the chooks had got in and decimated the peony roses and the other green shoots. The roses survived, yet could not find a focus for themselves, and their perfume was lost in the wider raunchy smell of fresh milk, cow shit, hen shit, the resin of the pines, the exhaust from the tractor.

'Everything is half made,' Natalia muttered to herself as they came through the gate.

Pearse was on the verandah. He screamed at her, jealous of them both. He had been *left*! She was useless for his needs and visiting people she had no right to visit, since Magga Trout had *rung* him – to tell.

She could have said he was battering the wrong person but she no longer responded, for his anger had deadened those delicate shoots; those buds, she thought, that had grown and flowered in one evening.

'I have spent some hours with the woman you love and whom you were to marry. I had never considered her before, but now she is my friend.'

In the face of this treachery from Margaret and Natalia, Pearse could only gasp and wheeze.

The father would not speak to his treacherous son, and so the son and Charlotte got into the trunks that had come from France and Switzerland. Both were dressed in feather boas, rouged cheeks, powder, the long trains on their dresses glittering with seed pearls and sequins, boas floating in the mud, and Benedict in his mother's old high heels.

What was this but Natalia's revenge?

They both carried bags and wore furs too, the endless treasure of their maternal past.

Natalia played stately gavottes on the piano. Brother and sister wound around each other composing steps under the light of the candelabrum Natalia had lit. She had drawn the curtains to keep this little world intact.

'Alison and I danced; the night before my wedding.'

She drank some apricot wine and smiled woozily out at the day.

Dionysius sat in a chair and watched them both, eyes bright with spiritual malice. Or was it simply amusement? Natalia couldn't think through the fog of wine.

Later the children paraded under the oak trees – down the long expanse of grass to the mud of the back paddock, the orchard stark and bare, carrying with them the dream of their dance, on their way to a meeting beyond the lichened gate. They leaned against it.

Pearse had been doing the winter ploughing and the frost would break up the clods. Charlotte and Benedict tried to get the gate properly open for him. He was Dad after all. Pearse came on, the tractor wasn't stopping for anybody. He gaped with disbelief at his son's rouged and powdered cheeks and blond hair, then snorted and averted his eyes and with another snort was past them. On the trailer was piled hay and an old ewe.

Benedict walked behind the tractor, trailing the skirt, the pearls less shining without candlelight, the wind ruffling the feathers of the boa while making an intricate dance of feathers in Charlotte's ostrich fan. Charlotte took his arm and marched along ceremoniously, her dark hair primped into a pompadour. The whole of history was crammed into her small body and self-satisfied face; she was riding her dream. 'Just imagine,' she ordered, 'that we are grown up and going to be married.'

'To each other?'

'No, you are someone else.'

The tractor stopped outside the shearing shed, the ewe, tied and bleating, was carried in.

'What'll they do to it?' asked Charlotte, who hadn't watched any slaughtering.

'I dunno. Kill it for the dogs. It's old and scraggy.'

They went to see. Pearse started to shear off the wool and dags around the ewe's rump. 'It's flyblown,' he informed Charlotte, with whom he still had close diplomatic relations. His son he viewed at best as a neutral power, more likely to ally with Russia.

'Poor old lady,' he told the ewe, his face tender.

'Let me see,' said Charlotte.

'She missed being crutched,' said her father. 'They breed in the dung, then go into the skin. Look at her, poor old lady!' The old lady showed her eyes, struggled and bleated but didn't try to get away. Not very hard. The maggots writhed with the Dettol.

'Whatta you want to get dressed up like that for, son?'

Benedict didn't know and watched the sheep and wished that his father had been like that to him, strong and tender with the fear of the knife that the face held.

'Are you going to kill?' asked Charlotte.

'We'll see. We'll give Ben a chance,' Pearse glanced at his son. 'A coupla days to see if he starts to mend, otherwise . . .'

'Dog tucker,' said Charlotte triumphantly, begging a kiss from her Daddy with a simper of love and predatory possession. The father straightened his back and his eyes looked tender. For a moment his lungs filled, straining with affection and kisses.

Benedict stood back to allow them to love one another and had to leave, down the steps away from the shed, trailing his train, the fan he'd taken from Charlotte in his hand, his grey eyes staring at the banks of cloud, the grey heaviness of air, his breath fuming before him.

He walked up the kitchen path. His mother was where she did her preserves and made her apricot brandy and wine. Her hair was limp and her face fat and sagging. She couldn't see him.

He went to the piano but the notes didn't lead anywhere. So he took his mother's box of jewels from the drawer in her dressing-table. Nothing was under lock and key.

On the top layer of faded blue velvet were the rings: cut diamonds, sapphires and emeralds glittered in antique settings. These were better than music just now as the blackened silver with rough gold was more than history: it had a note. He held the things, listening to the qualities of the rings and brooches, the old fire of the emeralds, the yellow sapphires on the pearl necklace, the clearer amethyst of a bishop ring. He stared into the mirror and watched his image disintegrate until he became nothing, drenched in the memories of pearls. He saw nothing, felt himself become nothing, except the layers of the past, the pendant fall of the sperm, from generation to generation to the last. For the last would close the chain or open another. Things were edging to mutation, so those grey eyes knew and didn't know.

The old man shuffled in and watched.

'What will happen to me?' the grand-nephew whispered.

The old man watched for the mirror view was necessary: these reflections and the deepest shelves of the sea the child swam in, and the golden light of the sea and the space that the sea flowed in. The conversion of Benedict's spirit fired him. He did not exist as he thought he did. This child of two forces.

'You will be a vehicle,' the old priest said, simply.

And the image through which the faces floated sank back into nothing until Benedict, like a tired woman after a court reception, flopped with hands over face while the maid did the undressing, and slept for a moment or two, to wake up shivering with cold.

The memory was now as deep as the deepest flow of his budding humanity, covered and concealed and hovering, one fish in the deepest current of his ocean where in time it would rise again with one face or another, one beast or another, one god or another.

'Well,' said his mother, 'what are you doing?' She smiled, but with a strained look as if she saw something for which she was certainly not to blame.

'You will be strong,' she said, to excuse herself. How else could you create, if you were not battered open? Creation was always preceded by rape. She stared at him, bemused now by the tender line of his lips, the curve of his eyebrow.

She gathered him into her arms, he shivering and half asleep.

Pearse was still in the shearing shed, filled up these days with antibiotics to help his chest. He of course got weaker, and now the grey clouds were breaking and beating down and passing through this room in a cold wind from the south, now blowing with thick flakes in it, and more passing the window, the house a ship beating up the paddocks until everything was a sea of whiteness in the gathering dusk.

'My lamb, my precious lamb who loves me,' said Natalia. 'How I wish we could leave! But we cannot. You are also Pearse's son! This place is everywhere! But you will win for all of us. This is Margaret's opinion and Dionysius'. That is what Margaret explained to me. For I was going to leave. But not now. The camps are everywhere and must be suffered.'

Natalia recognized she had poured the passing and confusion of her life into the boy. What would he make of it? She shivered at the heat of herself.

'And there is Dionysius in his room, a cold little room for a man who one day would have been an abbot at least. He doesn't mind, my lamb. But I am going to break the chain of history. I will destroy — all these dresses and fans, the ivory sets, the furs. I will destroy.'

She stared at the driving snow.

'Am I strong enough to live and die an *émigrée*? And you? You also have no country because you are Russian more than Scots. Charlotte. Dear little Carlotta? She belongs here and will change from doll babies to real babies. She will not even notice the transition. She will open her legs to some farmer. Oh, perhaps to one of the Fieschi twins. Perhaps at least that. But you? You will wander as Margaret said, making your music.

'Perhaps you will discover the point of this exile on this planet I have not discovered. "Blessed are the wanderers, for they shall wander and wander!" That is my beatitude, written for me. But you,' she fixed him with her large blue eyes, hard as steel tonight, 'you must find, must break through the circle we wander in like ants, like things on a treadmill. Slaves! Slavs! Otherwise, what point is there for your father or me if from our issue there is no resolution? Even Dionysius has not got all the answers. Not many. The only answer he has is patience, like a rock, waiting for a glacier to pick him up and carry him. You have experienced everything in your blood.

'All you need now to experience is the inadequacy of this place and this time, then you will be free.

'All you need to know is the fatal attraction towards evil of these communities, under the guise of good works. The collusion with evil which their devotion to refrigerators and cars and washing machines reveal! They love matter as they love their atomic bombs.'

Natalia was now more mad than drunk. The gates were open.

'Pearce will eat with his grandmother, who soon will be sent to an old people's home. She wants to go! Can you imagine that! She wants to be in with the end of all the aged. He will go to her and sulk and she will feed him roast lamb and she will make the gravy as he likes it — with lumps. Lumps!

'He is still a child and must be given special food. Then she talks to him about his parents. She sighs over him since he is her only grandchild. As I would do. We women fight for our men. Even though we are dried up, we need the other pole of existence.

'What have they done for me? Even my children do not love me, my little lamb, as I would have it. But what am I saying?'

'I will obey,' said the son eagerly, waking himself up.

'No you won't,' she answered. 'I never did. You were so much nicer when you were a baby, even four or five. But now?'

The snow fled along the paddock to silence the town.

'Your father will not eat with us tonight. But I will still prepare food.' She looked at her hands. 'Once my hands were white.' She stared at her still-beautiful nails. 'I will go and ask him to come back. As I have done in the past. I'll put a headscarf on so that I can feel like a Russian peasant going for her man. Then your father knows once again he is necessary.'

She looked at her son who loved her and his father. She told him to change. Tonight they would dress for dinner. He would wear his best clothes and they would drink some wine from crystal goblets that his great-granny down the road had given from her own supply of precious things – for the marriage.

They would talk about history. She met once Sartre. In Rome. She also met Count Ciano at a party, but he was later shot.

After dinner she would call in Dionysius and together they would discuss the Russian situation or perhaps tell fairy tales.

Then they would sing together and later before bed drink some hot milk with honey in it and one teaspoon of brandy each for Benedict and little Charlotte now nestling on Mother's breasts. Charlotte will go to sleep in Mother's arms warmed through and through with brandy and milk and honey and Mother will carry her under the silence of this snow to her bed.

The sheep must shelter under the pines that Daddy planted before the war when for him everything had been simple. And poor dear Pearse will be out late, despite his collapsing lungs, driving them into the home paddocks. Everyone will go out on the trailer to feed out hay. The dogs will be working tonight. Are working. Their barks come from across the fields, under the blanket of the falling snow as sharp as the cries of wolves.

6

Miss Crabtree, the piano teacher, had applied melancholy spots of rouge and dressed herself in a mustard dress to counteract her flushes.

The branches of the cherry-plum tree spiked out into the winter evening as did the prune. One branch appeared to point straight through the open gate to St John's Anglican Church.

'There,' said Miss Crabtree, 'is *your* godmother, Alison Black, going to practice hymns before the service.'

The tone of accusation made Benedict blush as he often did for no particular reason.

'Your godmother,' sniffed Miss Crabtree to divert herself, 'is said to be a Red. Red! And you know what happens to them. They are sent to the electric chairs. Like Julius and Ethel Rosenberg. Electrocuted in the same month Queen Elizabeth was crowned, June 1953.'

Sometimes the genius of her student so irritated her that not even a perfect chromatic scale calmed her Strauss-walzing hormones.

Alison Black vanished behind the deep-blue baize doors and faced the altar. The Queen might be dead too, she thought.

Edward VII had his Coronation Hall and George VI the Coronation Memorial Library. What would they build for Elizabeth? State urinals?

Alison rushed at the organ and belted out 'God Save The Queen', 'Rule Britannia', with embellishments, then 'The Red Flag'. And tried not to think of Hank she'd nursed in Noumea.

There had been Korea, but who could tell about that? The New Zealand boys were in the backlines of the fight. With the peace the Americans stayed and, on leave in Japan, Hank, now a colonel, recalled the little red-haired nurse he'd held hands with through many a sunset back in World War II and wrote a sentimental postcard – before getting back to his massage girl.

Alison had received it this morning. It had almost turned her around until she started pedalling the harmonium for the first hymn.

The vicar had mumbled through the prayer of consecration. Alison had adjusted her stockings and dreamed of Leningrad, and as the host was raised to several elderly ladies, muttered the real presence, 'Djugashvili'. Ferreted out by Natalia, a willing abetter. 'Stalin, Djugashvili,' Alison muttered as she approached the altar rail.

Only a fairy-book plotter could have thought of such a *nom-de-guerre*. Only the most arrogant who dealt death to millions could exist inside a name that wasn't his. With no name you did as you willed. No-one could call you to account. It was here that Alison parted company with Natalia who would laugh with pleasure at the consummate hypocracy of the modern Russian ruling soul: 'I call Trotsky, Lenin and Stalin before the Throne of Grace to answer for their crimes.'

No answer.

'Nobody Christened *that*, dear,' Natalia sneered.

'And no crimes,' Alison answered, refuting all the Hanks and America. 'It's all propaganda against my beliefs that will conquer. And even if you've resigned from the Russian-New Zealand Friendship Society, I am still president.'

Natalia let that pass since autumn was on them and with Alison she could read deep into the night.

She would wait for the evening.

On the days when she felt prophetic Natalia would watch for Alison coming across the paddocks, her mac flapping and a copy of *Permanent Revolution* or *Short History of the Bolshevik Party* hidden deep in her shopping bag. Together the two would sit and ponder the fate of nations, Alison playing Stalin and Natalia Trotsky or Bukharin or the whole Central Committee of the CP.

Pearse was drawn to revolution as any good conservative is. He fondled the idea and was appalled by it and would drink some whisky and peer out to check that his land had not been socialized.

Natalia ignored this member of the ruling class, and when missionary Alison asked his opinion he snickered at his favourite collie bitch and gently kicked at her. Nellie knew her powers and batted her dun tail coyly.

So the days passed until Alison was uncovered.

Mrs Baxter was consort and ambassadress extraordinary from the Anglican establishment to the Presbyterian League, the non-conformists and the Catholic imperial power. On that day she had come, with Sunday's hymns, to the house which Alison now shared with that new gym teacher, Paula. She had pushed open the door and walked in after hoo-hooing. And found on a table the book. *Das Kapital* was not familiar to Mrs Baxter, but the author was. She crept from the room sniffing conspiracy and the undoing of the Ecclesia Anglicana and the middle class.

She walked firmly down the street, left right, left right, right turn – up the path, through the door, down the carpeted passage and into *his* study. At such times Mrs Baxter was willing to concede that hubbie did represent God in some awful and un-defined way. Besides, he could commit Holy Communion which she could not.

She flung open the door, ready with the treasonous news, and caught him on his knees, his mild face pinkly serene. Mrs Baxter averted her eyes from the unnecessary spectacle. Then as he scrambled to his feet she advanced to meet him as the repre-sentative of the Most High: 'Your organist, my dear, is a viper in your bosom. The one who plays *your organ* is a communist.

Quite probably an agent of theirs.' Hubbie presented his quivering front for her inspection. 'You have a spot from lunch, the soup,' she informed him.

There was no doubt that his purity would see them both safe into heaven.

'A communist?'

The word spread.

Not that it was spoken, but the way in which hubbie, with mild and loving eyes, persuaded Alison to 'Think of God' – he could not bring himself to accuse – and the way in which his consort icily looked the other way spoke volumes. And Mrs Baxter let it drop to the authorities in the shape of Mrs Fergusson, Lady Mayoress, and the ripples stopped and turned into something like concrete. The town knew it had been betrayed.

Magga Trout, still in her odds-and-ends shop and well into her third childhood or deathless maturity, considered for a long time. She reread carefully the Apocalypse and came across the Scarlet Whore and the Bear from the East.

Alison Black had unpardonably beautiful hair, which she refused now to cut, falling in shimmering waves of bronze across her mild white shoulders. She did not age as women should who had no man. Her face was as serene as on the day she had stepped down from the train. The day Michael Pearse had returned to Natalia, who *had* settled down with her children, even though she was eccentric.

Magga Trout considered further and stroked the rabbit-skin vest she had made. Was it possible Alison was the Scarlet Whore? Magga sighed. And what with democratic privilege there was no way of finding out.

'Although that Senator McCarthy in the United States had found a way around it. As had the Australians, catching Petrov and his wife.'

She brooded further, waiting for the right formulation, and brooded so much that her clients who came in for a gossip and a reel of cotton were struck dumb by her silence. They waited and she pronounced: 'Alison Black has gone over to the enemy.'

'What can you expect?' asked the Lady Mayoress.

'What can you expect from a girl who ran away to the Army to "nurse" soldiers in the Pacific, as she says, but that she would come back with new-fangled Asian ideas like Communism.'

'And,' said Magga Trout, 'she is a friend of Michael Pearse's wife, the Russian woman!'

The saying came to Magga: 'Women without love turn to the Reds.'

Magga Trout organized. Within a week she had roused the League of Mothers and their rivals, the Mothers' Union, and the schismatic Oddfellow Ladies Lodge, with a few Doolans who feared Communism as much as hellfire.

They started at the Queen Elizabeth II Memorial Park. Not that they had told Alison they marched against *her*: you could not confront someone with the cunning to have formed a view! You simply launched the juggernaut and rolled it along the streets. And paused, significantly, outside the boutique where Alison Black, aware and sitting in dignity behind the costume jewellery counter, looked out at the placards – 'Down With Communism', 'God Is Our Right', 'Freedom For The Russians', 'God Save The Queen'.

'Down with Communism,' quavered a lady.

Magga Trout nodded agreement. She wore today her mother's seal-skin coat. A special string of amber beads delineated the death of her breasts or rather their atrophy. She protected herself with a large black umbrella and a copy of the Bible.

The ladies marched again since they had not been fired on. In the Presbyterian Church Hall the Lady Mayoress and her assistants were busy making morning tea with fresh scones and some brownies.

Ahead was the south border, the bridge and Fatty Dragoumis' Fish'n'Chip Shop, recently burned out.

And further?

Alison Black threw back her white neck and laughed. And put on her hat when six o'clock came and walked across the fields to Natalia.

'They say,' she said, cool and angry, 'that I am a communist.'

'Are you?' asked Natalia.

'I am what I am,' answered Alison, and that satisfied Natalia.

'It started with Mrs Baxter,' said Alison.

'Then beard her in her den.'

'What should I say?'

'Be dignified. Demand an apology. Stand up to them! Ask her if she is a fascist. Yes, a fascist, that she wants to control your reading?'

'Yes,' said Alison, 'I will do that.'

Dionysius was inside, warming his feet. 'Be careful, my child,' he said, 'that they do not force you to become what they hope you are.'

Alison left and Natalia wanted talk, but Charlotte was not interested in obtuse notions. She was busy growing into a young lady who read love comics.

Charlotte yawned.

'Put your hand over your mouth,' snapped mother, who secretly longed for the touch of velvet, the gay laughter of her youth, the golden memories of balls she had hardly been to. And besides, the town now believed her friend to be a communist. Very well, she would distribute her past to them all – her feather boas, her ivory dressing-table sets, her dresses covered in seed pearls and sequins, the fur-tipped and gauzy shawls, the paisley shawls of silk with intricate embroidery of flowers, birds, the delicate edge of lace fronds so like a flowering thing, to wrap around yourself after a ball in the Doria gardens.

Filippo was the eldest Doria son. He had wanted to marry her. Later he had gone to Abyssinia. In those days she was not political and would have married his corpse had they sent it back to her. Her darling Filippo with his black Moorish eyes.

She had walked in a paisley shawl one early spring morning in the Orti Botanici, the gardens of long-dead Queen Christina of Sweden. Filippo had found her up a side path enclosed by trees and the silence of the place. At the top beneath a eucalyptus she had leaned on his arm and looked across the city of breast-like domes, the bells ringing, the warm umber coming to life under the fingers of the sun, the swift arabesques of the swallows. Higher than the fountain he had said: 'Questa fontana,' and 'La mia Natalia.'

They had kissed, she tremulous and certain.

The old Countess had called for her to give the news, in her drawing room with the shutters pulled tight. They had offered her his miniature.

With her father she had fled once more. They had already fled from Paris because Mama was in the Père-Lachaise.

Natalia turned to Charlotte and explained this rot they moved towards. Her spirit was now caught by it, for this day and perhaps forever. Charlotte tried a polite face and waited to return to her comic.

But if the vanities were burned up, and with them the agonies of memory? Dearest Filippo! She had allowed him to hold her breasts once. How many years had he been dead – in the sands somewhere?

For that reason she must discard. And the pain of those beautiful things? She turned on her son who had finished his practice. Their destruction would burn into him. And if she was distributing her patrimony to the barbarians, they would loot it anyway if they got the chance.

She summoned the town through Charlotte – ever a willing messenger of conformity – who stood beside her mother in front of the open trunks, playing Lady Bountiful.

The boas heaped on one wooden chest fluttered in the cool breeze and some feathers escaped to be blown down the grass spaces and wedged into a mass of brambles.

The kids at first stood at a distance, unsure how to approach this treasure, but Natalia laughed and threw at them an ebony evening reticule.

'Tell your parents, that I, like Alison Black, is what you would call communist.'

The kids with their snotty winter noses and hacked-about hair moved in, not noticing Natalia's verbal inaccuracies.

The little girls seized evening dresses and put them on. They paraded before Mrs Pearse and Charlotte, simpering and queening, swaying their child hips. They sucked their all-day suckers, ogled each other and experimentally picked sequins and seed pearls off their gowns. They took dressing-table sets in old yellow ivory.

They sailed off across the railway paddock, feather boas blowing in the wind, some clutching their furs to keep out the cold while they danced and pranced or walked sedate, arm in arm, into the town and the gossip that must follow. So much silk was surely a declaration of war.

Leaning on his walking-stick, Dionysius left the room on the shearing shed. Benedict's eyes were sick with contempt for his mother. Not that he wanted to get dressed up in that stuff, but he liked to bury his head in some aging brocade or browned silk.

And now the remains were piled by Charlotte against the old car where his grandparents had died, down on the crossing one Friday night, and high priestess Natalia approached with the tin of kero.

She sprinkled liberally and threw in a match. The pyre caught and flamed as high as the smashed windows, singeing Natalia's eyebrows in passing.

Benedict left with the old man's eyes following him. He walked into the kitchen and on through to the front room. He took off the green baize and there were the white keys grinning up at him like his mother's teeth.

He raised his fist and smashed it down onto them as hard as he could.

7

Benedict knocked on Margaret McClean's door.

She opened it to him after first checking through a window, for the local kids had got bolder as the years passed. Sometimes they threw stones.

She wore a white blouse with the same old tartan skirt. A cairngorm brooch reflected a pasty yellow against her skin. Her face was thickened by drugs and pain.

Benedict stood in a green puddle of light reflected through the growing immensity of the macrocarpa hedge. She ushered him over the brass front step, polished to a sheen by Natalia who liked to perform some useful act for her friend.

'I thought you might come again soon,' she said, ignoring the time that had passed and now having to turn all her body to look back at him. 'You've grown taller.'

He shuffled. 'It's a nice place,' he said, shoving his hands into his pockets.

'Look around,' she offered. 'These rooms I keep clean out of habit, but I do not live in them.'

He poked his nose into the front bedroom where old Davie must have died – icy now with a white bedspread, a scoured pot under the bed. The bolsters were losing their feathers – a rooster quill stuck rakishly out, spangled scarlet and green. In the fireplace were splatterings from the starlings. Benedict let out a fart he'd been holding in.

Down in her room the cabinet radio stood where it had on an earlier visit. He bent down and twiddled the dial.

'Remember the concert?' he asked, a bit shy.

She nodded. 'It was the first time you knew other countries existed.'

'It was a freak reception, I tried again at home. To find an orchestra like that one: Bruno Walter and the Vienna State. "Das Lied von der Erde",' he told Margaret.

They had listened crouched together over the speaker, straining through the static for the voice.

'Kathleen Ferrier,' had said Mum. 'Once she spoke "Ewigkeit".' She could not sing it because she knew that it was forever. 'Oh, Mahler,' Natalia had moaned as to a lover, 'I haven't heard you since 1937.' Natalia's postlude had been drowned in applause and more static.

'Then you went to the coronation film with your godmother, Alison.'

Benedict nodded.

'So much pageantry. I went too, but by myself, and left just before the end. She seemed like a young nun taking her vows. Or how I imagine such things.'

And Alison with her white throat and emerald eyes.

Margaret didn't tell him of Natalia's strange fantasy: Alison, fur cloaked, in a sled galloping along a willow-dead road with the wolves in a pack behind her, and she, eyes open with strange golden flecks, was staring straight ahead to the snowy horizon. 'They caught up,' Natalia had explained, 'and ripped away the furs, and there were other wolves, watching.'

Natalia had shaken her head to dispel the vision and ventured a Freudian opinion from a book she had just read.

'It is probably early menopause,' she decided, giving up on the unconscious.

Margaret rocked, forgetting the presence of the young man.

'What was it?' he asked, his hands shoved between his legs.

She got up and took the pot of tea off the hob and stroked her cat, orange and black and quite undisturbed by the fuss – eyes blinking and closing. 'Yes,' said Margaret, 'old Tom is quiet. It was probably just a bad dream. Of this place.'

Margaret poured out tea and handed the plate of girdle scones.

'Yes,' she murmured, watching him stoking up to burst into manhoood. 'Yes. You can escape because within you there resides another. This I found because I am so deformed. The other is strong and beautiful, pure as a flame. When I am that being I know I have reached home – I am no longer caught by dreams. I am my Self. I believe it is that Self which dared to dive, as the ancient Greeks showed it, in the tomb at Paestum.'

She fed him another scone, piled with strawberries and thick yellow jersey cream.

Natalia sat in the rocking chair. 'Have I ever told you?' she blinked to remember.

Charlotte was still playing with love comics she borrowed from the mill girls. Natalia could scarcely credit such vulgarity, and to see Pearse thumbing through one for something to do! Of course for him anything Charlotte did was all right.

'I am worried about Alison,' she said somewhat defiantly. 'As are the Schenkles, who feel safe. Ruth says that Alison is becoming the town Jew.'

Benedict finished some Beethoven sonata or other. He would be coming in to warm his hands.

'But at least Alison now has company, with Paula Roberts sharing the house. It was fortunate Paula arrived to teach when she did. Even though gymnastics! But then, if muscle is required.'

Natalia stuck her feet into the open coal-oven door which once she thought to dispense with, but was now her chief winter comfort.

Her son came in and was struck by her thinness. Or was it simply a spiritual spareness?

'Strange, that it is now summer here and almost as cold as

ever.' She smoothed down her apron. 'If Dionysius would come into the house more often I could confer with him on facts, but he will sit out in that room of his. And Paula is no help. She believes too much in reason, while Alison has given up hers.'

'It's nice and warm,' said Charlotte, who paid a daily visit to charm her aging relative.

'Here I am with my father in the graveyard at Tokoiti. Who would have thought that Count Pytor Dashkov would have ended up in Tokoiti graveyard? And Mama in Père-Lachaise, which is quite acceptable – as far as the world goes.'

'Who was he?' asked Charlotte, immersed in dreams of sponge cake and lipstick.

'Your grandfather, dear.'

'What's a count?'

'Of no consequence and in truth in this world as foolish as a dinosaur out shopping in Milton. Now do not ask me what a dinosaur is.'

Charlotte sulked.

'But we have an apartment in Rome, in fact, two floors of a palazzo which is mine and will go to you, Benedict. To give you a *pied-à-terre*. Cousin Dmitri lives in it and sends the rent, which is low, to Switzerland. I fail to see why the New Zealand Internal Revenue should benefit any further from my existence.'

The children didn't know what this meant but were pleased for her. 'Yes, we had a sound heritage. But like Ozymandios, who cares now? Only desert! For some purpose though, I feel . . .' She patted down her hair, 'they cannot bear the notion of top although they are good at the middle in their way of things. Everything is middle here – but an unusual sandwich – no bread on either side.'

'I dunno,' said Charlotte, deep in a pash for Paula, who taught her class rhythmic dances.

'There is a lot to understand,' said Natalia, 'and it will undermine everything you have learned in Milton – if you ever learn.'

'I'm good at sums,' suggested Charlotte.

Natalia reached out a frowzy arm and called the cat, grey and macabre, with whiskers you could spit meat on.

'Come to Mother,' called Charlotte in an ecstasy of competition. 'Oosit, Poosit, Woosit. Come to Mother who loves you!'

Poosy came to Natalia, settled on her ample lap, dug into her warm thighs and glanced in cat manner at the fire and the dish by the fire, the fire itself, crouching and now purring and kneading, gazing and seeing, eyes like topaz and as hard.

'Horrible cat,' said Charlotte.

Natalia searched the early evening. Even Pearse was swallowed up in some back paddock.

'Tell us more,' begged Benedict, hair in a pudding basin crop so that, apart from his eyes, he looked like any of the town's spotty pubescents.

'What can I tell? I remember nothing.'

Charlotte smirked and admired her reflection in the windowpane.

'But you *were* talking,' her son insisted, his voice cracking into baritone.

'Yes, I remembered, for a moment, something.' She stroked the cat and like it stared into the fire, her pale blue eyes defeated by the glare of the burning coal.

'Yes! I was! There is . . . snow. And, Rebecca Weiss is arriving in New Zealand. Ruth has had a letter. It seems she is still grateful Hans von Leinon was able to save her. He got her into the orchestra. It seems so long ago – the war.'

Pearse sat on the steps of the shearing shed where the red wood was really splintery, and patted his dog. He had had her tubes tied up; the last litter had almost killed her.

Nellie battered her tail as a reigning favourite would, dog or human. She was getting a matronly spread.

'Still the best header,' said Pearse, 'aren't you my fat old lady?'

Nellie licked his hand, lolled her tongue, and put on a voluptuous expression which would drive Pearse to caress her tummy.

The grass was growing up the wooden steps and the wind blew open the door of the priest's room. Dionysius was at his table, writing into the twilight. Some magazine they published in Paris.

Benedict coughed politely.

'Mum was telling me about her family and some saint we're related to.'

Pearse and Nellie glanced at each other.

'Anyway, the Pearses are nothing to laugh at.' Pearse raised his voice and looked under the brim of his hat at the ruin of the car. Now part of a tree, he thought: the wheel, the blood, the iron absorbed and living in a new way.

The wind was blowing across the paddocks.

He glanced shyly at his son. 'You want to be a farmer?'

Benedict stretched his hands.

Pearse coughed and the air flowed, but seemed just now to dry him out.

Each note was a pearl on a string when his son played. While Mum played to break each pearl open. Poor old Mum.

At that moment Natalia poked her head out the window and called down to them that tea was ready.

Pearse daydreamed and then noticed his son had gone. For a moment he thought, permanently. But the door of the old codger's room was still open and he was sitting on Dionysius' truckle bed, waiting to help the old man up the grass track to the farm house.

'The Pearses,' said Pearse to both Dionysius and his son, 'came here a long time ago and *paid* for this land. They went to Gabriel's gulley for the gold rush back in 1866. That,' he said to Dionysius, 'is just twenty miles away, close to Lawrence. You remember? We took you for a drive.' The old man smiled and then closed his book.

'Yes, I remember.'

Just as good as those bloody Dashkovs, thought Pearce with irritation, as he launched into social conversation: 'Angus is getting married, Benedict, to your distant cousin Elizabeth – in the Presbyterian Church. But now we've got the Queen Carnival, eh, Uncle Dionysius? And Elizabeth is the Town Queen.'

Dionysius nodded in stately agreement: 'I will come with you, one day, to watch this carnival.'

'Yer,' said Pearse, a bit perturbed by that, 'yer, of course you can.'

8 .

Schenkles had a new record player that cost sixpence for three records. The little schoolgirls with white pudgy legs sat and sniggered at each other.

Karl met Benedict at the door. He was eight months older than Ben and had a freckled face, a large nose and merry blue eyes. No more children had been granted. Mrs Schenkle had had a breast off for cancer and it looked as if the other would go any day.

Snigger snigger went Karl and Benedict. One playing with his nob and the other with his foreskin.

The town was alight, this Friday night, with carnival decorations.

'What does Lynette say?'

'Next week,' said Karl. 'Tomorrow's no good. It's my Bar Mitzvah!'

Karl had got a new three-speed bike after the visit to the city.

'What did they do to you?' asked Benedict.

Karl clammed up.

'Come on.'

'Its a ceremony,' said Karl, 'like when you're confirmed. It means you're a man. The Jewish communist came. There's a cousin of Dad's now in Dunedin. Her name's Rebecca, she's a concert pianist except she won't play. She knows about you and your mum. She's real nice. Talks in a funny way. Real thick like. Not married either. She's going to write.'

Karl looked about at this goyim town and still didn't feel much different from it. They arrived at the Queen Elizabeth Coronation Park and changed into their togs.

'It looks bloody cold in the water.' Benedict shivered and snorted a bit with the fag – blowing the smoke out his nose in two long professional streams. 'Have a puff.' Karl obliged.

At the pool edge the water lapped black with leaves.

'Lynette'll be round later,' said Karl, who managed to crack a hollow sort of fart as he climbed out.

'I took her clothes off yesterday and struck my finger up. She's done it before.' They went to get dressed, neither daring to look at each other. Shit stirring in the bowels.

'I've got a packet of frenchies,' said Karl. 'I pinched them from Dad's drawer.'

'You did?'

'Yer.'

They walked back to the bike.

'She's gunna meet us down the road,' Karl said. 'It's all got to look casual. We'll go over to the river. Peter Black did it to his sister but she wouldn'd let him put it in properly. Lynette will or I'll bash her up. I've told her she's got to let you put it in properly too. And once we get good at it I'll pinch another packet.'

Benedict was reading the instructions: 'You roll them on and they give maximum pleasure.'

'I bet.'

They strode along pushing the bike past the swings.

'You ever done it, Karl?'

'Sort of, once.'

'I know a place on the river, upstream,' said Benedict. 'Dad sometimes goes there with a book.'

Lynette was hanging about the school gates and had brought along some apples and a bottle. 'I pinched some of Dad's whisky and put it in the lemonade,' she said, serene and flat.

The men led the way. Lynette followed at a discreet thirty yards so that no one would guess.

At Maxwell's corner the banners started: 'Support the Rugby Queen'. The Rugby boys were having a joke and putting up Tom Maxwell as Rugby Queen. Big burly Tom! And Angus and Terry for his princesses, dressed in blonde wigs and parading with the boys up and down the street in an open tourer, dresses flying in the breeze, tits big enough to bust. And Tom just as good as any man in a scrum and picked for provincial trials. Tom played lock, Terry right wing and Angus left wing.

The lock with his two wings burned past the Junior Natural History Society, a rare butterfly, rich with mutation.

'I've got a horn, Ben,' Karl breathed in his friend's ear.

'So've I,' Ben lied gamely.

The signals went down and a goods train came by, slow and steady, bound south for the freezing works. Packed on board were lambs, a couple of wagons of steers—wild yellow eyes, foam-flecked mouths, necks already knotted against the knife.

Lynette got off her bike, but Karl wobbled virilely on, careless of the rattling wheels. Just ahead, the lanolin-stinking Mill Stream and green frogs floating amongst the scum.

Lynette was back behind them with Karl again showing off. Into a rut and arse over tip. Not knocking anything essential, only a few grazes and Lynette bent over with laughter, her large white flat face crinkled, her neck stretched, and now as she stared helplessly at the sky tears ran down her cheeks and she bashed her hands about.

They hid their bikes down the side of the Toko bridge and climbed through the barbed wire, Lynette hitching her dress into her bloomers. On through the patches of cutty-grass, avoiding cow pads and the smelly guts of a dead rabbit – a hawk spiralled off watching them and returned amidst the crowns of the purple thistles to gorge.

Over the river was Benedict's house, white and snug.

Somebody stood on the porch. But he knew his mother couldn't see that far.

And into this new circle.

Angus had said he had a whopper for a kid his age and Angus had seen a few, what with the Rugby showers and them getting big Tom Maxwell to get a hard-on by laughing and telling him to — Tom's was twelve inches long and bloody looked it, Angus said. Benedict's was now six and a half and still growing, he hoped.

Lynette unrucked her dress from her bloomers and walked in front, wiggling her bottom, down the track close to the river, the deep pool where someone had put an eel trap and where Pearse on occasions had thrown an illegal stick of dynamite to see what came to the surface.

Lynette gazed moodily at the water. In case she changed her mind Benedict offered her a ciggie which she took with good grace and let him kiss her before she lit up. She took ladylike puffs and suggested they have a swig of lemonade and whisky. It tasted funny but warmed your stomach.

It was half past three and Lyn had to be home at half past five for tea or she would get it from her Dad. She'd been late two nights running.

Benedict led the way after he and Karl had told her how nice she was and how they both reckoned she'd win the talent quest. Flattered, Lyn followed willingly. Benedict was frightened and excited. With Karl when they had wanking competitions you just did it. Now ... Now you weren't boasting with Karl about poking it up someone, you were going to do it. Really.

Lyn was practising the song she was to sing with her sister Gayleen:

'Between two trees
There lies a story true,
A story true that I will tell to you

Was here that I first fell in love with Sue
Her hair was red
Her eyes were blue.'

Lyn's flat voice continued another couple of verses.

'Gee,' said Karl, 'that's great Lyn, I'll bet you and Gayleen win.'

'I gotta keep me voice in practice.'

They arrived at the rendezvous. The weeping willow was there as were the bushes at one side, secluded, with the river flowing just beyond. They sat down against the trunk, swigged and smoked some more, Lynette in the middle, Karl playing with himself and finally unbuttoning for Lyn to have a go at.

Benedict did the same.

Lyn puffed and sang and gazed moodily into the blue sky. 'I thought of singing "On Top of Old Smoky", but Gayleen always gets the third verse wrong.'

The boys put their hands up her bloomers and found their fingers meeting about the right place – where there was a bit of hair. Lynette opened her thighs a bit and stubbed out the cigarette. Benedict felt like shitting, but you couldn't leave at this crucial moment for Lynette had turned to dispose a moist kiss on his lips while Karl was pulling down her bloomers, she helping and arching her bum a bit off the ground.

'I feel so romantic,' said Lyn, 'with yous two here.'

Karl grunted and started on the buttons at the back of her dress. Benedict nuzzled at her breasts. In Angus' book that was what they did first.

To his surprise the nipples turned hard as they had done in *Hot Blood* when Lord Randly had started on Fifi the opera girl, and Lynette was taking long deep breaths as Ava Gardner did, sighing a lot and throwing back her head and gazing deep in Benedict and Karl's eyes as Jeanette McDonald did. Except Jeanette kept her clothes on.

Benedict got out of his pants, his Russian blood impatient, the Catholic-Calvinist squawks of the Pearses drowned.

Karl was red and stiff.

Benedict felt his balls tight against his shaft and the nob was right out of the skin.

Lynette noticed it too – with a great deal of interest. She played with it, pulling the skin over and letting it slide back. Karl pulled himself a bit and watched.

Then a cloud came over the sun and it seemed time to begin. Benedict let Karl try first, with his hand between her legs.

'Try that now Ben,' Karl said a silent moment later. 'Just one finger at a time. Show him Lyn.'

Lyn did and he felt her smoothness and slipperiness. She wriggled and moaned against Benedict's shoulder. 'Oh Ben, you've got such sensitive eyes. Is it true your mother is really a Russian princess?'

'Yer,' said Ben, breathing heavily and forgetting what romantic words he should use.

'Ooh, I knew it was true. Mum said she'd heard it from Magga Trout who heard it from the post mistress. Just like that, put it in like that. Just one finger, now two. Oh yes, my darling. Kiss me. Be romantic. Kiss me gently.'

Karl snorted and leaned over and kissed her hard and stuck his tongue in. Lyn gagged a bit but managed a sigh. 'Yes, just like that.'

Karl handed over a French letter to his friend. There was a bit of trouble as he tried to roll it on the wrong way, then tried again and this time got it right on and down. He hoped he wouldn't shoot – yet.

Lyn lay back, her head on her bloomers, her eyes half shut to show her passion and her lips slightly parted and she far away in a pearly haze with an orchestra playing in the background.

Karl whispered some directions to his friend who nodded grimly.

'Now, legs a bit more apart, Lyn, a bit higher with them, that's right.'

Karl had a good view and Lynette seemed to think she'd done her work. She was paralysed with romance.

Karl helped Ben. He guided his friend in, as you would any bull out of practice, and found the place. 'Now – push!'

Ben pushed and was past the lips and inside in the warmth.
'Slowly,' said Karl, 'she hasn't done it much before.'

Ben went slowly and found himself muttering at Lyn in English,
but she wanted something in Russian. All he could think of was
a prayer so he said that to her and Lyn was stirred to the depths
of her wild Miltonian soul. Ben started to accelerate.

'My Dad says you think of apples or a dripping tap,' said Karl.
Ben did so and slowed down.

'Ooh darling, say those things to me again in Russian. Ooh,
it's so nice, ooh you've gotta big Tom Thumb.'

She gave her lips with abandon and kissed his neck while his
toes took fresh purchase in a cow pad and now he knew he was
safe from something.

Everything was still except for the two of them and Karl's
quick breathing and the canopy of liquid green light. Benedict
wanted this to go on forever, for it was going somewhere even
if it had to be trapped in the rubber bubble at the top. 'Please
Devil,' he prayed, 'let this go on forever, I'll sell you my soul if
you like.'

The Devil smiled benignly. And Ben came into the rubber. He
pulled out slow and stared at the slippery frenchie with his seed
in it.

Karl was waiting to go straight in and he didn't need much
of a help as Lyn now lent a willing hand. She was open and wet.
She moaned and twisted and Karl was right, first thrust. But then
he was half an inch shorter so what could you expect?

Benedict lounged back, lordly, and watched it go in and
out – funny really. Karl moaned. Lyn moaned. That was that.

Karl pulled out, put a knot in his frenchie and threw it away.
Ben kept his, wrapped it in his handkerchief.

And then they saw the horse through the liquid shadows.

Angus, changed and looking left wing, rode to the edge of the
willow and looked at them. 'All yous kids'll go to gaol for this.
It's a crime at your age.' He laughed and fumbled with his fly
buttons. 'Wanta bit more, Lynette?'

Lynette opened her eyes wide and cowered. Angus was about

to get off his horse. He was off it. 'I'll show these kids a trick or two.'

Ben had with him his new sheath knife. He pulled it out. His face went white and his grey eyes looked nasty.

'You piss off, Angus,' he ordered. 'I'll tell Elizabeth on you. You piss off. I'll bloody knife you.' Angus wasn't to know that the blade was not extra sharp yet. 'You're supposed to be getting married,' added Ben.

Angus got back on his horse. 'I'll tell your bloody parents,' he said as he gathered in the reins.

'You piss off,' screamed the three conspirators.

The horse broke into a short canter and with several splashes it was across the river. Angus turned to laugh nastily at them, all naked. Then he laughed again, this time friendly.

They all knew they were quits. No one was going to say anything. Equal hands, equal cards, checkmate.

Lynette went into the water and washed herself, smiling lazily at the lovers displaying themselves to her from the bank.

Karl also washed. 'You ablute,' he said, 'before ya put it in again.'

So Ben followed and the cold water cleaned and awakened.

'Oh, no,' said Lyn, noticing. 'We've all had enough fun for today and I've gotta think of me voice for the talent quest.' Holding her bloomers, she stood beside the river and sang, her flat face tense with passion.

They walked to the bridge.

Evening was coming in the bridal train of twilight. The moths were out amongst the grasses and the occasional dragonfly, its wings on fire, reflecting the burning shell, gone, as Natalia said, to the other hemisphere, where he must follow it one day . . .

Lyn departed alone, so as no one could say that she and Karl Schenkle had been up to anything.

Benedict walked back along the tracks, the grass bending before him, the starlings coming to roost here and in the pine trees of the home paddock.

For some reason when he reached the willow he knelt, not

exactly to pray since he didn't know words anymore, but more to deposit his French letter in a small hole in the ground and cover it up.

He sat back and waited.

When he felt his belly stirring with hunger he went home.

9

The world is silent.

The Nazi war machine and the Allied war machine had ground and lunged at each other and finally, in that embrace of semen and blood, cogs and wheels, struts and lymph, a life-sustaining force had been reached and the orgasm of rust, decay, rot and dead dreams had fused in the womb for the new creation. Then the two machines, as intimately linked as spring lovers, had fallen apart and waited for the birth of peace.

The corpses, piled as high as the horizon, had been reduced to earth and on them flowers had not grown.

And time?

Over the bed the moon, now yellow and fertile as an egg, lit the plains of dream and the translucent face of the old Orthodox priest. And touched the memory of his great-nephew, mouth open in sleep and in the path of those wrapped in fiery cloaks moving still to the pavilions of peace. The dead cried out for his music as the spring cried for the flowers to grow. Had he met them on his way to birth, escaping the smoke and slaughter, the ovens and the gas?

He stirred and reached for his penis to comfort himself.

They danced before him, splinters of light or light itself.

'Rebecca Weiss,' he muttered to himself.

A stallion neighed to a distant mare and his flesh hardened with that sap of his age. 'Rebecca Weiss?' he muttered again, his dream touching into someone that he must know.

He struggled back into what might be another room of sleep. It was three in the morning and the wind blew softly. He got out of bed and the linoleum was cold on his feet. He put on his wool dressing-gown and slippers and glanced at the photos of the All Blacks and of Dad in soldier's uniform standing in front of a camel backed by an Arab and the Sphinx.

He slipped through the kitchen and out the back door. Nellie was lying in state on the doormat and gave a warning growl in case he'd forgotten.

He stopped in the darkness with the stars and the ruined car there, an owl swooping low over the lace work of trees. He took a pee and continued to the shearing shed and through to the room where the old man lived.

Inside the wardrobe were the old man's vestments. They were finely spun in the moonlight, with dust an essential part of their fineness.

The emptiness of the room embraced a sense of Dionysius and there was nothing of the homestead, now in ruins, that could not be fitted into the old man's truth.

Now Benedict is dreaming of the spikes dragging the earth into furrows, the seed falling in a thin stream from the boxes. Dad is wheezing away. At the end of a row, dust-covered, they'd suddenly not recognized each other.

His father had straightened out his back, normally bent over his lungs. He hadn't said anything but had taken his son by the shoulder and they'd stripped off their working clothes and strode through the mushy ground to the river and swam.

For the first time his father had let him see his body as proud as on that day he'd gone off to war. Nor was his father embarrassed by his son's naked presence, and he had looked straight at him and his sex.

The lights shone across the western hills and Benedict could see in the distance a flight of ducks.

Behind them the wind moved across the paddock in small storms of dust. 'Much drier than usual,' his father admitted.

And with the sun moving towards the palest of dun hills, the moment passed, as it must, and both of them knew something which would never be given again.

It was always fear, Benedict thought, as Rebecca's music clutched at his guts and the bitch whined and licked his ankles.

It was a time of night when everything was either so alive that you couldn't stand it or so dead that you floated with it in the wind in the pines along the home paddock.

You wanted to understand, being with it and nowhere.

And that was what he chose, awake now on the back step with a cup of tea, re-reading Rebecca's letter to Natalia, his eyes heavy with this strange dream and the blue shadows around his eyes like those he could see, but faintly, on the hills over which dawn must be coming; for the sun arrived at the moment of greatest decision.

Already in his shack down in the orchard, the rooster was swelling his throat and turning towards the east, preening between the white leghorns and the Australorps, middleman and lord of the harem.

Benedict heard him once faintly, as if clearing his throat, then again and again as his instinct told him the horses were pulling the chariot and their breath would soon be on the hills.

A goods train pulled out of Milton Station with a lonely scream. Down the tracks to another station no different from this one.

He went to his bed where the cat still snoozed through all revelation. Rebecca would come to stay with the Schenkles and that would be before Christmas – just.

10

Magga Trout's eyes began to glitter with dreams. The small set of brass scales and the silver scoop shone. The eucalyptus cough drops were discounted and the shop decorated with crêpe streamers. Then a notice appeared stating her support for the Town Queen. Hercules, her parrot, who had been banished to the sitting room, was back again on the mahogany counter cocking a ribald eye. Well might he! Magga Trout's dried-out pate was sporting a red wig which fell in descending streams of fire and lolloped around her ears to reflect the new fire of her lips – a bright shade of magenta which must clash: what otherwise was the point of it?

Up and down the main street the banners fluttered. The *Milton Herald* put out special bulletins on the events. The queens opened bazaars, kicked off at charity football matches, led hockey teams against other queens and ladies, hacked at each other's shins with blithe abandon, and sat on the ball when necessary.

The Plunkett Queen was assisting at a bring-and-buy stall outside.

Across the road the Talent Quest was being sponsored by the

supporters of the Town Queen, Elizabeth Fence, Angus the left-wing's intended. On the dot of eight-thirty it would get under way.

The Coronation Hall entrance was decorated with flowers about the mouldering gothic pillars. A red carpet was specially laid. Two posters outside advertised coming cinema attractions: tomorrow night Doris Day was going to do *On Moonlight Bay*. The film had been around three times already and Lyn was going to sing the theme song as an encore if she won.

Karl had a joke: 'I used to know Doris Day before she became a virgin'. Neither he nor Benedict knew what it meant.

Benedict flexed his fingers. Miss Crabtree was arriving with Mrs Baxter. He stitched on a smile. Miss Crabtree stopped to speak as did Mrs Baxter, who was most interested in his progress at the piano. 'Already up to *all* the Beethoven sonatas,' said Miss Crabtree proudly, but also knowing she must relinquish to a better teacher. To whom? There were rumours that the Schenkles' cousin, Rebecca Weiss, had arrived in Dunedin. Miss Crabtree was praying about the matter and awaiting Divine Guidance.

The flower arrangements swallowed up the ladies, wading through the glads and dahlias.

Karl arrived and they went in while Alison finished fussing with music on the Bechstein. As they found their seats Alison entered formally and went to the piano, her glorious hair in a bun, severe and practical, but showing her ivory skin to perfection, her cheekbones, her small-lobed ears.

The Town Queen moved to centre stage. She wore a long white frock and a white fur around her shoulders. The princesses were dressed in matching turquoise.

Alison's hands came down on the opening chords: 'God Save The Queen'.

The virgin before them raised her white neck like a swan and sang, in a soft little voice, her devotion to Flag and Empire.

There is so much evil, thought Magga Trout. What with the Korean War long over and one boy coming back with a certain disease. Unrepentant like Alison Black as to what he'd got up to, calling his Japanese whore a little flower. Well, with a worm in the middle. But at least the Working Girls' Club had disbanded, under management threats.

The performers came on to be announced – and there was Lyn, trussed up in pink and ruffles, her guitar decorated with ribbons. 'Like Shirley Temple in a whorehouse and down on her luck,' said Karl in a throaty whisper.

The lights dimmed for the first entry, Johnny Dash, 'The Cowboy from Lawrence': leather pants and a black cowboy hat, black silk muscle-rippling shirt, blue neck-scarf. The boots clinked right out of Texas.

Several ladies were jerking at lace handkerchiefs in anticipation. The Cowboy strummed up close to them and one or two could hardly restrain themselves from reaching for those bass notes and shoving them somewhere. Velvet and gauze grated on corsets. Sweat trickled.

'I dunno,' whispered Karl, who instinctively recognized plastic emotion when he saw it, 'why they can't make up songs about around here.'

Several irate ladies turned and frowned. The prayer must not be interrupted as the ceiling lifted into a night of desert stars.

Johnny Dash finished with them and the applause was terrible. They'd been transported.

Now the compere, Mr Fluck – whatta name! – was all ready to make them laugh before Muriel, the town contralto, came on in her long coffee-coloured gown to sing a couple of art songs.

Margaret, in her fur coat, McClean tartan skirt and solid brown lace-up shoes, crept into her seat. She wiped a drip off her nose, stern too, head sunk in her hump, brooding over something, hardly taking in Muriel, hands clasped in front of bosom, a gardenia bouncing about.

Muriel's hair was done up around her head in tight coils with many a tortoise-shell comb, the diva of the evening, gracious in her baritone-to-bass voice.

Alison accompanied – white with concentration. Schubert.

Karl was sniggering into his handkerchief. Several ladies lashed at him with disapproving lips. That Schenkle boy never did anything but stare at girls. Even poor Muriel Addle's bosom was not safe. And as for that Lynette! On stage with Gayleen, flat face wreathed in an imaginary mist of light.

Lyn strummed the guitar and let her face grow loose and thoughtful as she waited for them to settle down to her magic and be beguiled by it.

'Between two trees
There lies a story true
A story true
That I will tell to you . . .'

Benedict clapped, but not too hard in case anyone should guess. But what was the story true?

Margaret McClean closed her eyes and tried to find it. Beginning here: yes, all their energies were working together. It would take more than a bashing of tins to unswarm them.

So many mothers smiling and battering their eyelashes. Lyn wafted them right along to Christmas Day, not to speak of the crowning of the Queen of Milton on Christmas Eve.

Twang! The more musical acknowledged that Gayleen had gone flat and that Lyn, coming out of her dream of 'Between Two Trees', was scowling and nudging her into step.

The mums drifted off again. If they got home in time, it being Friday night, they could have a listen on the radio to Harry Strang's Dance Band at St Kilda, or Joe Brown's Late Dance from the Dunedin Town Hall. Who hadn't had a bitta shuffle around in the old days?

It was a funny night. Sort of warm sou-wester blowing outside.

A white Christmas? That would be lovely, like living somewhere else. And who cared anyway, if this was supposed to be summer. The bloody weather knew what was best.

One hesitates on the edge of all paths. Dionysius in the wool shed entered his own meditation. He watched the energies breaking and forming over the town.

One is faced with negation, he thought. It is a process of

attrition. Many thousands of years were needed to reach this point of experience, the Iron Age – the age of bits and pieces, rejected before – now the foxhole in which this town crouches. They will negate themselves almost finally, but not completely, since there is always the light which will shine out of fragments and will repair and make whole the casings of matter.

On his knees was a text of an early father. Dionysius could not remember whether Saint Gregory of Sinai or Saint Nilus.

Silence rained about him in dense sheets so that he could see only the inward point he strived for where Benedict Pearse-Dashkov, somewhere in his future, flexed his fingers and looked at the piano keys, white under the overhead lights.

The orchestra played the opening bars of Chopin's First Piano Concerto. In his black dress trousers, Ben felt himself ready. His hands came down.

Dionysius sighed in his meditation. So the boy would go to Warsaw for the International Chopin Competition.

Johnny Dash, by popular request, had come at them again:

'Mother, pal and sweetheart,
Three names I love so true,
Mother, there'll be no other
It's mother to the end.'

This guaranteed the Cowboy the votes of all the mothers.

The lights dimmed and the audience sank back into the occasion. The contestants formed a semi-circle and in came Queen Elizabeth Fence, regal although she'd had a couple of gin-slings backstage with Mr Fluck. But regal as an eagle.

Her hair was still immaculately shaped, noted Mrs Fence, who had given Elizabeth another going-over that afternoon. The lacquer was keeping all the sculptured waves in place, frozen over Elizabeth's forehead, who'd had time to put on a bit of powder and redden up her lips. The princesses bustled about their Queen, straightening and patting for the photos. Her diamanté crown sparkled as much as glass could under the competent electric light.

First they gave away third prize; it went to the conjurer. The town liked illusions, no matter how badly done. In fact, the worse the better; that way you can keep your feet on the ground. Second place to the McClaren sisters who sang about love and betrayal in a rather more mature way than Lynette and Gayleen. And first prize – Muriel thrust forward her bosom and then took the bullet in the belly – was the Cowboy from Lawrence.

Johnny Dash lept forward, chaps crackling and buttocks so tight that a carload of Bacchantes couldn't have prised them apart. Dark eyes lustrous and lips full-blooded, he thrust out his chest and kissed the Town Queen on the cheek, which was met by applause and a deep spiritual moan from the mill girls.

Anywhere else they would have ripped off their bras and come in a high scream – for him standing there alone, legs apart now and loins thrust out, guitar at the ready. Their souls gathered in great clusters around it, swooning and shapeless, willing on whatever he'd give them. An encore. One more time. Fuck Alison Black and her revolution.

Then the special prizes.

Muriel condescended with a tight-lipped nod and received a special leather-bound edition of Schubert which she'd been heard to want. Central to the town culture, which the organizers *knew*, Muriel became all diva.

Lyn and Gayleen were called forward, fixed doll-smiles, eyes rather glazed at the applause. Lynette was already on Moonlight Bay with Cary Grant and Queen Elizabeth presented a special box of chocolates, but Lyn would renounce them – so her gesture of acceptance indicated – for the good of her figure and her voice.

Alison was back at the piano, solid stolid Paula sitting beside her to hold down the music. Good old Alison and good old Paula.

Everyone sang 'God Defend New Zealand'. For what reason no one could be sure, except they were where they were. Maybe for the prime lamb and the thick butter you could rub over yourself, so one mill girl had confessed, and then do it. Imagine with Johnny Dash! Soft slippery butter on his belly and those thighs gripping you like a horse.

Margaret let her voice rise like a lark above them all, riding the storm she could feel. Benedict left the hall with her. Outside he saw his mother, who had come late. Pearse was in the car. He always vanished when Margaret was close.

'Take Margaret home,' said Natalia to her son. 'Walk her home.'

The two women kissed.

'Have you ever seen such a sky over such a small patch of earth?' Natalia demanded.

Benedict and Margaret crossed the road.

Wong's fruiterers was still open, Mrs Wong in her tight-bound feet, her small wrinkled monkey's face intent on her task, dressed in a shabby silk housecoat with a woollen scarf around her throat.

Margaret shivered and came back to herself.

And on cue from the Rugby Club came a cavernous roar. The Rugby princess, left-wing Angus, wig streaming in the wind, was going to pick up the Town Queen. Dressed in chiffon and waving a bunch of glads, Angus was clapsed to the bosom of the Rugby Queen Tom Maxwell, driving with one hand and swigging back whisky with the other.

Their cavalcade passed by, streaming with pink dunny paper, horns tooting loud and long. One of the boys threw out a thunder flash and a cat leapt to the safety of a branch, spitting, back arched.

The sky was still there with the galaxies bright beyond frost, but the mind of the town let the boys in with a grateful sigh.

Margaret, in her coat with the warm wool scarf around her mouth, stayed for some time, listening.

'In three days,' she began to walk again, 'there is the crowning of the Queen of Milton with the ball. It is also the vigil, as they call it in the old books, of the incarnation. In the trenches in France in World War I, on Christmas Eve, the German and French boys heard angels singing. And so all will be well.'

Margaret brushed her fingers along a holly hedge to reassure herself.

'Such skies and sunsets here,' she offered Benedict. 'Perhaps because of them they hold all the harder to things like chairs and new wallpaper. They are less demanding.'

At fifteen what could you say?

Margaret was singing inside herself like a thrush, buffed up against the cold, and Benedict felt a bit ungracious. He didn't want to walk back along the railway line by himself.

'Yes,' she muttered more to herself than the boy. Remembering too the mystery of the snake. Bottled on the mantlepiece. Brought back by old Davie from Fiji, golden baleful eye watching her through the fume of oil. No sympathy there but also no illusions. But she would still reach out her stubby fingers to the birds, feel the tiny pool of warmth in which their bones and feathers had their existence. And guts.

'And this is strange,' she told Benedict, forgetting her thoughts hadn't been spoken. 'There are also cats. Who are the enemies of birds. They too have this warmth in which their bodies live. It is like light but contained into a shape. When you are in the right frame of mind you can feel it, and on this flesh depends. And yet cats are cats.

'As people are people. But with people – because of my withdrawal – I haven't the necessary skill to know. Their thoughts are growing into such ugly shapes that perhaps I do not want to believe it.

'Or perhaps it was formerly so, when people lived more beautiful lives. As in the diver of Paestum. The book has arrived but the text is in Italian and I must continue to decipher it myself.'

'Dionysius says there's no more time,' offered Benedict.

Margaret might have started sulking at this difficult proposition had they not been secure now inside her gate.

'We will drink some tea,' she decided as they walked around the path to the back door. To Benedict she seemed taller, her presence overflowing into a bed of midnight velvet pansies and the grasses she allowed despite offers of Magga Trout's son through a hole in the hedge to cut the bloody lot down as a favour, like, and anyway they were all seeding in his friggin' garden, and his garden, which was used only to law and order, had started to sprout bloody docks, couch grass, cocksfoot and thistles, not to mention friggin' hemlock coming under the path!

Margaret put her hand on the back door and pushed hard. They were met by a wave of hot air with a good smell of burning coal.

She got down the blue cups and saucers and shifted the hob over the burning coals.

She drank her tea and munched on a coconut biscuit.

'And now,' she said, looking at the tea leaves in the cup bottom, 'it is time for you to walk home. Your mother will worry if you're late.'

Benedict left with a biscuit in his hand and a couple in his pocket.

'Be good to your parents,' Margaret called from the door.

Down the streets, the sounds of revelry from the barn-dance hardly touched the placid surfaces of brick.

Outside Queen Elizabeth Fence's house was the tourer that the Rugby Queen and his two princessses had disported themselves in. Elizabeth sat demure in the front seat with Angus half-flaked beside her. Beside the car was a pool of vomit.

'Hi, Elizabeth,' Benedict said.

Angus managed to open his eyes.

'Just a kid, dear,' Elizabeth whispered, so as Angus would not have to put on a social face.

Benedict crossed the road and began to hurry. Suddenly there was too little air.

11

The crowning and the following ball were on them.

'So many bloody events in one night,' Pearse said, getting trussed into his tails and fumbling about with the cufflinks with the Dashkov coat of arms that Natalia had presented to him. Natalia found them heavy and a trifle vulgar – but stylish. And no one would notice, or not approve if they did, since Pearse was an upright pillar of the community these days and entitled to a touch of gold.

Natalia pulled out her sable coat from the trunk and glanced at the long silk dress, French, that Ariadne had sent from Genève – for the *occasional* little evening, as she had put it in her letter.

Pearse was slicking his hair back with brilliantine and adjusting his OBE. They'd gone up to Wellington to get it from the Governor. The head of the Farmer's League, Pearse was fighting hard for higher prices and a staunch conservative in and out of bed.

The front door closed as Benedict left to walk across to the town.

The Coronation Hall was decked out in fresh flowers. The women had been busy all day with them, gathering bunches still with the dew on them—roses and dahlias, the late daffs and narcissi, the sprawling branches of lilac.

Benedict stood outside and waited for Karl. They'd done Lyn over at three, on the Schenkles' new wall-to-wall carpet.

He felt at peace while he watched the townspeople rolling up. He tried to see them as Margaret saw birds and cats who were natural enemies, but apparently not for ever since they were surrounded by the same warmth and light.

Was God like a cat? Charlotte had asked him, years ago. Benedict had though he might be.

'Hi ya!' said Karl, who had Lyn trailing behind him. Ten yards further behind was Gayleen, done up in gold with a new butterfly clip in her hair.

'Congratulations,' said Benedict, 'on your hairdo.' It was bouffant.

He stood up as well since it was public and his mother said you stood when ladies were around, and Lyn was radiant in a pink dress. No bows in her hair tonight and a touch of her mother's pink lipstick and face powder.

'Only talc,' said Karl. 'She told me.'

Lyn sniffed.

'Who do you think won?' asked Gayleen. She was ignored.

'Cantcha hear me or something?'

They sat down. The stage was open and the blue curtains tidied to both sides and held back by a blue cord.

Resplendent in brown, Magga Trout dreamed back to the gold rush and the aboriginal nigger, Black Andy, who ran from Dunedin delivering the mail.

Eeny meeny mino mo
Catch a nigger by the toe
If he squeals let him go
Eeny meeny miny mo.

Magga had thought of grabbing Andy.

The Lord Chamberlain entered with a blaze of lights. Magga sniffed to herself at the candelabrum donated for the evening by that Mrs Pearse, friend of Alison Black who was dressed, appropriately, in red tonight. There was a round of applause and she forgot the mists, the tussock that had grown where the Coronation Hall now stood.

Alison, noted Magga, looked nervous.

'And now,' said the Lord Chamberlain, his wig rucking around his shoulders, 'I give you the Mayor!'

There was fanfare of trumpets.

Magga nodded approvingly at the new scarlet robes, the chain of office glowing amidst the ermine. An expense well warranted when Queen Elizabeth had visited after her coronation. A whistlestop tour, a quick speech, and on to the next place. But leaving behind a strong sentiment, thought Magga, sizing up Mrs Fergusson the Mayor's wife in her best ball gown, crimped, descending at a precipitous rate from her expanding middle to small waves of tulle around her ankles.

The Grand Chamberlain rapped his staff on the floor and the heads of the dahlias and banks of narcissi about the throne bent and waved.

'I give you aspirants for Queen.'

The would-be queens all curtsied in unison.

'We will start with the third place. To the left of the throne of the reigning Queen will be as princess our one and only, and lovely' – the Mayor wattled and puffed – 'lovely Plunkett Queen, Nurse McDonald, who looks after the kiddies' dental health. Her courtiers raised two thousand pounds!'

The mothers gnashed their teeth when they remembered those baby smiles straight from heaven.

'Second place goes to the Country Queen, Miss Anne Prince, with two thousand eight hundred, who has deserted the counter at Hall's Chemist Shop to be second princess and to sit on the right of the throne of the reigning Queen of the Night and the Year, the Town Queen, Elizabeth Fence, whose courtiers raised four thousand.' The applause grew tumultuous.

'As a special favour the reigning Queen will allow the Rugby Queen to help with the occasional dubbing of knighthoods.'

Mrs Fergusson dug her husband in the side. In his enthusiasm he had got the order of things wrong. 'It's supposed to be after the Grand Procession,' she hissed, 'that Angus and the boys come on!' She could have kicked him she was that annoyed.

But the loyal subjects had seen nothing amiss and were cheering. More cheers as Tom, pissed as a newt, came striding in with his two princesses, Terry and Angus, dressed in wedding gowns, white veils, blown-up falsies, red lips and all pregnant.

The Mayor paled then rallied. But the ladies gave their approval and thrust out their dimples and bosoms and sweetest smiles at how boys, under it all, understood.

Alison Black stood up white-faced and left the stage; but Queen Elizabeth's mother laughed, as did Big Tom's and Terry's.

As if they understood 'Mother, pal and sweetheart', the boys wilted a bit and the fun was over. They trooped out to whistles and cat calls and the Lady Mayoress was seen remonstrating with Alison just offstage. She came back on with Paula and sat again at the piano, her face in a rage of concentration. Paula checked the music with nervous fingers.

The boys hadn't done much harm, reflected the Lady Mayoress, while they changed back into mufti, although Angus should be given a talking to.

Alison began the Coronation Music.

The Queen sank to her throne and the Mayor, assisted by a Doolan playing Archbishop, held the crown high above her head. The trumpets blared as it was placed on her head. Her white hands stretched forward to accept the orb and sceptre.

Alison finished with an overloud chord. Paula glanced at her but knew better than to whisper anything.

The trumpets blared again and the Mayor took the Queen's elbow while the princesses picked up her fur-trimmed train.

'Ladies and Gentlemen. Rise for the Queen.'

Which they did. In a hush. For Elizabeth Fence had become foreign and might order an execution for them, or dance a pavane with her favoured lord, kicking her legs high in regal abandon.

Muriel sailed to the piano and the children's choir, augmented by the League of Mothers, grouped about her. Alison struck up the opening chords of 'Land of Hope and Glory' and Muriel – a devoted subject in green with a spray of orchids – sang. Her throat strained open with the glorious words. The audience, tender and proud, started to mumble along with her. Angus' mum, the Mayoress, and Mrs Fence were openly weeping at it all.

Elizabeth walked stately down the ramp without a glance as to where her feet were, neck like a swan, descending to them from a great distance. She was the stuff of dreams.

Muriel, having wrecked her vocal chords on a couple of high Cs, curtsied deep and left to gargle out her throat.

Alison walked off without a glance.

The Lord Chamberlain handed the Queen her sword.

Natalia and Alison had refused to take part in the dubbing: Alison for the fury bubbling up in her, Natalia because she was tonight Natalia Dashkov. And it seemed that Pearse, with his OBE, dazzled by the light of her sapphires, was shackled to Natalia in a very final way.

Benedict shouldered out with Karl and Lynette. They'd managed to get rid of Gayleen onto one of her girlfriends.

Lyn's face was dreamy with possibilities.

'I really feel like it,' she whispered to the thick clouds in the south. 'It's so much more romantic when you know it might start snowing. I mean, it's like a miracle.'

It was ten thirty when the opening waltz sounded its first lingering notes.

The Lord Chamberlain helped Queen Elizabeth to remove the cloak and crown. Angus put down his whisky and stepped out into the empty floor. The dancers applauded as they made the first circuit alone.

Alison glanced at her card, the supper waltz was at ten minutes to midnight.

'Christmas Eve,' she mentioned to Natalia. A cold draught blew in through an open door and she adjusted her fur cape. Paula went to refill their whiskies.

The large reflecting ball on the ceiling turned and caught the light of the jewellery and layer upon layer the air was filled with smoke and now, from the kitchens in the back where the Schenkles were catering, the smell of turkey.

Natalia fanned herself as the band struck up the opening chords of the supper waltz, 'The Destiny'. Pearse took her arm and they joined the ring of dancers. The dresses flared and caught on each other, and then that soft hesitant step forward.

The trestles were hurriedly pulled out, the tables covered with white cloths. There was little to do before eating except to toast the Queen in the good green sauterne.

Alison stood with Paula, who swayed a bit. They were all flushed with the dancing and the booze.

Alison's red ball gown had been a gift from Natalia. Perhaps the fault lay with the arrogantly simple cut.

'The Queen,' said the Mayor.

Alison laughed and her glass shattered on the floor. New energy coursed through her. Her fists itched to smash into dust every brick raised over this swamp. She remembered as she laughed at them the snake on Margaret McClean's mantelpiece, eyes cold with the spaces between worlds.

The town looked at her, hair elegant but now half undone down her back, breasts defiant, her milk-white skin that had never known the teeth of a town male.

The glass ball had ceased revolving but an ultra-violet light burned through the men's tarnished faces, their balls tight for what Alison Black must finally get.

'What are you doing with decent people,' shrieked the Carnival Queen. 'Why aren't you married? We've known for years. You don't need to answer us!' Her small decent face flushed. 'Just being here you've wrecked everything. There are other pianists, Alison!'

Magga Trout tottered forward, her new wig falling judicially over her shoulders.

'In America they send them to the electric chair,' said the Sports Queen. 'Why don't you Rugby boys *do* something.'

Magga fingered her string of amber beads: 'Once we believed in virtue, and kept things clean.'

Alison smiled: 'Did you burn a few heretics?'

The Carnival Queen felt the taste of truth on her lips: 'You're nothing but a viper, Alison.'

'And a bitch,' screamed the Sports Queen, muscular arms tensed with the headsman's axe that would come down on that white neck.

Alison Black threw back her head and laughed in peals of delicate crystal and then, under the strain of the vibration, she shattered and fell.

She lay where she was, some blood dribbling down her forehead.

A small cut, thought Benedict Pearse, watching his godmother from the door.

Alison was helped up by Paula and saw her godson where he stood with clenched fists and his eyes grey as ice. She shook her head.

'You are a load of fakes and yet you talk about freedom, as if this was freedom?' She took the glass of whisky Paula got for her. 'What have any of you done for progress?'

'Who mentioned freedom, Alison?' boomed the Mayor, severe in his tails like a fat blackbird hopping amongst the voters. 'And haven't we freedom? Who talked about freedom but you? You refused on Christmas morning to toast the Queen. Have you cast in your lot with the enemy? Don't you care about our democracy?'

It was obvious she didn't and that by her denial she was compromising the Christmas goodwill and dirtying the miracle of falling snow.

Alison dabbed her lips. 'I am entitled to believe what I like.'

'And,' said Tom Maxwell, 'what will happen to us when your revolution breaks out.'

'She'd have us dead,' said the Carnival Queen. 'They kill off anyone who doesn't agree with them. Unless you get them first, like us in Korea.'

The band made a few tentative noises but was stopped by those who turned towards them.

Natalia Pearse, who had drunk some sauterne to calm her heart, started to giggle and stopped herself; she herself was within the amphitheatre with her two children.

'I do not see. . .' she heard herself saying in the voice of that English governess – how many years ago? Then on Sundays, lunch in the Hotel de Russie and a boat ride to Chillon, to the chateau where 'that lecherous goat Byron' as her father called him, had scratched his name into a pillar like any vulgar tourist out with his cut-lunch and camera.

'Don't you think,' said Natalia, 'that you are all being rather ridiculous. After all, Alison may not be a communist, she may be a republican like the Americans who threw out the English monarchy. Or she may be a committed socialist or a secret Irish Catholic. Or equally, a human being who feels.'

No one of course laughed, and Natalia was winging over the walls. 'I, for instance am a Russian. I had to flee in my parents' arms from one revolution and I have met in my time many people who chose for many reasons to be Catholic, Orthodox, monarchist, republican, fascist, communist – or for that matter, saints, in the sense in which Mrs Magga Trout would use the term. But until the barricades are down and we are forced to take sides we can exist quite amicably.'

This breath of civilization was rightly rejected.

'Whata ya know,' said Angus, 'that old tart Pearse is one of them too.'

At which Pearse, drunk and sick but loyal, belted him one. To everyone's surprise, Angus stayed on the floor longer than necessary and offered no comeback.

'I demand an apology,' yelled Pearse, bouncing up and down, breath flowing into him like air from the mountains, his lungs pumping clear and clean and him young again and the boxer he'd been. 'I demand an apology immediately for the insult to my wife.'

But attention was diverted, for Alison Black and her friend Paula had gathered themselves together and were about to deliver an ultimatum.

'We have paid our money,' said Alison, 'to attend this ball and we are not leaving even if you all do.'

Natalia disagreed with this. She managed a slow walk through the crowd, which stood aside for her, and stopped in front of Alison but also half turned so all could hear.

'You know, my dear, when one thinks about it, one would rather be stoned by this mob than accepted by them. One must take one's compliments, Alison, where they fall. And now I think I will leave this—gala occasion.'

She kissed Alison lightly on each cheek and walked on, without Pearse who was swaying and staring around him, ready to grab his rifle and leap over the dugout at the enemy. But the attack never came and so he followed her.

Benedict hid amongst the coats because if he were seen he would be taken home. Yet Natalia would not deny, for she was staring out of her pale-blue eyes with a high amusement her son had never seen before.

At the door of the Coronation Hall she turned to her husband. 'I think, Pearse, that we have just severed diplomatic relations and on Christmas morning. I will hear mass at the Catholic Church. It is only midnight. Do you wish to come with me?'

'Like that?' he asked.

'Pearse, like this, as I am, as I have always been.'

'I dunno,' said Pearse, but would follow anyway.

Alison Black waved to her friends then went over to the table, picked up a fork, speared some turkey and potatoes, hesitated over the stuffing, and returned to Paula to talk quietly as if nothing had happened.

Elizabeth, the Queen, nudged Angus and Big Tom.

'She has no respect. And tonight, of all nights when. . .'

It was evident that the Queen might sign a Bill of Attainder without noticing.

The band was playing 'Rock Around the Clock' as they returned to the bar.

But Alison signed the Bill herself. She had another couple of whiskies and started rocking and rolling with Paula.

Elizabeth the Queen developed a headache and had to leave at once, and anyway Angus was planning a late late do with the boys. Some of the other girls remembered presents to be wrapped and the Doolans were already at Midnight Mass.

*　　*　　*

The boys got the girls home and then back to the Rugby pavilion, all their gear still there, radio on, plenty of smog from the roll-your-owns.

They stood at the door, swaying about and farting with the beer, looking at the field they played on and didn't recognize.

So back into the warmth with the photos of past fifteens, the decorations the lads had won in the war, the parade after the war, the past presidents of the club in their blue and gold blazers, the cups they had won from other towns.

The showers were right through the door and bloody hot as Angus knew who'd taken one to wake himself up from the ball and Elizabeth in a peeve. The windows had steamed up.

The boys roared with laughter as Big Tom fitted himself again into his wedding dress with the veil, as did Terry into his brides-maid's-cum-wedding dress and left-wing Angus into his, smacking Tom on the rump and Tom laughing like a drain and bashing at them with the bouquet of gorse and geraniums.

All dancing around, passing on the whisky bottle after a good swig to keep things up and going and getting out the ball and trying a few passes and a few more chug-a-lugs. With the club president glowering down at them, dour old bugger, from his framed photo.

Then out the door and Big Tom, prop, with the left and right wings on either side of him, dresses hitched up and right on the ball, which they sang. 'The song of the Rugby Men':

'On the ball, on the ball, on the ball,
Fifteen stout fellows and all . . .'

Shit! What came after that? Roaring it out anyway for what the fuck did the words matter?

Tom tried a punt at goal and over it went, the leather lost in a drift by the hedge and the veil that separated them from the town or married them to it continuing to fall; and now chasing the Rugby Queen around the field, all roaring with laughter and falling about, and old Elizabeth, Queen or no Queen, would be getting it legally soon and probably a bun in the oven. Elizabeth wasn't saying, nor her mum, though her dad pissed at the pub had let it out sideways a couple of days ago. Bloody laugh that wedding would be!

Now forming a line-out and Angus throwing in and the ball out to the five-eighth and on out to the left wing or some bugger and haring along and over the line. Try for Milton!

Back in the clubhouse Tom fixed his lips with a simper and someone put a record on – Elvis the Pelvis, 'Jailhouse Rock'. They danced around and smoked a few more fags.

It was three in the morning with Angus spewing hot and steaming in the gutter; but on around a corner and who should they see at the street end with her dog squatting for a shit but Alison Black, changed into fur-lined boots and her parka.

Tom, as Rugby captain, let out a yell and set off, kicking the ball ahead for the team to chase, and Alison, still a bit tiddly and fired by the vision into which she was cast, was thinking of what she could do about Milton and herself, when out of the snow falling around her came the veils flying with the speed of descent, the faces rouged, the lips fixed in a grimace, red and dripping with lipstick and spittle as they chased towards the goal which must be her.

She screamed and ran as fast as she could, on down the street and past her house which she forgot existed, since it was only in the fields, at the thorny edge of a ditch, that she would find safety from them. On and over a gate, tearing her leg on the barbed wire, her breath coming in gasps as she ran, clumsily now for the wolves would soon be on her and this was what they meant by suffering for what you believed?

But it was not a stoning as Natalia had suggested. It was something else.

The ball was punted over her head and bounced in front of her on the crust of snow and they on her, kicking and thrusting forward with her to the goal, suddenly ripping, their balls tight in the air and holding open her legs and Big Tom yanking up his wedding dress and she crushed by him and the veil in her mouth.

Just as suddenly he found his mark and thrust, someone else holding his hand across her mouth and slobbering over her. They were battering her with their release, everywhere, everywhere it felt. Someone laughing, but that was her laughing as her mouth got free of the hand and veil and she could laugh: with this vast field curtained off from the town which far back in its brick houses had just won the war against her.

Suddenly the ruck lifted itself off and would have liked to lie and get back its breath and adjust its clothing and find again the bouquets, but she lay with blood around her thighs.

Alison's lips had crumpled into pink crêpe paper, her arms were stretched out like streamers, and the scrum horsed around to show it was all a joke that they must forget at once. What better way than the Rugby ball, a few feet off? Yellow leather, really wet.

So the snow fell and Alison Black raised herself in silence. But had been kicked in the head and could not remember the way home for now there was nothing but this fire over which she must crawl towards the ditch where she would be safe, forever in sleep with this sick feeling she had. But safe from Japanese bombs falling on the hospital. Safe with the men she was nursing, and Hank with third-degree burns on his chest.

Now she was among them, her hair singed and her skin blistered, her bandages ready and her salves. She touched them and murmured words to be brave and stroked their foreheads. With them she went to sleep, waiting for the morning.

The falling snow was better than conscience for it covered the footprints, the spots of blood, the trail she might have left had people taken more seriously that she was worthy of a search on Christmas Day.

In the club Big Tom roared out:

'Oh! My old man's a night man, a night man, a night man.
He goes round the dunnies all night,
And he comes home in the evening, the evening,
I give him a plate full of shit.'

The boys held another court. Laughing and fooling about they put Big Tom, shickered as a goat, under the showers. Some passed out then but all knew they were sleep-walkers when Big Tom was laid out on a rug in front of the open fire and on him Angus, the first, with rouged cheeks and blonde wig, half-deflated falsies grating on the splintery floor that belonged to the Sports Queen's mum.

Terry poured whisky down Tom's throat, and then with Angus to break him in, Big Tom was royally shafted – white arse, hairy hole and all.

The others blundered around and waited their turn.

Big Tom was that quiet he could have been dead, though his eyes opened with the first thrust.

There was nothing anyway to say since now he and they were safe from Alison Black. Better than an oath, one crime wiped out another.

The walls of the pavilion reached the stars, better than any concentration camp. But during the consecration, snow was rubbed from the window and a face looked in.

12

The choir had been rehearsing for weeks and was managing the chanting quite well. The incense was thick about the altar with Father O'Fee, tall and golden in the middle of it, feet hardly touching the ground. The language was Latin, and in that way you were removed from your swearing and jokes, desires for profit, hatreds and meanness.

You could go to the other place where you were not those things.

Natalia at least believed this and at the 'Incarnatus Est' sank so low that Benedict, watching from the back, thought she'd never manage to heave herself up again.

He shoved his hands deep in his pockets, for the snow had brought a freezing wind with it, and hoped Gayleen hadn't told on Lyn. He turned his thoughts back to the altar. The lamb was once more defenceless before man.

Benedict left into the darkness for another circuit of the town.

He could easily have gone home. Their Christmas tree would be lit up and the presents laid around the base for the morning, the cat on Charlotte's bed and Nellie on the rug in front of the range. But instead he traced the anonymous line of streets. He flexed his fingers. It was hard to imagine Rebecca having been in a camp. She'd been betrayed in Paris but she'd survived because some German friend of Mum's had got her into the orchestra. Three years after the war's end, two of them spent in a nursing home, she had faced Germany with Mozart, Piano Concerto in D Major, K537. But her hands had refused to play and she'd left the stage. He was now learning it. One day he would play it with the Berlin Philharmonic – for her.

And for a moment, when he had sat with Rebecca and she had told him what he already knew but had to be told, he heard himself in the Waldstein he had played for her, singing like a bird before the storm, playing with steel and love in a flow that could only purify as the years passed into another holocaust? After all, it had happened to Rebecca.

'You will be great,' she had repeated.

He shrugged his shoulders. The sheep were in the home paddocks. Pearse had shifted them yesterday after sniffing the wind.

Unsure why he walked, Ben turned down another street, past Alison's place, and ahead the paddocks opened to the sky and the hills beyond.

Then he felt the shape, running and falling, and saw a few geraniums near the gate and a piece of white satin fluttering. His mind went into a blank and fear caught him as he began to run, faster and faster, the trees, the hedges, the emptiness urging him on.

It had to be someone's room and the only one that he knew for certain would contain a human being, contain what he had sensed and not crack, was Margaret's. So he rushed for her house, shoved open the gate and ran around the corner, skidding, cannoning into the walls and into the kitchen sobbing for breath. He found her flat out on the ground as if in a faint, arms stretched out with the fire low, and in the corner a little crèche she had made with candles lit around it. Sparrows and waxeyes with an occasional gold finch and fat thrush cheeped on the curtain rails.

Margaret returned from wherever she had been. She listened

as she picked up her thick duffle coat from the arm chair. 'I've been out rescuing birds who were not prepared, as Boy Scouts are told to be, for this night.'

He told her, in gasps, his story, which anyone else would have laughed at. But Margaret understood and pushed him ahead of her out of the door.

She walked, or rather shuffled, with a scarf around her lips, to keep the cold from her lungs. He talked, but the snow absorbed his voice. She pretended to hear since he was letting off steam.

They pushed ahead through the deserted streets, blanketed cars – not even headlights to tell them this was civilization.

He tried again to explain as they approached the place. But standing at the farm gate with the barbed wire looped about it to discourage kids, the smell of fear, the heat of flesh had gone. It would have been in Margaret's power to know. She would have caught the edge of such things and followed the sense of it to the ditch, but a blanket had fallen thick and white and had absorbed the traces and the vibration.

'I don't know,' she said, 'what you saw. There is a great confusion here and the loser always wins. Something bad, yes, something, very bad.' She started to cough a little. 'But it seems to have gone back up the street.'

They walked again, she leading like a gun dog, pointing with her snout. Stopping for a moment to catch her breath, following again the shape which was already absorbing the victim as the scrum made its way up the street fast this time; real fast in their passing of the ball and their kicking ahead; running as if out training, chests strained, not seeing but together; Tom holding up his wedding skirts, the bouquet dropped somewhere, the veil streaming and his dick red with Alison's blood.

Margaret clasped the boy's gloved hand.

She did not mind the pain in her lungs since that she could feel around her was greater. 'But paid for, paid for,' she mumbled – on a night like this when she must be a pillar of flame, if God willed.

They were past Maxwell's corner.

Ahead, the long straight road that led along the plain, with the avenue of blue gums at Milburn visible now through the squalls that were blowing from a closed sky, and the waves beating down on the sea beaches of the plain.

'It is still this way,' she said. 'And what it is, whatever it is, will soon manifest itself. I am not afraid but you are young.'

They were past the Queen Elizabeth Coronation Park before she stopped.

Here there was a light flickering dimly from around the back of the Rugby pavilion, and here there were cars: the open tourer of the Rugby Queen and his princesses, snow thick on the front seat, the muddle made by tyres in the snow, the flowers, the streamers damp with water, the yellow pool of piss, the gate open and the light from the clubroom.

'It is here,' she said. 'But what I do not understand.'

She took his hand. 'If anything should happen, or should come at us, run, because all they can do is kill me and that is very little. You will run?'

She looked at him with eyes as fierce as a wildcat's, orange and flickering. He was forced to bow to her superior understanding which Dad would accept would not be cowardice in the face of the enemy.

They crept along the path until they came to the door which they dared not open. Margaret climbed on a convenient fruit box, brushed away some snow and looked. She turned her face away, puzzled and compassionate, for nothing fitted what she had felt. She did try to stop Benedict from seeing, but could not as he had to.

'Yet it was not that,' she said, taking his hand and leading him away. 'This is not what I felt.'

She led him home.

Dawn would soon arrive over the eastern hills that separated them ineffectually from the sea.

She put the kettle on and brewed some tea – brandy in it for them both – and telephoned his parents. Then she directed him to Old Davie's bed and changed in the bathroom into her flannel nightie. In the morning before he left for Christmas Day they would search for more birds to feed.

She sat on her bed which was the sofa and put on her glasses. She read from her family Bible, sighed, turned out the light and got into bed.

There was nothing to say.

13

Natalia looked out of the kitchen window at the peony roses, lush and unblackened by some miracle.

Today was the inquest on Alison Black's death, which might decide on murder, rape, or death by misadventure.

Didn't these communists believe in free love and had she not been walking the dog late? Had Paula heard anything? No, she had not. It had all taken place too far away, besides which she had had more to drink than Alison, taking a couple more whiskies before retiring. She could not be sure if she'd plugged in the earplugs or simply crashed into sleep.

It was true that Alison Black had participated in sexual intercourse, but then she had been at the ball, as the town pointed out, and she was undoubtedly drunk, very drunk. What was all that fuss she made but the effects of booze?

Unfortunately no one could decipher the thoughts that had frozen into Alison Black's head that night.

'Yes, it is obvious to all,' said Mrs Fergusson, 'that the poor girl was unwell, possibly through the effects of too much whisky which she was seen to be drinking. And age creeping on and . . .'

What need to finish? Women without husbands did become

peculiar and were subject to virgin laws that froze the furnaces of their hearts and left them smouldering – the thoughts of love creeping through the wet ash like the trail of a slug, soon covered in more ash and dying of it. All that much was obvious and so the sentence never needed to be finished. Alison Black, with her flaming red hair and her skin still white and fresh, and looking ten years younger than her age, was accepted back into the town in its compassion.

And whatever the verdict, death by misadventure or perhaps justifiable rape by the town males acting on the darkest cries of their wives – hands grasping and tugging at their buttocks – they knew, all of them, that out of the outrage that marriage and food and boredom had produced, a sacrifice had been decked out. For that beautiful creature had affected not to see the red erections offered over the years and instead had chosen Paula and lived with her, a vestal-virgin college of two, and what did not belong needs must perish. So she was offered at the right time of the European midwinter solstice even though the seasons were reversed and it was summer.

At the twice-delayed inquest the issue at stake was life and death, but no one would have guessed it. The Rugby club was open for the spring season. Had never been closed since they'd got going again in January without Angus, away on honeymoon. Big Tom had married in a hurry, the Sports Queen, and they were well settled into a house on the Rewe Road. The Sports Queen was already in the family way.

How then had Alison died? The town paused in thought again that day. Had the shock to her flesh been enough to make her think she was an animal that must chew grass, crawl across the ground and find her refuge in the ditch amongst the thistles and grass, the spoor of wild rabbits, the occasional possum, the hedgehog snuffling its way along? And there, because she preferred the white of her former virginity to console her with the coolness and lightness of its touch, she lay down to be covered in dreams of white?

If she was not raped and murdered then where was the man – men perhaps, for there was the question of mixed sperm in the frozen vagina – who had been offered her flesh? And what could virginity matter when she had been caught out in the act of *lèse-majesté*? Yet no men came forward to say that it had been them. And was there any reason to suspect that it had to be this town of Milton? After the Cowboy from Lawrence with his red and rubbery lips had thrust his groin at the town, all was possible. Cowboys were riding through every lady's sleep and might be found down some side street or in the ditch where Alison had died.

This made it more difficult. If they could not find the lovers, what was the town to do? Alison had opened her legs in a car, got out pissed and fallen into a ditch.

They'd found her dog the next day down at Fergusson's farm three miles away, the lead wrapped around a collie bitch and both satisfied with the gifts they'd offered each other.

Paula had resigned at once and left for Dunedin. Not that you could blame her with that happening to her mate.

It still seemed spring by two o'clock, with the stone warm, the first bluebells bursting into flower under the hedges, the narcissi and daffs and jonquils thrusting out their perfumes, the birds singing, the eggs laid, the hens clucky.

A soft wind blew from down south where the Antarctic was. Perhaps the icecaps were melting too. A strong gust flapped into the sky the fish-and-chips papers outside Fatty Dragoumis' new shop.

The mill girls would not presume to attend the inquest but were roaming about outside. At least the eight-to-one shift was, dressed in new white hats with accessories.

The town that afternoon was, to Natalia, like a toy that could be picked up and arranged as she wished, and this Milton soul – less than an antheap – would today be confronted. Natalia had visions of Madame Roland and the French Revolution – 'Liberty What Crimes Are Committed in Thy Name' – and also, on a minor key, Edith Cavel – 'Patriotism Is

Not Enough'. She buttoned her gloves and went to the car with Benedict who would accompany her. As would Margaret.

Benedict was wearing a new suit his mother had ordered from Vienna, capriciously, and paid for out of her Swiss bank account. She remembered that boys in Geneva had worn several suits by the time they were fifteen and this one was in hunting green. Also boys went riding and some hunting. But then there was no Hunt here, so perhaps he should be sent to school. In the city?

Farming was doing well. Pearse, it was tipped, might again be asked to stand for parliament if his lungs lasted. She looked at his son. Since some time before Christmas his spots had begun to clear and she no longer found those sperm-filled handkerchiefs he used to toss into a ditch where the dogs nosed them out and fell to snuffling and lathering before bringing them in triumph to the house.

No! Some change! Men needed experience.

She stopped at Margaret's gate and found her standing on the kerb, smiling from her patient face at Natalia who she knew would make a fool of herself today. Margaret rode beside Benedict and clasped his hand, her short nails biting into his skin.

They arrived at the Presbyterian Church where once Margaret had been destined to make her vows with Pearse.

Natalia let Margaret out before she parked the car. This caused a stir amongst those who had been invited as witnesses and those who had come to offer opinion, or, it was hoped, hard facts.

The ladies wore their cheaper cony, with a few younger ones in fashionable monkey pelt. Natalia Pearse was in her Russian cony with sable collar and a black dress. On the collar was a circlet of rose diamonds, a matching ring on her finger and a miniature at her throat of her mother – painted on ivory when she was twenty-two and doing something in Saint Petersburg. It was all very strange, this descent towards the soil.

And the rest of the family! So few letters. Dmitri, not married and reputed by Ariadne to like boys, in Rome in her palazzo. One could not remove relatives, they could be more embarrassing than a personal disease.

But today she was ready, with the washed-blue sky, to do

battle – ready for the torture chamber, the firing squad, and the blood of the guilty washing the ground. For that must be the penalty for murder and rape? And surely when the violation was that of a lady, the penalty would be higher – perhaps quartering. It was High Treason when a princess of the Blood Royal was raped, so why not Alison?

Natalia tottered her way through the mill girls into the grounds of the Church.

And if Alison Black was not strictly a lady in the sense that one would find her family in the *Almanack Gotha*, she had been in the spirit. For that laugh, those gay eyes, the slender throat, that good taste in clothes . . .

Not that Alison's good taste extended to the house she shared with Paula. She would clutter the walls with those hideous ballet pictures by Degas whom Natalia's father might have known as he had once met Picasso. No, not Picasso, it was the Renoirs, good simple folk, the kind of people you didn't find these days. They had called on the Renoirs in their country place and had been received very kindly. Papa had brought away two paintings and these hung somewhere or other – was it Rome or had she lent them to Ariadne?

No, Alison was not a total lady. More important, she had been *alive*.

Natalia glanced at Benedict, in the middle between her and Margaret. The young man started sweating down his back as they walked up the steps to Munroe Hall. For he caught from his mother the memory of a time when men had connected with other dimensions – as audibly as, elsewhere, insects whirr and click against the midday sun.

And the ages fell, so Dionysius had written, moment by moment, note by note on the scale. The wheel turns faster and faster, sparks and flame shooting off from the wheels of a chariot and Natalia driving the new car. It seemed she'd always been driving to the inquest with her weak blue eyes, needing glasses but refusing them since focus did not improve matters.

Pearse had had a tantrum. He didn't want to know what the coroner would decide.

Benedict had walked through the iron gates, the trees straight and green with birds circling out far into the sky and he himself no longer a boy but unsure if what he knew made him a man or something more substantial.

What did you say in this court with Mr Lucas, the coroner up there, and the jury gathered to hear the evidence? Ruth Schenkle had been billeted as had a couple of people from Balclutha. The rest were native Miltonians.

Margaret, her head resting in her hump, took Benedict's hand.

'Don't worry,' she whispered, 'we must wait and see if we are directed to say anything. We do not know who did it, we only know what we think, and . . .'

She knew and he knew they were not going to be directed by anyone. These men were neighbours or kinsfolk and her conscience could not allow them to suffer for no purpose.

People looked out the window and seemed to doze as the afternoon passed. Muriel Fieschi patted Natalia's arm and left for the city, duty done as Alison's cousin by marriage.

At the end Natalia stood up to defend her friend's memory.

She was given the Bible to swear on.

'What particular light do you think you can throw on this unhappy business?' said the coroner, wearily stroking his chin. So far no light had been thrown. Much had been offered as conjecture, but Alison was buried deeper than anyone had suspected.

Natalia gazed down at the town; the vicar's wife in the second row beside the Presbyterian minister's spouse, the lawyers and their wives, the reporters, Magga Trout with her jaundiced skin.

The afternoon was rapidly declining and someone's stomach was rumbling for want of a nice cup of tea and a slice of fruit cake.

It was not the bar of history at which Natalia would have preferred to stand.

'I have this to say,' said Natalia, 'that at the ball as it was called, Alison Black, who was my dear friend, was selected as a scapegoat, not because she refused to drink a toast to the Queen but because her sense of life and her passion for it separated her.

This she called, as did you, her Communism. The toast was the occasion and what followed was inevitable. I have no doubt that the agents of the town decision were at the ball and that they acted in the interests of this town. I have no evidence to offer, only observation, that what has happened fits in perfectly with the town.

'As with lack of evidence, the lack of desire to know, all fits in perfectly with this town.'

Margaret's face was showing its pain, for she might lose this friend if ever Natalia even suspected what she had seen, and that she was now acting as a kinswoman of Tom through her mother's family.

She had pity for that coroner man, for Tom, for all the others in their rapes and their secret passions. What point was there in dragging out the secrets that would only tell against some, leave *them* in prison with no hope of release or hanged until dead and thus permanently beyond what now she knew did exist within their muddled minds and the stranger paths they trod in their dreams? For in Tom as in Alison there was an immense possibility. Oh, not as these church people would have it, by flying into the clouds and there receiving benediction from a plastic Christ surrounded by plastic angels and singing hymns that the congregation of the Milton faithful sang, but in diving into the centre and finding there your real face – like the Paestum diver.

But if they were told the factual truth, then the town would find a new scapegoat, plait the rope and the ladies would wail as Big Tom hurtled through the trapdoor, his neck breaking if he were lucky, or otherwise choking on the rope.

And now dear Natalia was thrusting out accusations and Benedict's white face had cracked open. Minute by minute Margaret felt him growing and expanding under the pain of their decision, as she had from the moment her spine, the straight source of her back, had grown tubercular and was cut, leaving her as she was now.

'I have seen in my time,' said Natalia, 'the Nazis and the Fascists, and the attraction of the small to the mass and the mass becoming the mob, and this town is more mob than town. Frightened and insecure with no roots. Believing only in surfaces and the morality of façades and ugly small façades at that. It is waiting for the moment in which a leader will arise and, if it is not the Jews you turn upon, then some others who will do. The first victim was Alison Black. Others no doubt will follow should you be disturbed enough. Then you will march in your uniforms and start your concentration camps, for there is nothing in you that has striven to avert this. And that is the truth!'

Then Magga Trout stood up, righteous in her dotage and prophetic garb, eyes sparkling and ready for battle – or the immolation of error. But Margaret pre-empted her.

'This is not the time to show hatred,' she said. 'What Mrs Pearse says may be right. What do we know of truth?' She swayed and groped for words. 'I do not think,' she murmured, 'that we can know because we are not used to it. But Mrs Pearse is from overseas, and having seen in those parts what can happen to people, may see what has happened here and I think we should listen to her.'

The coroner had given up on his inquest. The Bible lay meekly on the green baize.

Natalia looked about her but was met only by stony glances or averted eyes. She knew she must concede this battle. For the experience could not be conveyed where it had never been recognized, and that question had never been answered except in silence. She returned to her seat where she stopped: 'I wish only to add that Alison Black is dead and that no one mourned her and few attended her funeral. She warranted only small headlines in the papers, and those because she was the victim of snow in summer. But I know she was more than that and that she died because you all knew that. But *that* cannot be shown. For she is dead and cannot speak for herself.'

'So why don't ya shutup,' called out the Sports Queen, red-faced and muscular for battle.

Margaret took Natalia's hands and held them. They left as the coroner's jury brought in a verdict of 'death by misadventure'. They hadn't even retired to consider the matter.

Natalia got into the car.

'Why did we come?' she asked, settling back behind the wheel but uncertain where to go.

Benedict sat, irrevocably separated from her or any community, for he had chosen his silence above the laws by which men regulated their ant heaps. The separation was pain. He was leaving for the second time the security of a womb. He did not know that at that moment, but in later years he would recall accurately the emotion, and know that this was what had happened. Then he simply felt miserable with what some deep part of him had decided, coldly and dispassionately.

They drove off, with Margaret now in the front to give Natalia directions. Not that she needed them, but it was a comfort to be told to turn here left then straight on and up the hill to Tokoiti with the little house where Natalia had once lived.

The cemetery gates were in front. Natalia put her foot down on the accelerator, narrowly missed a marmalade cat rolling in the dust, and swept into the cemetery yard with a clash of gears.

There would be no flowers for Alison. Paula had fled.

They walked along the rows of neat graves. Lying on some marble slabs were glass bowls where linen-white roses swam, decaying into green and yellow mould. The headstones bore the names of the town – the Stuarts, the McCleans, the Fergussons, the Trouts and others who had arrived and finished here.

Above the unknown dead there grew a wild profusion of buttercups, wild seeding grasses, docks and couch. All a bit like Margaret's garden. In time all names were writ on water, thought Natalia with a degree of satisfaction.

The headstones leaned more drunkenly in death than ever their owners had inclined in life to either vice or virtue.

'What has happened?' Natalia called back to them, her blonde hair blowing free as in a moment of irritation she had let down the severe coiffure she had created for her judgement on the town. And gazed down at her father's own neglected space.

Only Margaret was at peace and used to the silence of grass, the orchestration of the wind through the husks. Yes, the husks as much as the seeds provided music if you listened. She smiled at the late westering sun and sat to rest on a substantial angel whose reinforced concrete wings would support her considerable bulk.

Benedict stood by, hands in pockets. He hadn't been to the cemetery before but felt himself thickened and strengthened by the compost of these unknown humans.

Margaret and Natalia gazed at the young man, also sensing in him a hardening and a decision as he flexed his hands and drummed out a scale on an angel's wing.

The women stood silently. Not that they could wait for ever on that late afternoon when the town was spread under their breasts and the boy suffering again the thoughts of his age.

They both observed him picking at a late pimple on his chin and squeezing out the yellow pus – wiping it on his handkerchief, absent-minded and a bit gapey from their attention.

They looked back at the town, and being above it didn't improve the dun and the mathematical precision of streets.

Margaret looked severe. 'What did you expect would happen, Natalia?' She wrapped her thick alpaca scarf around her head and fastened the top button of her coat.

The young man was wandering off, the paths ran in many ways, and stopped in front of some wild poppies.

'They grow wild in Italy,' said his mother, coming upon him with Margaret resting on her arm. 'I remember wheat fields like a sea of red. With patches of cornflowers. Around Monte Cassino.'

They found Alison's grave. It had not yet been concreted over. Bertie Fieschi would see to it without a doubt.

There was a plain wooden cross and a piece of cardboard noted her name and the date of her death – as determined by the autopsy. The date of birth was missing and Natalia bent down with her fountain pen and added it.

'I wish,' said Natalia, 'that I could think of something to say for her.'

Margaret gathered her breath.

'I wish,' said Natalia again, her Russian spirit wallowing a bit, 'that I could find the reason for it, although I should not expect to, never having seen the pattern myself.'

'You make it,' said Margaret, unexpectedly severe. 'You start at the bottom and work your way to the top. Like that myth where the young man kills the minotaur beast and comes out holding onto the thread – into the daylight. *That* is a great truth.'

'I am like Penelope,' announced Natalia, undeterred. 'I stitch and unpick day by day, waiting for Ulysses to come home from Troy. Except she had a kingdom no matter how small – Ithaca *is* a rather barren island. And she had suitors.'

Natalia looked startled when her son started to snort.

'I am not past the age, young man,' she informed him, and giggled herself. Alison wasn't having such a bad send-off after all.

And yet if the river is time, thought Benedict, swollen with your memories and you hold onto the log which is *you*, you have already drowned in what has happened. 'You hold to nothing,' Dionysius had said, and 'When you hold nothing you are free.' But how could you think like that when you hadn't reached the bloody point?

Natalia was having a bit of a cry into a cambric handkerchief that had been sent during the war. Ariadne, uncertain what the New Zealanders who were her allies might lack, had sent six dozen.

Margaret was not sniffing in sympathy as ladies generally did. Rather, she was pointing her snout of a nose towards the tears and observing them. 'What are you going to do, Natalia?'

'With what?'

Margaret shrugged at Benedict and it seemed that both women were giving him the once-over as they would any young beast. They looked then, together, down at the white smudge of gable that was the Pearse homestead.

There was no point in lying.

'Benedict saw what happened,' said Margaret. 'He saw something in that paddock where Alison was raped, and got frightened.'

It was obvious that Mother was about to ask him what he thought he was doing out in the middle of the night – but restrained herself.

'He saw something,' Margaret continued. 'You see he also has this gift. I know, because I have and can sense things and see sometimes what I would not have seen had I been married with children.'

'What did you see?' Mother demanded.

Benedict did not know what to say so opened his mouth.

'Stop catching flies,' Mother snapped.

'It was a shape,' Margaret went on. 'I came out with him and felt the presence of it. I did not think of Alison, since I *knew* her. So we followed the shape, which was what I felt it to be. And at the Rugby Club we saw what is was. The Rugby boys, the followers of Tom. We saw Tom Maxwell being – ravished – by his friends and that also must have been inevitable. I knew later why that had happened. As did Benedict. When we had news of Alison. They had raped her and fled. Then they had got on Tom, who must have been first. They were protecting each other. No one could talk then. No one.'

'Devils!' said Natalia, white-faced.

'Men,' said Margaret, 'no better and no worse than Germans or Italians or Americans. But it was only circumstantial evidence, for we never saw the rape. Nor did we know she was in the field – by then in the ditch.'

'Devils!' said Natalia, swaying about and looking at them both as if she had not seen them before.

'I am telling you this, Natalia, because it is time you were shocked out of a selfish preoccupation with your failures, and playing about with madness. Do not think that I have not observed! Grow up, Natalia! Be worthy of my Pearse and of your children. Enough of your snivelling. It is time you were knocked into life.

'I loved your father,' Margaret turned towards Benedict, 'and three times when I was whole we lay together. Which you and Karl have experimented with, with Lynette.

'I also have my memory, Natalia, of an evening when I too was perfect. But have you ever thought to ask me about my suffering when you tell of yours with Michael Pearse? Have you ever thought, over these years?'

Natalia shook her head. 'No,' she said, 'I have been blind.'

'Yes, you have,' her friend told her. 'Not that it matters now that your eyes have opened. So you are caught as am I and Pearse, but we must act to redress as best we know. Did you think that the smoke and fire of the ovens, the smell, which I have smelled, and those places where they were sent whose names I cannot pronounce . . . The whole earth is covered in . . . Did you think that was contained in one country? It is everywhere. Everywhere!'

'Why?' asked Natalia. 'Why here? When I escaped here – for safety.'

'We are not strong enough to hold back what would come at us from this town if they knew the truth. They would finish us, Natalia, and for no good purpose.'

'And Alison?' asked Natalia.

'Who would give evidence but your son and myself? And what would that town have to do?'

Natalia's eyes softened as she allowed her coat to hang free. 'I feel years younger,' she announced.

'It has always been thus,' said Margaret. 'That, I have gathered.'

'Yes, yes.' Natalia sat down suddenly on a clump of thistles and grabbed at them.

Margaret did not offer sympathy. She coughed once or twice with the rising damp and rested herself on the wall of a small tomb that the Mayor and Mayoress had built for themselves.

'Yes,' said Margaret, summing things up, 'we must understand that we matter. Our townsfolk cannot believe that, for then they would have to stand alone and grow alone. As we three have. Or have begun to. Yet, I have also been shown that people, no matter how unnatural, have still this cocoon of light around them in which their shape is held. I had not thought it possible but that night I saw it. Can you imagine? I was shown that men have souls looking in on the Rugby Club! I cannot understand why there. Yet it was there!'

Natalia had stopped grabbing at the thistles and was now pulling them out of her fingers, one at a time.

'I am not here to save you, Natalia, you must do that yourself.

But you must think of this boy, begin now to think in proportion to his gifts.'

'I know,' said the mother, 'but I do not want a saint for a son, I want a man who can live.'

'And see?'

'Yes, that is his responsibility.'

'Yes,' said Margaret, breathing a sigh of relief, 'it is. And there is Rebecca Weiss.'

Natalia picked herself up.

'I think,' she muttered, 'that Ailson would be pleased that this conversation has happened over her grave, and it is worth more than flowers, and more, as you say, than judgement. So! So?'

They stared at the red earth.

'It would have been better,' said the mother, 'if it had been men who talked here, like this. But where do you find them? Not any man I know, and Dionysius is past it.'

They walked down the grass path, the two women in front leaning on each other's arms. In the car Natalia reached for the packet of cigarettes left in the glove box. She lit up. 'Do you smoke?' she asked her son, who nodded awkwardly and took one.

'Come to my place,' said Margaret from the back seat, 'for a brandy. There is still some. Old Davie liked to take a spot on difficult days.'

Natalia manoeuvred the large car out of the gates. At Margaret's she sat with the orange tabby on her knees and had several spots.

'Pearse is a good man,' said Natalia.

That night Natalia and Benedict told Pearse all they knew of Tom, the Rugby boys and Alison.

Rebecca Weiss decided to settle in Dunedin, where Benedict was sent to school.

14

The school stood on a hill and that was its sole eminence, although it would produce honourable men who ran business in the city or the university; all cricketers and Rugby men. Within the walls decency reigned.

So he grew like a weed, sullen and resistant to them, but the jackboot, however, was never far from the soul.

One afternoon he had been swimming, during a free period. A class was in progress there and the gymnastics teacher, with muscles and the fluid drive of a tiger, decided to amuse himself.

The Jew Strauss had a bulbous nose, spotty white skin and pus spots around the hairs on his cheeks. He smelt altogether stale.

The gym master had ridden many times to villages within the pale.

The Jew Strauss was frightened. He waited at the beginning of the diving board, his maroon satin suit wrinkled around his circumcision, his white-stale skin crinkling and blue as he put a foot on the wood and gripped at the coconut matting with his toes. He sidled a couple of feet. He could almost sidle to the end.

He whimpered.

Living was to stay afloat.

The gym master ran to his glassed-in office. He returned and crouched on the concrete swinging the cane, tapping the Jew Strauss and then a hard swing into his buttocks which at the very last stopped, although the Jew expected it and his anus had tightened in anticipation.

The school boys split their sides and hoped Strauss would delay more.

The Jews killed Christ, as the priests said. And would do anything for money, so those who had turned them into userers said.

('Yes,' said Rebecca Weiss, 'it is as well to recognize it, for it is in us all.')

The bamboo swung backwards and forwards, edging Strauss up the board. 'Come, come,' yelled the Cossack with a grim smile. 'Come, Strauss, the water won't bite you! Though I might!'

Swing swing went the cane.

Strauss stumbled off the end, hands half-raised, stepped back by a miracle and was tottering between the land and the water.

The schoolboys howled.

'Try again,' said the gym master.

This time the Jew crawled up the coconut matting, feeling the stick swishing about him in arabesques of power, lightly tickling his maroon buttocks. His face tensed with will to arrive, to achieve, and he reached the edge.

He had held a Parents' Evening enthralled with his rendition of two Beethoven violin sonatas only last week. But that was last week.

He reached the edge and with a connecting swing was launched out into the air, where he hung for eternity it seemed, tongue out, arms tensed, face in rictus, then landed with a splash. And surfaced.

The schoolmates roared as he dogpaddled to the edge.

'Well, Strauss,' smiled the gym master, 'not so difficult after all.'

Over this there was not even silence, for nothing had happened.

('What can I say?' Rebecca said, but broke open a bottle of

cognac to toast his birthday. For his hands and their soul would play against this one day, and for the Schenkles, for Alison and Natalia and Pearse and Margaret.)

Pearse, in the days and months following his son's exile to the green fields of learning, stared incredulous at the lights of Milton just across a few bloody paddocks, and got on with his land.

He himself in the last grips of his illness, for he could not survive the shock that he had put himself back in a dump which wasn't just that but was also a bloody Gestapo cell – so to speak.

Pearse was close to death, but he had little Charlotte and there was old Dionysius outlasting them all. Bugger him! But no offence meant.

And sometimes he and Mum sat together and held hands on the back porch watching the sunsets in their violets and golds and their crimson palaces which they both strained to reach. And the break of trees he'd planted back in 1934. Now the green tips caressed the lowest clouds so that his land and heaven were one!

'Sentimental, aren't I?' he demanded petulantly of Natalia, 'to think of that?'

She shook her head and held his hand tighter for Pearse, she knew, was getting ready for the voyage.

He couldn't manage the tractor any more, though Tom Maxwell, Big Tom – him! – helped.

It was all too much, thought Pearse. And in those days just after the war when all was rosy and you thought of building on here and there and hadn't, you could still look at the car Mum and Dad had died in. Now the oak had grown into a tree with a few shrubs and wild rose. The seats, or what had been seats, were a favourite laying place for the chooks; a few cats rolling about at his feet with the smell of trees and the wallflowers and the concrete path as it had always been; still splattered with hen shit since the chooks had learned to fly higher and were buggered if they were going to let their wings be clipped – the sentiments Pearse approved of. No fence kept them out. Not that there was much to peck.

And Charlotte now a woman.

Pearse was dressed in his new tweed jacket that night, for some reason, and a pair of brogues Natalia had given him last birthday.

There was Charlotte reading her historical romances on the verandah and keeping an eye on her old dad. Charlotte now a woman, though Pearse averted his eye, his inward eye, from the fact, otherwise how could they cuddle anymore?

Nothing funny had happened to his little Charlotte.

Pearse massaged his hair with the raw onion that they said stopped you getting balder if rubbed into the roots good and hard . . . and tried to breathe.

It was Charlotte who looked up from her book, who noticed; and who came close; and who whimpered, holding onto her breasts and staring at her lover of fifteen years, for whom she was the queen, the dove, the perfection of woman. Who had always loved her as she was and as no one else had, not minding that she preferred cooking to listening to music on the radio like Benedict. Not minding that she liked living where she was and always would.

So for a moment, in one of the brave acts of her life, little Charlotte stayed where she was and watched with him the golden palaces of the sun, the courts of heaven etched in the colours of that Antarctic sunset.

She watched with him the red clouds piled high which meant good weather tomorrow and star-filled sky tonight – so full of light, so large was that expanse, so large were both of them on that path leading out to their land. And the trees in the home paddock which Dad had planted, 'When you were just an idea, Charlottey, my sweet.'

Such a good break against the weather, she thought, and leaned over to kiss him before the cold south wind arrived to tell her that this was death. But as she kissed, something in him gurgled and she leapt back. She screamed at this for it was as if somebody else had taken possession of her dad and was belching at her to stay away.

She screamed until the hens fled from her and Natalia came running from the new kitchen, hands floury from some meat patties she'd been making for tea. Natalia saw what had happened at one glance and felt within herself a wild loss and a wild release. For all the chains were now gone and Pearse whom she loved had left her to her own devices.

God. How she did love Pearse, with his lips soft as a baby's, his hair falling out and the long vistas of light that cut a swathe across the grass through all things living and dead and along the long avenue of oaks and pines, out to the side paddock that led to the river.

She could feel him walking towards the water not knowing that he walked. She watched, unable to stop him, unable to call him, her eyes as open as they could be, yet of glass, for she could not move or see further than his disappearance from her; nor could she see what he was going towards but something. Something better, dear Lord, for he has suffered in his ignorance and tried. And she knew in that moment as her insides were seared that he too might be going nowhere, never having gone before on any journey. That he might stop at the water and not know he must embark on the waiting barge and leave for the sea. So she called after him. 'Darling. Darling. Don't loiter. Keep going Pearse! We won't hold you back.'

And he turned and smiled and went on.

The dusk was on them. Now Charlotte howled around her skirts which brought Natalia back to her sanity, or at least her normal self.

Natalia looked down at the body. It was time for it to die.

She glanced at her hands, still floury, and wiped them clean on her apron and her fingers still good though wrinkled by garden and kitchen. She had always looked after her nails. They shone like moons. But she must push back the cuticles.

They were going to ring Benedict tonight, to wish him happy birthday. She poked with her slipper at some clods, trying to understand, but gave in and sat on the step and held Charlotte who now needed her. Yet, also being a woman, Charlotte knew they would have to do something. Since it was her dad she wasn't going to run away.

Natalia knew too that she must move but she could not force herself.

She tried to make an accounting of things but the strange

balance of his death would not allow it. She remembered his illness and the jars swimming with his green sputum which he coughed up during the night. He had felt guilty that his body could produce such muck and emptied it down the dunny as if it was his illicit boyhood sperm – when he was blameless of all things that the town swam in, as he said, like a bloody sewer. After Benedict had got away to the city, Pearse resigned from the School Committee, the Rotary Club, the Farmers' League and even at last, from the Returned Servicemen's Association. He kept himself for the land and in the few moments a day when he could breathe he would stand still and look at it or Natalia if she were in range.

In the nights he and Natalia would hold hands and he would say . . . 'Do you remember?'

Not always nice memories, but taking her back through their life together, and he facing things and trying to explain, what with the shrapnel wound and Margaret, that his temper had grown short. He confessed he still loved Margaret. They had cried together over it all, and his not being able to bear seeing her as she was now.

Later he remembered his boyhood sins and wheezed them out to her, everything on his conscience. 'I even thought of trying an Arab boy in Cairo, though mind, Mum, I wouldn't have kissed him.'

Yes, everything had come out, and she in her acceptance had absolved him as well as any priest.

They could find, it was true, no explanation for their lives, but did accept that there was one as there was for the grass growing. They didn't know why they hadn't built more onto the house and expanded the meadows, to include flowers, but they would sometimes sit in the orchard at three in the morning and might as well choke in the open as anywhere else with Charlotte inside sleeping, and the codlin moths buzzing around on feather wings like hummingbirds in the pale green petals of the Granny Smith they hadn't bothered to spray, for it was special . . . those small hard fruits, those delicious white-green petals with their perfume already so desirable as you were, Mum, with your lovely giving to me.

And now this death which was the end – for the dream was over that had bloomed for one night under that tree but lasted so many years.

She reached out and took Pearse's hand which was still almost warm. She supposed that his heart had given out, looked again to make sure and stood, brushing Charlotte aside as only, for a moment, a product of their love. She leaned over and kissed him full on the mouth, then on the forehead, then shut his eyes.

She would lay him out before women came, with food, to get a foot in the door and offer sympathy. As would men with hats off and offers to help with money.

At that moment Big Tom walked around to the back door looking for Pearse. Tom had run a bit to fat and had bought McClaren's farm down the road. So all were again on good terms – Sports Queen pregnant again and had baked a cake for Mrs Pearse, her neighbour – all 'unky dory.

Big Tom was all understanding and Natalia, suddenly, had wanted to throw herself into his arms. Tom lifted Pearse up and a bit of air belched out. He grunted and adjusted the weight in a fireman's hold so that Pearse's head lolled over his shoulder.

He walked slowly through the house and laid him down on the spread Natalia had tatted over one winter. Then he stood respectfully back.

'That will be all, Tom, thank you,' she heard herself saying and Tom, awkward, left the room, forgetting whatever it was he had come for – probably the loan of the tractor.

She could get the clothes off her husband with the help of Charlotte who, being a woman, must face her father's body.

It was dusk and Charlotte, for reasons known best to herself, had put on the outside light which shone dimly through the curtains into the bedroom. Which Natalia looked at and saw she had made cozy for them both with the twin beds of veneer mahogany, the white washbasin on a mahogany stand that she liked.

'Come darling,' she said, 'you must call the doctor for mother and you must also ring our dear Margaret for she will want to help us.'

'You don't need to ring,' said Charlotte, who opened the front door as if expecting visitors.

Natalia pulled aside a poplin curtain.

Trudging across the paddock, her shawl over her head and held around her mouth, was her friend.

Natalia pressed her face to the window to witness. 'Go now darling, and ring the doctor.'

Tears streaming down her face, her cheeks and lips taut and aching, Natalia blundered out the door, tripping on the top step and that loose board but recovering herself, and out into the paddock. There, amidst the long streamers of gorse, she was held by Margaret and then she held Margaret and together they rocked. And got themselves back through the gate.

Together they laughed and cried at the privilege of their love. Margaret could not speak for the cold until they got inside the front door.

'Thank God the house is warm,' said Natalia, 'for your lungs.'

'You always kept it warm for him.'

Margaret took off her duffle coat and her shawl of bright pink wool.

She stood small and humped, looking down the passage to where Natalia had banished the relics of the Pearses' Celtic dream – the dirk, the triumphant stag, Edinburgh in mist and a chieftan.

Margaret took her friend's hand. 'Let us go to his body.'

Cousin Annie had grey hair and a pinched face from too much church-going which so far had not brought her joy – not that she expected it. She allowed some boarders into her scrubbed domain to assist her income, which had already been bumped up with a pension from the Labour Government which she nevertheless spurned at each election in favour of the Nationals who had won her heart.

That night her first cousin once-removed, that foreign boy

from Milton, was about to smile on his birthday cake with its marzipan icing that Annie found too rich. His mother had sent it up on the bus for the occasion. And *who* had collected it but Annie? Wearing now a particularly delicate shade of puce to help the celebration and pouring out a lemonade.

He was seventeen and doing well with his school work which would serve more in life than belting around on the piano, although he did play some nice tunes on occasion.

Otherwise he sat and read scores like you read a book, at the plywood desk *she* had made in the woodwork class. She suspected he played with himself. They all did. Not that you could say, but you could prowl as was right in your own home, and that kept them on their toes.

And what could you expect?

Cousin Annie went to find matches to light the birthday cake. She sniffed a bit. With the money from his board and her other boarder, Tony, she was within months of getting a return ticket to Scotland and the Banks and Braes o' Bonnie Doon without dipping at all into her savings. Sniff the mists, then home to Dunedin.

What was this? The phone ringing?

She patted her bun and went to answer in the hall – no seat there, which discouraged too-long conversations, although she'd allowed a composition of some driftwood and dried grasses from the ikebana class at the Tech. She listened and shivered through her autumn-tinted cardie, asked details and gave condolences. Then, being a practical woman, rang the railway station. Should she go and pack for him? But that was putting things off. It was half-past six.

Instead she went to the birthday boy sitting with Tony. There should have been a lot of friends here tonight and blown-up balloons to make it festive. There were a few lying about that she'd snaffled from the Tech Christmas party. No use in leaving them there to be thrown away.

She sat down beside her cousin, and although not in sympathy with people pawing at each other, took his hand. He looked at her.

'I have news for you,' she said in a grey, distant voice. 'Your dear father . . .' he was a dear although he had teased her so and once pinched her bottom, before the war and marriage of course, 'your dear father . . . your dear father is dead. At a quarter to six this evening. His heart gave out so the doctor says. Your family is waiting for you. There is a train at nine-thirty. I will ring and book a taxi.'

He stared at the birthday cake.

One day he might be handsome, she thought. Not in the Miltonian way — too arrogant about the nose, too heavy and too tall and too thick in the lips with this sudden sensual droop to them which she knew was only an attempt not to cry. And those grey eyes! Altogether they would make some lucky woman happy. What with the farm and the money the Russian woman was said to have stashed away in Europe and not paying tax. Annie did admire a dodge like that.

Tony was blushing and fidgeting. Said nothing, which was the habit of their age.

Benedict stood up and pushed his chair back.

'I want to walk,' he said, searching into the distance for something. Tony with his red lips and merry eye was no help. His father was alive and would live forever or until you were ready to get rid of him.

Benedict went to the hall for his school coat and scarf and went down the steps. Not really thinking, but wishing that Dad and he hadn't been fighting like they had for a couple of years, and that he had said that he loved him. Arguing too over his allowance, 'which bloody isn't enough, Dad'.

'Bloody is,' said Dad. 'And anyway don't swear at me, I'm your father.'

He walked to the esplanade and along to the end seat where you could watch the waves foaming and sweeping up to the concrete wall. The moon was getting full and the sea responded.

He sat, hands in his pockets, and shivered. Then he went back to Annie's.

She was waiting for him at the door.

'We will have a cup of tea,' said Annie. 'All of us. And sit quiet.'

She didn't talk about Pearse when young and oh so up to tricks with poaching fish, the police after him and Cousin Annie risking her reputation to hide a sugar sack full of illegal trout in her house in Spencer Street, Milton, now rented out. No, she didn't try to unthaw him, for then he would cry and what could you do when men cried? Better he kept himself like this.

The clock on the mantelpiece ticked off the quarter hour. Tony went off to do his homework.

Cousin Annie had switched off all the sitting-room lights, leaving on only the sidelight she'd made at the Tech. It was time to put on her electric blanket.

'I'll pack for you,' she said.

He went along to his room and sat on the edge of the bed, wishing he had a fag. Tony came in with a packet of Rothmans and a quarter of whisky that they glugged in turns, talking about school and Rugby. Annie came along and lit up as well and said nothing about the illegal booze. On a night like this it was nice to know that boys were still boys.

The taxi honked outside and she and Tony went with him. She pressed five pounds into his hand and said she would be down for the funeral. To ring if there was anything she'd forgotten to pack.

She waved but did not expect him to look back.

'Six bob,' the driver said at the station.

The train arrived with steam, a screech of brakes. The furnace door opened, coal was shovelled in, the fiery sparks belched and whirled, a smoky orange light glared before the door crashed shut again . . .

He got into the second-class carriage behind the engine; that would get him there quickest.

He'd told Annie to ring home and say no one was to meet him, that he'd walk along the railway line as he always did.

The guard waved the red flag. This was the Midnight Express so they turned the lights off to let people get on with sleeping. He watched the city passing him.

Later he tried to move his bowels but his body wouldn't do it. He pulled up his trousers. The guard was waiting outside to click his ticket.

'Nice night,' said the guard. 'You home early for the school holidays?'

Benedict nodded.

'We're on time. For a change.'

They arrived. He opened the door that let him down onto the tracks and set off with the suitcase.

He was at the Mill Stream, the cinders grinding into dust under his shoes by the time the train passed in a rush of icy wind and tooting for the crossing ahead.

Everything was small!

He started to run towards the homestead light, tripped once and lost his bag and ran faster, snorting up air through his mouth. He could look over his land, and then, Jesus, the homestead!

His blond hair flopped over his eyes as he made the wicket gate. He stopped to wipe the sweat off his forehead and look at the gorse hedge Pearse had had to cut back.

The bloody dogs were yelping, having picked up his scent.

Mother was standing at the front door. She held out her arms and he went to them.

'Your dear father is in the drawing, oh, the front room. Your father.'

Mother and son walked through to the old kitchen and sat beside the coal-stove fire.

'Death,' said Natalia.

'We laid out Dad,' said Charlotte.

'The funeral will be Monday morning at eleven,' said Natalia. 'He will lie with us until the time to leave.

'The undertaker,' she went on, 'found that rather peculiar. He said most people wanted a "beloved departed" out of the house as soon as possible, but I told him that this particular corpse was the man I had slept with and made children with . . .'

Suddenly she was far from them both.

'I told him my husband and my children's father would stay with us until it was time for him to go into the earth.'

At that Charlotte started to wail. Yet it was lovely the way Mum and Margaret had washed Dad, so soft and respectful of him, so loving as they washed and shaved, stretched him out, bound his jaw, hardly more than a bag of bones when you saw him without his clothes.

He might awake at any moment.

She half thought he would and maybe smile at the joke of it, but he didn't.

It was like being a nurse.

'*We* laid him out,' said Natalia. 'Together. *His* women.'

Benedict listened to them, not confused by the different cries from Mum and Charlotte, which came from different stages of their womanhood. For little Charlotte would always face things bravely, even though it might not be given to her to understand what they meant.

He looked at her and saw that she was grown up. Her boobs weren't all that bad either, for a kid almost fifteen, with nice brown hair after the Pearses. She slumped a bit as she sat, which Mum at once noticed and told her to sit straight, like a lady. There was some lack of spine in girls at fifteen. They would stoop and glower as Natalia herself remembered, but the stage passed. She drew in a shuddering sigh for the peculiar road she found herself on, and it only ten past eleven at night.

Margaret came in from the new kitchen, Dionysius on her arm. He paused peacefully at the door and then wandered towards the rocking chair.

'I've heated soup,' said Margaret, 'which Mrs Trout sent with young Mr Trout. There are also cheese scones from Muriel Addle. The rest we can keep for people tomorrow, coming to pay respects and more food with them, I expect. Perhaps a casserole we can put in the oven for tomorrow night's tea.'

She took Benedict's hand and squeezed it.

He rang Rebecca. 'I am not going back now,' he said. 'Not to school. There isn't any point, is there?'

'No,' she answered. 'I will come to Milton.'

'Tell Rebecca,' called out Natalia, 'that she should come and stay with us.'

Benedict nodded back to his mother.

Dionysius rocked by the fire, his eyes wide open like an owl's, watching.

The atmosphere of mourning got on Benedict's nerves.

'I need a walk.'

'Don't worry about the farm,' said Natalia, busy with more mundane thoughts. 'Angus has offered to look after the land with Tom. It will give us time to look around for a manager. Your father would not want anything to be let go.'

He stumbled out the back door and through the open gate, with the wind whipping along from the south and blowing away the river mist. He went, he did not know why, to the old car, to look inside.

He remembered, at night, sometimes, he'd seen his father doing the same – peering into the wreck and tracing the shape of the windows, the wipers, the twisted engine parts, the collapsed pistons. Sometimes tearing at the weeds around the rotting wheels.

He went to the shearing shed. A bale of crutchings that would fetch a fair price in Japan was open. Mice were rustling in the rafters.

He leaned against the sacking and would have buried his head and wept but instead grabbed at handfuls of dirty wool. When he surfaced he was like a sheep, new-shorn and trembling.

He walked back to the house, drank the soup and said goodnight.

In his bed he twisted around, waiting. The house was silent when he dressed and he crept out of his room covered by Margaret's stentorian breathing.

In the front room, beside the piano, they had fitted in the coffin, open still with a candle burning at each end. Dionysius was sitting beside it, face washed as clear as water.

Benedict crossed himself, took the other chair and looked at his father's hands crossed on his chest.

Natalia had thought of putting a Bible in them since the corpse would have rejected a crucifix, but could not pretend with Margaret there to keep her sane, so Pearse had instead the company of his war ribbons and his OBE for services to farming.

Benedict tried to understand what this meant – not the body but the absence – but couldn't find an explanation and grew colder as he tried. He would like to cry but he was, as Margaret said, now head of the household.

It chimed four-thirty and he knew he must sleep, for all the callers who would arrive when the news got around. They'd come to drink tea or whisky or sweet sherry, view the body and talk about Pearse's good life and the shame of it leaving him and him so young.

Then he heard someone — as did the old man, who looked expectantly at the door.

Maybe it would be Pearse's spirt. But it was Margaret who shuffled in, her nose still a bit red from the brandy Natalia had insisted on her drinking with milk and honey.

'I haven't been here,' she said, 'since the day he left for the war. This room is different because Natalia has made it so, although the house as a whole is like it always was.'

She ran her fingers along the polished rosewood piano. But if Benedict hoped for miracles from them he was mistaken. Enough the miracle of death tonight.

Margaret took in the silver candelabrum, the brass candlesticks, the watercolours Natalia had painted one feverish spring, the chairs, newly covered in autumn tones, the painting of Countess Dashkov, Natalia's mother, and Benedict.

'I will go for your mother,' she said.

Margaret herself was unafraid of death for she would walk through that door straight-backed in the soul's freedom. Sooner, she guessed, than Natalia.

Natalia sensed her friend's conviction and was ready for life whatever way it would fall. It was time to break free although her wings had grown thick and her breasts too heavy.

'And why not here?' she said, finally reconciled.

Benedict flexed his hands while the two women arranged themselves.

'You know,' she went on, 'I had hoped he would die on our anniversary – the night under the tree.'

'Instead, Benedict's birthday,' Margaret reminded her, smiling.

It was obvious that the conversation would remain elliptical and Benedict allowed them to look at each other and make room for Charlotte who heard them talking and came in, wrapped in sleep.

Natalia moved to the sofa so Charlotte could put her head on her lap and stretch out under a mohair rug Margaret fetched from the bedroom. Natalia relaxed where she was in this stationary boat, the grass of the land lapping almost to the front door.

Benedict flexed his hands. He looked down from his hard-backed chair to his father; the face was as peaceful as a child.

Natalia looked too. She had seen the face before, as had Margaret in earlier days. Sometimes after their lovemaking, sometimes when the moon was full and they had taken out bedclothes and lain together in the orchard, rocked by the soughing wind, the grating branches.

For the last time Benedict touched his father and the strange emptiness he held. He put up the lid of the grand piano and sat at the stool, fiddled with the height adjustor and ran his fingers across the keys.

Margaret and the old priest smiled encouragement. Charlotte snoozed, her hair smoothed now and then by mother.

He tried out a few chords, the opening of the Waldstein. No one made any suggestions. Slowly, hesitantly, he reached into memory and returned with the first long piece he'd learned.

'Für Elise,' announced Charlotte, who had battered at it too. 'Dad loved listening to me play that.'

Margaret closed her eyes.

'"Jesu Joy of Man's Desiring",' Benedict said. 'I used to play that for Dad.'

He remembered on the last note the waves sweeping around the rocks as they had yesterday – solicitous, like a housewife out with her broom. And began on a Chopin nocturne.

'Rebecca says next year I'll be ready for the International Chopin Competition. In Warsaw I think it is. Or maybe Moscow. So I won't be returning to school. Rebecca will be staying with us. We'll have to work four or five hours a day to get me ready. I stand a good chance. It's a matter of polishing up my technique.'

The women knew he was telling his father.

'You have the rest,' Dionysius said.

'Yes,' agreed his great-nephew, 'I've been given the rest.'

He glanced at Pearse as the candlelight flickered across the rosewood and lit his high cheekbones.

Benedict had got dressed up, Natalia suddenly realized, as if this were a concert performance: a silk shirt and black trousers she'd had made to measure by a Roman tailor.

He waited, crouched for a moment over himself, then straightened up, sensible to his decision and to the water beginning to run, which must lead away from here. And began to play.

'The Pathétique,' muttered Charlotte a moment later, pleased with herself until shushed by Mother.

The knowledge of Rebecca Weiss began to flower again, and the knowledge of the places that Margaret could not name but knew of. And the earth too, that his father had worked.

Pearse and Natalia were reconciled, the fractures healed, the elements in balance together with this passion of the first movement. Which lifted to the second and suddenly flew into the heart like a bird buffed up and singing.

No, not that, Natalia decided. The peace of this moment.

She accepted and reached over and placed her wedding ring in Pearses's clenched hands.

The old priest closed his eyes, for now in each of these sounds was measured his own understanding. As opaque as his skin, the inward light shimmered against the silence he had become.

And somewhere or somehow this touched the town's sleep and for a moment shone clear through to all of them.

It rocked Pearse in his death and his family in their wakefulness as they followed the last note of the second movement.

Benedict looked at his father and at Natalia. A grey light was above the hills with a flock of early starlings.

He began to weep.

The old man coughed quietly.

'Michael Pearse's death is over.'
He pointed to the hills where night was breaking around the sun's ascent.

GOING HOME

1

He had three seats to rest across while he wandered through the dream city of London and reduced it and his memories to ash. He knew it had to be that way and he sniffed in the perfume and menstrual smell from the woman across the aisle as a temporary benediction. Then he turned and looked out the porthole. If he were a bird, he would see the plane reflecting harshly against the dying sun as it burst through the air, taming currents and riding them like a falcon. Yet it was alien and he felt that the more as the cabin lights came on and he imagined the skulls of his neighbours and below them the blueish haze of blood and nerves. Were they, perhaps, the meal of this unnatural creature whose steel skin would outlast them and the journey?

The captain announced the descent had begun. He was running them into time again and away from this false balance above both light and dark. The porthole showed early stars and these with diamond hardness reminded him of real things as, without warning, the plane was over the mountains. In a sweep of glacial wind he had tramped over snowfields like these. Even this same moon, a wafer-thin host in the sky which was now impaled on a spur of rock.

His heart slowed like an animal's in hibernation as a metallic voice told him to put on his safety belt and adjust his seat to the upright position.

Ahead was the flat land of Christchurch airport and the runway lights stretched out to capture the lumbering contraption he was borne in.

He found a room. And asked if they could send up a bowl of soup with some toast.

He ate as he washed and changed into warm pyjamas. Outside a single tree bent into the westerly wind and its full canopy rustled and hissed at the mountains. These were bent over the plain, black and dense with the energies of frost.

I am twenty-seven, he hold his mirror image.

He sat on the bed to watch himself from the distance that the glass created. His eyes, sometimes green like those of a forest cat, peered back at him with a trace of malevolence.

They had yet to understand since they looked only on living things, or had not seen closely enough the blundering of moths and stray birds. But they would learn. They clouded over and grew inscrutable with some deeper awareness, which he, the one who looked, did not share yet.

He got into bed. As if in a cocoon he retreated back to earlier stages of life. His memories hung on him still, attached like a thread to a twig. And the darkness was alive with the presence of his heart beating and his animal warmth flowing around him. Before sleep he wondered what his family would be thinking of the returning exile. Then he dismissed the thought since he had no ideas about anything any more.

Mrs Fieschi tilted the venetian blind to exclude the excess of light. For the house, on the edge of a hill and among high trees, was bathed in violet, under the arch of a rainbow formed between showers.

If she had opened the door to her terrace she might have discovered that her garden was as on the first day of creation. Drops of water united, rose by rose, the circles and verticals of her flowers. Even the high hedge, usually heavy with leaves, was floating towards the extremities of its reach. And chrysanthemums, bronze and gold, yellow and copper, bent under their weight towards the drawing-room door.

But the door was closed because too much light would fade the new carpet as well as Mrs Fieschi, who now smiled at her sister, her brother-in-law, Mr Farquar, and assorted portraits, photo and oil. 'Well, it's hot today. Almost an Indian summer.'

Mr Farquar, broad-shouldered, stooping a little, cleared his throat and looked at his gold watch. 'Ten minutes and we leave.'

'I can't believe it.' Mrs Fieschi impulsively pulled apart the usual two slats of the blind and peered out. She turned away dazzled by a burning chrysanthemum.

'I am sure,' said Mrs Farquar, her sister, 'he will be as excited as we are!' She shifted her large beam around the chair and smoothed down her floral silk dress.

'But we're going in five minutes,' said Mr Farquar, when Mrs Fieschi suggested a quick cup of tea.

'I feel a bit cold,' she said.

'The season.' Solidly rooted in the landscape, Mrs Farquar presumed all causes and effects to flow from variation in heat and cold. 'You always get a cold in March. You used to even when you were a child.'

'Yes, I'd forgotten.' Mrs Fieschi was pleased to be told and ran to touch the frame surrounding the picture of Nicholas. She did not bother to look at George, but was annoyed. 'I do not know why he couldn't get away from the farm. His twin brother arriving home after five years and he skulks in the mountains. His behaviour is peculiar.'

'Fiddlesticks.' That was Emily at the door. 'He's always been that way.' Emily put her hand on her belly and with unbecoming coarseness, Mrs Farquar thought, felt for the baby to jump. 'Nick'll probably settle down soon like the rest of us.'

'We are sometimes late marriers,' Mrs Farquar said, who had no children as a result, but would always defend family tradition.

Mrs Fieschi patted the handbag Nicholas had sent four years ago. She was wearing his earrings and a brooch from Russia as well as a Persian scarf. The mementoes she was decked in with idolatrous precision drew her, for a moment, into abstraction. She glowed like a minor deity who demanded sacrifice.

'What I can't understand,' said Mr Farquar, somewhat querulously, 'is why he's given us so little notice. What will he do after he's seen us all? I can't think at all . . .'

Mrs Fieschi noticed for the first time, it seemed, in months, her husband sitting on the sofa, polishing his glasses and smiling at her frostily.

'At least he is coming to the family home. So many people shift into smaller places when the children leave the nest, but I have never believed in doing that.'

Mrs Fieschi was surprised to hear her husband's view, but accepted it, along with what he had added to her inheritance, as of good quality and quite possibly exceptionally well matured.

'He has an English accent in that tape he sent,' Mrs Farquar said.

'Put on,' said Emily.

Her aunt gave a broad understanding beam at her niece's belly and let the remark pass without comment. Nothing was threatened by a little spirit shown on inconsequential matters.

Outside the day lowered from autumn and Indian summer, almost to winter.

Nicholas half hoped the plane might eject him from its belly. Like an egg. He had dreamt last night that he was hurled, white and foetal, his head between his legs, deep into the soil. Today he wore buff-coloured trousers made of thick linen and a solid jacket to keep out the cold. He looked down at the peninsula and the sea, both alive, earth and water viewing each other with equanimity, neither having been converted even temporarily to the cause of man. The city was small enough for each house to be identified. That was his house down there.

Across the causeway, the church. Further on and over the hills of Tomahawk, the cemetery, the crematorium. And the Pacific Ocean beating in where the city council let out sewage: memories of grey French letters in the lucid water. The Pacific now broke into the mouth of the Taieri River.

They were so far down. He smiled at the smallness of his memories. There, the island, brown-backed, lay across the river. The channel was to the left of it just now. And then the three miles of white beach. And on the hill, overlooking the estuary, Miriam's house curved onto the land like an animal. And beyond that hill, only a glance away it seemed, was the lagoon and the fresh-water pond. And the bridge he had wanted to dive from once. It had been painted a dull red. The shadow of the aeroplane crossed the river and leapt over the towering rock cluster above the church, looking ready to fall on it should the wrath of God demand it, on that side of the river.

Nicholas sat back. Among these familiar things must be the instruments of his decision.

'Dunedin's a pretty little city.' The air hostess stood beside him with a basket of sweets and patted her yellow skirt. 'But I suppose you'll be going to the lakes for trout fishing.' She came back and sat down beside him for a moment. 'And the autumn colours are very nice. Still I'd rather be on the island run, if you know what I mean.'

He didn't.

He felt sweat waiting under the top layer of skin.

He feared he would smell sour.

He shrank deep into himself and became a kernel.

The wheels were locked into position and the fields hard under them.

Suddenly he saw a child's doll in a backyard. Caught by his eye with no hands to defend itself, the cheeks were cracked and red and the eyes surprised.

Nicholas supposed the journey was bringing him to those who loved him and his heart drummed back into rhythm with the discipline of the earth around him. The hostess patted his knee and offered a paper handkerchief soaked in eau-de-Cologne. 'I know how it can be. Sometimes you think you'll never make it.'

The plane turned slowly on its own weight and pointed its blunt nose at the airport terminal. It swayed one wing and then the other. Mrs Fieschi gripped Mr Fieschi's arm. Her face was stretched on a frame such as she pinned her tapestries to. What story would begin now? And who would make the first stitch? She would of course. Her nostrils, flared like those of a dog in the hunt, opened even further to catch the perfumes and scents, the odour that she would recognize intermingled with five hundred others if it swept by in the wind.

'Oh, he has come. This is the plane.'

The group moved close to her.

Her neck slackened back with satisfied knowledge. 'It's been a long journey. Only one night's rest. I suppose he'll be tired.'

'Fancy five years of tripping around,' said Mrs Farquar, dumbfounded. 'Why, he left in 1958!'

Mr Farquar measured the time on his watch against the gathering shadows. He nodded. 'Only five minutes late.'

Mrs Fieschi found her husband's hand around her waist, which gave her the necessary support not to weep yet.

More people joined them and stood around patting hair into place or nervously fiddling with fly buttons. Mrs Fieschi looked delicately the other way and then the door was open.

The hostess came down the steps putting on her gloves, bag neat against her waist. Some people at once gaped at the clouds as if the sight could not be sustained.

'Nice place, this,' said Mr Farquar as they were pushed against the glass.

Because she was first in the three lines of reflections, Mrs Fieschi managed to elbow some room, adjust her scarf and brooch, and, with panic, fish for her compact and lipstick. She found them and shrugged her bony shoulders, laughing to others around. She had dyed her hair for the occasion and as a result it was a little stringy. But youthfully black.

Mrs Farquar smiled sourly as she surveyed this handiwork of vanity. But now was indulgent as Muriel leaned against Bertie's shoulder and with languid swooning gestures displayed her handkerchief to wave or weep into.

With Nicholas home all pieces of a jigsaw fitted into place and the fact they had ever been mixed up or out of order could be ignored. Mrs Fieschi lifted her face to the sky for the benediction which clouds in their innumerable possibilities could bring her: the torso of a god, the trailing of her own hair when she was young and had brought this child into the world.

Mrs Farquar observed Muriel appearing to 'let go' and hastily scrutinized an unknown woman's coat. The material, she observed, after a few moments of blindness, was floral, and loud. Mrs Farquar was content.

And Muriel now stood like a duchess about to open a bazaar. The sun withdrew into cloud.

Someone was on the top step. He was wearing – it looked like boots, a thick long coat, and a green scarf. He carried some leather hand luggage. He was not moving. He was watching them all. A bit, thought Mrs Farquar with a laugh, like sheep in a truck on their way to the abattoir. She recalled once seeing a sheep being slaughtered. The knife bit deep into the flesh and sliced across the jugular. The blood was very fresh and because she was young it had reminded her of something you drank.

'There he is,' said Mrs Fieschi, her face crimson with triumph. 'There. See. He is talking to that hostess girl. Smiling. He is *smiling* at her.'

Muriel pushed to the open door, her arms opening and shutting like a sea anemone, her scarf flapping over her throat, the pieces of jade in her ears jangling.

They followed the road leading around Saddle Hill.

At such height it wasn't necessary to talk to each other and as miles passed the journey gathered him back into them, so that they almost wondered why they were having a party to welcome home someone who suddenly didn't seem to have left at all.

'The river has been wrecked,' said Mr Fieschi, remembering fishing outings with George and Nicholas. George had always sat in the back because he liked it that way.

The father and his two sons had gone to a pool, deep in the

flatland and – unexpected in a downsurge of light and willow – an old bridge hung in pieces of spar over the water. Light caught in the umbrella willows.

Sometimes George would go swimming up beyond the bridge, his red hair bobbing and sinking.

'And here we are,' said Mrs Farquar.

The two cars rushed along beside the sea. They turned into the drive, under the arch of laburnum and wistaria.

The dog came running up to Mr Fieschi and jumped on him. 'Down,' said Mr Fieschi. 'Look who's here. Nicky is back.' The family dog, golden and old, full of memories like a blocked drain, wagged his tail politely and bounded away toward Daphne and Emily.

'Come here, Sam,' Mr Fieschi called anxiously. 'Come here.' The dog did so. It danced arthritically around them all, surrounding them with the magic of its circle. It looked at Nicholas and then it whined.

'He knows,' said Mrs Farquar. 'You see. He knows.'

Nicholas stared at her fat face expanding under the light and the grey leaves, caught by the shadow of the maple tree and the sudden gale of golden dead leaves.

'Knows what?' demanded Muriel.

'Nicky!' shrieked Emily. 'Nicky darling!' shrieked Daphne.

Mrs Fieschi swayed.

'And,' shrieked Emily, 'George got away from his bloody sheep. About bloody time, too. You would think he was having an affair with some nice ewe.'

Mrs Farquar chortled louder than usual to dispel the fear that a deep crack had opened and suddenly shut again – with her foot stuck in it.

'Where *is* George?' asked Mrs Fieschi.

'Go on,' said Daphne. 'Go and find him. I saw him down past the pond.'

The second garden level had the pond, surrounded by Cecil Brunner roses, whose wild streamers brushed, greengage-green and fern-green against the deep green water. Carp and goldfish swam among the depths.

Nicholas stopped to throw ants' eggs onto the surface and watched the thick lips of the fish. Near him a piece of unhewn marble lay under a japonica bush. The apples of that shrub, yellow and viscous looking, waited to be picked. A larch shaded a spot where they had buried Lulu-Penelope. They had made a cross, George and he, and both wept as they lowered their cat into her resting place.

The second level was divided from the third by a thick, high laurel hedge. Under it grew pink geraniums and winter roses, pale waxen things, with death in their petals and in their thick stems.

Between the levels were the steps which George had laid in stone and brick; on either side a boulder from the farm. Their natural shapes had hardly been disturbed. They stayed as guardians, stained with rain and lichen.

Beyond, George was merged with the gathering evening light. Around his feet lay chips of wood, and the axe rested between his legs, the handle firmly in his hands. His gaze was slow and gave nothing for a moment. Then he quivered and seemed to glow. His thick taurian neck knotted with muscle. His face reddened.

Between them was the grass, but for the moment, before they were joined to each other, the ache was such it stopped them in their tracks.

Then George's arms came out.

They were just in time, for Mrs Fieschi was rootling among the plants of the second garden, her skirt caught by roses. 'Come on now, boys,' she called, sprightly as a bird.

'We are coming,' Nicholas said. 'Go back to the house. It's too cold here. You'll catch a cold.'

'It's almost dark, too,' his mother replied. 'These early autumn nights. Really it is winter but we don't like to admit it.' Her voice, like a long skirt, trailed behind her.

George blew his nose. He pointed to the hut. 'Let's have a cigarette before we go up.'

The hut was dark, but in a corner a candle had been lit. Beside it was the fat-bellied Buddha which looked as if it had been given a perfunctory rub.

'I knew you'd come here. Down here. I didn't want to say anything with them. You know how it is.'

'Come on, boys,' called out Mrs Fieschi, safe at last in the drawing room from which she had escaped only for a few minutes. 'Hurry along. It's teatime.'

'So you're back.' George peered at Nicholas carefully. 'I've waited for you a long time.' He lit a cigarette for his twin brother and handed it to him. 'It's been a long time.'

Nicholas nodded woodenly and George took his face in both hands. 'What's happened to you? You look thin. Kinda dried out.'

George inhaled and blew smoke out through his nose. He glowed against the darkness, suddenly strange and powerful. He took Nicholas and rubbed his back and chest with his hands.

'You're cold all the way through.'

'Stop it!'

'What's the matter?'

'It's the travelling. When you travel over so many countries you get out of touch. You feel strange. Time doesn't matter any more, George. You just drift. I'm still in the plane. Perhaps it's still London for me.'

George wasn't satisfied but he damped down his force and took in his paw the hand of his twin. 'I feel complete now,' he whispered to him, and rubbed that hand against his cheek. 'We mustn't separate again like this.'

'No.' Nicholas shook with agreement and laughed a moment. Then George kissed him gently on the forehead and held him tight.

'Come along, boys. What are you doing down there?' Mrs Fieschi's voice was sharp with suspicion. She remembered seeing them both go into the shed when they were fourteen and she had suspected things which she did not, of course, allow herself to clarify.

They left the shed together and layer by layer they grew lighter – and heavier. Shade by shade, what they were to the others fell like a mantle over them. And George could say as they approached the half-open French windows, 'Why didn't you send me a card for our birthday?' And Mrs Fieschi could hear this and prepare at any moment to arbitrate between them. She had forgotten how much they had fought as children, and the terrible beatings they gave each other: two forces which seemed destined to be locked in combat all their lives. Except these odd moments when they were gentle and in harmony together. They came arm in arm into the room. The two girls gave them scornful looks. They had started their tea.

2

'So! Here you are.' Mrs Fieschi surveyed the boys' bedroom. 'I dusted it myself. I wasn't trusting the woman to do it properly. She is a little slapdash. I changed the sheets too. I haven't touched anything. Not even the wallpaper. Everything is as it was when you were both here.'

Below in the hall, Mr and Mrs Farquar trumpeted goodbyes and Mrs Fieschi trotted out.

George pointed his mind at Nicholas and waited. 'Have a bath,' he said.

Nicholas began to take off his clothes. George unpacked the bags. In one were presents, wrapped carefully. Each package had a name. George piled them together by the pillow. He hung up the three suits Nicholas had brought with him and threw his dressing-gown over the chair. The jerseys he put away in a drawer, neatly enough, the socks and shirts in another. At the bottom of the case he found a pair of underpants and socks smelling of sweat. He sniffed them without thinking, and as the smell he remembered was of his twin he was comforted. George undressed too, threw open the cupboard where he kept some clothes and found the gown he used to wear.

'I can hardly fit into it now. It's all this bloody manual labour.' He pulled the gown across his chest but could not cover the red hair curling over his breastbone. 'Come on now, let's wash ourselves.'

They locked the door as they had always done to keep the girls from running in.

'You get in.'

'No, you get in George.'

George scratched his balls in perplexity.

'You get in or I won't give you your present. You'll like your present.'

'But Dada poured in all this essence of pine shit for you.'

'I want you to have it. I want you to have it first. Come on now.' Nicholas was at the bath. 'Do you want your hair washed, George?'

'I was going to wash it.'

Nicholas took the shampoo. 'Get in and duck your head. Go on. Duck your head.'

The suds frothed up and George became an exotic oriental god.

Nicholas broke it down with his hand. 'Rinse,' he commanded.

With the steam and the perfumes, Nicholas could have been a slave in a bathhouse. He looked pliable enough for it.

George, his buttocks misty pink, stumbled to the lavatory. His bowels were swimming with strange sensations which he wanted if possible to expel from himself. He looked back at his brother edging down into what was still hot water.

Sweating a bit he sat on the lavatory. As he flushed away his unease, there was a tap at the door and George put a towel around himself and went to answer. He returned with two whiskies. 'Dad,' he said.

Nicholas drank his down like medicine, expanding through such loving acts.

George took the empty glass.

'I brought you paints. Really good paints. And brushes.'

George blushed.

'And also some prints from the Tate. Some of Blake's.'

He stepped out of the bath.

In their bedroom their parents were taking their evening sherry. The high tinkle of crystal glasses touching at the lip brought back the men from their silence. George flexed his hands. His brother yawned, at ease, and reached for his dressing-gown.

Nicholas had not slept much for two days, and when he looked at these party people he was unsure whether he dreamed them or not. They could also be souls awaiting their judgement. Water and sky had come at each other and parted, dripping. The harbour was blood-red and wave leapt on wave, holding each other's fluidity with a sexual desperation.

The children of the town were too busy with cocktail chatter to notice the antics of nature. They had become simple in their desires.

'It must be good to be back.' Someone grabbed an asparagus roll and nibbled the extruding green tip.

'I'll bet ya pleased to be home,' said Gloria Whinstable, toying with her sherry, pale as babies' urine in the bottom of Mrs Fieschi's second-best sherry glasses.

The Whinstables had just arrived.

'Must be good to be back after those other places. I was in Sydney last year. I took a trip when Fred was at a law conference.'

'Wouldn't trust the old tart these days. Too bloody independent by far,' said Fred.

Gloria sipped babies' urine and rolled it around in her mouth. 'Spanish, I'll bet,' she said to Mrs Fieschi, 'not that I would know about thatatall!'

Mrs Fieschi had lit some candles in a candelabrum. Society bridled at the romanticism, but was pacified when they heard some Chopin coming over the loudspeaker. Chopin by candlelight was okay.

'You're looking like a corpse warmed-up,' Gloria told him confidently.

He laughed at her sharp laugh and she retreated from him to the safety of Emily. They had both taken a course in Zen Buddh-

ism. And Gloria, out of the void, a BA in English at some uncertain moment of her past.

'So,' said Mrs Baxter the vicar's widow, not seeing Nicholas
who was caught between a gold-and-blue vase and the heads of
flowers from the garden.

'So?' The wifeless Professor of History admired an Etruscan
amphora.

'So I killed this rat. Imagine, in my bedroom, with his cheeky
face and that awful thick body, fat as could be.' She flounced
her curls. 'It reminds me of another story. When Jimmy was a
priest at Milton, among those awful farmers – at times I feared
for my virtue, particularly from the Chinamen. One never knew
what they were thinking, which I still find disconcerting – not
to know. In fact I am convinced that that poor Alison Black was
done in by them. You remember that.' Mrs Baxter lowered her
voice. 'She was a *cousin* of Bertie's.'

The clock in the oak-panelled hall chimed with German stur-
diness, seven times. Nicholas wasn't surprised, for in the plane
time had hit the curve of the horizon and fallen back on itself.
Moments later it could be morning.

He reviewed his life. One volume of bad verse, one mediocre
novel, a good job in an English publishing house.

Around him, and like him at this moment, the party folk could
have been reviewing each other's lives. Sometimes the veins which
were close to the surface were ready for the knife.

'Bloody cheek,' said Gloria Whinstable of something, securely
deep in her third whisky.

Nicholas slipped away to the garden.

The family friends preferred the room and were drugged
enough by the occasion to forget that doors could exist. Behind
glass they could not see the levels of the lawn. Or Nicholas, as
he left them. Conversations rose and fell with the monotony of
prayer – broken by an exclamation or joke.

By the pool a fragile wild light rode the back of his father's carp
and the seven steps into the second garden assumed the precision

of geometric forms. The two stones from the farm – the guardians – were fluid, and menaced only the night they had sprung from. He ran his hand over them, feeling surfaces and tender planes, the obscure velvet of moss and the rough-chiselled edge where George had begun to chip before he realized that they were perfect and had leapt, in their own way, out of the bondage of matter.

But he walked past because the illusions of permanence might make a net in which brighter plumed birds than he could be trapped. The net swept high tonight and the gold-backed fish offered reflections of apparent depth.

The third garden beckoned. And there was the hut.

George and he always drifted back to it for their rites of mystery and profanation. He looked into its open doorway, half expecting the candle to be alight. It was always left on a saucer as Mrs Fieschi was frightened of the dark, but nevertheless insisted on keeping her trunks there with schoolgirl essays and old clothes. Among the feather boas of an aunt the mice had made nests, but for some reason no one thought to stop them or even to set a trap.

He struck a match and stumbled forward.

The Buddha had belonged to Alison Black and for that reason Mrs Fieschi had held on to it along with her volumes of *Das Kapital*. Sometimes she even polished him and put him back on the shelf, puzzled at herself. Now he glowed in brassy glory which did not disturb his presence. The kingdom of the hut was his, and everything necessary for life, from stored apples to books, over the years had found itself here. Most things in time got mouldy or mildewed and slowly turned back into earth. That accounted for the rotting smell. Yet here he felt the possibility of many things he did not wish to recognize, so he left with the candle and even shut the door, as a gesture to the inhabitants, who would return to contemplation of the inwardness of things, after politely assuming forms for him while he looked.

The willow tree was down. George must have returned to finish off the job sometime after his bath. The chips lay scattered over the grass and the log with its tassles of twigs and leaves was crushed into the mud. He stepped by a heap of humus, piled high with grass clippings, and before him, growing out of the wall, was the pear tree they had carved their initials on. The fruit hung heavy and golden and he could see in the soft flesh the busy jaw marks of wasps.

He had come, he realized, simply to vomit.

It was not a controlled act. The food, like bilge, had slopped around his stomach for two days and got no further. He had no time to bend over before his mouth, by itself, opened, and the muck leapt out of his throat into the air. It deluged over a fuchsia bush and splattered against the native trees. The force was such that he followed that part of himself into the mud and lay sobbing beside a pool that smelled of rancid chips.

At last he could smell.

He could weep, too, and snarl to himself and scratch. He wanted to pee but he could not get up. He lay instead with his head in the middle of a clump of rich grass. The Southern Cross was directly overhead. He rolled over, and as he expected, there was George.

'I'm sick,' he said. But couldn't force any more out.

George was not a great one for ambiguity and merely smelt the vomit in the air and nodded.

'I can't get up and I'm dying for a pee. You'll have to help me, brother.'

George did.

'Look at the stars.'

George didn't bother. He had stared at them so often that their geography was embossed in small points throughout his mind. Instead he held Nicholas by the waist who managed to undo his fly and shake himself free from his cold and sticky underwear. He urinated in short intense bursts – between the shudders that ran through him. George held him carefully, as he would one of his animals. His hands were strong and direct and his concern dispassionate so he could be of the most use.

'You'll have to change.' George rubbed a vomit mark on his brother's shirt. 'All this finery,' he said, 'fucked up.'

*   *   *

Nicholas sat on his bed while George fetched things to wear.

'Thank you, George,' he said. And dressed.

He walked down the stairs.

He adjusted a smile onto his face.

He saw her.

She was, in the silence of the party crowd, deep in herself.

He sucked his teeth and tasted a bit of vomit stuck in a cranny.

George was behind him and Nicholas could feel the solidness of his brother's body, built for a time and their shocks. George was propelling him towards his desire even if he did not know it, as a low shudder moved out of his loins and gave Nicholas the power to move.

She was wearing her long black hair loose over her shoulders. Her waist had thickened and her breasts were full. He could feel her white thighs under the peasant dress she wore.

The last stars in the sky burned out the jets of gunpowder.

She was in his arms and did not bother to smile.

Nicholas and Miriam drove across to Tomahawk beach.

Flies rose around the headlights and were caught with the freezing mist into icy dances. She noted in the lagoon the white body of a swan lying among the thick weed, head tucked under its wing.

They walked side by side on the open shore, two small figures between the headlands. The autumn tide swept in against the rock and on to the white beach.

He waited for her to speak her first word to him. She had pulled her cloak around her and was watching the breakers rise high and pull fast away, as if in revulsion at their finished act. But another always followed.

Far above on the headland was the crematorium. She took his hand. He wanted to say I love you. Have you loved me?

She wished to tell him she had cleaned the house, inch by inch, scrubbing until her hands had blistered, but the distance between them was still there so they walked together up one of the inclines.

At the top she shook her hair free and pulled him further away from the lip of the sandhill until they were standing waist high in the dune grass.

He lay down with her, but because it was cold did not expect to feel her naked body. Only those parts which were necessary to break the silence. To defeat the waves.

And they were both ready.

Later he lay back to look at the cross of light. The mist billowed above their heads onto the land, damp and stinging with the sweat of the sea.

She held her hand over her belly, certain and intransigent.

'I love you,' she said, above the waves, 'I really love you.'

'I had to write,' he replied, 'and tell you.'

'And George?' she asked.

He shook his head.

3

She dropped him at the gate.

It was easy to see from the line-up of cars that the party was still in progress. Someone had put a rock record on. Probably Emily, to frighten them all out of the house. But it hadn't worked. He could hear the thumping feet and the screams of gaiety. The end of the war, any war, could be celebrated again. The garden was deep and ready for the adventurous middle-aged adulteries of the town. The hut had seen in its time most rites of the flesh.

'Miriam's gone,' he said, rather unnecessarily, to George, who appeared.

'Why?'

'Because – because she has a headache. The coast road's a bit nasty at night. I want to get away from here,' he said a moment later.

'Why?'

'Does there have to be a reason for anything?'

'There's a taxi dumping someone just around the corner.'

A moment later the headlights held them both.

Nicholas was stuck by a dribble of sperm in his underwear.

They got in. George gave an address.

'Have a good time,' said the driver on arrival. 'I don't suppose anything goes on in there. Looks too flash.'

'Dada and I put up the money along with a couple of others. Cousin Charlie didn't want to as he reckoned it wouldn't pay. But it is paying.' George was pleased with his surprise.

Nicholas followed George in to the sauna and was hit by dry, searing air. His heart reeled in its beat. The sweat burst down his back. He lay on his towel and felt the poisons his system had accumulated rise to the surface. He dozed.

George shook him. 'That's enough. Ten minutes is enough for a starter. You'll be able to stay longer after you're used to it. Come on. You can have a go at the hot and cold baths. You'll feel real good. Jump into one, then the other.'

They dived like porpoises and floated on the water.

Like the guide to some paradise, George took him into the Relax Room.

Someone appeared and began on George's command to knead his brother's body. And then he left.

George, his breath stinking of whisky, nudged Nicholas. 'It's eleven o'clock. Tom says you need a good working over.' George leaned loosely against the wall. He grinned through his teeth, and his thick red lips slopped open. It was the same grin when he pulled the lambs out of their mothers or killed them for meat. He painted sheep with silver light eating their fleece, and he made money until he almost pissed it.

Nicholas closed his eyes again.

'Wool prices have fallen this year,' said George. 'Did you see in the English papers? Not so much money to play around with. Still we're lucky, we haven't any big debts to pay off. The farm doesn't need any improving.' He belched in a satisfied way. 'I was with the boys yesterday. Rough lot of cockies. All brassed off about the prices they got. They wanted to get pissed out of their minds. All their old ladies lined up outside in the Chevs just about having heart attacks. Saw their old men up in court on disorderly charges. Good thing Dada's off the bench! I got a bottle of whisky for us. We can go home if you like.'

Nicholas did not move. Every part of him sank into waiting. Even his lungs seemed to stop.

The air was silent and, hanging like ripe pears, were the faces of Miriam and George. His own face and theirs joined and fell away again.

'Before us all the masks of men groan and sing as stones lie on the sand, storing the heat, and letting it pass with the night into the winds which are sent to carry it back to the sun.'

He remembered the farm on the plateau where George stayed.

'I am he who is reborn through the singing the wind makes through my own empty ribs.'

He half laughed at the hallucination.

Then he saw the graves of his grandparents out on a paddock close to the stone mountains. A willow and an ash grew there, but they hadn't reached the fence top because the earth was barren.

He could feel himself in this strange moment, swimming, and also in another moment, if one factor changed, drowning. And George was there, dozing.

'George, listen! I'm dying of leukaemia. That's why I've come here. Because I am dying.'

George half opened his mouth to say something. They dressed together.

'We'll go to Grandma's house,' said Nicholas. 'She left it to me and I should go and look at my property.'

They walked on to the street. The pavement was littered with sweet papers. They both pulled up the edge of their collars against the wind.

'The house will be cold,' said George.

The taxi pulled up and George paid.

Together they looked over the railings. Grandmother had made brick paths to take herself about her small demesne. She preferred a bed that could hold only the number of plants she could grow acquainted with personally. Each path led somewhere: to a flower, to an underground nest of ants where she had placed offerings of honey to give their tiny bodies energy for the winter work of patrolling her clods of earth.

Nicholas, the mood still on him, could feel the house open to him. It was two storied and the old woman had lived mostly on the top floor. The neighbourhood, except for the large Anglican church, was depressed, filled with students, peeling wallpaper, and sentenced by time to a general damp. But the old woman, off her farm and with memories of her own, did not mind. And now, if her grandson was right, she was there at the opening of the house, as in the middle of a lotus, her face wrinkled and alive with more wisdom than Nicholas could find in the pale, fading generation her own womb had nurtured.

'She's still here,' said George, and stroked the gatepost timidly. His brother pushed ahead to meet her.

The walls of the house had been painted yellow ten years before, and among the weatherboards the wistaria grew until root and rot mingled and worked together for the privilege of holding up a brittle sparrow's nest.

'I can feel her here.' George grabbed the key and rushed to the lock to fumble his way into the affections of the old woman. 'I've often been here since she died. Why didn't you let Mum rent it out as she wanted to? It would have been money in your pocket.' His blond-red hair flamed under the hall light. 'I paid for the electricity and the gas. I didn't want them turned off.'

They wandered down the hall, past the stairs. A green baize cloth had been thrown over the oak dining table and the darkness smelled as she would have wished. Every hole in the house, each cranny still had its lavender bag.

The downstairs rooms were empty, the wallpaper faded discreetly into beige.

Nicholas took the stairs up to her bedroom where she had lived out her last week, wheezing with pneumonia. George was waiting for him, hunched up on a chair in front of an electric fire.

'We'd better get some drink into us,' he said. He passed over a bottle after draining the top two fingers into a cup. 'I tell you, it's a pity prices have fallen, but the old woman wouldn't have cared. I wonder why she left you the house?'

Nicholas pulled his coat more tightly around him.

'I suppose,' George went on, 'because she liked talking to you. She found it difficult to understand why our dad didn't go back to the farm when Uncle David was killed in the war. It was too much for Grandad.' George shifted closer to his twin. 'She frightened me sometimes. It was her eyes.'

He looked out of the window over the Rugby field. In the vapour lamps it was all a vile yellow shade.

On the bed was the old woman's eiderdown. George threw it across to his twin who still shivered. 'Put it around yourself. You'll catch cold after the sauna if you don't keep well wrapped up.'

George was searching for words. He looked at the bookcase, at the upright Steinway the old lady had ordered musical relatives to play. But the vision of what was to happen held off, so he drank some more. 'This place is like a fortress,' he suggested to his twin. 'I feel drunk. All this bloody whisky.' He put down the bottle. 'I really like Miriam. I've been going down there quite often. I pay her some money for a room and then I feel it's okay to go when I want to. She has old Charlie Katana staying. He's a permanent. You remember him? The old fisherman. Well, the roof of his house fell in and he doesn't have any money to fix it up, so he came to Miriam. You remember, her grandfather employed him. Now he says he'll be dead in a year. He can see real good, he says, that he'll be dead in a year if not before. He does a bit of carving sometimes.' George scratched his hair and a shower of dandruff settled on his collar. Like a monk, he was losing at the crown.

He went to the sofa opposite Nicholas and stretched out. 'I wouldn't mind taking a nap.' He retreated towards it as hopeful as a child. He curled up tight but the trick of forgetting eluded him and the warmth of his body spun off him. 'Well, anyway,' he opened his eyes sulkily, 'when do you want to go and see Miriam?'

The bottle reached the quarter mark and Nicholas sat, waiting. Like a fish that was hooked but had to be played slowly or the line would break, slowly, slowly, George was approaching the bank.

George could feel Grandma as she grew decrepit and her pleasure was the few bulbs she had ably planted. She focused all her waning sight onto them. Each leaf she examined with minute pleasure and she even took to watching the ants and earwigs with a magnifying glass she bought in Woolworths.

Mrs Fieschi had wondered, carefully locating the thought at the edge of her mind where she would not be required to give it full attention, if her mother-in-law was losing her hold on the reality that Mrs Fieschi, like all the ladies of the town, bore witness to from the moment of their getting out of bed. But her mother-in-law had taken no notice. She was being drawn closer to her few flowers. Finally she was pulled down through the stems and into the experience of earth.

A few dried leaves in the chimney rustled, reminding George that to understand you had to be open. But George felt angry and his anger reached as far as the dirty muslin curtains and out to the new vapour lamps. The leaves dripped onto the pavement.

George stared at the carpet through the thin layer of whisky on the bottom of the bottle. 'I suppose she left you this place because it was here she'd talked to you when you were little and it was here she died. Whenever you sit in that chair or lie in that great bloody four-poster from the farm, then you have to think what she was and what we're not.'

George would be able to say anything. He was drunk and was snorting with unease like a cob fed too many oats. His lips flopped with the drink. They were wide open for the truth.

'I came back,' said Nicolas.

George snorted with fear. 'Why do you have to be so bloody melodramatic. You're always so sure of what you have to say. What bloody divine right have you? You let the old lady down. You didn't sleep here after she was dead. You were fucking around in London. But I did, to keep her happy. You bloody went away and left me.' He threw the empty bottle at the heater and it smashed against the hearth behind.

'You know why I'm back. I've told you, George. You know. I am dying. I have leukaemia.'

But this admission was also a defeat because George was sunk in remorse and his eyes were frightened like a child's. It was because he was learning something of himself.

'Whatdidyasay?'

Nicholas waited again.

When he was little Nicholas had walked with his grandfather, that silent and sometimes elegant man, to look at the salmon, come home to spawn.

The sea lay two hundred miles away and some of the fish were old and ulcerous from the struggle, for they ate nothing on the way upstream.

He had lain on a shingle bank under a willow and seen everything that he would ever know. He had seen the bodies of those for whom it was the last season drifting bloated on the current. His grandfather watched these with sombre eyes and when one of them brushed against the bank he pushed it out with a stick so it could get that much closer to the waves and endless motion which, for some, was the peace of God.

Later that year the fire had come sweeping across the plateau. Some thought it was Miss Daisy Crawford burning off, like the old fool she was, when the wind was blowing.

It reached the Fieschi run and swept along the tussock, dried by the last summer and a rainless autumn. Great clouds billowed ahead of it from the burning fleeces and the fat of the sheep. And they ran in circles, milling together in the middle of the fire and were roasted as they ran. Above them blew carrion birds.

In the evening, ushered in with smoke and a red sun, he had walked with his grandmother into the holocaust. His granny had put on a clean white linen pinny and a clean dress which the help had ironed for this moment, early in the day. 'Fires,' the old lady said, 'always burnt out. Now, Ethel, iron that well.'

The ashes crumbled into dust and he could feel the heat they kept. Behind them, the dogs, who wanted to investigate, howled and barked. The ash was too hot for their pads and they feared their mistress had got the better of them. But they calmed when she gave them an angry look.

The old lady stopped at a sheep with its belly burst open. The foetus had popped out to the flame and the womb was a black wound in the flesh with the lamb holding by a powder-thin cord to its mother.

At each one she stopped and counted. Then she told him. 'Your grandfather cannot bear to do this, to count his dead. So I must do it. Fifteen!' she muttered. 'Already fifteen just in this paddock. "The Lord giveth and the Lord taketh away." But one of these poor brutes was enough for the altar Abraham built. One ram. Might have been an old ram.'

At a spot where the fire had curved around for reasons best known to the wind, a ewe lay. She added to the count. 'Thirty-five,' she said and knelt down because, although the fleece was burnt and some patches of skin were blackened, the eyes had moved.

Grandmother knelt in the ash, not minding that she was scorching her stocking. 'Quick. She'll die soon.' From the pocket in her pinny she took out a sharpened knife, eight inches long almost, with a point like a stiletto. 'Slit her open.' She pointed along the belly she was feeling with her hands, despite the flesh there being blistered and hard. 'Cut along there.'

'You do it, Gran.'

She shook her head.

'The poor beast has kept herself alive for this long. She will not feel pain now, but she will want to know we are going to rescue her baby.' She turned to her grandson, her white hair lank, and she wiped her hands. 'You slit her throat and she will think she is being killed, that is all. What do you think? Any woman, any beast who is of the female sort is born to give birth and to nurture her young. She is the earth, even this black hateful earth. She is the tree that grows always in the place it was planted. Now, you do it.'

'But I am only ten,' he had whimpered, and stopped because she didn't think that it mattered and she was old and experienced in things. He took the knife out of its sheath. 'Now,' she said. He held it on the swelling flesh. 'Cut half way down. Half way down the blade. No further. Straight in and move along to its birthplace. Move slowly and that way you'll miss the womb.' She knelt between the back legs of the beast and held them wide apart and he pushed the knife in.

For a moment the ewe struggled; it was running back from death. 'Take no notice,' she said. So, he pulled the knife along. And Gran, tears running down her cheeks, reached over the guts and patted the ewe's head and told her what a beauty she was and what a good mother. He stopped at the back legs because there was no further to go. 'Good,' she said, and pointed to the womb. 'Cut carefully. Carefully. Like a surgeon. Good.' Her hand dived into the opening and both hands reached around for a moment and then pulled out the sack. She took the knife and cut that, and cleaned it off quickly with her pinny. 'Take off your jersey,' she said.

She wrapped the lamb in the pinny and then in the jersey of good thick wool. She held it close to herself, prised open its mouth and sucked, spat out muck, rocked it quickly. Held it so it would feel her heart and want to live.

A feeble sound, thinner than high, came from the throat.

And his grandmother, his dignified grandmother danced on the spot like a Spaniard and then ran across the black ashes and the patches of bright, burned clay.

The dogs saw them coming and they yapped and barked, running in bushy circles of tail and nose. 'It is worth it,' she puffed at him. 'Your grandfather will bear the loss.' She held the small body close and ran in short bursts, her bottom swaying from side to side and her head stuck forward like a goose. 'Hurry. Run ahead of me and put the milk on, and open the oven of the coal range, we'll keep him warm there. Open it so it's not too hot. The milk is by the range, ready, in case – tell Ethel.'

And he ran fast among the lolloping and barking dogs, chasing them and being chased around the side of the house, all of them skidding together on the gravel as they strained to reach the step up to the house first.

*   *   *

The burial ground which was to begin their history had been chosen at the place where grandmother had found the lamb.

The first to go was the old man, crushed by a boulder. The service was in the house – some Presbyterian parson had arrived in a little car – in the room they called, from memories of other days, the supper room.

Also from some memories whose origin it was difficult to tell, four candles were placed around the coffin and, with his face smashed as it was, she kept the lid open for herself and the children to see him.

The only son left was Bertie, the magistrate, with his wife Muriel, who found it all a little primitive. Her father-in-law had made his own coffin some five years before and it was not of good wood; the other, for his wife, was stored in the barn until she would need it.

The old man's son walked in the procession with his wife. His mother, like a guide, walked in front, her shawl whipped by the wind.

The sky was grey and dirty with snow that might fall.

Muriel Fieschi struggled across the tussock in her townish high heels, her soles slipping on the mud and the fresh sheep droppings. She clutched her new beaver fur coat and looked sourly at the ground ahead.

Later Muriel remarked to her husband that she herself would expect rosewood, and she would never expose people to the unpleasantness of her dead face, no matter how well the undertaker applied cosmetics.

And in this case, where the face was smashed and had only been washed, it was obscene. And to cut from that dead body – with the kitchen scissors – a tuft of hair for the son – absolutely pagan. There was, when she considered the matter, no real need to see the dead at all. 'Let the dead bury their dead,' she said to Bertie Fieschi over a glass of sherry when they were back in civilization.

*   *   *

George was staring into the glowing bar of the heater, entranced by it. He skidded on the trough of a thought and his body twitched as the dangerous edges were surmounted. He thought of the fat topaz-eyed rams dragging their balls along the skyline.

Nicholas thought again of his grandparents' graves. They had been blasted with charges of dynamite.

He went to the Victorian mirror that Gran had peered into as she grew older to guess how long she had left. The teak frame now suited him. He examined his double, line by line, because at any moment in this night he could be changed.

George, as a counterpart of this scrutiny, had sunk into a light sleep.

Nicholas turned on him and shook him savagely. 'Wake up. You're not getting away with it that easy. Wake up.'

George did. 'So what's the matter?'

'A lot is the matter.'

'What?'

Nicholas sat and remembered the letters he had written over the last month. He had even sent a letter to George that hinted but didn't say. Most of the letters had gathered dust in his bedroom in Chelsea.

He had not written to his mother because Mrs Fieschi would get the feel of his words and convert them into the ammunition of love: He must return home – to her. In sickness every man becomes his mother's child. And she would be racked by his energy flowing away from her outstretched arms.

All the letters were written to himself, even though one or two had been posted to other people. This city had not received any. Each brick and plate-glass window was dense with the thickness of the Dunedinites' lives. He could have written one hundred letters from the centre of this knowledge, but each would have been ignored, or the charge of his words drained to nothing by the platitudes they lived in. He had hoped otherwise, for one second, between his sweat and the locking of the wheels on the Taieri Plains airport.

'Do you remember, George, when we were sixteen, our trip into the mountains above Te Anau? We almost killed ourselves

– walking over a bluff when the mist came down. Do you remember, because you were born first you walked first, and so you would have gone over if we hadn't stopped, and I would've had time to stop before the edge. Do you remember?'

George stared ahead squeezing his groin.

'What do you see, George?' Nicholas knelt beside him and reached out with both his hands to stroke his brother's head. 'What are you looking at?' George's hands clenched tighter around his balls.

'George, you must look at me.' Nicholas prized away one finger and then another. His brother's hand was again a piece of statuary which had to be caught before it fell, and held against his cheek. 'Listen to me.' He rubbed his brother's hand against him, and then thrust it through his coat and pushed it against his heart. 'I am afraid, George.'

George looked at him.

'I can feel this death in me, in my bones. That is where it starts, I believe. I turn cannibal on myself. I eat myself. George, please touch me.'

George caught on. Nicholas rested his head on his brother's lap to be cradled by his brother's hands. He could smell lanoline in the cloth of his trousers. Then he wept. And believed what he had just told his twin.

George lifted his brother to his feet and kissed him.

'We'll stay here,' said Nicholas. 'We can go back. Later'

'I see,' said George.

He helped Nicholas off with his jersey and his other things. 'Step out,' he said, and held out his hand for Nicholas to lean against him. Then he too undressed and lifted his brother onto the bed. He lay next to him and pulled him so close that every inch of flesh was receiving the warmth that flowed, wave upon wave. Together the firmness of one and the lightness of the other, neither in heaven nor hell nor on the earth, were united, as twins in the womb of their mother.

From that ancestral bed, rocked by the shadow, in the presence of their grandmother – whom they smelt in the musk of the house, and saw in the light from the one-bar heater she sat before

– they looked down to the small paths that had brought them back to the same place as children before the dark.

Nicholas wondered if tonight were the moment of his change.

For George this was evident somewhere, but the thought stayed beyond his horizon and he could not put a precise shape to it.

'You mustn't tell them.' George squeezed his stomach. 'I wouldn't have told them. I would have written to you to tell you to come to me, and would have stayed on the farm with the animals.'

'We'll go to Taieri Mouth,' said Nicholas. 'Miriam knows.'

'The river,' said George, 'is really beautiful, at the Mouth, with the seaweed in it.'

The University clock beat the hour.

'We must sleep,' George said, 'because we'll have to go home before morning, otherwise Mother will think it's an accident and phone the police. But I don't care. I'll do what you want.'

'Before morning – yes.'

George snuggled close to him and pulled the eiderdown up to their mouths.

4

Mrs Fieschi smiled down at the sleeping head and sighed again, allowing a few tears to sparkle around her eyes.

Down in the hall the clock chimed twelve-thirty.

Mrs Fieschi leaned forward over her boy, clutching her floral dressing-gown. She touched his cheek. Behind them George had woken up and lay watching. Quiet, for George, who usually greeted the day with a roar of pleasure.

'You are terrible, George. You and Miriam dragging him off on his first night home. Heaven knows what the guests thought. But boys will be boys.'

She took the breakfast tray from Mr Fieschi and put it down on the bedside table. She had opened a tin of peaches and now they were in a bowl with fresh cream Daphne had brought up from the dairy after her women's meeting. Also Marmite on toast which Nicholas had always liked, with extravagant helpings of butter.

'Wake up.' She sat on the edge of the bed, light as a leaf. 'Wake up dear. You were late last night, but I heard you and George come in. Around six. Where were you? But, don't tell me. Out with some of the young things. What you can find in town until

six I'm sure I don't know. Did Miriam drive home? I suppose
she did. It's a long way for a girl by herself. George, did you
offer to drive her?'

'No.'

Nicholas opened his eyes and his mother was placated.

'Now, eat your breakfast. I'm keeping you in bed for the day.
The others can wait. Some people enquired last night and I told
them you had to go to bed as you were exhausted. No need to
say anything else.' She went over to the window. 'It really is
winter today. Such a bitter southerly. Bertie, you'll have to get
them to come and turn on the central heating.' She sat down
again on the bed. 'Just fancy, in England it will be spring.' She
straightened the coverlet. 'I've heard that cousin Charles' house
in Somerset is very beautiful in that season. My mother always
said she preferred Somerset to any other county. Of course,
people could afford service then.' Her fingers touched her nude
ears where emeralds had graced their antique setting the night
before.

'And how is Miriam? Does she have a phone number down
the coast?'

'Yes.' He began to force-feed himself.

'She is looking after Charlie Katana,' said George. 'You remember him. He used to sell us fish.'

'Oh,' said Mrs Fieschi, pleased by Miriam's maternal display
though slightly off-put by the fact of Maori, 'I suppose it is very
good of her. But old people like *that* should have the *sense* to
find a home that will care for them.'

And then Emily and her husband arrived, talking loudly to
cover up the fight they had had in the car. Peter, her husband,
looked to be waiting on the final social crown, a coronary throm-
bosis. 'So, I suppose you'll be thinking of some work to do. Soon,
I mean.' Emily measured his body with a firm glance. 'Time you
settled down, Nicky, found a nice girl.' Her voice was like a well-
drilled canary.

'And,' said Peter, 'if you're thinking about business, I'd be only
too pleased.'

'We'll leave you and George to get on with your breakfast.'

Mr Fieschi reappeared with another tray. 'We'll be having lunch. Your mother is keeping some for you both.' The family, led by Mr Fieschi, left the boys and descended the stairs, talking over party incidents and especially the colour of cousin Minnie's face. She had been boozing as usual.

'Nicholas,' said Mrs Fieschi much later in the day, 'is interested in Miriam. He will need an exceptional girl.' Mrs Fieschi had been sensing the atmosphere and made frequent excuses to visit the boys who were sitting up reading some rubbishy detective novels. Before, Mrs Fieschi had thought of Miriam as 'that girl', and frequently put the adjective 'strange' before her name.

'But,' said Daphne who had called in with some fresh scones, 'she's funny.'

'Miriam,' said Mrs Fieschi, 'is, at the moment, living by herself.'

'What about George and her?' asked Emily, who having contemplated adultery could also consider with some equanimity the probable fornication of her brother.

Mrs Fieschi brushed back her hair with a sudsy hand. 'Miriam is a pianist and artistic girls like that are always difficult. I was artistic once myself. But I have grave doubts if George could win her as his wife.' She ignored the implications of her daughter's remark with an ease which secretly delighted her, and gazed fondly at the expanding belly which today seemed so much bigger than yesterday. 'All will be for the best.'

'I think,' said Emily later in the evening to her husband, 'that Nicky's maturing. He doesn't have all those half-baked ideas about changing the world. I really thought he'd take after that cousin of Dad's, Alison. And, God knows, it didn't do her any good.'

5

Miriam awoke at eight on Easter day.

Nicholas slept through the alarm and she was pleased, because her face was heavy and she could feel rings around her eyes. She bent to kiss him. And in that flow of warmth her whole body lit for the day.

In the kitchen Charlie Katana would be sitting in the smoke waiting for the range to start pulling. She could smell manuka wood.

Outside, the cows, heavy with milk, were wandering over the hill to the byre. She envied them their udders. Her breasts felt swollen – but that was Nicholas. Sometimes his mouth and teeth were rough on her as if he wanted to force her paps to produce for him.

She slipped into the house shoes George had made for her from brown doe skin. At the window she leaned out, forgetting the chill she might get, and smelled the lilies. The grass had dew on it and was thick enough to harvest.

She threw a shawl over her shoulders and opened the kitchen door. George too was asleep, snoring loudly. He had worked late at night after they had gone to bed.

Charlie, bent in the back, his face brown and wrinkled, sat in front of the fire, watching his pipe glow.

'I've put on the porridge,' he told her.

She nodded as he relinquished the place next to the fire, the woman's place, and sat in a rattan chair at the door.

'Happy Easter,' she remembered.

'Yes,' he said.

She pulled the bubbling porridge onto a cooler spot. And took from the sideboard the plates rescued from the *Marguerite Marabord*.

Everyone had come to Crystal's Beach to see the wreck. Everybody had been saved, and so there was a certain merriment over which the Presbyterian colony of Milton was at odds with the Catholics of Taieri Mouth. But eventually, mirth won. And it was at that moment that Miriam's grandmother, Jewish, from Vienna, was welcomed by the women because she dirtied her hands with them over the vat of soup, helped to change nappies, made good strong tea and put brandy in it, despite the fear of some that it would aid the devil. But, Mrs Roberts said: 'They will be cold in their stomachs so.' And with that display of her inferior understanding of their language, and with her pink silk skirt, the women were captivated.

In one picture was a young Maori boy, eyes alight. Charlie Katana when he was eight or so.

Miriam wandered away to the upright Bechstein, its carved pompous feet drilled with borers.

'The tea is ready,' the old man called.

She heard the door to the dunny open and shut. That would be Nicholas. She could see George sitting at the range, yawning and stirring the pot. The old man had let the collie off the chain and it raced to and fro.

The toast was ready on the table. She had been dreaming and they laughed at her. Even Nick was there and the dog was jumping up on his chest and licking at his unshaven face.

'Happy Easter,' she called to them.

'Happy Easter,' the twins replied.

The old man was telling about the shipweck and Miriam's

grandmother. And the hill had more trees on it in those days and only one cow, called Daisy.

Captain Roberts hadn't gone around to the wreck because there had been trouble on the island. A man had been knifed and the Captain, who didn't need any magistrates, had gone out to see about it himself. The man who did it was bent over a barrel and given forty with a riding crop. Roberts had stayed the night there drinking with the men and joking with the whaler he had beaten and who was real cut about. They rubbed in whale oil later. The man he had killed was part nigger and nobody liked him. They took him out in a cutter and dumped him for the fishes.

'So I rode with Mrs Roberts to the wreck,' said Charlie. 'She was a pretty sight, her hair all flying out behind her, and she whipped up that horse to get us there in time.

'The boat was a mile or two out, on a reef, and some of them sailors, naked as the day they were born, came swimmin' in, and Mrs Roberts, she laughed to see them get in safe. She knew French because she was a lady. The Captain said all real ladies knew French. She even taught me a bit.

'It was a great sight. They were whores arriving from France too late for the goldfields. They came to the shore all decked up in feather boas and fluffy skirts. Mrs Roberts knew what they were but she told the women of the plain that they were French ladies, which impressed them all.

'How they chattered! Like bright little birds. Never stopped talking and joking with the sailors and diving into trunks and "O la la-ing".

'One of the sailors had a pipe, he was a hefty boy. He sat on a rock and started to play his pipe. And a few that had been given hot tea with some of Mrs Roberts' brandy in it – they danced a sailor's dance. Big men some of them was, with bare feet, and thick toenails, like shells. Must come from all the stubbing they get on board.

'So we all had a picnic. There was a priest on board, a strange fella with a beard, and a brown cloak and sandals – I remember those girls calling him "mon père", real devout they all became.

'One rummaged in her trunk and found a tablecloth and some

of the sailors set up a table. You would think the devil had appeared, those Milton women were real shocked. But they couldn't tear themselves away from watching.

'The table was set up by a narrow gut, and the water once swept right up, the way it rides high in those rock guts, and washed around mon père's feet.

'Those Milton women all thought that God was answering their prayers. They expected the Frenchman to be swept away into the sea and drowned. Some were waiting for a monster, the Great Leviathan they said later, to reach out and devour him and his pagan ways.

'The wind blew a bit cold but when he raised his hands with the bread stuff the sun came out and shone right down on him. But the sailors and the French whore girls hadn't known that the Milton ladies thought their worshipping wicked so they didn't take it as a sign that God was on their side.

'And those Milton women stood like a gaggle of geese. One said she'd never thought to see the day when a bloody Mass was celebrated on Mr Crystal's beach, and him an Elder of the Church who should have stopped it.

'But I told her Mr Crystal had rowed out to the ship before it began and it wasn't his fault. She told me to be quiet, Maori boy, and don't answer back to your betters.'

Charlie Katana chuckled and slurped tea.

'Then everybody coming with us piled on board a dray Mr Crystal lent us and we set off for home.'

Nicholas wiped his mouth.

'It's a good story.'

The old man smiled at them. 'And now you'll be ready to walk around the river for your communion.' His eyes slanted away in thought. 'It was because the Captain bought Mrs Roberts the piano from the wreck that your mother met Mr Kraus, Miriam. He was a piano tuner. He played the violin real good, too.'

Charlie Katana scratched his white hair and sat on a dry patch of clay and rock, like something grown out of it.

The hills went straight for the sea, dipping a curtsy before plunging into the water. The river had eaten out a passage through them.

On the church side there are four fishermen who share Doris. She milks the cows that Charlie now watches – cow after cow is dried out and sent off to grass with a spank on its rump.

The church has closed its doors except for three festivals a year, and sometimes, when kneeling at the communion rail, one of the faithful will see some rat shit and remember to tell off Doris, who cleans for a small sum.

The bell began to ring.

They walked down to the pew the Captain had donated.

Miss Carew from the store had manned the harmonium and was belting out some simplified Bach chorales, as well as 'Christus Lag in Todesbanden'. The two altar candles had been lit by a server the rural vicar brought with him.

Now the vicar entered. The chalice and paten were covered in the fair linen cloth which Miss Carew's aunt had sewn. Miss Carew ironed and starched *everything* the vicar would need, herself. It was a matter of pride that she was at the organ, that the vicar was in the church's vestments, and that little Miriam was there with what looked like the Fieschi twins. She missed a couple of notes as she craned her neck around like a middle-aged turkey. Yes, it was the Fieschi boys, so Nicholas was home from his trip.

'Kyrie eleison. Christe eleison. Kyrie eleison.'

Miss Carew was surprised at the foreign language but used to the innovation of young men. Personally she couldn't see what was the matter with the Book of Common Prayer as it had always been, but then, if the young fussed around with things, they imagined it was all thought up by them. And it kept them off the streets.

The young rural vicar coughed and raised his hands and approached the altar: 'Almighty God unto Whom all hearts be open, all desires known and from Whom no secrets are hid, cleanse the thoughts of our hearts by the inspiration of Thy Holy

Spirit that we may perfectly love Thee and worthily magnify Thy Holy Name . . . '

On either side of the cross the Easter lilies rose out of a foam of maidenhair. The perfume surrounded the cross like incense at the intersection of the vertices.

'He hath burst his three-day prison,
Let the whole wide earth rejoice.
Death is conquered, man is free,
Christ has won a victory.'

So sang Miss Carew, the rural Vicar and one or two of the more musical farmers' wives.

Moment by moment, to Nicholas' surprise, they were gathered back into what he thought lost among the debris of childhood.

Perversely, because she liked the tune, Miss Carew played 'Christus Lag in Todesbanden' once more as the priest left the altar with his server.

'Happy Easter,' Miriam whispered to Nicholas.

Outside, the place even in winter had received again its blessing. She knew that the land, for this morning, would hold them in that promise. The sky was clear and distant blue like ice with the sun firmly planted in it.

'Let's visit my parents' grave,' said Miriam, 'and Grandma and Grandad.'

A corner of the church grounds had been designated the yard. Trees had grown up, luxurious broom with yellow ears, and the manuka brush in flower, with bees still tumbling in thick, yellow pantaloons through the light.

Nicholas watched the shore and thought of the often-grotesque flotsam that the ocean could carry, it sometimes seemed, for ever. Even a beer bottle, in its currents and tidal disposition, would in time become the sense which the water, with no particular desire, would imprint of itself.

The yard with these few bodies was also broken down.

A jam-jar with flowers had been kicked over. The moss on the Captain's grave almost excluded his identity with that of his wife. Only the stones, together, spoke of their rumbustious intimacy, with Mrs Roberts leaning gaily, in Viennese fashion, towards her husband's erect nonchalance.

And Miriam's mother's grave? It was by itself, a slab of concrete. She had been born and died when the first flush of adventure had subsided and most people had found themselves confined, by the wisdom of the land, to its surfaces.

'I ought to pay someone to look after this, or do it myself.' Miriam was on her knees pulling up daisies and scraping moss.

'Lovely day,' called out the rural vicar, in a friendly hurry. 'Happy Easter.'

Miss Carew, well bundled up against the cold, rubbed one wool-stockinged leg against the other. 'Come and have a cuppa.'

They left the graveyard and the church, both gathered back into their closer relationship with the hill behind.

'They ought to do something about the bridge.'

Miss Carew had been bounced several inches into the air by a passing car. 'One day this bridge will simply cave in and it could well be my luck to be on it. People shouldn't work on Easter Day. That was one of Doris' boy friends, I think. The pigman . . . Yes, the pigman.'

Miss Carew kept a small grocery store and managed the telephone exchange. She also managed a sitting room with a polished brass fender around the fire and a fat tomcat called Geoffrey.

The clock ticked loud and bossily; the photographs matured into the yellowing wallpaper. Here, one of a longboat out after a whale. Another of a picnic around at the pond just over the hill from Miriam's. The picnic, Miss Carew said, had been given by Mrs Kraus to those who were connected with the whaling business. Strange that. Men so close to the sea yet they didn't marry. The Captain never married again. She remembered him, a little, when he was past his best. He used to sit outside the store and take a drink.

'And now,' said Miriam, 'there is just the old brigade left.'

Mrs James, Miss Carew's widowed cousin, handed around the warm scones which exuded cheese.

'And how is Charlie Katana?' Miss Carew poured another cup for George.

'He's fine.'

'You should tell him to sell his boat. He could get a bit for it. And to lock the door of his cottage. Even if the roof has fallen in people won't take anything if the front door is locked. Otherwise they do. So would I.'

'I'll tell him.'

'And, Nicky dear, what are you up to? Just back from your trip?'

'I'm writing a bit.'

'And George is painting, I know that. Well, it's really quite an artistic colony,' said Miss Carew.

'Yes,' said Mrs James, kissing the cat, 'getting real classy.'

'And how are your parents, Nicky? They should come down and stay with us all for a few days. The weather is surprising. Doris says it is the atom bombs in the Pacific. The French always were a little pushy. And then the wreck. They say Doris' mother was the result.'

George looked at his hands, thick and straining with the cold. He would like to paint Miss Carew the colour of tea or fresh coffee, with butter skin and lollipop cheeks, holding an Easter egg. He laughed to himself and screwed his hands tighter.

'So,' said Miriam, putting down the cup, 'we really must go.'

They watched the island, heavy and lumpy in this fine air. It was shaped like a whale. The whale was there because the Captain had blasted away the connection to the mainland. It was a strange thing to do, to create an island.

They took off their shoes and socks. And Nicholas with his suit and tie, she in her church suit, paddled through the sand and spider's web. They followed the curve of the water until it met the sea. In the shelter of a tree trunk they sat down.

'I love you,' he said.

She pecked him on the nose, found some weed and threw it at him. It draped around his neck so that with his black hair and green eyes he was a sea god caught by the tide out of his element.

He chased her along the weaving line of the water and inland to sandhills and hillocks with mysterious paths half-closed by the autumn growth of lupin. 'Bitch,' he shouted and filled his lungs with good air. He tackled her in the lee of a dune and fell on her and mock pretended her death with the slippery weed.

George was somewhat behind — not far because the young collie jumped onto them, licking and nuzzling and breathing fumes of cooked liver over them, squirting some yellow pee against the sand skidding around imaginary obstacles and rolling over to play at being dead.

George whistled shrilly. They could see him carrying a bundle with him. Scarves, a wrap for Miriam, gloves and a coat for his brother.

'We can walk down to the rocks,' said George. 'Charlie said we should have a picnic at the pond. He's buying some sausages from Miss Carew.'

They reached the lagoon. George's ruddy face flamed against it.

'Come on,' called Miriam.

The lagoon was sunken farmland and took the sewage that leaked from the dry lavatories of the weekenders.

For George that was a wonder, the smell that water could make with the ocean so close and the clean pond. Where on one miniature cliff, like in a Chinese garden, one aged rata tree had caught the shape of every passing century.

They had gone after eels here in that long-ago summer.

The dinghy prow had cut through the saffron-yellow water, and at the bend where the dead trees were and the birds roosted — the steam rising through the dead branches — they waited.

They had hit it with the oars to stun it, and the serpent, no longer ruling his world, was caught on the point of the spear, its yellow eyes penetrating.

Nicholas had flicked it by mistake into the boat.

The twins had screamed with Miriam and jumped on a seat and lashed down the shaft of the spear at its malevolence and hated every inch of its black stinking skin and its bloody side.

'It wants passage,' George had thought as it curled itself in a knot around the shaft. He thought he saw a cunning. It was forgetting pain and concentrating its strength on something else.

'Throw it back in!' he screamed, and heaved the spear with the body caught on it into the water.

They rowed away fast, the boat covered in slime and blood.

George recalled the eel eyes and the instant of terror when he had thought flight wasn't possible. Flight had compressed itself into thrust and stab, rising and falling so that the eel head would sink in defeat.

It must have died.

'This place never changes,' he said to Nicholas, who had put up his coat collar. Miriam was ahead of them dragging a length of seaweed.

'You remember the eel?' George asked his brother.

Nicholas had found a glass float from a Japanese fishing net. He threw it into the sun and caught it as it descended. 'Yes, I remember.'

They walked back over a small bridge. Above, on the telephone wire, a kingfisher in cobalt wings and black head fretted over the patch of water. Now, even after midday, a few bullfrogs croaked at each other.

They wound past the brown barn house with the bank of succulent daisy, cream and scarlet, and onto the grass track around the hill.

Charlie was waiting for them. The fire was going and the old man had spread out a large piece of paper, some sandwiches and cups. The black billy tea stewed.

Nicholas left the others to talk and wandered over to the rata. There had been a fall of mud and rock and one root, close anyway to the air, was left naked. He pulled at it.

Miriam brought him his cup and waited.

'It's nothing, really.'

'About what?'

'I feel cut off.'

'Do you want to go back to town?'

'I don't think so.'

Charlie was calm in the agitation of the other three, suffering the unease of birds wondering whether to migrate.

'I'll tell you a story,' said Charlie.

They sat and ate.

'Once the herons came here all the time. Long time ago that was. But one year when the Captain was real drunk – he got that way towards the end – he said he didn't believe in eternal life or anything at all. He believed in his bottle. That's what he shouted: "I believe in the spirits in here. No more in that other stuff. I can't taste it. It's all lies."

'In those days there were still places. Holy places. One was on the island. Now sometimes, bad whalers went there and things happened. The Captain went there when he heard about it and he spat and cussed and did everything but do his shit. Nothing happened.

'Then he went after the white heron.

'Well. He waited around here by this rata tree. He waited. And after the sun got up he saw 'em. Both. Wading around the edge of the water looking for food. Two beautiful kotuku. And he sited up on one. Bang. Got it in the middle of its breast. White feathers went all directions. And it fell down to die.

'Well, then it came time for the Captain. And when that time come the other kotuku must have heard about it, because it come back here and waited. And the minute the Captain died, this bird rose up as if it had to gather up the part of the Captain he didn't believe in, and then sped off along the waveline. He soon vanished.

'Now, we believe that kotuku was taking his soul to the beginning of the next world. It came back specially for him because he was the Captain. That's a story isn't it?'

Charlie began to eat his piece of steak and sip on the black billy tea.

'Why did he come back?' asked Miriam, for all three of them.

'Because the Captain cared, that's why. And sometimes one kotuku will come back here. But never two.'

6

The wind was blowing cold from the harbour in Dunedin, the sky was greyer than the feathers of the seagulls fighting for scraps of bread on the grass and wheeling about the gaunt war memorial.

It was the first of June so winter was reaching its meridian.

Nicholas dozed off in the bus, as he often did in the afternoon, and woke up close to Taieri Mouth. His mother and father, his uncles and aunts saw his face, pinched and blue. They asked what the matter was, and he had to see a doctor. See a doctor or – what? 'See a doctor or else.'

'You must have picked up a bug.'

'Does Miriam feed you properly, and what are you up to there?'

'I don't think I like it at all.'

'You should be getting a job.'

'Cousin Charlie said you were to come on the paper. Your father had to wave my shares around under his nose to get it. Where is your sense of gratitude? I sometimes wonder *why* you bothered to come home. We never see you. It is as if you didn't like us. And don't sit there saying nothing. Try and think of something to say.'

'I had better see a doctor.'

'Yes, yes, a doctor. Get some tranquillizers. Tranquillizers will help, also vitamins. You are probably run down. We are all run down. It's the winter.' Mrs Fieschi loosed her hair from an ornate clip.

On the way back a tide-running wave drowned his memory of her. The bus accelerated down the slope and up the incline before the next rolled in.

Nicholas got out. Miss Carew was seeing to her provisions.

He walked slowly up the path.

Charlie was deep in the porch with the dog. 'You're not as fit as you were.' And chuckled with pleasure as Nicholas handed him a small parcel. 'Tobacco, eh? Encouraging an old man in bad habits.' Charlie played with the string.

'You're cold?' Miriam, two weeks back from a concert in Auckland, with good reviews and an offer of a concert in Paris, stood by the toaster. His resolve to be irritated was swallowed up in need for her.

'Warm your feet.' She motioned at the fender of the freshly blackened range.

'How was the afternoon with your family?'

'Bloody awful!'

'What did you talk about?'

'About how ungrateful I am. And what are we all up to down here, it isn't healthy. And I am disappointed that Miriam hasn't made you see sense?'

Miriam poured him a cup of tea and buttered more toast.

He went to her and put his hand on her and felt her thick nipples and soft breasts. He kissed her.

Sometimes she wished to be unconscious of what was beginning in her. Her concert had been prepared for, worked for, all the technique there; but a new clear stream had flowed through her. Not as good as the national star, Benedict Pearse-Dashkov, but better than before, Rebecca Weiss had thought.

Now? She looked at this man whom she loved, whom she often held when the nights stretched into the interminable blackness of a country winter. Whom she wept over in his sleep. And then got up to create with her music the silent shores she felt he walked along in his dreams. She knew his search. As did George. George painted hunks of timber and flat canvas, and out of them came an eerie effect of Nicholas and his knowledge.

But for Nicholas, to whom all gifts should have been given?

She gave in to his fingers as they touched her face.

Myrrh is mine, its bitter perfume,
Breathes a life of gathering gloom,
Sorrowing, sighing, breathing, dying,
Sealed in a stone-cold tomb.

And what escapes from that death? Or any death? She could feel her womb contracting against this fear.

So she busied herself with small tasks that could be given object-love. She turned the toast until it was golden, she spread the butter as if it were caviar. Then she washed the dishes, each plate carefully, and went on with cutting up the stewing steak. Since everything which happened was an interlude, she could see in the onions, which made her cry, the fact of time: the rings would break up one by one in the stew and dissolve into a rich gravy. She would put a few cloves in the stew. It was good, with a teaspoon of vinegar to flavour the meat.

Nicholas Fieschi's Diary, 1 August:

We follow the law of our being, willy-nilly.

George has painted a picture of my death mask.

George doesn't know what he does but he is preparing me, with Miriam, to stand firm against the love of my family.

I try to believe we are all ultimately one. Although each believes in its autonomy, it is maybe no more real than one brain cell is real if alone.

But another part of the 'me' I know less about sometimes engulfs me with a flood of death. No, not of death, but desire to escape time — the endless growth and dissolution of living things. Life! Existing through shape, conforming sometimes to heaven but mostly to the ideas which develop out of man. They mostly seem imprecise enough to cause the inventors' destruction. Like this place? Like myself? Like this century? Like their fucking nuclear weapons.

Yet here each of us will assume a theme, and the melody will reach a conclusion.

Even dissonance has its own means of reaching into silence. Miriam?

Moment by moment the music leads her out of the room, leaving the river mouth, the pond with the rata tree, the dirty lagoon stinking of cow piss.

She goes to where she is formless. That is it. No beginning and no end.

One night I woke and because I had the warmth of Miriam's body beside me, her flanks smooth and warm, her breasts heavy against my side, I wasn't afraid to wish not to go on for any longer than is necessary.

Yet a flower reaching its full bloom, its perfume caught in the warmth of the sun, is pain to me. To feel those petals crumple is pain, as is the guts of a rabbit spewed out on the road. That is the same pain. And a fish flopping and gasping. That is my death.

He stopped writing and noticed her hair. It was the texture of spring darkness, as familiar as the brass fender or the red spot on the range where the flame concentrated its strength on the lid.

'Be happy,' she whispered to him, her arm around his shoulder. Together they watched the bus crossing the bridge and followed the headlights illuminating some sheep feeding on the hay line.

'Would you like a drink?' She bought him a whisky.

Charlie and George had another bottle they kept down at the fishing shed.

'The others will be in soon, for dinner.'

Nicholas looked out of the window again. 'I don't see anyone.'

'Charlie went to the fishing shed. Just a while ago. He's been there a lot lately.'

'I'm going up to town tomorrow.'

* * *

The old man had a fish wrapped in newspaper, its snout sticking out with little sharp teeth like a steel saw. It was a grouper that the men had given him when they came off the boat. Doris had been there too, looking tough in gummies and a sweater full of holes. She had given him a comradely kiss on the cheek. He had had Doris one afternoon in the sandhills, just ten years ago. What had she done that for? But she had and he didn't mind.

Charlie took off his gummies at the door. He put the fish on the table and sat on the rocking chair they thought he should have. He knew there was trouble. He sat and rocked back and forwards.

The dog settled down by the range batting its tail, smiling around and scratching a bit, licking itself tenderly, yawning.

There was a smell. He could smell something that was in them all.

Charlie lit up his pipe. The stew was bubbling and the smell was good.

Sheep were huddling together on the hillside. George opened the door to listen. Sometimes there were marauding wild dogs to be stalked with a rifle. But it was just the moon and the river winding silver through the dead banks of the land. The bridge was black. He imagined the struts were bones, together forming the skeleton. He thought he would paint that and returned with the idea to the table and his sketchbook and began working. The moon shone with a special force when the sea was working up for a storm. He called out: 'Charlie, is there going to be a storm?'

The old man was surprised in conversation with Ruia, his wife in his thoughts. 'Yes,' he called, thinking that mullet were riding on the tide and remembering their wild yellow eyes as they tumbled up the river.

'He says there'll be a storm,' said George.

Nicholas spread out the cards and began a game of clockwork patience.

'I'll go for a walk,' said George. 'I'll bet Charlie forgot to tie the boat for a storm. It needs more rope. And the door of the shed should be padlocked.'

'He doesn't keep anything important in there.'

'It doesn't matter, Nicholas. He'd be upset to lose anything. It's the principle.'

The door closed.

'He's going to drink,' said Nicholas. 'To get pissed again.'

Miriam wasn't in the mood to commiserate with him. Or to agree it was because his twin was dying that George sometimes drank himself silly.

Nicholas took his coat and ran for the door.

The laburnum hung branch by branch into the night, but the curtains were drawn and it was no longer reflected in the windowpane. The gravel was hardened by the frost. Far off, in the spangled night of the lagoon, bullfrogs croaked fluently.

He walked through the mob of sheep on his way to the hill top.

From there he could see the lights of the city. Dunedin flickered and glowed on the cloud like a city under gunfire.

In the other direction, south to the Nuggets, the lighthouse threw out a burst of incandescent white, and another. Tonight all water slopped under the winter light, every movement was languid. The landscape slowly froze. Further away, the Antarctic marshalled its wind and fog.

Below, in the perfect bowl of the hills, was the pond. The heavy palms dipped almost to the water. The bullrushes in one small corner rose stiffly like copper spears.

Far below on the road, George was shuffling along and whistling to the dog, more to punctuate the night than to command obedience.

George was climbing over the gate. The three gum trees around the house rustled as he came up the track.

Just then, as the light in the old man's bedroom went out, Nicholas saw the bird coming down the river, skimming along with wide wings, its feet and bill yellow against the silver night. He wanted to call to George and then decided against it because it might be only in his mind.

But it was the kotuku, now struggling in towards the beach, now higher in the penumbra of light, and suddenly above their house.

George had seen it and was running.

The bird hung in the air. Then, with one long wingless glide, slid down the air to the pond.

George reached his brother as it rose on stilt-like legs to wade out among the rushes and stand resting beside the calm surface.

'It'll stay the night,' said George, puffing and clapping his hands together. 'At least that long.'

The bird, if it saw them, did not bother to receive them into its concentration, but tucked its neck back and became still.

George pulled at his twin's sleeve. 'We must tell Charlie. He'll be real excited. Tomorrow I might be able to take a photo.'

They jogged down the hill together and through the flock.

George burst through the door. 'A heron has come.'

Miriam clenched her knuckles. 'A heron?'

'I'll tell Charlie.' George knocked on his door. 'Just think, Nicholas saw it all the way. He might have been the only person to see it really fly. He probably was.'

'What is it, son?' said the old man.

'A kotuku, Charlie. A kotuku has come.'

The old man was silent for a moment. 'Who saw it first?' he asked.

'Nicholas, and then me.'

Charlie was half out of bed, pulling on his thick army surplus coat and the army socks.

Miriam had wrapped herself in the shawl.

The air was clearer than glass, the stars ice in the vault of distant rock where the moon was held captive.

The old man knew all about this. He was more interested just then in this hill to be climbed, and whether he had the strength to find out about the bird which had arrived among them.

And as before, the heron took no notice.

Charlie pretended not to see it too clearly. He pretended to be more taken by the flight of an owl from the rat-infested surrounds of the lagoon. Or the path of a marauding gull, gusted out of the inland country, the memory of food in its erratic, slaked flight.

Nicholas awoke at seven, sweating. He reached out to turn on the heater. The air was crisp. It breathed.

He hadn't heard Charlie come in and the storm had frozen back into a calm morning with hints of broken glass.

He tapped on the door and opened it. The old man raised his head from the pillow. One eye, beaded like a bird's, stared unwinkingly for a moment.

'I'll light the fire, Charlie. You stay and rest.'

'Yes.'

'You were late last night. We didn't hear you come in.'

'I was late.' Charlie closed his eye again to think.

'I'm going for a walk.' Nicholas returned to Miriam. 'I'll see you when you get back from Dunedin.'

He left her sunk inwards like Charlie.

As he walked down the path a headache began. The hill-line where he had looked down on that bird was a coarse mixture of grass and horizon, and the path, anyway, led down to the river. 'Fuck the bird,' he said to himself – and lit a morning cigarette.

He was awakened by the dog, paws on his chest, dribbing sand down his open shirt. Nicholas shook him off and belted him across the nose. He yelped and ran away.

'Why'd you do that?' George appeared over him, his hair very red this morning.

'Oh, fuck off.'

'What's the bloody matter with you?'

'Nothing.'

'Miriam's in a mood, too. Bashing around in the kitchen. She's left for Dunedin.'

George held out a raincoat. 'I saw Mrs James. She told me to go on up again and get a couple of coats. Miss Carew swears there's something blowing up, her back is giving her merry hell.'

They walked.

'It's a real island we live on,' said George.

'And you've never travelled, George. You've got no farther than Dunedin.' Nicholas let his headache unravel into pleasant accusation.

'It doesn't matter to me whether I travel or not. What matters is the plane leaving the airport. That matters. That they go. If they stopped going I think I'd go mad.'

'Really?'

'Don't be sarcastic.' George munched heavy chocolate, mushy and frothing around his lips.

'But if the world blows up,' said Nicholas. 'If we were all that was left. Then we would be the new cradle of man. We New Zealanders.'

'Shit!' said George.

Nicholas laughed. George took his arm and they marched along making fresh footprints while the dog dragged a branch and chased birds over the sheen of water and sand.

In a barren bit, near a flat rock, George stopped. 'Tell me,' he asked, 'what the doctors say – in Dunedin.'

'The same as in England. Pills, potions, remissions, but probably only a few months before the going gets hard. Just now, okay, because the transfusions keep me going.'

'Do you talk to Miriam?'

Nicholas stood on the flat rock.

'*We* don't talk so much now,' ventured George, sitting at his brother's feet. 'I hardly believe it any more. Seems that when time passes it can't be true because I'm getting used to it.'

'It's true.'

'Yes.'

'It's true.'

'I wonder what will happen to me afterwards,' said George.

'I don't know.'

'Do you believe in an afterlife. I mean, will we meet again?'

'I don't know.'

'I feel it,' said George. 'But what do you think?'

'I don't know. I'm not the fucking Delphic oracle.'

'I know we'll meet again. After you're dead. I'll find you somewhere.'

They walked on.

'Well,' said George, 'this is the place Mrs Roberts must have stopped at with Charlie Katana.'

He was sure because of the intimacy of light, the sweetness of the stream. They paddled up it.

'Nothing changes,' said George. 'I'll bet this is the same as it was.' They sat beneath the rata trees, leafed but flowerless.

'Let's sit for a bit longer.' Nicholas pulled his coat around him.

George laid his head in his brother's lap. He was thinner, his hair longer. His large white forehead was half covered in red curls as was his neck. His neck was marked by razor cuts and he had a small red spot under his left ear.

George was defenceless against him and even in sleep would never think to put up the shutters of his mind. His face twitched and quivered as his twin implanted him in his own visions and hopes, as deep as he could through that defenceless membrane of skin and bone.

George grew readier with the months. He must tell their parents. And what else? What more must he do?

Nicholas stroked George's hair and ran his hand across his face. Other things were decided, too – underneath. But George was suffering. The lines around his mouth were dense with the activity of acceptance. George, who lay crushing his belly, moved his head.

'Time to go.'

They followed their footsteps back.

Once or twice they found a depression far from the sea and kelp rotting against the discoloured sand. The dog liked those places, sniffing busily over every inch of ground before finally lifting his leg.

Far out to the south horizon, sunlight was a livid bronze. The winds which came from there were short and gusty.

They came to a small stretch of sand, held in place by rocks.

'Look at it,' cried George.

'We'll pretend it's summer,' his brother said.

'Why?'

'Let's pretend it's summer.' Nicholas began stripping off his clothes. George munched some chocolate.

'I'm not coming in. It'd kill me. Look at it, practically fucking ice.'

Nicholas unbuttoned his shirt and pulled down his trousers.

At the water's edge the dog was barking and scuffing up sand. Nicholas took off his underpants and threw them onto the bank of shingle. The dog, looking for a new role in this theatre, seized them and carried them in triumph back to George.

The dog did not act alone.

Miriam was tracking their march.

The dog barked among the wavelets, dying – and yet not dying enough – to swim out with Nicholas.

Still unobserved, Miriam examined him. She brushed her hand over her mouth as he ran from the waves and began to dry himself with a coat. His back was white, his buttocks now thin, his legs firm but thin. He turned and his phallus was shrivelled.

'Why?' she muttered to herself.

The dog was licking Nick's feet as if they had wounds.

She moved back down the paddock. Over the sheep droppings and the wool on dock stalks, her footsteps became strides. Almost running she reached a barbed-wire fence and pushed through onto the road, leaving a piece of her coat fluttering on the wire. Her car accelerated down the dust road.

'Miriam will be home,' George considered. 'If her appointment was at ten.'

'She might have stayed to have lunch with someone. Or to see a film.'

The lagoon, filmed with sludge, was streaked with shining phosphorescence. It rivalled the sea in its complexity and potential.

The track led the two men above all this, and the smell, mixed with a land-blowing wind, wasn't so bad. But Nicholas was still uneasy.

Then George stopped and Nicholas bumped into him. George grabbed his arm and pointed to a mound where some weed and rushes had made a precarious atoll.

There, sedately moving along the edge as it gulped down a small frog, was the heron. Ignoring the stink, the mud, the eels, the innumerable odours, its downy body had landed in a rush, so that the brown slop had touched those pristine white feathers. And it had stayed.

This was no mistake.

'You sodding bird,' George whispered, when he realized. 'Get away from here.' He wished he could find a stone to throw at it so that his notion of truth would win out.

Nicholas could say nothing.

And the lagoon quivered with that bird; the whole nature of this seemingly rotten kingdom was altered.

'What do you believe now, George?'

'It's only three,' said George, 'and we've not eaten at all. I'm bloody hungry.'

The herd was moving up the hill. Doris patted one with her willow stick. 'Goin' to snow I reckon,' she called out from under the brim of her modified stetson. 'I'm milking the ladies early.'

Nicholas thrust his hands deep into the pockets of his overcoat and followed George, who was walking ahead to encourage him. George let him enter the house first.

Miriam was waiting for them, rocking to herself and reading a magazine. George caught her atmosphere and slunk past with the dog. 'I'm going to draw,' he offered by way of explanation.

'Come back for tea, Georgie dear,' she called.

'Don't you want to know where we've been?' asked Nicholas.

'Your hair is wet,' she said. 'You'd better get a towel and dry it, or stick your head into the oven.' The flame roared in agreement.

He took a towel from the rack above the range.

'We are hungry.'

'Well?'

'Could you make us something?'

'Why don't Mumma's boys get off their arses and do it themselves?'

A cold south-westerly had started to frill the edges of the view. He looked down the hill.

Against the gathering darkness which would set in at any moment, he saw four figures struggling up the hill.

'They've come,' he said.

She pushed the pan quickly to the centre of the range and lifted the lid back on with the poker. 'Why today?' Her voice had lost its belligerence. She was bewildered by some sequence of events.

George was on the edge of the bed.

'They've come,' said Nicholas.

George nodded. 'You couldn't keep them away for ever.'

They returned along the passage.

At the end of the hall was a photograph of the Captain in a bowler hat, clasping a harpoon, ready to repel any attack that might come from that direction.

Charlie waited with a blanket wrapped around himself and his new slippers on. He began to rock on the chair.

The person who knocked did not like to make a sure presence, or *intrude*.

George dealt out some cards and Nicholas gave each of them fifteen matches. The knock was repeated. Miriam rose and looked back at her lover, then opened the door.

'Miriam dear,' shrieked Mrs Fieschi on a key lower than the gusting wind. 'We were over at Milton visiting Natalia Pearse.'

She tripped inside. The phalanx consisting, as usual, of Mrs Farquar, Mr Farquar and Mr Fieschi, all followed with correctly interested smiles.

'How nice it is, Miriam dear. So homely.'

Everybody shook hands, but the old man who saw them with bright eyes relapsed into another world.

'How are you, Mr Katana?' Mrs Farquar called out as if she were still on the opposite bank. 'How are you?'

'He's fine,' said Miriam.

'Yes, yes,' said Mrs Fieschi, kissing both her sons with a devotional equilibrium unusual in her.

Mr Farquar was carrying a basket.

'We brought some food,' said Mr Fieschi. 'We thought perhaps we'd have a picnic afternoon tea with you.'

He put the wicker basket down on the table. The contents were discreetly covered with a fine-linen cloth.

'Of course I remembered the place from when we were *all* here for summers. But so long ago! I remember your mother, Miriam, and myself, walking along the beach to the rocks, with you in a pram. We both pushed like mad through the sand and then one of us had the bright idea of taking the pram down onto the hard edge. It was low tide and we almost ran with you.'

In the time it took to speak, Mrs Fieschi had got rid of her coat and hat and patted Mr Katana.

'Now, do let us see the place. It's been so long.' She glanced around the kitchen at the polished fender, the black stove, the wood, the dog, her children.

'It's a nasty day,' Mrs Farquar informed the gathering as she devested and began to lay out the picnic.

'Now Miriam and Nicholas, do come and show your old mother the layout of the place.'

'In here,' said Nicholas, with George behind, herding them quickly, 'is the other room – where we sit sometimes. Where Miriam practices.'

'And the concert went so well,' said Mrs Fieschi. 'I read a review. Who looked after you boys?'

'Charlie cooked one year for a shearers' gang.'

'Such good reviews. You must play to us before we go back.'

Mrs Fieschi saw the family photos, a piece of whale jawbone lying athwart the fireplace.

'And this is our room,' said Miriam. 'Where Nicholas and I sleep.'

Mrs Fieschi frisked around the bed to the window.

'What a marvellous view. And such lovely mats, Miriam. Where did you get them? I can remember when women used to do this sort of work. But now I should have thought we had all grown too lazy.'

'My mother did them.'

'And your grandmother, Mrs Roberts! I remember being told her crochet work was a joy to the eye.'

'I've kept some. In my mother's trousseau box.'

Mrs Fieschi immediately admired the oil painting of the ship with funnel and sails driving by the island under a gale. 'That, I'm sure, was painted by your grandmother.'

'And my room is in here,' said George.

There, there was dust, the smell of dog, paint tubes, the chrome yellow open on a chair dribbling solid.

A painting stood on the easel.

Nicholas hadn't seen it before. It was a half profile, with Miriam, eyes long and black, seeing into the silence of her lover. He was there as a nude shadow.

'Really, George. One would never think, dear, from looking at you, that you could paint such morbid things.' Mrs Fieschi looked closer at other canvases. One was of a mask, and since she had never seen the face of Agamemnon, not even in her deepest dreams, she did not recognize. 'Morbid, dear, but the gold colour is nice.'

George blushed and said nothing, but his hands showed what he was thinking.

'And here's one of you,' George said to her. 'There.'

It was an old woman patting her dog and gazing out into the dazzling light of her garden, as if that were a source of terror. The view marched down to the ruins of the shed. The way was flanked by creatures bearing swords of incandescent flame.

Mrs Fieschi bridled.

'And what are *you* doing?' she asked Nicholas.

'Writing.'

'He's writing some poetry,' said George.

'You must show me dear.' It was always Mrs Fieschi's intention to keep things balanced.

'They're not finished yet.'

'Tea is ready,' called Mrs Farquar.

In the passage they met Mr Fieschi hovering under the eye of the Captain and his harpoon. 'So much history, Miriam. So interesting. You must be very proud of the house. Real character.' He patted her arm, and each – to the other's surprise – smiled with understanding.

'Times change,' said Mr Fieschi. 'Perhaps that is a good thing. But I am suspicious of the word progress. I think most things are, underneath, quite the same.'

'Yes,' she said.

'Will you play a little Mozart for me?'

'Yes. I'll play you a sonata after tea.'

Mrs Fieschi held the door open and patted her hair down.

'We mustn't stay too long, dear. What with this storm. But the weather will be behind us.'

Miriam listened to them all.

'You are looking a bit better, Nicholas,' said Mrs Farquar. 'I expect this rest is doing you good.'

'Still,' said Mrs Fieschi, 'you must decide sometime to come back to civilization. Now there is something I want to say to you both. Let's go next door while we have hot tea in our cups and talk a moment.'

Nicholas and Miriam went.

'I don't want to interfere with either of you. I am a modern woman, but I do worry about you both. Perhaps I can help. Nicholas.' She opened her purse.

Her conversation would be composed of riddles or pregnant silences. There was no point where her authority could be disputed which would not appear as an unprovoked attack. 'Here,' she said, 'I've saved a bit out of my pin money. I'd like you to get out and have a good meal. There is a good restaurant at Milton run by a Jewish man, who lately lost his wife.'

Nicholas took the money because he did not know how to refuse. He loved her at this moment with a kind of ache.

'And,' said Mrs Fieschi, whose gift had given her the right to speak, 'I do wish the two of you would decide something. It's all very well living together, as I suppose you are. But there are other factors.' Mrs Fieschi's hand briskly dismissed all factors except herself. 'Your father and I feel you should both reach some sort of decision about your future. Why don't you come up and have dinner with us next week? Say Thursday. And we can talk privately then, about what should be done.

'Now, let's get back to the warmth. The tea is excellent, Miriam. Do you make those little Viennese tarts your mother was so fond of? Pastry that would float away if one didn't eat it right down.'

Mrs Fieschi caught Mrs Farquar's eye and they both understood whatever it was they had agreed on to understand. The older men looked down at their boots until George told them about the heron. It was a good conversation piece. The heron could be done to death and forgotten. It came so infrequently.

Which reminded everyone of the time. Mr Farquar went to the door and looked outside. 'It's getting dark. That jolly storm. The radio is warning shipping. Up to point eight winds down south. Scuttle home.'

'Such a comfortable house,' Mrs Farquar boomed, folding up the fine linen cloth and putting away the thermos which they hadn't needed. 'I'll leave the bits and pieces to you young people. Always have good appetites.' She laughed and patted the dog who seemed to like her.

Miriam waved as they vanished down the hill. A delegation which hadn't heard any Mozart after all, because it had forgotten, to ask again once the ground was secure.

'What do those people want?' Charlie Katana asked, not recognizing them.

'A lot,' said Miriam.

George poured himself a whisky and put on a record.

'What are we going to do?' asked Miriam.

'Go to dinner with them next Thursday, I suppose.'

The clock chimed eight. Miriam went for her coat and Nicholas got his.

When they reached the top they went on. She gave him her hand. They climbed over boulders into the shelter of a cave that looked out to sea and the squall swept by them.

'What is it?' he asked.

She shook her head.

'You want to leave me?'

The fear in his voice made her smile.

'You know. I thought I would like to be married in white. You remember?'

'I'm in the way?' His voice was quiet and not bitter.

This worried her.

'No.'

'It is?'

'I love you, Nicholas. Concerts can wait.'

'Until I am dead.'

'Yes. We have a bridge, Nicholas.'

'Yes?'

'I'm pregnant. The night you came home. I wanted to get with child by you on that night.'

'My child?'

'Yes.'

They took each other's hands. Finally, with her teeth chattering, he came back to himself.

Later in the evening they sat with George in his room and he showed them the painting that Mrs Fieschi hadn't seen. It was only half completed. He told them it was the child. He had known by her looks and because of the way she held herself. He was pleased. A nephew was good.

They drank from a glass George had in the room.

The child in the painting had blue eyes. It looked at blue light coming from behind bars – a prison, or birth, none of them could be sure. There could have been a candle inside the skull because there was a light in them which did not belong to the natural body.

'It's a terrible painting,' she said. 'It's so good.'

George belched with pleasure and the dog batted its tail.

'You shouldn't drink so much,' she told him.

'You know,' she told Nicholas late in the night, 'Charlie Katana was my grandmother's lover. Doris told me. He could even be my grandfather.'

Charlie Katana lay in his bed and dreamed he had got himself down the hill to the boat. There, he found snow on the ropes. The wet had tightened the knots but he was strong and he cut them and Ruia, his wife, jumped on board.

Mrs Roberts waved them off, wearing a lace hat.

He went on out into the sea and with Ruia he sailed right into the path of the sun.

But he held back in the dream, in sight of the land.

The dawn had shown itself on the horizon and slowly extended to the shoreline. Some seagulls screamed above the sea-fall.

Nicholas watched the windowpane. He remembered the young gum tree around the side of the house, dressed and took a sharp penknife from the kitchen. On the bark he carved as deep as he could: 'Nicholas loves Miriam'. And then: 'Nicholas and Miriam love their child'. He carved that so deep that it would grow with the tree and expand with the years. He kicked his way back through the snow.

Miriam gave him breakfast and noticed his quiet. She waited for him to speak. At last when George was there, he did. 'Can I take the car? I want to go up to town. Stay the night. Come back tomorrow.'

He drank down the coffee to give himself time.

Then: 'I think, if you don't mind, we should move back to the city soon. I'll go for a transfusion again. I have the symptoms. It's time for blood.'

Miriam blinked and bent over the range. 'Ring up a piano tuner. I'll practise on the old Bechstein there. And for God's sake light some fires to air the place. Charlie can have the back room. George, you could sleep in the bedroom next to us.'

When Nicholas was well down the hill, Charlie took them to

the tree. The raw wood was wet. The names were cut in a quarter of an inch. The heart Nicholas had cut was secure.

'You having baby?' he asked and laughed.

She nodded. 'Charlie. Nick is dying of a disease. But you mustn't say anything. It's going to be hard. We don't want to tell his parents yet.'

'They're not nice?'

'My parents are not nice for this,' George said.

'Nick is a dying boy?'

'Yes.'

The old man's face worked. Then he stared deep into Miriam's eyes. 'The baby will be special?'

'Yes.'

7

Nicholas arrived at his grandmother's house.

He had seen the doctors at the unit as soon as he arrived.

He wandered into the kitchen. The cups George and he had drunk from were still on the table, and a newspaper covered in milkstains. He walked upstairs to the bedroom. On the floor was a pair of dirty underpants – his own. He got into bed. And although the room was cold, and the fire he had made out of boxwood was in ash, he slept on his back with only a blanket covering him. And that was caked in sweat, and a residue of soap from the cursory washing Mrs Fieschi's help had given it after the old lady had died.

He thought before sleep of his child. Each aspect, each tangent of their relationship resolved around Miriam's womb. Tonight he felt empty. He must train himself to wish a little less each day. And then he was sleeping.

He dreamed he was in the yard of his grandmother's house, standing against a stone wall. And he was listening to the Kyrie eleison from the church next door. He had lost contact with those syllables except for the last Easter service, and he was puzzled he should be naked, with the sound of chanting under the high vaulted arches of a chapel, the fan ceiling, the narrow extending windows of ruby red, indigo, gold, green. The glass was thirteenth century and the unyielding statues of stone. Their faces he would have passed by, when younger, but now he was held by their severe peace. They saw what was and were content.

He longed to see outside and his longing hardened him where he least expected it. It was not to be put down by death. He needed Miriam and so she came in a red dress carrying white flowers.

Outside, it was close to dawn he told himself in a second of consciousness. The street would be empty and the tarseal hard, hard enough to break glass and the bodies of children. The hearts of his children's children.

There was fragile web-like sky which might shatter to let in angels.

He told Miriam. 'I may not survive to die without being destroyed by the fears of my parents.'

But all he could feel in answer to these thoughts was the gathering force of blood and the direction of blood through the shaft to the tip. Even minute surface veins laughed at him with the glad singing of blood.

'What do you want?' Miriam asked him. 'I have to play to my baby.'

'I too,' he answered.

Music jabbed at his flesh like the thongs of a soft whip.

Someone was singing: on that day when heaven and earth will tremble, and we will be judged. He didn't believe that, so he sung to himself though, as always, his voice was out of tune and grated along the rise and fall and hesitated in the intervals, like a bird with one wing clipped.

And as for the Agnus Dei. Who is the Lamb and who is the God that designates the Lamb? How precious is blood and who weighs it? Who decides what is good and bad blood? Or like all comedy, is any man's sacrifice just an excuse to create a pattern?

And would the music help him to find a rest in some sphere above the earth where he could learn to do without his body? Or did the music simply create his soul for the time it played?

The cathedral faces of glass and stone had no answers. They saw and were satisfied.

The thrust and jerk of his loins, the flesh biting and itching towards the smooth belly of Miriam – that was not in their field of vision.

Somewhere a voice with the sweetness of a bell finished.

Miriam rested her palms inwards across her breasts. The house moved and jerked into a spasm of life that lifted the web, spun by the night, and his flesh arched into the sky, higher and higher until the unbearable height was directed into the arc of the music, and followed and, perhaps, surpassed it. Yet both were in each other – in the drops of notes.

Sound was flesh.

For one second he saw.

Yard by yard the house assumed an identity again and shook and quivered with the ache of dawn, and everything, table, empty jam-jars and the two coffee cups, stained wood and open windows were surrounded by air now, and breathed.

Miriam was no longer with him.

She had become the earth in all its forms and he had found a potent womb. His decision would bear fruit. He knew now what he had to do.

So the light found him without even the blanket which he had hurled into a corner. He lay hunched like a man stopped by a bullet, his heart held to the mattress beneath him, and to the stains on it from his grandmother who had died there and been ineffectually laid out there.

He opened his eyes. He rubbed the bristles on his chin. The room stank of cigarette smoke and semen. He found a cigarette on the mantelpiece, lit it and enjoyed the pain of inhalation and the thickness of his throat.

At that moment the alarm clock burst shrilly and quickly through the room, ripping away the vestigial memory and focusing this smell.

He walked downstairs and was met by the neighbour's cat.

'It's six o'clock,' he told the animal. 'At eight I must be at the hospital for the transfusion.'

He went to the lavatory. His body, damp and shivering, was forced to accompany him, and he ordered the muscles in his belly to contract against his bowels.

Morning was morning. Ritual was ritual and childhood was the best armour against the inflooding knowledge of things. It would regulate.

With malign humour the house awaited the first eructation of wind.

He pulled some dunny paper and wiped his belly and strained again. The hard turd protruded and he held it where it was for a moment, his arsehole king of the process, his mind king of the arsehole. Then he let it slide with ease into the waiting water, long and emptying in its effect. After that he farted with growls and crackles. His own small thunder.

He looked as he wiped himself, drew in a long breath and enjoyed the rich stink.

'So you die,' he told himself as he took a shower, 'while you are still warm.' He rubbed soap over his belly, slowly and rhythmically over his groin. The small movements of pleasure told him this would be so.

He made coffee and sat in front of the gas fire.

The cat progressed to the window and in one fluid leap, in which both beginning and end were held, vanished.

8

The breath of pain. Its cool ability to please itself. The prima donna of sensation – the cut, the jab, the dull ache.

It drained off his fat, it stopped his kidneys from functioning properly.

Those thin intestinal membranes had made a treaty with pain, and for its cessation would become neutral territory: they would not suck the goodness from the potatoes, the frozen peas, fried fish sticks, jelly puddings made from Miriam's grandmother's invalid recipe, milk and a drop of brandy, after-dinner mints, nor the soft cheese for lunch.

All this allowed him to get to the bathroom, most of the time, and shit it out the other end.

Sometimes to sit by the fire.

Sometimes, towards dawn, to get out of bed and write away that hour.

George gave his back and buttocks a good spirit-rub most mornings and evenings, and emptied a bowl of vomit, if nothing would stay down.

Illness. This Wednesday.

'It's almost spring,' said the old man staring into the fire.

Nicholas tied the bow on his pyjamas and reached for his dressing-gown.

The effort cost him his breath and he waited for the heavy beating of blood through his head to quiet. A dull ache started behind his eyes.

Charlie knew what Nicholas wanted. 'Come here, boy.' He held up a bottle of whisky. 'Come to the fire and I'll give you some.'

Nicholas swore to himself and took the few necessary steps. He fell into the chair.

Charlie wiped the sweat off his face with a new red handkerchief Miriam had brought him.

Nicholas took a sip of the drink and slept for a while.

When he woke up it was seven o'clock. Miriam was sitting opposite. She wore a deep green gown which billowed out from her belly and she smiled to see him. She went to the bed to pound the mattress, the pillows. And plump up the blankets.

'Do you want to get back in?'

He shook his head and picked up the glass.

'Don't drink too much.'

'It's only a wee drink,' Charlie said. 'Keep out the damp.' He hacked a cough out and spat into the fire, then sat forward watching the sizzle and bubble of his phlegm.

Miriam was going to the opening with George. He was exhibiting five paintings in a discreet corner.

George moved silently. He watched everything around his brother. They said little to each other that night. But the weaker comforted the stronger with his eyes. George knew what his twin wanted him to do later, and accepted what he was offered.

His brother was looking into him and he could not shift his eyes.

Miriam, hardly breathing, watched, and showed only a second of surprise and hurt.

They left, and the old man was again in his dotage, with a look around his eyes that corresponded with no explicable thought. 'We all make our own way,' he muttered to himself and to Nicholas. 'Now that there are no ways of knowing what they want. Since we don't know, we've got to decide ourselves.'

He stopped. Miriam had told him to keep the fire stoked up, so he shovelled on more coal.

'What are you saying?' asked Nicholas, half out of a doze.

He thought of George. Even in pain they were united. They had been spanked together and almost always caned together for the same crime.

George felt pain and smashed a vase or a cup.

After a long shuddering sigh his eyes took on clarity.

Now he, perforce, must hold and nourish.

Nicholas had helped him not to forget. One day he gave him some scarves, another day a larger sports coat, another some ties and a few jerseys.

George had walked down the freshly raked drive, patted the dog at the doorstep and with him viewed the carcass of the garden.

The family was in the sitting room.

George could not think of ways to lead up to the conversation so he blurted it all out at the door, standing there with his fists clenched in the pockets of his overcoat. 'Nick has asked me to tell you he is dying. He has leukaemia – that means cancer – and he is dying from it.'

Mrs Fieschi had been tranquilly reading a history magazine with large, well-considered prints of houses and people.

'Really,' she said, letting the magazine fall onto her knee and withdrawing her stockinged feet from the fender. 'What did you say, George? I didn't hear you properly. What about Nicky? They never came to dinner that Thursday I asked them. And if they think I will beg and beg they are wrong. I will go to see them out of duty, now and then.

'One must have a break. Two weeks skiing has done me the world of good. Even just watching. Now, why are you aiding and abetting this situation? Even you . . . not working. What will become of the land, our investment, under some manager?'

'He's very good.'

'But you were always like that, the weaker of the two. Led by your brother.' Her small white face was trembling with anger.

George was thrust back to the door by this onslaught. So he turned to his father who had been writing a letter. 'Tell her what I said.'

His father began to gasp, choking on air. His mother, her eyes small and intent, watched every intake. By her expression she seemed to will on the suffering.

'I don't believe it,' Mr Fieschi finally got out. 'How can I believe that?'

'You must.' Towards his father George was tender and he could walk to him and take both his old hands and warm them in his own. 'He knew when he came back from England. That's why he came. He told me that night. There isn't any hope. He wanted to die on his own earth and he needs to be left to do whatever he has to do now. But he wants you to know – it wouldn't be fair otherwise.'

His mother was coming at him, small and determined. She slapped his face so hard she almost fell, and George, from habit, caught her.

'How dare you bring this news! How dare you tell me, his mother. How dare you tell me that the one I love best is to die!'

'I'm sorry,' George mumbled.

'There must be something to be done. We must get him to the best possible doctors. He must go into a hospital at once. I will ring cousin James and arrange it. A private hospital, of course, where he can have his own room, and television. And a bar, if they'll let him drink with his *complaint*. So many drugs seem to stop one having a drink. Or, I could bring him home and nurse him.'

'He doesn't want any fuss. He doesn't want anything at all.'

'My daughters would never have treated me like this. He must be brought to his senses. Nothing is incurable. He may not have been to the best doctors. There may be some method of holding things up. They say there will be a cure for that soon. I read it in a magazine. What magazine was it? It had an article on his complaint.' She sat down, numb with realization. 'My God, I threw it out. How could I have thrown it away. It was one of my woman's magazines. But which one. Which one?'

'He's been to the best doctors. He's asked me to tell you because he's getting worse.'

'I remember,' said Mrs Fieschi, 'something about sterile rooms and drugs which do something, but he would have no immunity. It is a modern technique. Some people have lived several years – behind glass. Or months. I forget. And radioactivity.

'What have we done to deserve this? Why isn't he at home with us? I will go at once and tell that girl to pack herself off somewhere else, with that smelly old Maori. I'll have him here . . .'

'He's married,' said George, seeing his mother in rags with long fingernails and scraggy bare breasts, stalking love in her hatred.

'Married?'

'Yes.'

'Then what can I do? She has . . . When?'

'Ages ago. And Miriam is pregnant. Five months.'

'She is pregnant. By whom?'

'Who do you think?'

'So that is how she got him?'

'That, you might also say, is how he got her. Or how they got each other.'

'How long have you known all this?'

'For months.' George walked to the door.

'Wait,' his father said.

'No,' said Mrs Fieschi. 'Let him go. I have nothing more to say to *your* son.'

'We must see Nicholas now,' said Mr Fieschi.

'I am going,' said George.

'I order you to take us to Nick. Remember, I am your father.'

George knew his father ordered because he had to feel some-where some authority. And that he had to be respected in his wishes so that in time he could also stand against his wife – if possible!

*   *   *

Miriam had been playing when they arrived. She stayed at the piano and watched from there.

'We've just popped in for a moment,' said Mrs Fieschi. 'George brought us down.' She plumped the blankets and pillows. 'I see you've taken down a wall. Granny would probably think it was an *improvement*. She was all for space. So nice for you all to be in the same room in the evenings.'

'Would you like something to drink?' asked her dying son.

'Yes. Some sherry. Keeps out the cold. And Miriam, my dear. You and Nicky have gone and done it. We must have a drink in town *soon* so you can tell me what you would like for a present.' Mrs Fieschi thought it would be indiscreet to mention also a baby in the same breath.

Charlie Katana thought she was declaring her intentions.

Nicholas was soothed by her chatter. After they left he himself wondered if he were as ill as he knew himself to be. Then he realized her stratagem. 'They'll be back,' he said.

Miriam nodded and returned to the piano.

His mother caught him for one day. And Nicholas went to a new specialist for more tests. Neither Miriam nor his mother spoke.

The two women watched each other, and Miriam could not fight for him. It was against the nature of their freedom in one another. Even now.

Only the old man could look fiercely at the boy, and he might not speak. He was as immovable as the island with seaweed and birds, fish and shells, the rock hard against the water.

'You are looking better,' Mrs Fieschi told Nicholas. 'It will be nice for Miriam to have an evening out tonight. And George too. With his silly paintings. I'm afraid I can't really take them seriously, even with this news of an exhibition in London.'

She pecked his cheek. 'I'll pop in later with the prescription.' She glanced at her watch.

'You must drink up, Mr Katana. Tea is very nourishing, with

brown sugar, on cold afternoons like these. I am pleased we got you, Nicholas, to see other people. These drugs do wonders. The girls have been very worried but I've told them to be positive.' She pecked daintily at a scone. 'And you must keep a dressing-gown on.' She found one across the bed and gave it to him, pleased that it was one she had bought. 'Now, things may get a little worse darling. But so much can be done.'

Mr Fieschi nodded. 'I've been reading everything there is to read. There is a possibility of recession for months, even years. But you must put yourself in the care of a good doctor. Under constant supervision. James has written to somebody in New York, and somebody in Moscow. There are new drugs. All over the world people are working.'

'Do you mean I can hope?' Their son thought he saw them for the first time in months. Or ever.

'We want the best for you.' Mrs Fieschi touched her warm Fair Isle jumper. Dear Bertie had brought her another string of pearls to help her along. Pearls!

And they left for the chemist because he must rest. They did not want to kill him with talk.

Miriam scooped her breasts in her hands.

'We are in a state of siege and that's not easy on the nerves,' she said. She laughed and lay down beside him and using her mouth eased away the hard mask he had grown over that afternoon to keep himself safe.

Leaning on the pillows above him she stroked his forehead with her fingers and straightened up the blankets so that they covered his chest.

She closed her eyes for a moment. 'They love you.'

'I'm getting weaker. I might give in to them.'

'Then sometimes it is a good thing to run. But how you run,' she looked at him, her eyes clear beyond the pain that was gnawing at her, 'is your own decision.'

Under the blankets she touched him again, lightly and carelessly. In the lack of words she knew a decision was being made.

'Time will tell,' he finally said.

She got up and sat staring into the fire, running her fingers through the fringes of the shawl. All their things had to be looked at. It might be the only time she could imprint each on her memory — for later.

She faced them: the bow window, the white curtains, the rug George had made for him so his feet wouldn't get cold if he wanted to sit on the edge of the bed, and the wood floor she polished in fury and desperation.

She looked back at the thin face, so thin, with its prominent cheekbones, the beard clean shaven, the black hair even blacker with the sweat in it.

His desk was placed so he could see out of the window. If he awoke he could write a bit and feel he was somebody.

Because he was now asleep she allowed herself to weep into her hands. The tears ran down through her fingers. Soon she stopped and gulped in some air and held it until she could feel that the next breath would not be a sob.

Nicholas woke at six and went to his desk. He lit a cigarette and rubbed the burn marks he'd made. Then the cat came in and sat beside him on the floor. Her eyes were inscrutable even as she purred and rubbed her pelt against his legs.

He toyed with a pencil and faced the clean sheet he laid out each evening. But what could he say? Only that walls of his personality crumbled and needed to crumble further. Yet he was frightened now because he was being drawn deeper into the earth. And to be awake might defeat it.

Miriam slept.

He thought: 'And I am only trapped if I allow the event to take its own course.'

Mrs Fieschi sat close to the window, where it was chilly but where she could see every movement of her son's face, which was again disappointing . . . Too calm: it should have responded to her enthusiasm for the new drugs.

The old man? His eyes, in the hour his mother spent in the house, were direct and clear, watching each movement she made, to and fro, rearranging the spray of maidenhair fern and violets that Daphne had brought, a week before, as she left for a holiday in Fiji with hubbie.

In the dusk, outside, people passed by in the hesitant colours of early spring. At home she had painted the boys' bedroom, put in new curtains, and had sheets airing in the hot-water cupboard.

'You see,' said Mrs Fieschi, 'I was sure they would find something. This drug may even get you back on your feet.' She did not think to ask for how long. Nor what the price might be.

'It's a beautiful season, Miriam.'

Their eyes met.

Miriam was drawing close to the time when her body would demand a protector. Mrs Fieschi was sure of this. She and Mr Fieschi left. It was seven o'clock.

Nicholas glanced at the bottles on his bedside table. The old man sat with him and together they drank whisky while Miriam changed.

'Very pretty,' offered Charlie, as she swirled in the gold dress and sipped gin and tonic.

And George, his beautiful blond-red hair curling to his shoulders, swung Miriam around as if this were a little dance.

Everyone laughed.

It would be that sort of evening, George assured them all. He had been offered a show in London and this was an evening to celebrate. What better evening could there be? Charlie shuffled to the fire to stoke it up. He listened to their feet on the stairs.

Nicholas hobbled to the window. He saw her, her arm in George's, her body heavy and wobbling with the baby, laughing up at the moon, her throat firm and beautiful. They turned and waved to him.

Charlie sat beside the bed. Nicholas picked up the vase of flowers his mother had arranged and one by one threw them into the wastepaper basket.

His eyes wide open, the old man saw everything. He hobbled over to Nicholas with the bottle and filled his glass.

'I have put some money in an envelope for you,' Nicholas told him. 'Enough. So you can leave Miriam and George to be with each other.'

Charlie hugged his red jersey in agreement. He took the paper bag with the money in it and put in inside his singlet, where he wouldn't forget. He poured another wee drink.

'I was goin' to go, too. That night with the bird, and the storm.'

'Go where?'

The old man came close to him.

Nicholas closed his eyes.

The images flooded into his brain, one by one.

Of that night, and other nights of many years.

The wind!

It hit across the sandbar into the estuary.

Most boats were sheltering far above the bridge.

At the channel the fresh and salt-water clashed.

Charlie's boat was old and the paint had sunk into the wood.

There he was cutting the new ropes George had tied on the night of the storm. Hacking them with a tomahawk because the fibres were waterlogged and George had never learned the trick of tying things so they could be released in a jiffy. Charlie's oilskin flapped about his legs and his sou'wester practically covered his eyes, but he was laughing, and with each laugh was younger. And at last that boat was free and Charlie jumped from the jetty to its deck. He started the motor and pointed it seawards.

But the boat was powered also by his will as he caught the crescent, cross-current and lotus swell, passing over each one at the confluence. And then the island appeared on his right. He passed by into a screaming wail of sea flecked with dissolving ice. It stretched forward in layers of upraised water.

Charlie Katana looked back at the land until a cross-cutting wave slammed over the prow.

So he turned from what could be held, touched and owned. And that storm was left behind. The motor, of course, turned more slowly. It was low on petrol and he had no more. It was acceptable that he should have forgotten.

And behind, the land had become Aotearoa – the long white cloud.

The sun emerged from its winter sleep, beat heavy on the cabin-roof, and raised what paint there was into bubbles. Kelp, uprooted from the ocean bed, drifted by with sometimes a shore bird perching on it. Charlie sat on a box behind the wheel and didn't notice a squall beating landwards with seagulls riding its currents. But his tongue responded to the rain that washed some salt from his face. Sometimes his lips moved of their own accord as the nerves continued to pulse.

The chill of night opened his eyes to darkness. Around the waterline the nails had been loosened by the swelling seams and were floating out with the caulk. In the hold where once he had thrown his catch the air stank.

He took off his clothes for the heat of his change was physically overbearing. His chest was lean, the nipples sunk into the thread of muscle that crossed the bone. Beside him was his woman, Ruia, younger than he, with strong eyes and black hair falling onto her stretch-marked belly. Together they searched the water and the sky for portents. She sang as they looked, a chant of a few notes that changed imperceptably with the rhythm of the swell and the sudden dark back of a shark.

With Ruia he began to find a horizon. He slept with her. The ocean became a lake reflected in her eyes. Over this lake the heron flew from a setting sun. And as he watched the bird he was drawn into the feathers and through them to its small, beating heart. And so he was carried over the last day. But even as a corpse he was singing what he remembered of truth, and the song went on, while the things which die, died.

At last his tongue burst through his teeth.

New stars inevitably appeared.

At midday two seagulls flew over. They had been blown from the island colony whose guano allowed life to a few bushes and searched for shelter now on the waves, less and less in the air. They landed and fell, but gripped, and swayed with the boat. They could not hope for easy food, for the fish here were of the deep. But they saw the body and in their lust stabbed at each other, their neck ruffs raised. The wheel turned, and with enough strength to power their fear they flew onto the mast.

With the morning they had absorbed the geography of their kingdom, and like all colonizers they recognized everything before them as belonging to their will. Food was food. They marched forward, wobbling lightly from one yellow webbed foot to the other, all power held equally. Before the heap of flesh they stopped, the desire for sole dominion again on each one. Then one of them broke and thrust its yellow-black beak into the right eye, half closed with parchment skin. The empty socket ran with a watery substance. Small drops of blood congealed rapidly. The gulls were unafraid. They looked right through the other eye and stabbed again, and fought and squabbled over the scraps of this delicacy. The flesh on the cheeks and belly and loins were tough. After this they were well fed. They stopped to sleep.

When they awoke a whole mountain of flesh, bone and gristle awaited their decision as to its demolition.

The old man was muttering.

Nicholas pulled himself up on the pillows.

'The chance only comes once,' Charlie was saying to himself. 'That night was the chance for me.'

They exchanged looks as Nicholas picked up a bottle of barbiturates and one of pain killers.

'I mustn't take too many,' he said, 'but with a few whiskies it'll do the trick. I read up on it, months ago.'

The old man poured a good tot from his bottle.

'Now I'll get dressed.' said Nicholas. 'I've put everything I'll need on a hanger. The one at the end.'

He got out of his pyjama top and waited for Charlie to help him with the trousers.

'Now, I'll lift myself. Pull them down to my ankles, right down.'

Charlie shook his boy's shoulders. 'Now you be brave.' He gave him his clean underwear.

Memories cascaded in and he desired her more than anything. Weak as it was, his sex had lain in wait and now made the final absurd statement of its truth. He and the old man both stared, and Charlie grew tremulous and shaky as if this were also, like the heron, a mystery of which no amount of living could finally take the measure.

Nicholas finished dressing and Charlie brought him a mirror so he could see if his hair was tidy enough. Nicholas sorted out the pills and began to swallow them with the whisky. The letters had been written – months ago. He told Charlie to fetch them for him and to put them prominently on the desk. He asked forgiveness – if forgiveness were necessary – and swallowed fifteen barbiturates with another glass of whisky. And with what strength he could summon, thanked the old man in the hug they gave each other.

Then he held Charlie's hand, and while he did so the pieces of his reason fell into place.

Nicholas remembered George and thought of the thrust of George's flesh within Miriam as they hastened to make another child. He felt their living until their old age and death – in his heart. Spring would follow. It was here. The laburnum at the Mouth was in flower and the orange bells of the abutilon.

His loves were with him. He carried them all at his breath as he felt the wave rise and fall, the stream carry him. And, as he was caught in a deeper trough, he placed his hands on his chest, his lips curved firmly together.

'No snivelling,' the old man muttered.

He looked again at the breathing. The boy was going, he decided. There were certain shivers and tremors. But too slow. He took a pillow and put it over the boy's lips. Something rose in him, crouched like an animal about to spring, and forbade that he be the one to decide the moment of passing. So he picked a blanket off the bed and wrapped himself in it and waited.

Nicholas could see the heron. It was about to leave that stinking, smelly lagoon. It took off low to the water and arched up above the trees in a trajectory of white, glistening feathers. It was across the hill and over the pond. The white bird neck was outstretched, the beak pointed to a sun whose light was reaching him. Its heart, small and pink with blood, beat steadily and more steadily.

Then came the sea. The sea was all things and the bird flew above it. And was it towards darkness that this white beauty fled? Was it possible? Nicholas Fieschi sighed during his dying and knew that it was not.

The car, with George and Miriam, drew up to the kerb as the clock struck twelve-thirty. They said 'Thank you'. Laughed. Blew kisses. Stumbled to the gate.

A couple of daffodils were in bud in the miniature flower beds.

George inserted the key quietly.

They crept up the stairs.

The old man was behind the door, hidden in his blanket.

First they noticed the face.

Then the shallow breath.

Charlie Katana pushed the door shut. He handed them the letters as if he were a postman. She took hers. And screamed. 'Nicholas?' And was silent. Then: 'Ring a doctor. Oh God.' She clutched her belly as if she had a tumour. 'We must do something.'

George ripped open his envelope.

'My dearest brother, When you receive this I will be dead. Look after Miriam and my child well. You love her, and you know what to do. I will think of you in those moments we both know. I love you.'

Miriam was entranced by Nicholas's face until George stepped towards her. 'Stop,' he said as she turned, searching for help in the air, in his eyes, in a phonecall. 'Stop. You knew.' He took her in his arms and kissed her hard. He held her tight into his belly and chest.

'Like this?' she asked.

He took her to the bed. 'That is my twin. We must do nothing. Nothing.'

The old man crouched back in his chair. The breathing, at last, after what could have been hours or minutes, slowed into a gasp. The breath left.

George looked carefully, then kissed his twin. He supported Miriam to do the same, then let her go as she howled with the old man and threw herself onto the corpse. Later George took her off, and she scratched at him and tried for his eyes.

He got back from her and waited. Then slapped her hard. He carried her to a chair and sat with her and the old man, waiting for morning to come.

'I will be goin', too,' Charlie Katana said, 'into that Home. But tonight, something has been good to us.'

They waited for the sun, then rang cousin James who came into the room, halted, and preferred to see nothing. But he signed the certificate then, as it would be easier and Nicholas, of course, would be cremated.

Miriam returned to her chair at the window and drew a shawl around herself and watched the old man sleeping. Then she remembered the body and pulled herself together. She found some soft cloths, a basin and hot water.

There were scissors, bandages, a clean scarf. A house carried with it the stuff of death.

His body hadn't yet stiffened. They took off his clothes and with soap and water washed his corpse clean of its death sweat. George shaved the light beard, tied the bandage around the penis, lifted his legs while she pushed cottonwool into his rectum.

Neither could believe the silence.

They touched and held only emptiness.

They handled Nicholas as if he were a god transferring a last knowledge through their working with him.

Miriam tied the scarf around the jaw and on the eyes she now put coins.

They remembered the nose and laughed a little that there could be so many exits for the body's fluid.

They left him naked, but covered with a sheet, and Miriam went to take a shower.

George rang his parents.

Miriam heard what he said and her heart broke just to hear the words, but healed again as she remembered their child.

She got into a black dress, took her shawl, and sat down again at the window.

9

The Fieschi family was in the drawing room waiting to cross to the church.

The house, as Mrs Fieschi's acquaintance described it, was 'pleasant'. And there was the view which distracted.

That afternoon, however, they faced inwards to the empty grate of the fireplace.

Now Mrs Fieschi managed a smile at her sister, and Mr Farquar who, broad shouldered and stooping slightly with the shock of it all, cleared his throat and consulted his watch.

'Twenty minutes and we leave.'

'I can't believe it.' Mrs Fieschi impulsively pushed open the usual slat and peered out.

Mrs Farquar was sunk in thought which, although it did not have a precise direction, was concerned with what her friends might say when the season of sympathy was over.

'He killed himself, poor boy, because he was out of his mind,' she said aloud. 'It is probably from Bertie. What with that cousin of his in Milton, Alison Black.'

Mrs Fieschi, fragile and bitter without knowing it, swung around at Mrs Farquar like a wasted flame searching for fuel.

'My son did not kill himself. He could not kill himself. It was an accident. My son! My son!'

'You have George.'

Mrs Fieschi didn't deign to reply.

'I don't understand,' Mrs Farquar took a handkerchief from her husband and dabbed her eyes. 'Why should a member of our family kill himself? Or,' she added hastily, 'how did he mistake the number of pills? I blame that girl.'

She, after all, had informed them coldly he was dead by his hand, whatever the death certificate said.

'I blame her,' said Emily, delivered and trim, her arms across her breasts. 'She didn't want him to go to hospital, or for us to help — to make him see sense. She wanted it all her way.' Under the impetus of her rage, Emily tottered further into the room. 'With that disease he could have gone on for ages. James told me. In hospital, being really looked after. They have a sterile room where he would have been behind glass. And this drug — they can carry on for ages. By then they might have discovered a cure. After all, leukaemia might be the next.'

'Stop,' said Mrs Fieschi. 'Stop.' In her agony she pushed herself tight against the back of the chair and closed her eyes.

Emily was surprised and, of course, hurt. 'I was only trying to help.'

'Well,' said Mrs Farquar as spokeswoman of the older generation, 'say nothing. And how is your father?'

Emily followed her rising voice out the door. 'He's weeping into his pillow, I can't stop him.' She broke down herself and the tears fell into her wet handkerchief. 'Poor Dad. He really cares.' With this accusation she was sucked back into the passage.

Mrs Farquar preferred to concentrate on her sister and stored up the accusation for a future reprimand.

Mrs Fieschi stared into the empty fireplace, empty that was except for a vase of arum lilies Emily had put there to hide the grate, and the telegrams and cards which Mrs Fieschi read and threw away at once. As far as she dared.

'Say something, Mu,' suggested Mrs Farquar. 'Get it out of your system.'

Mrs Fieschi transferred her gaze to a photo and twisted her hands around a small eighteen-carat gold cross. She had put it on a long chain around her neck to proclaim the faith of her family, living and dead.

But the dull gold did nothing to soothe her. 'What can I say? I cannot even weep,' her brittle whisper continued. 'My Nicholas.'

'He's passed over,' said Mrs Farquar. 'We've all got to some day, Mu. You'll see him again then. So will I.' A wave of nostalgia and surprise ran up her body and knotted in her throat. 'And,' she suggested later, 'we have our memories. When he was a boy – not so long ago.'

With that she erased from her mind the last year or two. As an aunt she could afford to be selective. 'He had good parties when he was young.'

'Yes. And we were always welcome to meet his friends. Nice girls – and boys.'

'Why?' – the question was finally wrung from Mrs Fieschi – 'why did he turn against me, against all of us? What did we do? Why didn't he go into hospital? Why is he dead? Why did he have to die? My son. Why?'

'The Lord giveth and the Lord taketh away,' said Mrs Farquar. 'Blessed be the name of the Lord,' answered her sister.

In his bedroom Mr Fieschi lay on top of the quilt, wearing his best black suit. And watched the small crack in the plaster which kept him anchored to where he was. His hands, fine and smooth, with carefully-cut and sanded nails, lay by his side.

Mr Fieschi admitted his son had killed himself. Muriel would not look, would not come into the room to look. He had, for a moment, and seen Miriam. And said something. To her and to George.

But later he had gone to the undertaker's parlour. And Nicholas was in his coffin. Yesterday, that was. And the face he saw yesterday? So defenceless he feared to kiss it. And wrapped in a light white shroud. Mu had wanted that. That sufficed. As long as she knew he was wearing it. And that the coffin was closed before the service.

Why had he not placed in his hands something precious of his own? Even his wedding ring?

Now it was too late because the lid was screwed on.

But, there must be something to do. To talk to Miriam, his daughter-in-law? Yes. His daughter-in-law. And ask.

Would she want to tell, after Emily, after his own dear Muriel had shown their sure aim, their superior knowledge of where scapegoats could be located? Even on the morning of a death?

And George had turned them out of the house.

But he would forgive them, being solid as a rock.

'So many shocks,' he murmured at the crack in the ceiling. 'So much coming out.' And Mu his wife, she usually so meek, had turned tiger as soon as she was in the safety of her own home, and accused him of murder and rapine, the plagues of God. Then she had wailed to herself when he had offered a sherry.

And Miriam? He had told her of the funeral arrangements, standing there, his hat in his hand. And she had been sitting with a tartan rug about her legs and George standing beside her, as if she were the Queen and George a courtier. And he, the poor, allowed into a feast to pick up the crumbs.

She had agreed to his arrangements with a barely perceptible nod of her head. She had accepted his apologies with an even less formal motion. He wondered if she heard, or did they count so little with her that only a fraction of attention could be given — and then, once.

He blew his nose and tried for magisterial dignity. He was head of the family. He would have to support Muriel. And perhaps Mrs Farquar.

This small lie helped him to stand up and see a green streamer of rose curling on another, more woody, and that was sure to wave right into this room when the days brightened into summer. With God knows how many heads of blossom.

The hills were succulent with the rains. Out of the window

— he dared to look — the garden. Beside the fish pond the cat lay heaped about on some sun. This beautiful garden. But what time? The brief season would be over and everything would be caught into the net of memory.

He coughed and thought he would pull down the hut-shed thing at the bottom of the garden. Perhaps he could build a summerhouse he could use for writing in.

So, far above all that was hidden, he bade adieu to his son, the garden, the admittedly short time in which he could indulge them all, and walked steadily to the stairs.

Mr Farquar glanced at his watch. 'There is another ten minutes and then we leave.'

Mrs Fieschi drank a small cup of tea with thinly-sliced lemon floating on the top.

Mrs Ruby, the help, had retired again to the family kitchen-cum-sitting room and sat in the chair Mrs Fieschi usually sat in, close to the picture-window. There, she got on with her knitting, glancing now and then at the cups and saucers, the plates of scones, asparagus rolls, some biscuits with cheese on them, topped by a dyed-green cocktail onion. Also pavlova — light and frothy and brittle with sugar, dry on the surface, damp underneath and glutinous — into which everyone sank their teeth, and for a moment, Mrs Ruby was convinced, died from sheer pleasure.

Mrs Fieschi had told her not to make things too extravagant, as if she needed to be told that. She tapped with her knitting needle on the bottle of sherry Mr Ruby had given her to bring as a mark of respect. It stood with the whisky and brandy, and the other two bottles of sherry that of course had foreign names, as if what they made in Auckland wasn't good enough.

'Poor souls,' Mrs Ruby thought, remembering them in the next room.

There, the sun had slyly moved to penetrate a bent slat and injected light onto the mahogany tea cabinet, the 1790 blue vase with gold splashed wildly across its blue enamel flowers, the chrysanthemums arranged in it, which were extraordinarily late this year. They tossed their heavy yellow and gold heads around the light or inclined, flaming, towards the gloom of the yellow picture seat.

Mrs Farquar had shifted attention to the radiogram, and followed without blinking a knot in the wood. Followed it right to the inmost point where it waited for further diminution.

Mrs Fieschi, her hands tight in her lap, had turned to stone in the centre of the moment. She was absorbed in the latest picture of her son and held it tight in her lap.

The lips, she thought while she waited, were a little thick. For her, just right. And his nose, a clean delineation of bone, a family characteristic. The green eyes were his own. No one else had green eyes. Sometimes brown or hazel. But his eyes could be like emeralds. Or, with tiredness, moss-soft, reflecting a shadow beneath them, he could have been a young god fresh from the bed of love.

And he had cut the cord between them.

It should have been her death that was the second severing. But he had held the knife and it had fallen with its sharpened steel edge. And he had gone so far that she knew, whatever happened, however she would pass over to the other side, he would be somewhere else. Perhaps nowhere except in the shadow of him that would grow faint and fainter.

He had denied her her immortality. Stripped her of her knowledge, the hymns of glory she sung each Eucharist, the flesh and blood she nibbled in memory of her Saviour. He had even destroyed her God. And what hope was there of knowing? He had escaped knowledge; had fled through its piled-up eminence. He must have. She shuddered at the horror of it. He must have, otherwise he could not have done what he did, which was in defiance of every law she had conceived of. He had experience of something. They could never meet again because he . . . he had fled away towards something she could not see.

And then she felt rising from herself the purest feeling that stretched taut every nerve of her body and rose to her head and on, she thought, so that she was taken over and breathed through by this sense. Her heart stopped, and between one beat and its recommencement she recognized the flame as that of hatred, so beautiful and so searing she wished to die, and knew that if she did she too would escape, as he had. And the room she sat in would be as it always had been, dust, made into shapes of beauty to deceive and destroy.

The kettle on the stove puffed some steam and suddenly shrieked. Mrs Ruby of course saw to it, with a startled grunt.

'What?' said Mrs Farquar.

'Kettle,' said Mr Farquar. 'Boiling.'

Mrs Fieschi relaxed.

'You must be a bit warm,' Mrs Farquar observed as she saw beads of sweat on the wrinkles of the bereaved mother's forehead.

'Yes.'

Mrs Ruby, back in the kitchen and oppressed by the grief that was being carefully shut into the other room, opened the window and took a deep breath of air.

People were already arriving at the church. Mrs Ruby took the pair of binoculars and hurriedly adjusted them. It was that Miriam with George. Neither had come to the house first. For a moment she thought of going in next door to tell them, but decided not to. Her fat and specially powdered face pursed itself up as she tried to decide what she felt about what she had seen. Finally, with a sigh, she approved, patted her flowered dress, and allowed a quiet and discrete fart to ease out between her legs.

Miriam wore a brown and green maternity dress and felt herself to be solid with the child, and solid with the affection of George and the way he took her elbow and guided her up the steps into the anteroom to the church. Her face in two days had lost flesh and she received images of the world through layers of shock. She had tried to play music to bring herself back but had heard it from a great distance.

Inside, she was caught into the odour of Anglican sanctity;

well-polished floors, candles hastily snuffed, the covers of prayer books.

Mr Fieschi had always been a generous patron in things financial, and the church burial of his son was obligatory. As long as no questions were raised, which they were not.

There was no one yet around so Miriam lit a cigarette. It helped her to face the coffin.

The pews of polished wood could have been from any antique waiting room, as could the ivory crucifix above the lectern – very chaste and sexless.

She wondered at that cauterized Christ and which particular heaven he would preside over. But she would rather have a man who still could understand the pain of her. And thrust up her, even in this late time of her pregnancy.

She gathered her dress about her and climbed the three steps to the chancel.

The coffin was on the royal-blue carpet.

At last she was beside it.

She rested against it.

Stubbed out the cigarette.

Watched light in its patterns from Victorian stained glass.

'There is nothing,' she told George.

'I know. He left that morning. I felt him close for a bit. Until we read our letters. Then nothing.'

'You should go for your mother. Take her arm. I am all right. I can manage by myself.'

'I know,' he said, 'and so can they.'

At that they both stared at each other, and recognized for the first time that together they had reached a frontier, and together crossed over it.

'I could marry you,' George said.

'People will come soon,' answered Miriam. 'They always like to come early for funerals. In case it starts without them.'

She hauled herself up and walked to the altar. In the sanctuary she lit a taper. As the first flame, shaking, rose new in the air, she transferred the flame along the row of candles on either side of the cross. 'This can be our contribution,' she said.

*　　*　　*

Charlie Katana did not read the papers and did not know they had asked for no flowers. He pulled his coat around himself and tied the scarf which George and Miriam had given him, of yellow cashmere with stripes of grey and red and fringes. It was a gay scarf and he shuffled a little faster down the garden of his new home, between the newly planted flowers: polyanthus, dusty miller with thick green leaves, and a border of crimson pansies.

At the bottom was the kitchen garden and a tap with a damp patch around it. Here Charlie leaned against the wall and felt in his pocket for the nail scissors and the rubber band. He glanced at the high polish on his best black shoes. There was no one around. The old gardener codger had been lured off by a screeching nurse to play at quoits.

Charlie knelt by the violets and began to cut. Then he put the rubber band around the stems, sprayed them out into a real nice bunch and shuffled out onto the street where his taxi was waiting.

'Where are you going?' asked one old man, spitting slyly.

Charlie paid the taxi driver and told him to come back when the funeral would be over. Then did up the top button and arranged his scarf, the colours fluttering proudly in the breeze. Miriam and the rest were there. George a bit hunched up. The priest reading from his book.

He walked down to them and on past them and past the priest to the chancel.

He was stopped by the lid. He had not thought that it would be screwed down and it made him angry.

But he showed respect and instead placed his good-smelling bunch of violets on the wood.

Then he returned to his friends in the front row and smiled at them.

Because he sat down with the family, no one thought to comment.

And the violets held them. For who can ignore the purpose of a whole life offered to the death of another?

BURNHAM CAMP

1

The tracks stretched away in a flat line down past the signal box and on to the embankment, that looked in the heat as if it would fall onto them, as soon as the train's hooter shattered the deceptive quiet. Beyond the embankment that had been built so long ago that no one knew any longer why, was more ground and the line of the horizon. You could follow the rails until you hit against arid blue. Then you were suddenly pulled back into yourself and the station was present with the metal roof cracking and groaning under the sun at midday.

Trains passed through on their way to some destination or other and it seemed as if the only life were here, around the station, poured in from the sky to this bowl, with the hope of a few people to make something of it.

It was difficult to look at those red clays the rails ran along.

The Stationkeeper could. His eyes were as hard as the sun and he welcomed into his sight and for the mesh of his thoughts, those things that were the same each day. He stood now, waiting. Sweat poured off him when he thought of the trainees, for this was an Army camp whose land lay across both sets of rails and down a road. He looked at their water tower jutting up above the trees in the distance.

They came because their birthdays had been drawn for National Service. Sometimes one left in a coffin with a flag over it, on one of the trains that stopped. It was always a boy from the green parts; they were softer.

He straightened up. Rubbed his left hand. It had been shattered by a German bullet in World War II. Today was 4 January 1967, so it had happened twenty-three years ago.

At the edge of the platform he spat and stood waiting.

He gave in to the heat. The sweat trickled down into his eyes and blurred the vista of dried grass and gum trees hanging above their roots. The only patch of shade was a hole in the station wall that said 'Men's Lavatories'.

There were two uprights with yellow stains running down the enamel that started where the highest pissed to. And one lavatory, stuffed up to the top of the bowl with used pieces of newspaper. The smell didn't put the regular soldiers off. And the trainees had bladders like everyone else; when they arrived most had to piss from fear of what might come or from excitement that it would.

There weren't any lavatories for women, who if they got desperate, could saunter across the tracks. There, where the grass was long, they crouched while a row of magpies arched their long white necks and cackled together at such pallid flesh.

In shade on the platform was the station-keeper's cat. Its eyes were dull copper against the glare, its fur lay close against its skin, and it growled to itself, watching for the flight of some dazed bird too close to the earth.

The keeper flicked his fingers and waited too for the night and his kingdom among the broken-down huts, the wastes of grass and bramble, the lumps of concrete and rusty pipe.

Today was the last Army train. When it came back in three months the station would close.

Down the road he could see the Colonel walking towards him.

*   *   *

Colonel Leinon limped as he walked by the rifle range. It was a reminder that he had rather less bone in his right knee cap.

His shadow travelled in front of him and he kept his eyes on it as he passed the red flag hanging at the firing range. A niggle of pain shot up his groin and way out of the skin. The Colonel relaxed and put on his sunglasses. The grass now sank into dusty white, and further away from the road, into a deep, crackling brown. If it were a powder barrel he would have thrown the Black Russian he was smoking into it. In resonance with the thought he moved his fingers to the red-hot ash, stroked the tip and smelt with pleasure the thick callus burning on his fingers.

After the flame had started he would lie on the Army green around the Memorial Gate and watch the flames leap from blade to blade and bush to tree and on to the edge of dryness and bareness. And why not? Let the whole plain burn. And those National Servicemen on their train. Let them be stopped many miles away by his conflagration. And when they arrived find only the Army acres secure; an oasis in the middle of ash and grit.

The Colonel took off his sunglasses and his eyes opened with deliberation against the soft glare of the dust road ahead. Where the Army control of the road ended he listened to the water from the artesian bore. That water had kept the camp open for three more years, because lack of water was the first excuse for closing it.

Who in war asked about water? But they thought they were at peace. Peace did not exist, as justice did not exist. Only a battle for truths.

The water ran clear and cold down towards the tunnel fifty yards away, and slow, as it was pumped up to the tower.

He threw a small fistful of gravel onto the calm surface and expected it would stay there. As if the world could ever stay the same!

So, he smiled to himself. Even the trains roared through the station to somewhere else. He should change the points and force them off into the siding, or let them hurtle against the embankment. And then let them see what the centre was like.

Where do you go now? From here?

The Army had already given back the land and now roofing iron flapped and grated in the wind around the bomb site, except for the row of huts, the last parade ground, the last quartermaster store, the last armoury. And his headquarters.

The Goverment had thought of making it into a camp for children needing the sun. And now they had decided the camp would be a Borstal for louts! Perhaps he could stay on – hang a prisoner now and then or wash their dirty feet.

He lay back in the long grass at the edge of the race and pulled off his clothes. He lowered himself in and shuddered against the knife-edge of the current.

'Lotta.'

He shouted the word up to the canopy of grass above his head. The cicadas swaying on the thin stalks of green and dry stalks were silent.

'Lotta.'

His testicles pushed back against his groin. He felt the hardness and tightness. First they were in the lower stomach somewhere and then came down to make a man. His were retreating from him. When he had had enough of water he lay back in the grass.

Lotta's idea was to return to Vienna, or Wien as she called it now that her Austrian personality was ready to re-emerge like a butterfly from the chrysalis. They would settle in a small house in the suburbs, or better still, in a chic apartment somewhere near the Woods.

He had found her in Köln.

She had been looking for fuel that day, circling the perimeter of the Cathedral. There was no wood, but the stone walls, blackened and smoke-stained, the gaps in the windows and the rose light from the west windows through which the faces of saints stared as they climbed through to the postwar world, were benign in their blessing of the wastes around them.

They had gone to the Rhine and watched British soldiers repairing a bridge. Lotta's hair had been a straggling brown shade, and in the sun which touched the lights in it she had seemed to him beautiful then. 'I sleep with them,' she had said, pointing to the soldiers. 'Of course, only with the officers. They can get me more food and heating.' She had wept at the thought of her affairs. 'And my son, little Franz. He died in Berlin. A bomb! I carried him into the bottom of our garden and buried him myself as if he were a pet canary. And Franz, my husband . . . He is dead, but you know that. On the Russian front.'

He had clutched his coat to him and pressed his hand against the wound on his chest. The flesh was raw, but the bullet had been removed. Now it smelt stale. There might be gangrene developing. 'Poor Hans,' she said, having often seen the same gesture in other soldiers. 'Here we are talking tragedy, but we are alive.' She glared down at the brown water.

She slept the same night with a medical orderly, only a sergeant, but got the penicillin.

Now Lotta was as fat as the lambs the farmers sent as carcasses to England. She dripped with enjoyment at the sight of food. It fascinated her and he could see her remember Berlin and Köln whenever she was doubtful about feeling hungry. Memory set her salivating. And now she was safe, all her memories buried under layers of comforting fat.

Dear little sister, Lotta. His sister? How could people be such fools! He raised his buttocks, white and firm, and pulled his shorts on.

Ahead was the station, approaching and retreating on the heatwaves. He tightened his finger around the leather grip of his baton and moved through the waist-high grass as if it were a sea opening before him, and in his wake the day moths, fluttering in small circles of dust and vermilion wings, sank back into their territory.

The station mocked him in its determined displacement of his wishes.

He remembered again and his anger brought bile to his mouth. There must be no gossip. That was why he wasn't wearing his uniform.

His feet sank into the dust of the road and he paused to feel it between his toes. Then he saw the butterfly, hovering over some ragwort. He had no time to see its colour properly as it rose and swooped across the grass, for the keeper was there in the shadow, squatting and watching with his damned cat.

The Colonel raised his arm as the butterfly came, swung, and connected into the middle of the long yellow and black body. He lengthened his stride and swung the baton again to rid it of the corpse. It fell ahead.

The Stationkeeper looked at the dead thing on the steel rail and vanished around the back. On the wood of the Colonel's baton a few yellow egg sacks, like miniature caviar, were drying in the sun. Of the body from which they had been wrenched, only the wing tips quivered.

The Colonel stopped before the second set of steel-bright tracks and the vista south from where the train would come.

He climbed onto the platform. There was a thermometer above the park-size seat. The smell from the urinals curled around his nostrils and he wrinkled them. He pushed away an empty lemonade bottle and flattened the straw under his sandals. Where was the broom the Stationkeeper cleaned the place with?

Behind him, another smell joined with the stale air from the urinals. The smell of beer that had been in someone's stomach for a long time. The Colonel breathed in deeply.

'Hot day,' the keeper said.

Colonel Leinon turned around and balanced on the tips of his toes.

'Yes.' The Colonel stared past him up the siding where the dry green algae had climbed from the rails up an old wagon.

'Too hot.' The keeper's spit sizzled on the rail where he had expertly directed it; the butterfly wings of red and gold were burning with colour.

'Well.' Colonel Leinon smiled at him.

The Stationkeeper peered at the thermometer he had nailed to the wall. 'Ninety-four.'

'Yes.'

'Going to be hard on those boys. That asphalt you stand them on's hot enough to give anyone a headache. No girls for them either. It's not healthy for young men.'

The Colonel raised his baton, cut through the air, and crossed the sound of its descent with another cut.

'And you?' asked the Colonel.

The dry heat had done things to the man's skin. He had a long straight body, close to six feet the Colonel calculated. But his left hand was twisted around like a sparrow's claw. Better to have been amputated.

As he watched, the Stationkeeper put a finger into his mouth and dug around a tooth near the back for a piece of meat. The Colonel could feel the grave eyes on him as the operation was performed. At last the keeper grunted with satisfaction, drew out a stringy bit of beef and flicked it out to the sunshine. What did Lotta see in him?

The Colonel moved closer as the other sat on the slat seat.

'I have told her this cannot go on. I do not wish to think further on it. You are the gardener for my house. Not the stud for my sister. She has said she will not see you again in this way. Unfortunately the garden must be kept up. This she insists on.'

The other looked at the straw beside his boot.

The Colonel felt his anger rise easily before that submissive shape. 'I was amazed and disgusted that my sister,' he paused, 'my sister could behave in this way. In my house too!' He began to walk up and down, his lean neck growing red under his tan. He wiped the sweat from his forehead and did up a button on his shirt. Suddenly he wished he had worn his uniform, then the words would have drilled deeper into the body of the other. 'It is a sign among many of the way this camp is running down. All because this camp will finish in three months. And,' he pointed his finger, 'you take advantage of a foolish fat woman. It's beyond me.'

'Is it?'

Colonel Leinon stepped away, his back arched. 'Is what?'

The other shook his head. 'It doesn't matter.'

'What doesn't matter, man?'

The keeper could feel the Colonel's nervousness and the sudden accent emerging with it, strong and Germanic, and his brown face and eyes were intent on the other's face. 'She said a lot of things about you. Seemed funny, some of the things, for a sister to say about her brother.'

Colonel Leinon moved a step closer. 'What did she say?' His voice grew quiet. The echo of it on the station was cold.

The keeper thought him calm because he could not see the Colonel's baton behind his back inscribing little arcs through the air.

'Nothing much I suppose.' He chewed out the words and drawled them slower and slower until the last tailed off into the blurred silence he had been gathering around himself.

'Good fellow.' The Colonel placed his hand on the other's shoulders and felt the hard fibre of muscle beneath his shirt. The intention was there and the other crouched for a second under his power.

'We would talk to each other,' the keeper said, 'about what she did when she was young. I was in the war, so I know how hard it was for her. She needs company because she lost her little boy — in the war you fought in. When you were my enemy. The enemy of my country. She told me that.'

'True,' said the Colonel, feeling himself limp and heavy with the heat and the similar weakness of the other.

They both needed an enemy again.

The keeper had walked into the sun and was squinting down at the camp with what seemed the insolent pride of the conqueror. He belched. He, too, was depleted of emotions. He did not need them, so his straight back suggested.

But then, neither of them had any experience whereby they could firmly recognize what must happen.

The Colonel picked up some paper and pushed it into the waste basket.

'Don't you ever clean up?'

The Stationkeeper scratched himself and bent towards the lemonade bottle.

'What's your name?' the Colonel asked.

'George Kaufman.'

'Well, George. With a name like that, it wouldn't surprise me if we could call each other fellow countrymen. Why don't you clean up the station before my boys arrive? First impressions are important. Yes.'

The Colonel walked to the platform's edge and stared down south where the smoke would appear. The afternoon dropped its balm of light and fullness onto the earth of the plain and the camp was covered in a flow of golden honey. He could hear through that soft haze the pump drawing water to the top of the tower and the soft downward rush as it spurted out into the pipes. And on the lawn of his house the sprinkler moved in slow circles. The air around its orbit would be thick with spray, breaking up the light into rainbow discs.

'Yes,' he murmured.

'What?' asked the Stationkeeper.

Colonel Leinon turned, a soft look on his face. 'My sister is a slut. She cannot do without a man. She has always been like that.' He reached into his pocket and brought out a ten-dollar note. 'Now take this for your trouble.'

The Colonel was surprised to find himself on the ground, and even more surprised to be helped up.

'Don't say that! Not about her!' The keeper offered his words as an explanation.

The Colonel rubbed his cheek and the other was happy with some memory. The Colonel took his baton and hit at a blowfly emerging from the urinals, steel blue and bulging with vomit from the handbasin. 'Clean this up.'

The other scratched the black hair around his navel.

The Colonel tried to stop a twitch fluttering in his eye.

'Clean it up.'

The Stationkeeper walked for a moment to the end of the platform where the path began that led up to his cottage, and farted, moist and soft through the stains of oil on his seat.

'I'll have you for this,' the Colonel shouted.

The Stationkeeper had space between them, and laughed, louder and longer than the Colonel had ever laughed.

'You fuckin' fool, this place is closing down. You're finished.

She told me,' he ended almost tenderly, 'that you were finished. She knows there's no Army for you to go to now. You're gunna retire when it closes.'

The Colonel raised his baton and loosed the edge of it with all speed across the other's shoulders.

'Shut your filthy gutter mouth.'

He wanted to leap across the rails to the safety of the road to the camp, but the keeper held him by taking off his shirt. Inch by inch he uncovered himself and turned the weal towards the Colonel. 'You've marked me.' He rubbed his back and stood tall again.

The Colonel, propelled by some force he did not understand, reached out his hand. His fingers were stained by blood, the same colour as the dollar bill.

The keeper clicked his fingers and the cat bounded from a hiding place beneath the platform. The keeper's eyes changed under the influence of the light and became grey and empty, the skin smoothed over his face.

'This place will go, so must we. In different ways.' He picked up the cat and held its fur against his naked chest. 'We all have to pay for what we do. That is something Miss Wagner says. We must pay to the last drop.'

The cat reached up towards his face, its ears flat against its head. The keeper took no notice. He was absorbed in the density that the plain laid over its burnt-out soil and black rocks.

Yet, against him everything sprang into movement. Even the trees, stilled in the spirals of heat, danced with incandescent leaves and the dust on them shook. The cicadas flew in wild gyres, falling at last into the resilient clumps of bramble and grass.

'They will be here soon.'

Against his will the Colonel nodded.

The Colonel rested again at the stream. He could hear the noise of some insect burrowing into him. He ran his hand across the

swelling on his cheek and bent to rinse a large brown handkerchief in the water.

The station was squatting close to the earth, with yellow side-
boards peeling and glistening. Under that heap of rubbish no
creature stirred. He shrugged and bent towards his face in the
water. His eyes were bright with strength. Lotta's, by comparison,
were filmed with the sludge of her thoughts. They sailed by in
stately procession: food, sheets of silk, handsome young lovers
climbing into the crevasse between her thighs, Chopin by moonlight with the songs of nightingales.

He grew nostalgic. Lotta would be angry to know he knew.
He picked up a stone and placed it across his navel.

The noise from a car engine against the counterpoint of his
thoughts suddenly stopped their weave. He poked up his nose
through a clump of thick grass and sneezed as he breathed in the
dancing pollen.

It was the Padre. His car belonged to the Chicago gangster era.
The engine had been given a rebore while he was on holiday —
it purred and snarled as the wheels bounced up and down over
the ruts in the road. Through the windshield the Colonel could
see he had changed his glasses. Now the thick black frames split
the face in two and claimed the forehead for themselves. So much
for the dominion of his eyes. His face was pale as usual and, with
the exertion of the day, tinted into pink patches.

The front window was open and the Colonel could hear the
Padre singing. The Colonel chuckled. Cracks he had felt open
in the earth he carefully tended shut again. Everything was normal. The Padre was taking his Sunday morning run in the car.
As far as the far side of the crossing and back again. The Colonel
considered asking him to lunch but dismissed the idea. Tonight
was the party for officers and it would not do to seem too eager
to favour anyone. He himself did not go often to mass and neither
did Lotta.

The window had been open into her bedroom and he had seen
them as he walked around the garden. Lotta had thought he was
still on leave, which at least gave her an excuse. The claw of the

Stationkeeper was fastened onto one of her nipples and was dragging towards his lips that fat pendulous breast. And the hard fibre of his back was kneaded by Lotta as he moved his lips along her solid thighs and stomach.

What he had witnessed was not love or lust, but the exploration of alien territory. The Colonel felt a shiver at this thought.

One bullet could have finished them both as her teeth sank against his neck, where by instinct she knew the flow to his brain was carried. The Colonel had found himself about to shout, but suddenly, by some feat of strength, the keeper lifted and impaled her as deep as was possible on his knees, and while the sweat beaded by the light fell from his chest they were joined as tight as any carpenter's join.

No bullet was needed.

Colonel Leinon opened his eyes. They seemed to swim in a mist of his sweat. He stood up to smooth down his trousers. The flag flew crisply out from the pole. His stomach rumbled.

The water ran at peace with the banks. His reflection in it now rested quietly in the storage tank at the top of the tower.

But the mood did not last as he stood in front of the barracks. He sniffed in the heavy scent from the gum trees that fell straight through the brown burned leaves.

Lotta, if she had been with him, would have held his arm, and her eyes would have sprung into life. She had stood in the shade almost on the spot where he was now before the last batch arrived and had inspected each door, open onto the cooler air. She had peopled each bed as she walked through and imagined the face on the pillow and the family at home, beyond the plain, who would be waiting for the first letter. She never stopped at the yellowed pin-ups: sharp tits martyred by drawing pins and pouted lips receiving unexpected bounty.

He sat down. The mattresses hadn't been unrolled. The windows looked to have dust on them, like the attic windows he had peered through as a child – the slats of the bed he rested on were the same kind as the nursery chairs he had sat in with his brothers and sisters.

He could not imagine a day past the end of the camp. He had requested the place, and who could refuse him? He had served with distinction; first in Korea against Communism, then in Malaysia against Communism, then briefly in Vietnam against Communism. At times Lotta had upbraided him for landing her in a country which dedicated its energies to monotony, equality and Rugby. And, as he thought, incoherence when faced with life or death.

But it was for those very reasons that he found New Zealand a suitable place, and Burnham Camp the epicentre of the country's emptiness. Natalia Dashkov had been right to encourage him into this exile, along with Rebecca Weis who kept inviting him and Lotta to stay with her.

For him there was a logical progression from the Wagnerian uniformity of his homeland – Austria, once – to the grey monotony of his place now. And yet, in the more perverse days of his youth he would have approved of their submission to surfaces and their passion for obedience to stereotypes. And perhaps it was for this, and other sins, that he found himself with only a railway line to link him to the cities – to which he could only attribute symbolic interest.

He broke his mood, brought his baton down with a dull thwack. The puff of dust drifted into motes among the sunlight.

Outside the parade ground was a sheet of asphalt, as vast as any sea, and that dulled the insistence of the voices that spoke to each other from the deeper shadows of his memory. He saw for the first time how the process of demolition had gone. The light was now the colour of no living thing, and seemed embued with a ferocious will to highlight the rubbish around him.

He stepped over the white line that indicated the beginning of the parade ground and from a doorway, over at the colonial house which did for headquarters, his new secretary emerged. She tottered to the rail and raised her fingers to the sun. Whether this was an act of worship or of imprecation he could not be sure.

Charlotte Pearse was Natalia's daughter, and in competition with her pianist brother had become literary. Between jobs she had offered her services at a dinner party given by Natalia for her son's return from a tour. She wished, secretly, to experience office routine, smell the sweat and bad perfume of the gaggle of Army girls who serviced the office, and see whether or not they shaved their legs; then she would write poetry for the magazine whose editor she knew.

The Colonel made for her.

Charlotte blew on her nails and deftly recapped the polish before spreading her fingers for him to admire. They were a deep vibrating green.

'Storm green,' she said, giving him a short hard look, looking also towards the hut he had left, across the sea of asphalt. You could not discount homosexual tendencies in a man over forty.

Sadly, since it would have made a nice stanza in the long poem she had underway, no young soldier came hesitantly out of the same hut. But she could suggest the possibility. German war criminals and heroes were fair bait, as she had decided when he and Lotta had arrived at the farm for a vacation.

She also felt sorry for him. He had given up his office for her. *His* office was now a hole. Masochistic?

'It will set an example to the troops,' the Colonel said, accurately deciphering her thoughts. 'I want a lot out of them.'

'What?'

He could hardly say of endurance, since they endured the most frightful deprivations and seemed to enjoy them. They also showed by various feats of strength that they were not to be tampered with.

He moved into the shadow beside Charlotte. Suddenly he didn't care any more.

'What, I wonder, Miss Pearce, and what I want to know, is if they are capable of overcoming.'

'What?' asked Charlotte, who half expected something on Nietzsche to follow. She also felt a pleasurable tingle of interest.

'Me, Miss Pearse. I want to know if they are capable of overcoming me, or whether they will fall on their knees and worship me.'

'Why should they?' asked Charlotte.

'Because they have been trained to worship idols.'

At this they both laughed, as neither could possibly be serious. The small electric clock on the wall, which punctuated seconds and hours, could never stop to allow them to find out what the other might mean.

'What will you do when this is all over?'

'Old soldiers never die; They only fade away,' he hummed at her.

The squad of 'soldier' typists was marching across to them. 'I'll make a new dress tonight,' she told him, 'for the party.' But he had gone and didn't hear.

She was in no mood to collect first impressions of the soldier-women, so she returned to her air-conditioned office and put on a record of Johnny Dash and quoted to herself a line of her newest poem, that she was writing as she went along, about – Now: 'White-like spectre of old virginity she soldiered to cut a new pattern of experience'.

'I'll make a new dress tonight, and sew a live rose in its hem. A live rose,' she promised Johnny Dash, with his floppy sensual lips – now in America. She reached into a drawer for her vodka mix, prepared for office emergencies. The bite of the lime juice reminded her of poor Captain Cartwright, whose wife had fled. She had said they were all going mad.

Colonel Leinon stopped at the entrance to the garden. The birds were asleep in the elm trees. The sprinkler threw out large drops like over-weighted tears onto the roses and green grass. Poppies and tulips were against the walls of the house – loyal sentinels spiralling to the lush peony roses around the steps. The sprinkler had been on them, and in the shady parts the water could have been glass from the drawing-room window, shattered and falling like hail onto the petals.

And through that window he could hear Lotta at the piano, trilling like an overweight canary some snatches of Strauss, and now, the theme song from *The Merry Widow*. Fortunately the blinds were drawn and he could not see her, reigning queen of the camp since the Brigadier's wife had left with the Brigadier, and the Doctor's wife, the Anglican priest and his wife, the usual officers and their wives.

He wiped the dust from his forehead. The wood-carved barometer in the hall registered, as usual, 'Very Dry'.

Lotta was now playing a little bit of Bach. She had never managed to balance herself and hammered first the right hand and then the left, and she was hampered by her wedding ring; it was more stubborn than her will. Today, to play the piano, she had tried to twist it off, but her flesh had swollen around it.

She was wearing a red Thai-silk dress, and her dyed blonde hair was draped, in a youthful way, around her shoulders. She also wore an apron, signifying her exertions in the kitchen. Her thighs made him think of two expanding pipes driven into the hills of her buttocks.

'I have bought off your station lover. I cannot allow these young trainees to suspect that it is possible to communicate across the lines. And I do not like tulips. They are thick lifeless flowers, sickly and too dependent on water. Tell him that tomorrow, and tell him to trim the edges of the lawn.'

She turned so that he could see he had hurt her. He inspected her face, as if it were separate from her true identity.

'I slept with men for you,' she said.

He was suddenly drained of words.

'I remember my husband telling me you raped a woman in Poland. Held her down, you and your friends. You all lined up to show what virile young dogs you were to each other. What well-tempered steel.' She shut the well-tempered clavichord. Suddenly she was old, just for a minute, before she remembered that they were going to Wien. 'Think,' she said, 'in just three months we will be free, with a pension. You with new medals and a new passport.'

She smiled towards the mirror where she could see herself. 'We will make it in time. I must have some peace,' she added, 'in civilization.' Then she touched his cheek. 'Why, he hit you for me! He hit you and you've got a nice little bit of swelling!'

She blew her breath onto the wound. 'Remember Krannebitten

where I met my Franz. Both of you, naked on the green moss and eating, what was it – yes, paté and some bread with wine. I was so young and I saw you both. I had never seen men naked before and when Franz stood up I knew I would love him. You stayed on the ground. Were you embarassed, dear Hans?'

He remembered. She hadn't blushed, but her thoughts changed the quality of light coming across her shoulders. Her skin taut-ened at her throat. He remembered her among the larch fronds up there, high above the Gasthaus. She touched with her finger a small green cone and held it lightly in her hand.

Lotta wiped her fingers down her apron. He saw by the flour marks that she had been baking. She moistened her lips, moved a blob of lipstick onto her toungue, and flicked it down her throat.

He stationed himself in front of the fake-marble fireplace.

'Forgive,' she said. Offering him her fingers. He nibbled.

'Poor darling,' said Lotta, seizing on the cat as the nearest prop at hand, 'you are hot and want to be cool, in Vienna with the other pussycats. Somewhere near the Woods so you can go hunting.'

The cat was convinced, and rubbed itself around her legs and cried to the Colonel.

'Nice pussy,' said the Colonel, to make conversation.

Lotta paddled to the window and as her hand stretched out for the cord he saw the soft brown hair in her armpit; and he smelled her. He put down the whisky he was pouring and backed to the door. She could not help it, he knew.

'Dear Hans,' she said, confident of her powers.

Softly she pulled down the last blind, and then, as Charlotte's blue Morris Mini accelerated by, she poked her nose through the pink tassles to observe.

Hans Leinon was held no longer.

'Come here, Hans. Come here. My love.' She did not turn around and spoke instead into the canvas of the blind or possibly the glass behind it.

'Come here.'

*　　*　　*

Hans Leinon lay curled up on his bed. Everything in the small room which had been shut up against moth, dust and beetles now was open. The highly-polished surface of the wardrobe reflected the window and the view outside; the drawer with his socks was open, as was the box he kept his papers in.

The air was sticky. He stared at the ceiling, because of the black spider he had squashed there, just now. He inspected the death and thought he could see the remnants of eyes, and bright-jewelled fangs.

Neither the crucifix hanging above his head nor the picture of Lotta on the chest of drawers was enough to hold his mind in the well-beaten paths of thought. He felt quite young and spry as a result, almost as he had been in his philosophy class or talking to that charlatan, Karl Haushofer, about continents and destiny. The dogs were baying in his memory of course, and covered the silence of heaven in the face of dead men, tortured men, evil men, men who wished for repentence and punishment for their sins, men who knew that none of these were possible.

His gaze, vacant and controlled, drifted from the mirror back to the ceiling.

And who was mercy for? Rebecca Weiss? Himself? The young genius Benedict Pearse-Dashkov. Natalia Pearse? The shatteringly bad poet, Charlotte Pearse.

Didn't events have within themselves, as part of their outfolding nature, their cause and consequence? He had learned that in philosophy class, and Hegel, the philosopher, had said something of the sort. But some things cried for their own ending and waited, as crafty as a spider, to leap on the victim of their hunt. Neither crucifix hanging above his bed nor pictures of Lotta on the chest of drawers could stop the necessary pursuit.

And that was why he could not forget.

Poor Lotta could not know that he waited – for destiny?

His mind narrowed down onto the splotch on the ceiling and he saw again, first as if the ceiling were a screen and then as if he were in his past and had never moved, the eight faces, lined up against the brick wall.

There, by a cherry tree that was in flower, he was standing, waiting to give the order. His hand brushed up on a spray of flowers, perhaps to remind himself it was spring, that it was the season for being alive, not for having a brisk pattern of bullets lodge in your bowels, belly and heart. There was only one squad and they were behind the machine-gun.

His fingers were digging at the layer of green skin that separated the sap from the air, and as he brought up his hand, a figure came rushing over, dressed in black. It was the priest, picking up his skirts and waving around a small box as he came over the field between the trees and through the wild flowers.

All the villagers were hostages for good behaviour, but someone had slipped up. They swore and wept, said it couldn't be them, that it was a village further along, that they were all good Poles and loyal to the Germans. But a soldier had been found knifed in the river that ran through their village, and that village had to bear the suffering. The example mattered. Only the example. It was better for the innocent to suffer, then they would be more vigilant in the future for the welfare of their guests.

The priest was still running when he looked back from the brick wall, once part of a house, to the eight young men and the eight graves they had dug. They had been pleased at first, when the spades were handed to them, to have something to do.

One at the end looked about eighteen and had a red handkerchief around his neck, and his father snickered to him between wetting his lips. Another had a boil coming up near his nose; one in the middle had dark hair cut short and large brown eyes. He alone knew the Captain's fear, and his soft smile at the day allowed Captain von Leinon to raise his hand.

Two opened their mouths, showing the fillings to him.

As he shouted out the order the priest was coming closer, waving his arms in the shape of the cross and calling out something, but the Captain's ears had begun to buzz and the squad was getting edgy. His hand came down at the same moment as the rapid stutter from the machine-gun.

The boy in the middle had shouted something but his mouth was plugged and the force splattered the wall behind him.

They all crumpled on their backs, but one, still moving, stared blankly at the patch of earth, his blood dripping onto the earth and spotting the blades of grass that had not been stood on.

The Captain walked forward with his revolver out to give the *coup de grâce*, but the father had leapt at him. A blast followed from the machine gun and the father threw his back into an arch against the sky.

The one not yet dead turned onto his side, his fingers twitching. The pain had reached the point where it was no longer felt and that peasant face had suddenly reflected a distant peace. It made Captain von Leinon stop and fire between his eyes.

He had then walked along, kicking the bodies into their trenches as the squad lit up cigarettes and the priest stood where he was.

They had lain in all sorts of angles in their graves: the one who had shouted something was on his back.

'Well,' the Captain called out. 'I thought no-one was coming to the funeral.' After all, he had been only twenty-eight and assumed he would live forever.

The priest squinted as if in pain and muttered another prayer as the Captain stood in front of him, idly swinging the revolver. 'I was coming to give them the last rites of our Church. They are Catholic. I suppose you find that difficult to understand. I was not running to see them die. I was running to give them the body of Christ.'

'Well,' said the Captain, feeling suddenly light-hearted, 'they don't need that now.'

'Yes,' said the priest. 'And the old man, too,' he added after a time.

The sergeant came up and threw a small knife at the priest's feet. 'Who was he?' he had asked.

'The butcher,' said the priest.

The squad picked up the shovels. The earth fell in silent land-slides and settled with a hiss.

The Captain returned to the spray of cherry falling down towards the grass by his hand, and stroked the petals. 'It is a beautiful tree, Father.'

The priest walked to the graves and sprinkled water onto the face of one of them before the next shovel of earth covered it up.

'It is a beautiful tree. So strange to see it blooming in the middle of the war, so very strange.'

'All flesh is grass,' the priest had said in a loud voice as he stood over the butcher.

Captain von Leinon's blood ran easier. 'It is war,' he had said, replacing his revolver with a dull thunk into the brown leather holster. 'You killed and in return you had to die. This will serve its purpose. Disobedience will not be tolerated. Nor will subversion. You must learn to obey.'

'For what?' The priest began the first decade of the rosary.

'For being allowed to live in these times,' he had answered.

The priest suddenly switched to the flat tones of the mass, his prayers had stopped or they had grown louder. 'You have done murder. Remember that when this war is over. You may never be brought to trial, but you have denied life and life will deny you.'

The Captain turned as the women, six of them, came running across the field, through the orchard and over the flowers.

'They have come from the church,' the priest said, 'where you put us all.'

'Get them away,' Captain von Leinon shouted.

But the women, like will-o'-the wisps, evaded the wooden arms of the soldiers. One touched the Captain and she drew back as if he were on fire.

'Well,' he had asked above their racket, 'what do you want?'

Colonel Leinon sat up and the splotch on the ceiling became empty of meaning.

He watched himself in the mirror. There in the face that was his he could see his end: lines crossing and recrossing over his skin, ice-blue eyes fractured by the effort brought through looking too far in the future to find the shape of it. The land outside might be in the hands of his enemies, of those who wished for his final defeat. In the cracking of the rocks and snap of dried wood he thought he could hear their voices. And far above them, tendrils of the sun brushed across the red and brown earth of the plain, distilling the juices of herb and tree and raising them in dry mists.

He ached quietly, clenching his toes together and moving the long nail of the first one against the rough skin he could feel under his nylon sock. This was why he had lied his way into the New Zealand Army. To find a place like this. Lotta thought they all knew he was Wehrmacht and not SS and even approved of him. At least this was the Colonel's suspicion – a romantic figure in a landscape that bred only sheep.

Lotta came into the room.

'Well?'

Her hands were on her hips and her eyes were flashing.

'Well?'

He raised his arms towards her as if to be picked up and tucked into his bed.

'Poor Hans, what is the matter?'

He shook his head as she cradled it against her belly.

'Come,' she stroked behind his ear.

'Yes?'

Lotta allowed herself a smile of victory. They were speaking in German for the first time in six or seven months.

'The war is over. A whole generation has grown up and married, with children, and they know nothing about it. All over the world, in America and Germany and Austria and England, no one cares any more. It is just history to be read in books. No one cares at all. Neither must you.'

'Come.' She knelt beside him. 'We will have a special treat.'

She went to the window and peered around the edge. 'There is no one, everybody is asleep. And the train is still far down the line, huffing and puffing, with all your boys sleeping too.' She drew the curtains across, and flicked a blowfly out onto the marigolds and pansies.

From under the bed she took the box. There was dust on the lid and she blew it off carefully to avoid dirtying the satin finish.

As she sat down beside him, the Colonel appeared to come

out of a deep sleep. The muscles in his face tensed for a yawn that never quite erupted. He belched discreetly in his throat. Lotta opened the box, her fingers trembling under the weight of his interest.

She picked out the fine scarlet ribbon attached to a heavy silver cross. It swung to and fro, and the colonel followed its arc.

Lotta scrabbled for another and put it near his fingers. As he held it she too could feel its potency.

'Tell me why you got it?'

'You know what that was for.'

'Tell me again.'

'I won that on the Russian campaign. It was bitter cold. Colder than ice. I still can't forget the wind.

'I was ordered to take prisoners for interrogation. In front of Stalingrad. We had to pass through enemy lines. I remember bodies with their tripes blown out lying frozen. I didn't care whether I lived or died. It might have been a good place to die.'

Lotta was satisfied.

'And this one you won in Poland right at the beginning.'

'In the middle I wished to die.'

'But you were brave.'

'Ravensbruck,' said Hans von Leinon, adding a footnote to his history. 'I saw Rebecca Weiss and . . .'

'And saved her,' said Lotta. 'She said so, just a few weeks ago.'

'I did not join the plot with Adam von Trott und Zu, against Hitler. That is my shame.'

'And the cross, first class,' Lotta rattled on. 'Other races have gold or silver but we have our iron.'

'Yes,' admitted Hans von Leinon, before he became a traitor to his conscience.

'So brave,' Lotta crooned to herself and delved again. Her thick fingers fastened around a red velvet compact. She drew it out as if it were alive, and held the blue sash across her breasts, smiling at his submissive back.

'And this was your father's. From the Emperor to his loyal servant. And here is yours.'

'Adam Von Trott und Zu was strung up on piano wire, or

shot? I don't know. Rommel suicided. I survived!'

The Colonel was again young, and he had pale skin as smooth as alabaster. He wore his life with incisive courage.

'I was young,' he said.

'And handsome. Beautiful and hard.'

'As you were,' he said, a tired note in his voice as he slipped a beribboned medal over her head. The eagle hung between her breasts.

Lotta fluttered her fingers, as light as moths, over her dyed blonde hair. 'Come.'

The Colonel remembered again Adam and Franz and Rebecca Weiss. And Natalia Dashkov who had also elected to survive by running.

He had gone to Ravensbruck and had seen it and saved Rebecca by speaking to the commandant and using Adam's name. Then, he had refused involvement.

To forget, he bedecked Lotta with medals and ribbons of those days, of that day when he had waited, like a good Catholic, to break under the weight of his acts, and had not broken.

Lotta was willing to have them all around her neck. She clutched them to her melon breasts. She held his picture and kissed those young arrogant prewar lips, and the straight thighs, and the confluence of power which for him, in those days, still lay in his groin.

Which now exploded into heat.

In sudden terror he heard a fly as it limped from the ceiling to the bare light bulb.

'Now, now,' said Lotta.

She knew this mood too and she took off her clothes as he fidgeted and shook.

He moaned as she patted and prodded and touched. He lay still while her sweat dripped onto his chest. She was telling him that she loved him.

At three o'clock the corporal stood by the flagpole and sounded the bugle. The notes were high and pure and for a moment the whole camp achieved a sharp focus. But the new perspective was weaker than the old and sank back into it.

Hans awoke as from a dream and smiled. 'I must go.'

'Ach so,' said Lotta.

The Colonel reached into the open wardrobe and took out the hanger with his newly-pressed uniform. He dressed while she watched. She heard him slam the front door.

'Bathe,' she told herself. 'I'll put on my bathing suit and lie under the beach umbrella, close to the sprinkler, to wet my toes.'

From her room she could look across the dried-up paddocks to the swimming pool, fenced in, it was true, with nothing more aesthetic than barbed wire and corrugated iron. She couldn't see the water but she knew it would be blue, with a ripple of wind going across it, but she felt lazy.

From her dressing table she took an old pair of brass opera glasses and adjusted the lens to the high diving board. It was at the third to top step that she would start to see them, the soldier trainees climbing up as if this were the way to heaven.

They always looked happy and were brown. They were confident as they laughed up at the sun, raised themselves on their toes until they hardly touched the board. And then with the lightest of springs began to bounce higher and higher, always poised above the same spot, balanced against heaven and earth. Then, they were ready for the dive as they swung into the arc of the sun.

Some flew out, bodies bent high, others arched like swallows or crucified themselves in the air, or piked like a dolphin; all their white bottoms flashing.

She had told Charlotte one night after she arrived, when they were both tipsy. Charlotte had said she wanted to come and watch. Then she made some literary observation about the diver and the soul and the water of life. It was all mixed up and something to do with a painting of a tomb in Greece or Persia or somewhere. And men diving into God while still in their bodies. 'Diving into truth,' Charlotte had said.

Italy, Lotta remembered as she ran the taps of her bath. There was a young man diving into a pool, and after that you saw him with his Greek friends feasting in the afterworld. A pretty idea. Lotta liked literary ideas. It was a pity, as Natalia Pearse had said, that Charlotte felt she had to be in competition with her brother.

Lotta's eyes closed as down the plain the driver pulled the long greasy string which let the steam out in a brazen hoot. By the time she had sunk into her bath the white smoke was blowing around the trucks waiting to pick up the trainee soldiers.

2

Somewhere through the noise of the trucks rumbling up the roads, the contrapuntal stillness of the field in front of the Colonel's house, the lights in the soldier-trainees' barracks, a new sense of purpose came into the evening. The field, although overcome with shadow cast by the moon, was also caught in the strange white light of the stars, or perhaps reflections of dust. At any rate, something drifted over the ground, so that the dryness became softer and more yielding.

The window of the Colonel's sitting room was open. The acrid scent of tulips floated almost to the windowsill. The ormulu clock spread along the white-painted mantelpiece, the gilt falling from the edges of the cupid wings. Below, in the fireplace, a dozen bottles of Moët Chandon were in their silver ice buckets.

Colonel Leinon sat in one of the easy chairs near the fireplace. On his signet finger a gold and cornelian ring reflected the light from the candles on the piano. He watched the Gothic descent of the wax to the brass holders – that light also caught on the painting of Lotta above the fireplace. She had carried it out of her house in Berlin and the gold wire it hung on was beginning to rust.

To elevate the evening Lotta was playing a Chopin nocturne. The melody somehow collided with the air at the open window. Lotta's head inclined over the music; if the angle were a little different he wouldn't see her open mouth gaping at the score as she finished.

'Play something else,' he suggested, to delay the inevitable beginning to the evening.

Lotta reached to the top of the pile and brought down a Chopin valse from which the technical difficulties had been alleviated by a skilful arrangement. Even so, she managed only twenty bars before her knuckles showed white. 'I remember playing this piece for a little soirée. They said I should have made my career in music. So annoying.'

She tried a few notes. 'We must cheer up Captain Cartwright. His wife has left him, poor man. And the children! Perhaps you should take him aside. Talk to him.'

'Perhaps. And, Lotta, you must clean the nicotine from your fingers.'

Lotta dimpled.

The Colonel poured himself a whisky and squirted in the soda.

At the open window, looking over a lawn and flowerbeds sprouting weeds, Charlotte sat like the centre of a small painting, bent over the hem of the dress she was to wear, her face reflected in the mahogany table the Brigadier had left in the house for her to dine off.

The rose had been picked from the climber growing around the dead wistaria.

She pushed the needle through, stopped, and licked her thumb to remove a drop of blood. The last stitch was in. The thread could be broken. The dress was white and the rose sewed live into the hem. She poured another lime and vodka.

Tonight? She drank, staring at herself in the mirror. Why not tonight?

In her bedroom she pulled the curtains and slipped out of her clothes. Her body was good, her breasts firm. She was not running to fat. She would keep her figure as Dad had.

I drink too much. She waited for her reflection to continue but it was silent with her. I drink too bloody much and I've not been laid for six months. She touched a nipple. Prayers had been formed in stranger situations. I am a woman. I'm not waiting any more, she thought. Maybe too old for love.

She raised her glass and rubbed the blood blister until it broke. 'Up with love,' she announced, giggling to herself and her reflection, and choking over the last drops that had managed to fall into her windpipe. 'Fuck mother. And her big love story! The fucking Granny Smith!'

Mungo Picton was housed in the quarters for the unmarried officers. He shared the otherwise-deserted building with the Padre.

Now he was in his bath.

Captain Cartwright was waiting for him as he didn't want to go to the party by himself. Mungo was holding up a light conversation to keep him outside. If the Captain remembered his misery he might come in and that would be embarrassing because Captain Cartwright was such a prude.

Picton had been clogged up with dirt, orangeade and the cold pies he had eaten on the train with the conscripts. He had had a crap and now he was in hot water. Any man got a hard-on in those circumstances.

He tried not to let his irritation get the better of him and wondered if he dared to submerge and wash his hair. But he couldn't talk under water and there might be enough time for the Captain to panic and poke his head around the door.

'Could you take my silk suit out of the wardrobe?' He ducked quickly and washed out the shampoo.

'Is the party informal?' Captain Cartwright called out.

'Don't know.'

'Anything the matter?' called the Captain as Mungo surfaced for the second time.

'No.' Mungo splashed some water around.

'Have a good time in the city?'

Mungo laughed.

'You all right?'
'Fine thanks!'

It seemed to Hans Leinon he was sitting in the wreckage of a party that had already taken place.

Lotta was watching with him, the skin at her throat loose. She glided about the room on tiptoes, lifted a piece of parsley back onto the cucumber sandwiches. 'It feels like a play just before the curtain goes up.' She pirouetted. 'All the audience waiting.' She picked up a cream cake. 'See! They don't look burned at all. I cut off the edges. Snip snap.'

'This camp is a joke!'

'Thank God,' said Lotta, yielding to her creation.

'What are we here for, Lotta?'

'For their country,' said Lotta, impaling a pickled onion, 'even though they don't know it. Sometimes I think it is because they want to learn how we did it – in the war.'

'Just to kill?'

'No. That and, all the rest.'

Lotta returned to her nocturne.

'I think it will thunder,' she said, sniffing the air.

'I hope I'm not too early.' Charlotte, tired of standing at the open door, waited to be noticed.

'So nice to see you.' Lotta eyed the other's youthful legs and breasts. 'Do sit down dear.'

The rest of her conversation was drowned out as Lotta shifted gear to Gershwin.

The Colonel, with Charlotte on his arm, departed for the garden and fresher air. They stopped close to the elm tree. Charlotte stared through the bottom of her wine glass at the lawn and the stars. Both seemed equidistant from her.

'This,' said Charlotte, 'is a young country. It's not even a country.' She paused at her mother's treason but continued with only a moment of reflection. 'It's like being in hell or purgatory. I hope it's purgatory. One goes through that onto something better. Benedict,' she added bitterly, 'managed to get out.'

'It depends,' answered the Colonel. 'Look what is outside us.

Nothing but dried-up earth. The camp has water, people, order, a way of life, traditions. But because we do not beg, society shuts us down. Declares us redundant. Yet we can be free in our prison because we have each selected it in preference to other prisons.'

'But I want something else.'

The Colonel nodded. 'I understand.'

'Yes, yes.' Charlotte murmured to herself the line from a poem coming into her mind:

'We are soul-mates in the dead light of the moon, and we know the day comes with the mind, and the moon will leave the sky for us.'

'Beautiful,' said the Colonel, concealing a wince.

'Just now a cat came to see me. While you were fetching the bottle. It has freedom. Like the Stationkeeper. It was his cat, I think. There aren't any other toms around here.'

'And trespassers must answer for their crime,' he replied.

'Yes,' she said. 'But how can I answer for what I've never had the chance to do?'

'But we are all criminals in our own way.'

'Yes.' She walked towards the house. 'Lotta will wonder what has happened to me.' Lotta was starting to remind her of Natalia.

The Colonel leaned against the trunk and stared into the blackness of the hydrangea bushes.

'I know you are there, George Kaufman.'

The sky waited for the thunder.

'What are you hiding for, Kaufman?' He rubbed his cheek against the bark. 'Du weisst ich kann nirgends hin, wenn ich hier fertig bin. Ich kann nicht weiter rennen. Ich möchte nicht. Come out you bastard . . . creuz cruzefix, komm 'raus! Verdammtes arschloch. Komm raus! Du Krüppel!'

'Come home, Hans.' It was Lotta, standing on the porch. Charlotte stood with her.

Light sparkled from the candles to the dull wood of the piano and reflected a dull image of objects. Among them was Captain Cartwright touching a key.

Colonel Leinon watched Lotta.

Lotta was captivating Lieutenant Picton. Caught by good manners, he was managing a simper.

'It's a good party, sir,' said Captain Cartwright.

There was a hint of a question as Captain Cartwright waited for Hans Leinon to tell him what he should think.

The Colonel could hear Lotta shrilly picking wild flowers, somewhere or other, but certainly not here.

Captain Cartwright permitted himself a small giggle. The Colonel ran a sharp eye over his rumpled clothes.

'I didn't . . .'

'No?'

'Mungo Picton isn't dressed either.'

Mungo wore an expensive heavy silk suit in a dark cream shade.

'I hope you don't mind. Mungo took me for a drive in his car. We were doing ninety as we crossed the railway tracks. He said it would do me good.'

Between picking out notes on the piano, the Captain had been getting drunk.

'It's very sad that the camp is closing down, sir. I suppose it'll mean some big changes for you. But I suppose you'll be happy, pottering about.'

The Colonel leaned over the windowsill and poured some wine into a poppy.

'I'm sorry your wife's left you.'

'She gave me the address of a bank in the city, at the front door, to send money to.' Captain Cartwright looked anxious. 'I bought her a new fridge last year and took her for a trip to the islands. Why you think she went?'

The Colonel's lips tightened into a thin smile as he examined the creases of the Captain's face, pausing at the bags under his eyes, and briefly at the blue eyes themselves.

'First,' he said, 'I must define what man is. To me he is a hunter, the killer, the lover, and lastly, if he is given the chance, the lover of the bits and pieces of God he manages to discover. If he is very lucky he pieces some into a form, or perhaps is luckier if he never succeeds. He only lives from the moment he realizes that he is responsible for his pain and the pain he causes his life and the lives of those he takes away. He is subject to guilt, but this is bearable as long as he accepts it as a condition of existence.

'But he also begins to doubt whether there is justice or what he has called God or the order of the cosmos. His reason for feeling this? He has not been chosen to be attacked or punished or shown love to. God has ignored him: what is he to do, since he cannot believe, under his despair, that this is the truth?

'Then he's naked and feels shrivelled, with his eyes on the stars asking them to fall on him, so he will know he was created for a purpose, and that his acts have consequences. If he can know that, he will be happy to suffer. But he may be left without knowing, and so, not knowing that he has wasted his time, he may die into Nothing, and even this he will not know. This is the horror of men of my generation. And only a few escaped this. A friend of mine did. He was involved in the plot against Hitler. He failed and was shot or strangled by piano wire on a butcher's hook.'

The Colonel was aware that his words were carrying: there had been a lull in the conversation, and the others were being pulled into the radius of his will.

'The last chance may be death, if it is the last note of the coda; otherwise it is simply a note which happens to be the last.'

'I don't know,' said the Captain.

'I want,' said the Colonel, for a moment gentle, 'a death which will show me the things I was too weak to see until that moment.'

Captain Cartwright looked at him as if Hans Leinon were from another planet. The others forgot they had heard the Colonel opening a door into his soul.

'You have never killed,' continued the Colonel with a shrug, dismissing himself as philosopher. 'You have never ventured out and pitted yourself against the tide.'

'I've swum a mile in the swimming pool. It's deep. You can drown as easily there as anywhere.'

The Colonel was amused at the perspicacity. He flicked a speck of pollen from his lapel.

Captain Cartwright sank onto the windowsill and, as the pollen circled up into his nostrils, sneezed.

The other faces, caught into a moment of recognition of each other, rippled like a wind on silk before they composed their eyes into a party mood. Somewhere, far away, as Lotta said, the thunder rolled, and moments later a gust of hot air rattled some loose roofing iron.

But it wasn't calm. Charlotte could feel that now. Lotta, who a moment before had seemed like a fat, fluffy pigeon, preened and arched her neck towards the Captain, her eyes brilliant, as her cat called to her from the door, its tabby eyes brilliant with lust, its fur floating about it.

'Let's dance,' said Charlotte, putting on a record.

Lotta gathered herself together and gave the Colonel a glittering smile.

'It's a tango, Captain. "Hernando's Hideaway".'

Lotta took the Captain's arm and strutted a few steps around his limp body: she pulled him into the music.

'I know, dum! A dark, dum! Secluded place.'

She whirled and pushed, their clasped hands were tight and low in prayer to the maroon carpet.

'Now. Three forward, one back, sideways glide. Cross feet. Hernando's Hideaway, *Olé*!'

The Captain was anxious to obey. He was hidden, he hoped, in the hops and skips. Lotta caught him to her maternal bosom.

'Now I will lead. I will be the man.'

The Captain wriggled his groin to avoid Lotta's knee wedged between his thighs.

'That's it,' Lotta was saying, 'you do much better this way. Cross feet the other way, push head to side.'

They hopped and glided, their shadows reflected in some of the pink blinds that were still drawn against the sun. Lotta's hair had come loose from the pins and bounced over one shoulder.

'A rose, Mungo,' she called. He threw one to her.

'In your teeth, Captain. You are now courting. Rose in teeth.'

His teeth sank through the green stem and the petals, shivering, fell to their bellies and then to the floor.

'Now ready, Captain, the ultimate surrender. You must bend backwards, right back. Dum, da dum.'

She pushed hard against his chest.

Lotta assumed the pose of gladiatorial victor, her silver shoe daintily over his chest.

'You did very well, James,' said Charlotte.

'A victory, indeed.' The Colonel's voice broke the ice of their concentration and they laughed.

Lotta helped the Captain to his feet, took the stem from his teeth and dusted him down. 'You are a very good pupil. You learn very fast.' She took his arm and guided him to a chair. 'Sit here and rest.'

She wondered if the Stationkeeper was still watching their party.

Captain Cartwright seemed to have lost his tongue. He cast wild glances at Lotta's face as though she might be a sphinx whose riddles destroyed.

'Oh for a swim! For coolness!' said Lotta. 'I will be a mermaid in my next incarnation and sit on the rock all day in the sunshine, singing to the sailors.'

'What is the matter?' asked Charlotte of the Captain.

'My wife has left me!'

The Colonel himself felt constrained to yawn but to add no words, at least, not yet.

'What are you talking about? Who?' Lotta swam with the music.

'My wife. I was good to her but she's left me.'

Charlotte patted his hand.

'Write her a letter. Tell her how you miss her and want her back. Perhaps, if you apologize . . .'

'For what?'

Up the hall the lavatory cistern refilled and Lotta sang.

The rose on Charlotte's hem seemed on fire.

Lotta returned. 'It's almost bedtime?' She swayed against the hot air pushed before the clouds. 'No one to dance?' She held out her arms. 'I will dance then, with my memories.' She circled the room.

'Time for bed,' she said again, eating the last of the smoked-salmon sandwiches and dabbing her finger into the mayonnaise bowl.

Mungo picked off a petal and sniffed. The rose was dead. 'Oh Lord,' Charlotte whispered and clutched her stomach. She took the glass of champagne Mungo offered, and as she swallowed, it hit the spot and her nausea retreated, and she was off into the second phase of the wine, clear-headed and full of energy. It streamed over her. She thought of the swimming pool.

'Why not!' Lotta pulled the Colonel to his feet. 'We will look for swimming suits – if we must wear them.' They disappeared into the passage.

'The Colonel,' said Lotta reappearing with suits, 'must do some work for his speech tomorrow. The rest of us, of course, will go swimming.'

They straggled around the edge of the house. In front of them was the long field with the pines far to the side to act as windbreak against storms.

At the plantation, they split into two groups. The wind had altered and all the needles shuddered together, dropping their resinous scent like milk.

'A little too big,' Lotta confessed as Charlotte stood back to be viewed, in Lotta's second best.

Mungo undressed with Captain Cartwright. Again he was feeling randy, but now that the Captain was a lesser being than earlier in the evening, he had no qualms about his hard and allowed it to wave insolently in the breeze, though with no malevolent intent, towards the Captain. Captain Cartwright, immolated, and knowing his present status, peered down at his own limp vehicle.

'I feel great,' Mungo danced off among the trees. 'Fuck the Army, I'm getting out of this shithouse,'

'You have money,' the Captain called. 'You're the son of a landowner. What can I do?'

'Have a nervous breakdown,' said Mungo, confident that his youth would have its way. 'Bow to the inevitable.'

The entrance to the pool was a large green-painted gate. The fence was made of slats of wood and corrugated iron. Lotta and Charlotte surveyed the interior; the concrete under the fitful moon was grey, the water black and encompassing the sides as if to eat them.

'We had better go in.' Lotta approached with the authority of a herald. 'Who has the key? Why isn't it open?'

Somewhere, in the dark wood, Mungo was whistling.

'Perhaps we will just look.' Charlotte swayed against the slats.

'No, the men will think of something. Mungo will have an idea.' The whistling was closer.

Charlotte searched for a mothball that Lotta might have missed.

'Two nymphs waiting for entrance to the sacred waters.' Mungo was supported by Captain Cartwright.

Lotta bridled and smiled. Mungo was propped against the fence and found his eyes would only stay half open and he considered the flesh available through his long blond eyelashes. 'Ah, my Valkyrie!' Lotta picked her way across the path over the sharp edges of the pebbles imbedded in the tarseal. 'What you have is yours alone.'

'It's locked up,' Lotta trilled back. 'We can't get in. One of you must climb over the gate.'

Charlotte nodded. She gave Captain Cartwright a small push. 'You do it.'

He reached for the first crossbar of wood.

'Be careful Captain, you might hurt yourself. Mind the wood. It's dry.'

The wood and the Captain, obedient to her wish, gave way. For a moment his thin legs wriggled and coiled.

'Never mind.' Mungo flexed his biceps as he stepped over the Captain who was kneeling and breathing hard at the grass.

'No.' Charlotte pulled him away. She and Mungo looked up at the rolls of barbed wire around the fence top. She imagined his brown back and white buttocks whipped and bloody, his genitals cut and coiled into the innermost recesses of the rusty circles.

'Captain Cartwright is more sober,' Lotta insisted. She smacked Mungo on the arm. 'Stay here.' She approached the gate and called for admission.

'I feel sick. I want to be sick.'

Mungo stood beside her.

'No,' Lotta replied.

Charlotte shut her eyes as the Captain began to climb again. She opened them as he hit the top and balanced on the netting. He had one long scratch up his leg. His satin scarlet bathing suit crept like a skin disease to his bellybutton and covered it.

Then he vanished, but through the slats she could see his feet searching for a foothold. He reached the ground and Lotta took Mungo by the hand and led him to the gate.

'Well, what have they done?'

Captain Cartwright shook his head. His eyes glittered behind the safety of his glasses. They heard the splash from his dive.

'Come here, Captain Cartwright. We want to swim.' Lotta clasped Mungo's hand tight.

'Well, what is it?' Charlotte led the deputation as the Captain reappeared.

'It's padlocked. If you want to swim you'll have to climb over or get in through the gap in the fence around the back. It's very narrow.' It seemed as if he'd always known about the padlock.

The gap was narrow. The pine plantation at their backs was heavy with the strength of the wind. The women stood close together against the onslaught of the trees that were reaching their boughs out into the field.

'I'll go.' Mungo crawled to the corrugated iron and pushed. An edge caught him and cut into his shoulder.

'Come back.' Lotta pulled his legs and he slid across the grass to her.

'I'll sleep.'

'Yes, you sleep.' She watched Charlotte squeeze artfully around the bent tin and vanish. Lotta was content for the moment.

'Get my pants, Lotta. There's some brandy in the hipflask. I'm cold.' Mungo curled up like a puppy around his towel.

She walked carefully among the broken bottles and the used cartridges at the edge of the trees. In their centre was an assault course. The silence frightened her, even with Mungo's trousers in her hands and her hand deep in one pocket.

She returned. Mungo slept, his mouth wide open, ready to swallow the one star showing through the cloud.

'I will see you later,' she whispered to him. And was able to walk the first stretch, but she looked back. He was covered by her wrap. It looked like a pall, flapping and twisting. His head showed against the dark cushion of pine needles, but disconnected. A piece of rubbish thrown there carelessly.

As she ran, her thighs, soft and firm, rubbed light velvet against each other and sang their songs and kept her on the track up to her property, to the open window of her bedroom. Her arms flailed as she leapt from the clumps of grass to the smooth lawn. Caught in her momentum she resembled the windmill motion of children running faster than their bodies. She didn't see the Colonel watching her from the shadow of the elm, nor another shadow following him as he made for the trees of the plantation that ran like a sentry line up to the pool.

Charlotte lay back and let her hair uncoil and fall into the water below her, pulling her head down with its gradual increase of weight so that she sank lower in the water and trickles ran in runnels across her cheeks.

The water was warm and colourless. It remained attached only to its own life. The moon was a distant reality that had nothing to do with her or her presence in the pool.

Captain Cartwright, a grey shadow on the side, was watching her. As he must. There was nothing else to look at. Like a sea creature, he sucked in the energy from her body and expelled it again.

Above, the tips of the pines, tight and candle-like.

If the storm should slide over them, the trees would take the brunt of the attack, like any good forward position. After all, what did a few burned out trunks matter? But that depended on the lightning.

Captain Cartwright swam a length of the pool and his thin chest heaved at the effort. He displayed himself again beside her.

'I am the Lady of the Lake.'

The Captain tittered as the ridiculous stuff of her suit billowed up with air, making her pregnant in several unlikely places.

Charlotte paddled. The concrete wall, changed by angle of light and dark, zoomed off to its conjunction with the floor. There was no mystery in it, she decided, coming up for breath, just water in a tank. Not even the usual objects that found their way into such pools: butterfly hair clasps, buttons, sometimes a French letter, five-cent pieces gathering slime, that kids like Karl and Benedict had dived for.

'Why is it so clean?'

'Crystals to kill the bacteria – copper sulphate, chlorine.' He peered at her.

Even the white canvas of the diving-board, the coconut matting on the steps, were part of a luna debris, free of bacteria. The structure rose with a hard mathematical precision from its concrete base. Each cross-strut and support was built to withstand the white hurricane winds from the sun.

She sat on the edge and her hair began to dry. The hole through which she had crawled had vanished, or she couldn't see it. Around the fence top the barbed wire coiled like convolvulus, but without those stinking white flowers. The tin grew out of the ground and used the wooden slats for its climb towards the rust of the barbs.

'We must go.' She tried to stand but could imagine nowhere else.

'Wait here.' Captain Cartwright walked to the gate and peered out. 'It's safe. I'll go and bring you your clothes.'

He crawled through the gap.

Mungo lay sprawled across the grass and pine needles. His face was turned towards the plantation. His bathing suit, a small dark patch like pubic hair, was whipped by his flapping towel.

'Where is Mungo?' Charlotte said.

The Captain had brought Mungo's silver hipflask with him as booty. 'Drunk,' he said.

She obeyed and took several deep gulps. 'You look grey.' She handed it back to him. 'Drink and get some colour in your cheeks.'

He did so and lay down beside her and held the flask to her lips as if she were losing blood. The pool of water around her spread under them both and grew warm.

Charlotte waited for the Captain to return to her mind. For the moment he was in the shadows. Perhaps he had gone to the bathing shed. The floorboards the Colonel had discovered were infected by athlete's foot as well as some dried-up sperm. She could smell the lavatories. Around the entrance Lotta had placed a climbing rose in a tub. The flowers were large as cabbages, breathing in the sweat, shit, piss of the young. They gave off a strong, rich perfume: attar.

'I'm sorry your wife's left you.' She did not expect a shadow to reply. She allowed the palm of her hand to open and she held her mound of Venus towards the roses. 'A friend of my mother's read my hand once and said I would be happy. Alison's dead now, so I can't really trust that.'

She listened to the storm. The sky was black, split down the centre by one fork and another of fire. She felt the earth shudder down into its granite.

'You shouldn't mix drinks.'

Charlotte remembered again. 'Oh, it's you, Captain Cartwright. I'd forgotten.'

She didn't bother to turn to him.

'He's a bastard,' said Captain Cartwright.

'Who?'

'The Colonel.'

'Is he?' Charlotte Pearse stretched.

'I wouldn't be surprised if he was queer.'

Charlotte closed her eyes.

'He treated me like dirt.'

The Captain had a quiver in his voice. He leaned towards her and rubbed his face against her hand.

'I can't stand it anymore. I sometimes think I'll shoot myself, only I don't want to, it's too messy.' He touched her hand. 'No one will know, I won't talk.'

His hand moved to Charlotte's breasts. 'Everyone here thinks that he's run away from something.' He managed to fumble with her suit. 'No one will know.'

Charlotte shut her eyes tight, as with more strength than she could have imagined, he lifted her and slid the suit down to her waist.

'It's awful.' He ran his fingers across her belly. 'I have to make my own breakfast!'

'You must stop it. The concrete's too hard.'

He pulled her bathing suit down to her legs and clung to her, then turned demurely from her. She watched the slow exposure of his buttocks, white and wrinkled like a baby's.

'Do you want your wife to get you for adultery?'

'Yes,' whispered the Captain, rolling back over the concrete.

'Stop it James. Stop it. It's too hard. It really is.'

The Captain said nothing and Charlotte, in desperation, gave up and pretended it wasn't happening.

There was a thrust, a moment of cessation. The Captain began to move his buttocks and looked anxious. He stopped and felt for his glasses. He put them on. 'Is is nice?' he asked.

Charlotte found it took all her strength to control her backache, as the Captain lay with his whole weight upon her. She supposed he was afraid of grazing his elbows. To take her mind off it she began counting his movements. As she reached thirty-two they grew more violent, the glasses slipped from his nose and fell beside her head, one lens cracked.

'Bite me. Bite me.' Out of irritation she did.

The Captain opened his mouth and reached, with a furtive and determined acceleration, some kind of last glimpse of Charlotte, the camp, and his wife and children.

'I love her. I love her. I love her, bitch. Bitch.'

Just as suddenly, with a rather stronger thrust, the performance was over.

Charlotte, who apart from his lips and penis, had no sense of any interior conjunction, was left displaying a party smile.

He rolled away from her and stood up. 'I must go.' He put on his shirt, wrapping his cravat like a noose around his neck. 'I must go. My glasses?'

She handed them to him.

'Thank you, Charlotte. Now I must go off home.'

He suddenly ran the length of the pool. She heard him gasp as he crawled through the hole in the fence.

The moon came through a gap in the cloud, white like an eye. Outside the gate she could hear someone moving.

She saw a hand come through.

It held a key.

Now she saw what the Captain had seen.

It was the Colonel, his blond hair blowing in the wind.

She wondered why the Captain hadn't squealed as he bolted.

Colonel Leinon had found a rosary in his drawer. It had belonged to his grandmother. The beads had somehow collected moisture and were slippery to touch. He had swung them in the air like a prayer wheel, clacking against each other. Then he had jogged down the garden, vaulting the gate.

Beyond the plantation the sky burst into a yellow flash, like the reflections of a battle. He could feel himself freed in each cell and enclosed in the storm's dispassionate energy. His navel trembled. A breath of wind touched his forehead, drying the sweat as it formed. The darkness moved. He listened for the pulse.

He held the key to the pool.

And among the trees he could see a figure running.

Lotta's neck arched forward. She bounded and her breath came in gasps. At the edge of the lawn she stopped. Her relief was visible. He chuckled and stepped back as she patted her hair and walked towards the front door.

As she vanished he gave himself to his mood. Belches of laughter rose from his belly as the first drops of rain splattered like mud over his face.

He ran on. Mungo Picton slept like a casualty of war, his blond hair tangled with leaves and pine needles.

Hans Leinon went on to the gate and peered through. Close to the edge was Charlotte, the Captain on top of her. He felt his veins turn liquid and slow moving. His belly tightened. He willed the Captain to finish.

The thin legs shook and the face looked up towards him.

The rest followed as he expected and the Captain also ran.

Charlotte and Hans stared at each other while he undid the padlock and came to her.

He took off his clothes and dived from the side, scarcely raising more than a ripple, coming up at the centre of the pool.

Swimming a leisurely backstroke to the deep end, he hauled himself out and climbed the diving board steps, hardly noticing the new coconut matting on them, and found himself on the board.

He walked along it,

It was like a rehearsal for some event he didn't want to botch up, thought Charlotte, watching, her hair covering her breasts.

He bounced again and from the tip of his toes to the crown of his head he found the balance he needed.

The third was the last, and curving high out into the air, his arms like a bird's wings, he plummeted to the water. He was surrounded by it and did not fear his lack of breath or sight.

And when, at last, he came up, she was sitting in the same place waiting for him.

Hans von Leinon climbed out and crouched beside her.

She waited.

He saw that he had her attention so that he was able to take the hand she offered him.

They lay back together on his large white towel.

'Tell me,' said Charlotte, 'what you are hoping will happen.'

'It began when they were lined up against the wall. There by that cherry tree that was in flower. I was waiting to give the order.' The Colonel held her close to him for a moment.

'Tell me the story,' she asked.

She saw his face change as memory began to shape it, and she listened. He finished, and crouched over her.

She thought she might sob but she couldn't. She remembered again his beautiful dive.

'It was a beautiful tree,' his cold, dead voice said.

'You would be easy to love,' she said, and saw that he believed her. She reached up and brushed the hair off his forehead.

He kissed her and without pretence of paying court, lay on her.

Even in the universe there were empty spaces through which no galaxies moved, she thought, as she accepted him, and began to move away into her pleasure. When his sperm spurted into her she felt it.

Above their heads a night bird cawed.

The Colonel dressed and departed.

Charlotte left, sighed, and bent down to Mungo.

The third member of the trinity.

The wind was coming harder and the trees were bending and cracking under its weight. The lightning broke above her.

She prodded Mungo. 'Wake up, we must go.' She bent down and lifted him. Only his youth, like hers, almost like hers, could cancel out the night and leave her intact.

She tore the wrap off his chest. Mungo opened one eye and looked for the stars.

'Come on, you're coming home with me.'

He supported himself against her arm. 'What is it?'

'There is only you and me.'

'And the star?' said Mungo, offended and searching the heavens. 'There is a star.'

'Yes, yes. There is a star.'

They hobbled together across the field. She could see the light on in Lotta's room. Mungo took her hands as the water poured from the sky onto them both. Together they danced in a wide circle, their hair flying.

'Come,' she laughed and grabbed his arm.

Mungo lay back and allowed her to remove his trunks. He was slender at the hips but not bony like the Captain, or covered with old muscle like the Colonel.

She slipped out of her bathing suit and reached over to turn out the light. As she climbed into bed Mungo rolled onto his side and took her close to him, and seemed to be asleep again. She felt warm and cool and ran her fingers through his hair. She bent to kiss his forehead and pulled him close to her so that he slept against her breasts.

'Nice Charlotte,' he muttered.

The Stationkeeper held the cat inside his jacket and patted its snout to quieten any noise it might make. It was soaked through to the skin and smelled of earth warming up.

He walked carefully across the road and along the fence of the Colonel's property until he reached a gap. He pushed through and the cat, jumping down, followed. The moon sailed in and out of the storm clouds and finally into an open space of sky where it again looked tranquil.

The light too was on in Lotta's room.

His hands, as usual, tingled when he saw the dressing-table lamp and the pink lace around the mirror. He rested his head against the trunk of a tree and wished he'd remembered to bring some chewing gum.

Lotta walked on, slowly, drawing back the curtain to announce, so it seemed, the beginning of her performance.

One sudden breath betrayed her surprise and delight. She had left Mungo lying on her wrap, and, she confessed to herself, she had run away from him. But he had understood, and the storm had woken him up. She wished he would come closer but he never did. 'Dear boy,' she whispered, tremulously, as she dabbed some perfume on her shoulders – quite revived by his fealty.

She wore a blue chiffon wrap over her nightgown for tonight's performance, and as she walked to the window it swept in a train behind her. She waved her handkerchief towards the high diving board and the shadow, still and immutable, as if he were some presence from a timeless world, never breaking the calm of a god's observation.

So poetic. So gemütlich.

She sat on the window ledge, and as her throat loosened she took a breath that hardly moved her breasts, and sang his favourite song, 'As Time Goes By'.

In the railway yard, the Stationkeeper's garden was lush and fresh: the peas were ready, while the well-manured carrots curled against the young celery.

The storm had moved on, and the breeze that followed, like bridesmaids carrying the train, drew back the moisture into the air. Only the sweet peas had managed to hold the rainfall in their mat of flowers, leaves, and stalks.

The Stationkeeper went into his three-roomed cottage. In the grate of the fireplace were some empty cartons, and handkerchiefs stiff with snot from his winter cold.

From behind the clock on the mantelpiece he took the photo he had snapped of her cutting a rose. It was blurred and the edges had curled, but it was enough for tonight.

The sun streamed into Charlotte's bedroom the next morning.

She was sitting up in bed reading some poetry a friend had published.

'Where am I?' Mungo groaned and kept his eyes shut in case he wasn't.

She reached for the glass of Alka Seltzer. He drank it and opened his eyes, pushing his eyeballs further than his headache would allow.

'Who is it?' he asked, feigning the little boy and snuggling beside her.

'It's me.' She was surely herself again.

Mungo half sat up.

'Lie down or you'll be sick. I've rung the Colonel. He doesn't mind if you miss church parade.'

'What happened?'

'What happened?' Charlotte turned a page and sipped some coffee. Her contented eyes gave Mungo a warm masculine glow and he ran his hand possessively over her breasts.

3

The Colonel had finished breakfast and sat in a chair to digest the slices of browned dough that passed for bread. Beside him a cup of coffee had grown cold.

The water from the sprinkler could, during such a moment of recollection, create a sense of life on the yellowing grass. But even it was not sufficient to sustain the centre, and beyond the camp boundaries, impelled by the winds, the myriad forces of dried dust and grass swept into each other. Their intention had grown more intense as the weeks passed and the National Servicemen submitted to Colonel Leinon.

From his viewpoint in the middle of the lawn, he watched Lotta, secure under the shade of the elm. Her large white sunhat flopped across her face at a rakish angle, her cheeks were dappled by light through the leaves.

The roses had unfolded in the shade of the wall and were so rich in their display that he wondered if they were about to surrender to the whim of the season. The tulips had fallen to the gardener's shears and Lotta had cast glances of incredulity at the stems running with thick juice.

The morning was still ordered by the freedom night gave, and

Lotta, picking up her cup and plate and the rind of a gutted grapefruit, played her hands across the tops of dried grass to gather fresh water onto her fingers.

The Stationkeeper, busy amongst the debris of half-dead weeds and cut grass, smiled at her. He was content, the Colonel thought. Each day Kaufman spent a few moments studying his employers' faces. A second on Lotta, a minute on himself: it seemed he would decipher them in time.

The Stationkeeper bumbled to his feet. In the daytime his movements were ill defined.

Soon Lotta and he would issue forth again, she carrying breakfast and lunch for Captain Cartwright.

In the kitchen now, the Stationkeeper stood watching Lotta, and she in turn saw the dirt on his trousers where he had knelt to pull out weeds, and the string he held them up with, and his shrivelled hand.

Lotta presided with the authority of a priestess, Kaufman in attendance. She put the cloth in the basin, and cast a fond glance over Captain Cartwright stretched out like a plucked chicken.

'Now you are clean.'

The Captain smiled weakly and pulled up his pyjamas. 'I can do it myself, Lotta.'

'Absolute rest. Who knows. It could get worse.'

'Are you certain?' The Captain squeezed his fingers together.

'Yes.'

He raised himself on the pillows. 'Anyone would think I was dying.'

'You would have died.'

Captain Cartwright grabbed for the edge of the sheet.

The Stationkeeper watched.

'Come here, Kaufman, we will sit and talk to the Captain for a while.'

The bed was isolated from the mirrors, the faded flowers on the wallpaper, the marks where paintings had been hung and taken down again.

The Captain was isolated from his helpers by the carpets, and even when they both perched themselves on the edge of the inner-sprung mattress he was still king of his island.

'I don't want to go back into the Army. I like it here, just sleeping.'

'You must write Mrs Cartwright a letter. She will come back and look after you.'

The Captain slid down the bed.

'What do you do?' asked the Stationkeeper.

'Do? The Captain thinks of ways to recover.'

Captain Cartwright nodded.

'And,' asked Lotta, remembering her competitor, 'what does Charlotte read you?'

'Her poetry about death and love. We are going to start *The Waste Land.*'

The Stationkeeper looked down at the floor.

'I don't know what made me come to see you,' Lotta was saying. 'I'd been concerned after the party. But, back to the beginning. I had gathered flowers and was putting them in a vase on the piano and suddenly I felt . . .'

'Yes?'

'That something was the matter. I had a sense.' She searched for a word.

'Perceptive?'

'No.'

'I remember,' said the Captain. 'It's "intuitive".'

'Exactly! I feel you and I are attuned somewhere. I knew, on the night of the party, that you weren't well in your head, and then I did my best to cheer you up and take your mind off yourself.' She wiped the corner of her mouth with her handker-chief. 'It is the German in me. So I put the flowers in a vase and had a cup of tea. When I finished I was certain that something was wrong. I knocked at your door . . .'

'No,' said the Captain, 'first you met the Padre at the corner, but you didn't tell him what you were feeling, in case you were wrong.'

'*Ach* so! Yes. I met him and then I knocked.'

'I was being sick on the floor. All those aspirin tablets. I was looking first for sleeping tablets but she took them with her. They were mine. *I* had them prescribed for *me*.'

'You should have been lying in your bed. It would have been most unpleasant to find you dead with your head in the toilet bowl.'

Lotta glanced over the new curtains she'd run up with Charlotte's reluctant help, and the fresh roses. It was a cheerful room now. Dark, as befitted a sick man, but there were books, a table with a bottle of whisky on it that Mungo had donated on one of his infrequent visits. And a budgie that Lotta had ordered from Dunedin.

'Why didn't you phone a doctor?' asked the Stationkeeper, emerging from some cavernous trough. Lotta shrugged.

'We cannot afford scandal, not during the last month before the camp closes. The Colonel wouldn't want that.

'Instead I put my finger down his throat, and made him sick again. I also mixed salt and water and administered it at blood temperature. It is a very good emetic. Later I made him coffee and I sat down while he danced. I ran back for a record myself. The Captain tangoed for two hours. It helped keep him awake while his system cleared the drugs.

'What is the Colonel doing?' asked the Captain.

'Today we have the semi-finals for the platoon shoot.'

'They shoot at pictures of Asian coolies,' said the Captain, suddenly self-righteous. 'Underneath is a slogan, "This is your enemy". Charlotte drew my attention to it.'

Lotta leaned forward and he smelled her deodorant. 'There's nothing the matter with that.'

'Yes there is. You shouldn't kill.'

'It's right to kill nasty things.'

She went to the mirror to straighten her hair. Both the Stationkeeper and the Captain watched her, each differently, but in their own way implacably. Lotta, of course, could not imagine their emotions, and so, when she caught sight of them both, she was merely complimented by their attention to her coiffure.

'I like your wallpaper,' said the Stationkeeper, groping suddenly for conversation. 'I like stripes for a bedroom.'

The Captain opened his eyes and saw the walls as bars of a cage. Inside he could sing and chirrup merrily.

'She *is* drawing money out of the account. I rang the bank to ask them.'

'Don't worry. We will do everything for you to get her back. I shall write her a letter and explain . . .'

'No.' The Captain took off his glasses to show his determination. Lotta clasped her hands in perplexity.

'No.'

Lotta's cheeks reddened. She walked around the bed, swinging her basket as if she held his head inside it, wrapped up in a teatowel. 'You must write the letter then, yourself – or I'll be displeased and may take action. I may tell the Colonel he should have you seen to by someone.'

Captain Cartwright was impressed, and this allowed Lotta to kiss him on the forehead, and tuck the sheet around his meagre body, before leaving.

'Mr Kaufman,' said Lotta, deciding on the spur of the moment, 'can stay here and read to you.'

Lotta smiled at him as she felt for the latch to the front door. 'Read to him, George. Or have a man-to-man talk.'

She descended the three steps to the garden and reeled, for a second, under the impact of the sun, before she found and put on her dark glasses.

'Are you still there?' The Captain's voice was querulous, which made the Stationkeeper chuckle. For a moment he couldn't see where the Captain was.

'Read to me,' the voice demanded.

The Stationkeeper picked up the volume of *Paradise Lost* thrown towards him.

'I saw him,' said the Captain, 'through the gates, looking in. It was as if I'd been struck down with something.'

The Stationkeeper began stumbling over the long and intransigent invocation. It meant nothing to him, nor did the lordly ascendency of verbs.

'You may be clever, underneath. People sometimes are who have never learned to read, or watch television, or listen to records.' The Captain sat up. 'Let me tell you something. This place is out to destroy us. I know it is, that's why I'm in bed and that's why you look after me. Because you all know I'm the first victim.' He giggled. 'But I'll be safe here.'

Mungo smelt of aftershave lotion, and he wore the spotted silk cravat Charlotte had given him yesterday – some dust had blown into its folds. Charlotte's hair had caught in the slipstream of the car, like fine straw, winnowing.

The spasm of noise from the semi-finals of the platoon shoot had punctured their thoughts.

But now the camp was far enough away for her to stroke his head as if they belonged to each other. Above her, the sail caught by the wind moved into its own life.

It was a narrow lake, and the wind blew them along the length of it while they stared at each other's reflection, and he tasted the water: sweet, with a bite of iron and other minerals washed down from the valley.

'At night the stars would shine upwards and you would sail over them. Had you thought of that?'

He shook his head.

'The stars would be under our bodies if we sailed here at night. We would be on top of a whole galaxy. Are you listening, Mungo?'

He was watching them both in the water.

So they steered between ridges of rock like the back of a fossil and the sail lost wind.

They lay where they were, and later he made a fire among the rocks and cooked sausages on a stick of green willow. The skins blackened and fat trickled to the twig end and fell into small spurts of flame over the burning wood. He had bought a fishing

line and the thin, translucent nylon fell to the water in a long
fluid arch.

'This is where our land begins,' he told her. 'We could be
happy here. Please let's talk soon.'

'Not yet, later,' she found herself snapping.

'I'll leave the Army, buy myself out.'

She took his hand and led him back to the boat and their
clothes.

Mungo had to leave her and she clung to him, in public, but only
for a moment. The long grass around the abandoned huts had
begun to disturb her. A bulldozer had been excavating, in a
desultory manner, some of the foundations, and left the rubble
piled into hillocks, just like those on which thistle and ragwort
had already established themselves. It was a speyed landscape,
poised at a moment of fragmentation, waiting for the bricks and
concrete to be blown into dust, coating the broken glass and
hiding the rusted tin sheets.

The night wind would blow soon, and the air was soft.
National Servicemen were gathering into a group across on the
other edge of the parade ground, to catch the first breath. Where
demolition took place was out of bounds to them and she could
think at leisure. It was important to see what she and – and
Mungo? – would leave behind. Lotta, she recalled, thought of
the ruins as a bomb site. But there were no old women searching
among the gobbets of cloth and brick for broken cups or a spoon.

Across at the barracks the soldiers had noticed her. It was that
lot, hardening their eyes against the gloom to see her, who created
such wreckage as she was now among.

She leaned away from them as one whistled. The noise was
loud and peremptory, ordering her, as a woman, to come to them
and open her legs.

She smoothed down her dress and felt her neck redden. She
had to get back to headquarters, but first their thoughts had their
way with her, and she felt in her own centre the primacy of their

lusts. 'Pigs,' she whispered. 'Filthy animals.' The waste behind fed her hatred. 'Pigs, look what you've done.'

The response was another whistle, low and throbbing against her navel.

Her legs trembled as she forced herself across the asphalt to the verandah.

Colonel Leinon was giving the Padre a lift back from the shoot. They drove by stretches of grass that a month ago had been green. Now, extra water could be used only for the sprinkler in the Colonel's garden. It still turned.

But Charlotte's garden was dead. Only a few scraggy roses were alive there, and some wild-seeded poppies that grew on the new boundary between the oncoming brambles and the camp.

The Padre was polishing his glasses as a prelude to speech.

'We were wondering, the men and myself, whether, after the last exercise, a small ceremony might be in order.'

The Colonel waited.

'A ceremony of presentation. A small gift to you and Mrs Wagner – in appreciation.'

The Colonel ran his tongue rapidly over the unbrushed edges of his teeth. He braked. The Padre stepped out of the jeep and hopped from one foot to another.

Colonel Leinon shook his head. 'A lot can happen in a month, Padre.'

'Mrs Wagner is so looking forward to Vienna again.'

He looked, Hans Leinon thought with impatience, like a boy scout, an old boy scout. He should have been crying outside the gates of the camp, cursing those who sold themselves – to other gods.

Some, of course, crossed the boundary, and when they raised the body of God their arms dripped blood. But the Padre was merely a small man, out of small people. He did what he was told. After the camp closed he would go on retreat to a monastery.

Hans Leinon laughed easily and ran his hands over the grey stubble of his beard.

'Thank you for the thought, Padre. But we will all leave quietly.'

The Padre saluted the superior wisdom of his commanding officer, and marched away to hide his disappointment.

Charlotte had a fear of spiders and of webs that brushed against her, and the office was infested with the kind that leapt at its prey.

They arrived from the ceiling or wall. Wherever they were, they pursued their dinner with an inexorable sense of activity in the world. She would watch the spring in their legs as they tightened them, and, like a ballerina, found footholds in the air. Spiders that waited in webs formed part of natural hazard, those that hunted did not.

One was on her desk now, and in front of her on the blotter, a fly. A shiver of light coloured the wood a deep red, and vanished. She sucked her fingers frantically.

The spider jumped to embrace the prey, and was on it in a complete movement. She saw two small black fangs ease into the flesh behind the fly's neck. Both victim and hunter were still.

Colonel Leinon leaned over her shoulder and touched her freshly dried hair.

'You were swimming?'

'Yes. At the lake.'

'Come now,' he cupped her face with his hand, 'you mustn't be afraid.'

'Why not?'

'You are a poet. That species is reputed to look into the depths and never be frightened.'

'I am no different from other women.'

'No?'

'No.' He saw she was frightened. 'You are in love with Mungo Picton?'

'I don't know what love is. Perhaps.'

'You want him for marriage. It would please your mother, Natalia. She always said you should be a farmer's wife.'

She looked up at him for the first time that day.

'So she can spend more time in Ben's entourage.'

'I see he's released some Beethoven Sonatas. I've bought the first disk.'

'Yes.'

'Call me Hans.'

She shook her head. He knew she remembered the swimming pool, and the memory she had hoped to drown had floated up.

'My dear,' he took her hand painlessly and briefly, 'we of all people must try to be honest.'

They left the building together, with a soft measure to their step.

'Where do you want to go?'

They were bound for the acres just outside the camp.

She watched clouds carefully as they took the path past Lotta's window, as it seemed right to challenge the certainty they both now shared. If Lotta looked up from the meal they could see her preparing and called to them, then they would be proved wrong. But she didn't. Even the magpies among the elms, a parliament on any evening, were quiet.

He helped her over the barbed-wire fence and through blackberry bushes and wild thorn trees.

Below them was a gravel pit.

'Let's go down there.' She pointed at the empty rifle cartridges amongst the hemlock.

Charlotte waited while he lit a cigarette, then he asked: 'I want to know if you are pregnant. It is very important for me.'

Charlotte picked up a quartz pebble.

'My period's late.'

'I am the father.'

'No.'

'I am the child's father.' He sat down beside her. 'You know I must be.'

The thick green fronds of the plants they sat among smelt sour and acrid, like old urine. He stuck his finger into the sand as far as it would go but encountered only the drought that was everywhere.

'They put down a tap-root, these hemlock plants,' she said. 'I saw a soldier digging one up. The root is like a carrot, the leaves are like carrot leaves, but they're poisonous.' She could think of nothing else to share with him.

He kissed her.

'It is my child, but you will bring it up as Picton's. He has blond hair like mine, and blue eyes.'

She thought of men dictating their last testament. Like so much of the Colonel, it seemed Teutonic hot air. It was different, but similar to Natalia.

'Tonight I will come to your place and bring a parcel. You will give him the contents when he is twenty.'

'How can you be so sure?'

He pulled her down beside him, kissed her hard on the throat and ran his hand under her dress and up her thighs.

'Yes,' she said, fearful. 'Yes, it's true.'

'I will stay only a few moments with you, but you will think of me and how our child was conceived.'

'You bastard,' she said, hoping her period would start but knowing it wouldn't.

He began to walk up the bank. At the top he stood and looked down at her.

'Lotta has written a letter for Captain Cartwright to copy. It is to Mrs Cartwright. It is a plea for Mrs Cartwright to return to her lawful spouse. I am to dictate it to the Captain. Imagine, my dear Charlotte, the Captain would be dead if it were not for my Lotta's intuition. She, of course, owns his body now. We all must have our puppets so our voices can be heard. I suppose it is essential for both Cartwright and Lotta that he stays mad.'

In fact, the only aspect of humanity the Colonel could have associated with himself at that moment was pain – a niggle of pain around his right nipple and then in the centre of his chest.

Back along the road no curtain moved. There were only the blank windows – eyes to the departed middle-class soul – and interiors of flowered wallpaper, stains from the hands of small children.

Here and there, a length of ripped curtain material hung from its rod. Sometimes a window was open, and around it grew one of the ubiquitous climbing roses, the hallmark of the Brigadier's taste in flowers, which Lotta had faithfully copied. The gentler influences of the Brigadier's wife were marked by the choice of glass panelling for the front doors: a deer etched in acid standing against a mountain, some clouds, and for variation, a deer standing against a tree with a cloud. The animals were in various states of repair, some cracked from antler to antler, others with faces shattered by stones.

At Captain Cartwright's gate he kicked a half-perished ball into the middle of the lawn where on every other day Lotta emptied the stale water from the flower vase.

The Colonel walked softly through the dark hall into the bedroom.

'Captain Cartwright?'

The shape in the bed didn't turn. He moved closer and his heart accelerated. 'Of course he is alive.' He heard his own whisper to himself or the Captain, from a distance, and was jerked back into himself by the pain around the centre of his chest: short and sharp like a chisel working with a hammer.

'Heart,' he heard himself whisper. He felt breath pass out through his lips, and, in case it was his very essence leaving before its time – something he couldn't believe – he sucked hard and caught it, forcing it back into the net of veins and the soft capillaries, fluttering and opening like acute sea creatures.

He strained to see shape, but made do with movement and felt himself floating over the waves of carpet that flowed by beneath his feet.

Somewhere he heard a giggle coming from far off; a light had come on; he moved through that thick cloud towards it, but it veered from him and space became a nutshell; with him at the centre he was whirled back from the void into the cloud.

Someone giggled more foolishly.

Hans Leinon opened his eyes to find himself lying across the bed. Captain Cartwright was looking at him from the vantage point of an established invalid; his expression was professional.

'Are you not well. The heat of the day . . .'

'Get me a drink,' the Colonel told his subordinate.

The Captain scampered for the whisky bottle and poured out a generous slug. He returned holding his pyjama trousers up, individual brown pubic hairs sticking out from the gaping fly.

Colonel Leinon glanced at himself in the mirror. He looked as if he had just stepped out of a bath, even his hair was damp with sweat.

Captain Cartwright sat down beside him and laid his hand on the Colonel's forehead: 'None of us are getting any younger. We shouldn't strain ourselves.' With this advice the Captain climbed back between the fresh cotton sheets.

'Why is the light on?' asked the Colonel. 'It isn't dark yet.'

'You didn't seem to be able to find your way.'

'Rubbish!'

'I agree,' said the Captain, 'that one must enjoy the evening light. Mrs Wagner told me so.'

The Colonel remembered and took Lotta's letter from his breast pocket. 'I have here the letter my sister says you should write to your wife.'

The Captain giggled. 'Let me read it.' He took his time, scanning each word for hidden meanings. Finally he gave it back and giggled again. 'Dictate it to me. It will have to be in my handwriting. My wife would not be convinced by Mrs Wagner masquerading as me.'

'Your wife must have loved you – once,' said Hans Leinon, surprising even himself.

The Captain didn't deign a reply but put pen to paper expectantly.

The Colonel began:

'"My dearest Janet, I am most displeased at what you've done to me. It is despicable and cruel. I've given you the best years of my life, and now, when you are most needed by me you run away. You cannot run away from the best years we had together. Also, there are my children . . ." Are you with me, Captain?'

He wondered how Mrs Cartwright would feel about this passionate missive.

'Almost,' said Captain Cartwright, and finished writing out 'Ba ba, black sheep'.

The Colonel continued: 'I still need you, the house is too quiet'.

The line gave the Captain another thought and he began Eskimo Nell: 'When a man grows old and his balls turn cold . . .'

He listened vaguely to Hans Leinon, and occasionally where grammar or sense demanded it, corrected him. He wrote, for his own part, 'Fuck Janet Cartwright and the Army'. Hans Leinon droned on about 'new faith' and 'strength' while the Captain wrote with great flourishes, 'Hell Bitch', and ended with some free association.

' "I remain your loving and forgiving husband",' said the Colonel. 'Now, give it to me.' The Captain obeyed.

The Colonel, being well brought up, simply sealed it in a pre-typed envelope Lotta had supplied. 'I'll give the letter to Charlotte Pearce, the next mail leaves on the train tomorrow night.' He rubbed his hand across his chest. 'I suggest you say nothing of my – giddy spell – to my sister. It would worry her.' He left the Captain, fallen back with closed eyes, on the pillows.

At the corner he stopped. A quirk of the night brought from the barracks the sound of a guitar. Now and then a harmonica joined it, wavered a few notes and wheezed into silence.

He waited. Dead grass rustled and twisted against his feet with implacable infertility, yet the music played on, and the brown dust hues of the plain were reflected wherever his eyes sought to escape from them, and as the young musician played the Colonel began to know that his interior being waited beyond anything so mundane as exhaustion, and lived in a sense which only the initiated could experience.

But the empty window frames, the cracked glass doors, were obstacles to any vision. He looked away from the ruins where the Army had departed.

The plain, on the contrary, was prepared to receive whatever waste emotion or constructive act he chose to perform. Everything would be lost in it, baked by it, fired or broken and left as something less than ash. In some way he could never take up space there.

One single note drew him into a compact centre where all his actions were reflected in on each other with a dazzling sense of egoism.

And so his vision annihilated him for a moment as he realized how far he had to walk through that plain, and how far away was the water where that would dissolve. Yet the board and the pool continued to draw him, and if by a miracle he could let go of himself as he knew it, he would be saved in that dissolution when all walls are washed away.

Yet, with the sun gone and the music, and the field a mass of dried grass, rustling like the starched skirts of his childhood, he longed for a son who would be what he hadn't been and would triumph in his flesh over the weakness of his father.

So he walked, during the crisis of the moment, to the head-quarters, where he, after all, ruled the roost.

The flag was down from the pole and it was dark as he walked into his office.

The filing cabinet was the same green as the walls. It looked as if it were covered with mildew, but only in damp climates did things rot away. Here they dried out and kept their husk long after life had departed, like the artillery shell on his desk, of bright polished brass, that tonight pointed up at the roof as if its old power had been restored. He had had it with him since the Russian campaign.

The Colonel wiped his face free of sweat and left.

His preoccupations departed with the numinous quiet of the evening. For a moment he thought he saw someone watching him, or at least the shadow of somebody, but he dismissed such phenomena along with his heart attack. He dismissed, too, a sudden sense of defeat as he considered the other paths that he might have taken, or been led along.

Ahead of him, in the present moment, was the steamy warmth of the bathhouse. Silhouetted in the doorway one of his soldiers, plastic under the light, bent forwards and slapped his knee. The air around him was opalescent.

Hans Leinon pulled a comb from his pocket and ran it through his hair. He trotted forward a few paces. The steam drifted through the door and rolled into the night.

The men were singing, he heard them through the water hitting the concrete floor. He crept to the opening and saw one of them, naked, lying under the shower and soaping his belly. He was singing, deep in his throat:

'She's a lesbian and he's a queer.
Dear Colonel Leinon.
Kraut as they come . . .'

Colonel Leinon retreated to the point where the refuse water was discharged into the drain. There, an outjutting wall protected him and he could see through a hole into the shower.

A dark-haired soldier was in his line of vision. He spoke.

'Comes around at night when the guys are getting into bed. Doing his arse selection.'

The Colonel cringed but wondered if all relationships based on domination and submission were not a form of spiritual sodomy. This also disturbed him as he did not want to have to analyse himself in this light. There wasn't enough time left.

'I am just a poor Kraut
Who likes to knock about
With the Padre.
My sister's too big for me
To have a dig.
And so I frig and frig,
With the Padre.'

It was sung to 'God Save The Queen', and because Hans Leinon could not pretend to want a country he also laughed.

Cheers had greeted this new attempt, and for a moment the Colonel felt nineteen again.

'And his little talks about democracy.' The soldier imitated the Colonel on his first Sunday morning address. '"Democracy is not the best form of government, but all others are worse." Do you know, he cribbed that from a television show.'

The Colonel blushed and admitted it to himself.

'How can a cunt like that talk about democracy? I mean, everyone knows he bloody sucked up to Hitler.'

Someone else spoke with a trace of condescension: 'He'd love to drag us all off to war. Some people have got to risk death, like racing drivers, it's compulsion. It's the strange paradox of military men, they have never escaped from the nursery, and because they are crippled they have to stimulate life by risking death.'

Near Hans Leinon's nipple a pain started again. The water hitting the ground reminded him of Malaya – a raid against a terrorist camp to recapture five men. He had freed two of the New Zealand soldiers, no older than these boys. The other three had died under torture. He would include that story in his next little talk, a little reminiscence would underline the reasons for their training.

He applied his eye to the hole again. The one with black hair now lay under the water as if it were perfumed essence. 'Here we are, making up stupid songs.'

He sounded miserable, homesick for his girl, perhaps?

'*Your* stupid song,' someone replied.

They had taken fright and were allotting guilt.

'I'd like to throw him and his slobby sister into the bloody ocean, and leave them to float on her blubber to Germany or Vietnam.'

'He needs us.'

'I think you've got a point there, Tom Green. Are you coming?'

'I'll wait a bit,' said Tom.

'Wanking time?' asked the languid voice of his friend.

They came out to the dressing shed and the Colonel pressed himself against the concrete.

The remaining soldier was strangely white – perhaps it was the mist billowing up from where he lay on the floor. The Colonel felt he was in a dream, especially as the others had turned out the main light and the echoes of farewell to their friend already had jumbled into silence around his head.

He could see the soldier's hand poised in indecision above his groin, as if their joking suggestion was working a power on him. The soldier moved his head away from the spray and for a moment stroked the slack skin of his penis, then he covered himself, like a petal folding across a stamen. And added to this modesty by closing his eyes.

Hans Leinon felt pain. He also felt like a youth who watches his own brother naked in his sleep and who protects his secret thoughts. Yet the image changed, and just as easily he saw Green's whitish tripes stinking and oozing and mixing with the earth, presided over by the blue sky, and perhaps a cherry tree in bridal colours of white and pink.

For those Polish peasants it must have been an age between their sentence and being shot backwards into their graves.

The Colonel saw Green as one who had just fallen. He wept for him, for all men since Adam, and understood the warp that he had now exposed with his memory. No man could join another's life while enclosed in the chrysalis of a name and tribe.

He opened his mouth wide and gulped in air to keep himself quiet. No man could feel the reality of another's pain or need since the chrysalis was also the ego and it was driven by the laws of the jungle. Its false entity had masked from him his own compassion for himself and others.

He walked back down the changing shed to the entry, and looked in. He wished to be friendly, but when the other saw him he knew, by his eyes, that he couldn't be. It would be impolite to act out of the part they needed to put him in.

'Taking your time showering tonight, soldier?'

The other nodded and stood up.

The Colonel's glance travelled casually over him as dealers do at stock fairs.

'Enjoy the Army, soldier?'

There was an imperceptible nod of the head.

'What's your name?'

'Green, sir.'

'I see. Flex your arm, let me see how you're shaping. Good. Ready for the fight?'

'Yes, sir.'

The soldier's fear was back but was impersonal, and there was a wariness, as if he might spring back behind the curtain of water and vanish. The Colonel didn't want to provoke this, so he stepped out the door.

He let himself in without Lotta hearing and went to his room. He emptied out the top drawer of his chest of drawers and picked up the case with the medals. This he wrapped up in brown paper, along with his rosary and other bits and pieces and found some string to parcel them together.

Charlotte met him in her hall. She wore a light skirt and a blouse that buttoned up to the neck, with an old cameo at her throat, and had done her hair in a French roll. She motioned him into the living room. The remains of her supper were on the table, a candle lit, the curtains partly drawn.

'I've come with the things,' he said.

She took the parcel and stood facing him.

'I should tell you about myself, and my family.'

'Will you sit down.' She motioned him to a chair. 'Perhaps you would like a drink. There is some whisky. Also Martel cognac.'

Von Leinon noticed the tension in her face as she put aside his parcel, but he was too absorbed by the moment to think about it.

He ate a snack she insisted on giving him, drank wine and told her jokes. When, at last, he excused himself from the room for a moment, she stood up to distance herself from the relics he had spread before her. She couldn't take her eyes off the painting, a miniature of himself – at about sixteen, he said. His eyes were piercing and warm and his face was held together by a delicate but high bone structure. His grandmother had been a Hungarian.

Charlotte clasped her hands together and wondered how strong she could be. Then she remembered Natalia's clean sweep of her own reliques and the little girls queening by in Dashkov memories.

Through the windows the night, velvet black, held back the dead light from the stars. Her mind had been caught between his will and her own intuition that, being a sensible woman, she called common sense. It had remained inert at the centre of those two contrary forces, as everything around her caught into a motion so fast that she had almost forgotten who she was. He was a storyteller, a magician, she the hapless captive of his tale. And the story, she realized, had been told in order to imprison her in its meaning.

With what care he had led her through the geography of his mind, as if she were to live with him always! And, she would refuse him the indulgence.

He poured another vodka for her.

She let the medals slide through her fingers onto the Brigadier's mahogany table.

'You want yourself in me Hans, so you can go happy. But, Hans, that is wrong. My child should be free of your obsessions.'

Her face reflected in the polished wood.

Charlotte began to weep. She could see the snow wastes of the Russian front, the plains of ice across which this strange youth had crawled towards the enemy.

'You've made an old woman of me,' she said, to the handsome youth of sixteen in the miniature. She straightened out the medals as the Colonel sat down opposite her.

'I have been a man who hasn't given love,' he told her. 'That is why I accomplished nothing, and that is why I had to be here.'

She saw and wept for him, but at a vast distance, and went to her room where there was a bundle of her poems and would-be poems. She recognized them for the small green fruit that they were. She looked in the mirror at her pleasant face. She came back.

The front door was half open, and the night around them was comforting in the presence of moths batting against the window.

On a space, in the middle of a flower bed, she dug a hole, and beside it she made a heap of papers.

For the last time she addressed herself to his image. She took it from its frame and placed it on top of her offering. 'I don't suppose my poems are worth much but . . .'

She waited, kneeling on the dry earth, and he came beside her, his hand, out of habit in a crisis, steady.

It took only one match to start the bonfire.

She watched to see that it caught properly, and then dropped his medals, one by one, into the hole and covered them up. She covered them as a small flame crept onto the top sheet and the words sank into ash. The fire was away, leaping straight up with no strange twists or turns in the flame. The painting curled up, yellowed and burned.

She heard him walk away down the path and shut the gate quietly behind him.

Lotta had been preparing a salad for dinner: the pineapple and banana were arranged, the apple freshly cut and soaked in white rhenish wine, and the lettuce crisp in a wet towel, sliced fine and firm without losing its juice. On top of the pineapple she laid a neat circle of tomato and egg, quartered with ruthless abandon. A smaller bowl of potatoes lay white and glistening with her special herb dressing.

The kitchen table was covered by a blue cloth, and in the centre, two wooden candlesticks from Denmark.

She filled the wine glasses with sauterne. It was all that she could find.

The clock had moved to six. She had kept her eyes on the second hand as it reached the hour and thought, as it did, she heard the door. But Hans did not call out to ask how dinner was going, so it was her cat, or a board creaking. That took her mind off the salad dressing and she went to change into her dress for the evening. When she returned to the kitchen the beauty of her table forced a gasp from her, whose inspiration lasted until she sat down at the piano.

The cat arrived.

'Good pussy cat.' She had drawn her fingers through its fur. 'So hot for pussy cat!' The perspiration moved in runlets down her back, the silk stuck to her nylon slip.

'A lovely dinner for your father,' Lotta had announced to the basilisk eyes of her companion. 'Won't he be happy to have such a lovely dinner, with ham that pussy cats love, don't they?'

Her jocular tone was forced, for tonight she had exerted herself in response to some nervous fluttering in her breast. Tonight she wanted to prove to Hans, with her food, how much she loved him.

'Soon you'll be a lovely Viennese pussycat with a home in the country or perhaps in town. I wonder if things have changed much. And there will be lots of little birds to chase instead of those nasty fat magpies. Pussies can chase Viennese birdies without being frightened or being pecked.'

She followed the cat to the door and up to her bedroom where it jumped on the bed and stretched out.

She caught sight of herself in the bedroom mirror, and to be distracted from what she saw she reached for the opera glasses and trained them on the swimming pool. The sun had gone and only some vapour, pearl pink, traced out its descent.

The Padre was on the diving board and obviously regretting his decision. She adjusted the lenses and chuckled at his humility and white skin.

His bathing suit was a long woollen creation: he held the sides of it, frightened, as he tiptoed along the board.

She turned the glasses towards Charlotte's house and wished she had not.

In a dream she had walked down the steps and hardly needed to adjust to the heat. She had waved her amethyst ring with disdain as she clasped the knitting bag in her hand and set off across the field.

When she found herself at headquarters she had been surprised at herself. The typewriters in the girls' office were concealed under their black plastic covers. The doorhandle to the Colonel's office was brightly polished and had turned easily.

Lotta did not know what she expected to find, but seeing nothing relaxed her. She sighed noisily and sat down at the desk to do a row of knitting.

She blew her nose and felt dizzy.

Blindly, but with her other senses alert, she had pushed her way into the open and tittuped to the field nearest the boundary of the camp. She had sat down on the earth. 'But of course it isn't possible,' she said, startled, to the Stationkeeper's cat as it leaned and rubbed against her. 'It is not possible. Not *my* Hans and Natalia's daughter.'

But the cat, finding her, deflected her purpose. It was no longer simple to return and wait for the Colonel to come for his food. It was not even easy to sit where she was, although that cat gave her an excuse. She threw it a spare ball of wool.

'Is it fun, pussy cat?' She watched it bunt and throw the ball and catch it in its claws. 'It knows me,' she thought, 'through and through.'

Lotta looked at the wool, covered in burs. 'I might as well leave it here for you.' She picked up the knitting and put it in her flowered felt bag.

As she walked away the cat left his new toy and chased after her, jumping in the air in strange little arches and then trotting ahead, its tail straight and quivering.

'So foolish,' she said. 'I'm quite wrong.' But, strangely, her feet carried her over the grass in the direction of Charlotte's quarters.

A light shone from what she knew to be the dining room and she went towards it, blind, like a moth: the flowering snapdragons, the waist-high remains of poppies giving way.

The Colonel was leaning against a wall, a glass in his hand. Lotta shifted closer.

Charlotte was looking up and she was telling him something of importance. Her face was white. The Colonel, on the other hand, listened and was cracked open by her words. She had never seen the face he wore for Charlotte Pearse.

With a little cry Lotta fled the view, certain that, if they knew she'd seen, somehow she would suffer for it.

She ran all the way to the salad, the sauterne and the pineapples and banana, and the fresh crisp lettuce. She threw herself at them and began to eat, but suddenly she couldn't any more. Her stomach, the uneasy repository for her fear, pressed and ached.

In the bathroom, she wiped the corner of her mouth with the Colonel's face cloth, and sat down on the lavatory. She looked at the pattern on her frilly pants and the fold of fat from her belly to her thighs.

Her skin was still cold when she pulled the chain.

Afterwards she tried to sing while she changed her dress for a blue cotton cocktail frock and slipped into a pair of blue silk stockings she had kept from before the war.

The lawn had cracked and her heels broke the loose clods into powder. Her balance tonight was good, she swayed only on the downwards incline to the rough ground.

Ahead was the swimming pool, but she might have been making an entrance at an exclusive garden party.

Lotta held her handbag under her arm and pushed against her ribs. She kept her head high and still managed, by some radar effect, to miss the clumps of tussock. Her steps were dainty, but the bag was heavy, weighed down by the Colonel's Luger which he always kept loaded in the kitchen drawer.

She was uncertain why she required such ballast, for the weight was out of proportion to her, and of a different order, but she felt herself in control of the spaces ahead.

She scarcely glanced at the barbed-wire fence, but stood for a moment in front of the gate into the pool. Tonight, however, it was only a concrete tank.

She turned away from the only redeeming smell – the rose in its tub by the changing sheds – and moved towards the plantation. The pines were the same as those she remembered on a holiday at Kranebitten.

She wandered among them. Above her, the tree points were green and dark. The wind induced the tips to bend and sway and she herself swelled out with dreams and faces and memories, all gold of course, but such cruelty in their lips, and the lines etched in their faces – or masks.

The Colonel, she thought, in sudden panic, would understand this, since this is what *they* both looked like tonight – a little. Of course, not *really* . . .

But she was caught, so she ran from pine trunk to pine trunk. 'Go away,' she called out. 'Leave me alone. I'm just a housewife.' She took her bag in her hand and lashed out at trees and green branches born down with cone as if, that way, she would destroy them.

And found herself through a hole in the boundary fence.

She caught her breath and welcomed the flush of heat that spread around her nipples and belly. 'I must see a doctor,' she told the plain.

She skirted a rubbish dump and an abandoned car, plunged through the gravel piled up around a few dummy gun emplacements, and at last the road to the station was under her feet.

She looked up the track to the signal box. The signal flashed red as she stood on the platform. She dabbed some perfume on the pulse points of her throat and wrists.

The rails began to vibrate.

She stood close to the edge of the line, swaying with indecision.

Suddenly the engine light came into view; like truth, like dreams it rushed towards her.

Lotta forgot her worries.

The speed of the approach meant it would not stop.

She clutched her handbag, and with her other hand kept down her dress.

She was beneath the signboard which gave those who were passing the name of the camp. She raised a hand and found herself smiling at the brief, blurred shapes in the window.

She hoped that someone would look out and recognize her and wave.

'You wanting that train, Mrs Wagner?'

'Oh Kaufman.' She quickly patted her hair. 'I was coming to see *you*, but the train came through.'

He took her hand.

'I thought I would go and look at your new sofa cover.'

'It's red. It's the colour you said would go well with the carpet. It's got a kind of oriental design.'

She squeezed his arm as they walked down the house path. 'I've always liked oriental things. In Vienna I had a screen that came from the Imperial Palace in Peking. There was a rebellion and German soldiers were sent to protect the Europeans. I expect they looted it, naughty things.'

'Come in for a cup of tea.'

She pirouetted in the doorway while he picked her some carrot thinnings.

She hoped he would notice her dress.

'Do you like it? I wore it specially for this little visit. It goes with my blonde hair.'

He finished rolling up the hose.

I can have my own life, she thought as she plunged into an exclamation over the sofa cover. She sat down and bounced a little. The springs creaked as she settled into a corner.

The Stationkeeper went to the sink to fill the kettle.

'Are you going to make tea for me, George?'

He turned to catch the flutter of her eyelashes, and reached for the tea caddy he kept the biscuits in.

The kettle was blackened and burnished.

'The room is greatly improved. It is remarkable what we girls can accomplish with a little advice.'

On the mantelpiece was the photograph he had taken of her a few months before. He had put it at last in a bright-red frame.

'What can happen to us?' he asked.

She blushed like a young girl.

'How can I be yours while the Colonel is alive? He would never allow it. The Colonel is *alive* and I am bound to him by fate.' She was comforted by the idea of destiny. 'It is cruel. So cruel.' She picked up her handbag, deciding against tea.

Guided by the light of the torch he shone ahead of her from his doorway, she picked her way over a rake and reached the gate.

The dust road to the camp was like flour.

The light from Charlotte's room beckoned her, and to be an equal with it and with what she might see, she grasped the Colonel's Luger firmly in her hand.

It gave her the edge yet it was inconceivable to fire it. So, disdainfully, and although it was loaded, she dropped it, and hoped that the catch would continue to be effective after the grasses had covered it and rust had eaten through the metal and the bullets. She sailed out the gate and shut it.

She patted the bonnet of Charlotte's car as she passed.

Mungo would visit Charlotte as usual – later.

Everything would be as it was last night.

The Colonel must have got drunk.

And why had she put on a special dress to visit George? *Ach*! She patted the rhinestones inset on the ivory clasp of her bag. The moon still shone with its absurdly clear light. Over the field there looked to be someone running, and in her house the Colonel was listening to Benedict Pearse-Dashkov's rendition of the Pathétique Sonata.

She crept away but had to return for one last look.

Under the elm tree she sat down and shivered, wiping her face with the back of her hand. 'Dear God. Dear God.' Her mind baulked at continuing the petition, as she could not think what would complete her prayer. Instead she decided she would go to Dunedin for a medical check up. Mungo would drive her down as he had business with the Army – terminating his commission.

The Stationkeeper had followed Lotta down the road, at a safe distance. He could tell from her walk, and the way she was swaying from one side of the road to the other, talking to herself, that she was upset.

He waited for Lotta in Charlotte's garden, his cat under his shirt, and saw the gun fall from her hand.

And he saw Charlotte, sitting at a table, her hair undone, a bottle and glass in front of her.

He picked the Luger up.

The cat purred and cried, arching its tail and stepping proud through the moonlight.

4

Colonel Leinon slept under the elm tree, the leaves of which remained, with Christian hope, green and lush. He woke up and looked between the branches and saw someone staring out of the window. Bemused, he stared back, studying the light falling onto a pair of half-exposed and over-ripe breasts. Then he remembered where he was. He waved to Lotta.

It was time to visit Captain Cartwright, who tomorrow would be taken away. The Colonel walked off on his errand.

The gate swung in a shiver of wind.

He knew he would find the Captain at least the same.

As was his custom, he walked in through the back door. The smell of artichokes lay in heavy green pools around the sink. The hall, dark as usual, covered him like a cloak till he stepped into the Captain's bedroom where the budgie strutted and fretted along his perch, chirruping at a bell he rang.

Captain Cartwright was propped up by cushions and pillows, Lotta's angora wool bedjacket draped carelessly across his shoulders.

The Colonel had difficulty in seeing him in any serious role, but persevered.

'How are you feeling?'

'I am not at all tired, thank you.'

The budgie chirruped, 'Bloody bitch. Hell cat. Fuck hell.'

'It swears,' said the Captain modestly.

The budgie brooded.

'You need a holiday, Captain?'

'Silly,' said the Captain, picking up his knitting, 'I'm quite happy here.' He tossed a pompom aside for greater mobility. 'Knitting never seems finished. Each day it is as if someone had undone it during the night.'

'Like Penelope,' the Colonel suggested, and he sat in the easy chair by the drinks, pouring himself a gin.

He drew back the curtains.

The Captain clicked his tongue. 'I would rather have the curtains drawn, there's nothing to look at anyway that I haven't seen before.'

The Colonel raised his hand, possibly threateningly, for it seemed the Captain's monologue would stretch past the time he could allow it.

But the Captain ignored him, bathed now in light.

Colonel Leinon accepted that as a victim he was immaculate. The Colonel got up and put his half-finished gin on the drinks table.

The Captain called out, 'Goodbye,' as if one of them was going on a longer journey than the other, and giggled, while the needles clicked and clacked and clacked.

Hans Leinon was relieved, when walking out, to meet Lotta.

'How is our patient Hans.'

'He is patient.'

Lotta giggled and changed her basket to her other arm. 'I've made him some soup.'

'Isn't it too hot?'

'Vichyssoise. Anyway, he is a lot better.' Lotta addressed the listening shadow of the Captain in the window. 'And I've bought him a little present from town, just like yours.'

'A tie?'

'Yes.'

Lotta pecked the Colonel's cheek. 'I've left your supper on the kitchen table: some soup, fresh scones, a cucumber salad, cold lamb.'

'Mint jelly?'

'Yes, my dear.'

They parted.

Captain Cartwright jumped back into bed as Lotta sailed into the room.

Charlotte had told her about the events around the pool, the night of the party. But that only added to things. She could never again see the pool in the same light.

'What's the matter,' asked the Captain.

'It's about the pool,' dithered Lotta. 'Too difficult and not for invalids.'

The Captain poopooed. 'That,' he said, 'I know all about that. Charlotte told me too. They dive and then they come to a banqueting hall. Then there are lovers each holding an egg. I think Charlotte exaggerates. No one came to truth by diving, all you do is hit your head on the bottom.'

But it was still too much for Lotta. Because Charlotte had changed as had the Colonel. Fortunately Mungo didn't know and never would. Anything, really.

Lotta decided to spill the beans.

'Now, that's enough,' said the Captain. 'We are not *there* now.' He started crying.

Lotta fished in her handbag for a handkerchief.

'I'm frightened,' the Captain wailed, for a moment wondering about destiny.

'The Colonel is a good man, he will never do anything against the higher interest.'

By now, as the course wound down, all activity took place in the early morning, before the sun was too far up, or in the evening when it had set.

The morning after the visit Lotta and the Stationkeeper simulated happiness. They sat in deckchairs under the weeping elm and had their cup of tea.

For work, there were the peas to pod. In their white enamel basin they were an antidote to thinking, as was the shadow of the Colonel, descending to their level.

The Stationkeeper and Lotta watched his hooded eyes. Kaufman, who loved her more than anything else except his cat, could tell she was perturbed. She moved the rings around her fingers, looking for some stray light. She stared towards the swimming pool and wet her lips.

Even so, she managed to wave to the Colonel as he disappeared in the direction of the Captain's house.

For a moment the tea repeated on her.

'Tell me, George, did you like the tie I bought for you?'

'Yes.'

'The colours are the same for my three men, my colours really. I have always liked blue and gold and cream. Silk of course.'

The Stationkeeper belched quietly. 'What'll we do today?'

'We can start on the peas, but not too soon as they are for lunch. After that . . . You must understand, George.' She picked up his cup. 'It's because we are leaving.'

A long, well-polished black car swept by on the road, but Lotta was too intent on giving soft glances to Kaufman so as to fit him into the morning and the expense of boredom.

To the Colonel, waiting with Mungo in the shadow of the ruined house, the car looked like a hearse. It slid to the curb, the tyres flattening a scurrying lizard.

Colonel Leinon glanced at his watch. On time to the minute. He put his baton smartly under his arm and waited with a cultivated alertness. Mrs Cartwright could have been a visiting general.

A man climbed out first. 'This,' said Mrs Cartwright from inside the car, 'is the clinic doctor, Charles Davidson.'

They shook hands.

Mrs Cartwright, wearing the darkest of glasses so that not

even the sun could penetrate her disguise, stepped onto the pavement.

'I'm sure I'm doing the right thing,' she said, surveying what had been her house. 'This is not a mistake.' She took the arm offered her by the Colonel.

The procession formed itself naturally behind.

'I imagined Mrs Wagner would have been here,' Mrs Cartwright suggested.

'It might upset her nerves.'

'This is the only thing to be done.'

The curtains in Captain Cartwright's room shimmered as Mrs Cartwright opened her bag, took out the key, and fitted it into the door. 'Is the injection ready?'

'Let me go first,' the Colonel suggested.

The hall, dark and enfolding, sucked him in, and he felt like an advance scouting party. A certain weakness in his bowels and a slow cramp there told him he was excited.

The others followed him into the bedroom.

The budgie, struck by a ray of sun through a fanlight, was singing and swearing. It cocked its head to one side.

Captain Cartwright opened his mouth and put his hand over it. 'Janet? Janet. You've come back?'

She took off her glasses.

The Captain licked his lips and stiffened like a corpse in the bed.

Mungo lifted a corner of the curtain. He watched so intently he too could have been looking for omens.

The Colonel joined him.

Captain Cartwright had decided to placate. He held out his knitting for his wife's inspection. 'I've been knitting you a jumper, Janet. It will be finished in a week or so, when the camp closes. We'll be able to take it with us. To our next posting.'

The re-entry into reality was causing the Captain strain. His face was white and he sweated. 'I'm sure you'll like it. Here' – he pushed it towards her – 'take it now. Look at it.'

Who, after all, was to blame?

The doctor held up a needle. He forced it into the phial and drew back the plunger.

'I'm not having an injection.' Captain Cartwright shook his head like an animal with a rotten tooth 'This is my house. My house and Janet's. Tell them to get out, Janet. I suppose you have the kids in the car. Whose car is it? I saw . . .'

'For God's sake give him the injection.'

The budgie fluttered in its cage.

'Why must I have an injection?'

'Because,' said the doctor, with the smooth euphemism of his species, 'you're going to a rest home.'

Neither Mungo nor even the Colonel, whatever their purpose, could have managed such untruth. The doctor, however, was not annhilated by their cold looks. Beyond attack, he could afford, as usual, to feel nothing.

Captain Cartwright wondered how best he could delay them. Lotta must arrive soon. She would save him. With one thrust of her bosom they would be swept out of the door.

'Now, now.' The doctor, the needle dripping, crept towards the Captain.

The Colonel would harry and tear flesh, but he would never play false with it.

'You slimy creature,' shrieked the Captain.

'Hold out your arm.'

Captain Cartwright rolled away to the other side of the bed. He shook his head from side to side.

Mungo wanted to vomit because he didn't know what he should do.

'We'll commit you, Jimmy,' said Janet Cartwright.

Distracted, the Captain rolled his head towards his wife.

The driver leapt upon him, and forced out his arm for the needle. The doctor drove it in. Blood swirled and streamed in the cartridge.

For the split second it took for the doctor to press down on the cartridge they were part of each other. A perfect circuit was formed and the reason was sufficient – with an act of imagination.

'Lotta,' screamed the Captain, like a rabbit caught and antic-
ipating its broken neck.

The doctor massaged the arm for a moment.

'We'll have to admit him.'

The Captain didn't reply. He had become impersonal and the
Colonel, to overcome embarassment, thought of him as a corpse,
capable of eructations of wind, which might, in certain situations,
be moulded into language.

They pulled the Captain out of bed.

'It's for your own good. For the good of . . .'

The sedative was working.

'Pack his toilet articles. Make him put on the dressing gown.'

But the Captain had understood what he should do, the drug
had helped him to see. He held out his arms like a scarecrow
and waited.

The Colonel at this point left. He needed no further education.

Mungo watched while they sorted shirts, underpants, sifted
out a jock strap, a packet of French letters, and a sperm-stiffened
handkerchief. Into the suitcase was placed a suit, some sports
clothes, two jerseys.

'Will you please sign the Army release form.' Mrs Cartwright
addressed Mungo. 'Your Colonel expects you to cooperate.'

'Does he?'

He picked up the pen. There was almost no point in not
submitting – except for a second of illumination in the room,
emanating perhaps from the Captain's eyes.

For a moment Mungo understood. He placed the pen back on
the table, beside the three-quarters-empty gin bottle. 'You bitch.'
He said each word distinctly. 'You stinking bitch.' But his vision
could not take him past the moment. He could only comment,
like a good newspaper headline, on the situation.

Janet Cartwright took the pen back. 'It was only a technicality
anyway.'

The procession retreated down the path to the car. The Captain, in the middle of them, seemed to think he was on comapny
parade. His arms swung smartly.

Lotta was still shelling peas as the car came slowly by. Very slowly it seemed. Lotta walked to the curb and put on the correct smile.

Captain Cartwright, sitting by the open window, seized his last chance. 'Lotta, Lotta!' His head suddenly came out. He held on to the door handles with all his strength.

'Lotta. They are destroying me. Don't let them. Don't let them!'

He clung to her outstretched hand. She had no time to think. No time to reason what was right. She leapt forward. 'Darling. Wait.' She began to run. 'Come back you pigs! You murderers, bring him back!'

'They're taking me away.'

'Come back!' She ran across the dried turf, almost blown to dust.

The car merely accelerated. And she had no strength even to wave. She heard one last scream as the car turned up towards the station. She rubbed her bare feet frantically over the grass and managed to hobble back to the shade of the elm.

She touched her flesh to make sure it was real. Tears came in little trickles and she saw, for the first time it seemed, the ravage time had caused. The seed was in fruit.

'George.' She held out her hands to him.

Like two mourners after the burial, they returned to their deckchairs.

'He is a murderer, Hans Leinon. He did this. He hasn't changed.'

The Stationkeeper, as usual, seemed not to know.

'I can't sit down,' Lotta was saying to him. 'I must stand and tell him. He must be accused for this, he should be *executed*. Poor Captain Cartwright! Who will avenge him? They must be taking him away to an asylum.'

The Colonel was coming back along the road, and Lotta wished she had a shotgun. He could see from the way she stood that her blood was up.

'It was his wife and the clinic doctor,' he called from a safe distance. 'He is being taken to a private clinic. I didn't tell you directly. I didn't want to upset you.'

Lotta touched her wrist, the Captain's nails had left marks on her and the scabs hadn't yet set. She rubbed them so that her flesh could feel and bleed.

'I couldn't fight for him!'

The Stationkeeper picked up a rake he had discarded among the juiceless peonies.

Lotta showed her wrists.

The Colonel looked at the claw marks and then into her eyes.

And she stopped feeling for the Captain, for somehow she also, along with all breathing beings, was called into judgement on the Colonel, and she couldn't sustain the words that would rip and shred. And he stood too patiently in front of her, while Kaufman, faithful guard or executioner, stood by her side.

'I'm tired,' she muttered to the Colonel, to the sky and the circling birds. 'Where would it lead anyway? Love always comes to a dead end.'

5

He wanted the exquisite monotony of Bach – the necessary movement, the necessary resolution – but the only piano was in his house, and Lotta would come and sit, clap her hands or show him how to make a trill more effectively.

The twilight passed into dusk of the deeper sort, moths blundered from the trees and a bat circled and fled against the tide of life it usually devoured; the present immensity of those waves was too much for its belly.

The Colonel, however, knew no such hesitancy, and slapped his way through. He had remembered the small electric organ in the chapel. He opened the door and walked quickly down the aisle through the smells of incense and candles and the heavy, dead, present musk of the altar hangings.

In front of the cross was the Stationkeeper, gazing up at it, a rag and a tin of Brasso in his hands. His cat frisked and growled around the sanctuary steps, now and then leaping onto the communion rail and contemplating a further stage – the white cloth on the altar.

There was a further heaviness in the air which the Colonel recognized as the smell of cloves. In fact, carnations. The Padre had had some flowers sent from Dunedin, for tomorrow's service at six.

Tomorrow the final exercise for the trainee soldiers began.

Colonel Leinon turned on the organ, and while the machine whined and gurgled and the bellows sucked in air, he selected a Bach fugue.

The Stationkeeper finished the cross, picked up the cat and the Brasso. Because of the dark and the music, the shape of his thoughts could blossom.

The Colonel, on the other hand, wanted to talk to Kaufman, who directed all manifestations of life that passed through their land except for the cars which scuttled by on the tarseal. But he was caught up with the cat who would not wait, and now had jumped down and ran among the pews by the door, crying and yowling encouragement to its master.

Colonel Leinon turned the page and played on.

Yet it was here, in this stuffy chapel, guarded by the imitation Byzantine Mary, with the blood of the lamb carefully locked away in the tabernacle, that a free dialogue with the Stationkeeper could begin. Neither could act on any grand scale without perhaps a fatal blemish, but nothing grand was required.

'Do you have faith, Kaufman?'

The Colonel played a loud amen.

The Stationkeeper twisted a carnation head, adjusted a spray of fern he had found in a neglected garden, growing under a dripping tap.

'Will you answer me?' The Colonel stood up, but was kept from walking to the sanctuary and hitting out at the man.

Back home, Lotta was standing in the porch and calling to him. 'Hans,' she was saying, 'Hans, dear, the dinner is ready. There were only the peas to cook! It is time you put on a little flesh. Too much thinking makes you thin.'

The Colonel left the chapel and walked to her. He picked one of the last roses that had managed to bloom. 'For you,' he said, and threw it to her.

She reminded him of a little child waiting for the ball to be thrown exactly into her outstretched arms.

He laughed with her gently as they searched for another rose.

As usual the blinds in his office were drawn.

He had already gone over the last-minute orders with Mungo, who acted as his adjutant.

Outside, the soldiers were boarding the trucks.

'It's a long trek,' said the Padre, with enthusiasm. 'Two days over the mountains, then down to the promised land.'

The Padre did not mention the Colonel's latest arbitrary decision not to hold a passing-out parade.

The Colonel looked down at his desk.

'"Escape Prisoner of War" is an excellent name for the exercise, since the trainees will live off the land.'

It seemed the Padre was determined to hold his own service of commemoration. '. . . and in three days time we will all have dispersed.'

'Twenty minutes the convoy will leave,' said Mungo.

The Padre clasped his hands in prayer or irritation, then gave the world a bright Christian smile and adjusted his pack which was rubbing against his new shorts.

Outside, commands and counter-commands littered the parade ground as the trucks arrived.

Lotta heard the trucks leave.

She had invited Kaufman, who was also helping with the ideas Lotta had on packing.

Not that she had packed, because the Colonel had said nothing. It was as if he could see no further than this, his last command. But she kept the incinerator continually burning with old newspapers and a few old dresses.

'My memories,' she said, pointing to the wisp of smoke and smelling the strange stink of burning material. 'My past.'

With a sudden shrinking of the world, all points outside became equally close to each other and to her. The coming move, all events in her life, could have happened yesterday, or, she thought with a laugh, today. Even the swimming pool was now only a stone's throw away. She could see the diving board quite clearly and wondered why she had bothered with binoculars.

'I do believe my sight is improving,' she informed the Station-keeper, a trifle complacently.

The Colonel followed the trucks out of the camp. The drive to the drop-off point, at the foot of a range of low mountains, would take two hours.

He slept.

As they climbed the foothills, the cooler and lighter air woke him and he glanced out to the slopes where the rock outcrops protruding like the humps of prehistoric beasts caught in the sudden prison of the earth which had changed its mood.

Around them the long-woolled sheep grazed and pieces of wool fluttered over the fence posts. Yellow lichen coated the south side where the rains swung in from the sea.

Clouds were banking fast.

The lorries ahead belched out clouds of exhaust as the engines strained over the last climb.

'Hope they don't catch the storm,' said the driver.

The Colonel looked ahead. Some of the trucks had already arrived. He observed more acutely the clumps of snowgrass, the thick mat of spider web still sparkling with dew.

'We're here, sir.'

Colonel Leinon looked out again.

'They're being searched, sir. Random.' Lieutenant Picton saluted and stood easy.

'Sultanas in plastic bags up your arse, practically,' cackled the corporal. 'Have you no taste, Green? And cigarettes, too. Disgusting. Smoking your own excreta, practically.

'And you, bloody sweets tucked around your balls! Think you're going to sweeten yourself up. Bloody perverts. Sweets! Chocolates!'

'Right men, you can dress.' ordered Mungo.

'Considerable ingenuity shown, sir.' The corporal pointed to a soldier. 'Almost tempted, sir, to order an evacuation.'

The sky had discovered its edge and was decorated with a livid battle yellow.

Colonel Leinon waited until the last group was working its way towards the first test of their skills – a long scree, almost vertical for two hundred yards. He walked after them, to follow their progress for as long as he could, and stopped by a small corrie as his boots sank into the boggy green grass. He changed direction and was among thick patches of gorse, and suddenly on a rock promontory from where he could survey Burnham Camp far in the distance.

Then the rain fell, swinging onto his head like an axe, and what he hoped to see below him disappeared under a veil.

'They're going to be in for it,' observed the driver. The air replied with thunder and the collapse of the sky into bursts of violet lightning.

'We'll have to hurry. This'll start a flash flood. We'd better keep our eyes open.'

Lotta, who was easily infected by the Colonel's unease, had watched the storm sweeping across the ranges the trainees must get through. Then she had forgotten about it.

The next afternoon, as Charlotte drank tea with her, Mungo came running across the field to them.

Both women stood up.

'One of the trainees is dead. Fell over a bloody bluff. They've only just managed to contact us. They rang from a farmhouse.'

'Swept away?' Lotta shrieked, premonition confirmed. She grabbed a frond of the elm for balance.

'The boy's squad are on the way back with him. We've rung the family already. They want the squad to be the pallbearers. Some to carry the coffin, others for the firing party.'

Lotta rushed along with Mungo to headquarters.

Colonel Leinon was seated at his desk, his face drawn.

'Terrible,' Mungo lit a cigarette as the Colonel studied the photograph, 'I can't even remember him.'

'Poor boy,' sniffed Lotta. 'His poor mother.'

Mungo read further in the trainee's file. 'The mother is dead. He was five foot nine and a half, had suffered from no venereal disease, but as a child had chicken pox, mumps, measles, etc. Was aged twenty-one, and would have gone into the Signal Corps Reserve based in Dunedin. Was below par in gymnastics but a good shot.'

'What will they put on his tombstone?' asked Lotta, remembering that her small son had nothing.

'"He died for his country." That is what his father wants,' announced the Colonel.

Lotta was about to compose her face into solemn agreement when Charlotte laughed. It wasn't a happy laugh. It sounded like Lotta herself on one of her bad days.

'What do we care?' Charlotte appealed to them, as if their meeting place was Olympus.

'Yes, yes. We should have known,' Lotta agreed and giggled.

The Colonel held off for a moment, but the torrent of his mirth when it broke through soared higher than all the others. They were swept away in it while he bent over, gasping for air.

The arc lights were switched on over the parade ground, though most of the trainees had already left on the trucks for the station.

'I've bought the food.' Lotta posed for a moment as the queen of the feast.

Charlotte pulled back the curtains to see the parade ground the better. The night was a wall around it. In transit, she thought.

'Are the soldiers practising yet?' Lotta buttered some stale bread.

'No, but the corporal has come out.'

Lotta handed over a leg of chicken. 'Come, Mungo, my dear, you must eat. We all need our strength.'

'It's lonely now,' said Charlotte.

'Yes, yes.' Lotta handed a cup of coffee to Charlotte and

switched on her portable radio, and found some dance music. She had changed for tonight into a long skirt and fluffy blouse.

Mungo put his arm around Charlotte's waist. 'We're going to get married. We rang my parents and Charlotte's mother last night.'

Lotta looked skilfully surprised, and for a second stopped chewing. 'Congratulations, darlings. Of course I guessed.' She drank down some wine. 'Darlings!' She stood up and rushed for Mungo, diverting on charge to place a quick kiss on Charlotte's cheek.

'Hans!' She ran through to his office. 'They are getting married. Now come. Leave this place for good. All your papers have been sent to Headquarters. How exciting! Now, Hans, stop brooding!. Come and eat. You must eat!'

Colonel Leinon stood for the last time at his window. 'Let us toast their happiness,' he muttered to himself, and then, with a renewal of grace, strode through and brought the party to life.

Lotta opened the door. 'I feel like dancing!' She swooped down the steps and put down her champagne glass.

'Turn up the radio,' she said as she reached the parade ground. And realized she was too old to dance alone.

'Come, Mungo! Hans! Somebody. Mungo?'

Mungo walked down the steps to her. He was young and she reached for him as for one of her precious memories.

'Let us waltz.' She swept through under the arc lamps, simpering.

She picked up the edge of her dress and circled full into the amphitheatre that the parade ground had become. In the darkness there were, no doubt, thousands of spectators, ready to applaud her interpretation.

'Turn up the radio,' she cried back.

She began to hum to 'The Beautiful Blue Danube'.

Mungo held her tightly as, under the empty open doors of the huts where the trainees had lived, they swooped and dived and circled.

Lotta held her head back proudly.

As space drained off her memories, they were slowly becoming lighter and more distant from the headquarters and their friends. Then the door of a hut opened and from it emerged the funeral party.

They were holding a sawhorse upside down on their shoulders and the legs stuck out like those of a dead animal.

Both parties stared at each other in amazement, and Lotta was the first to recover. She took Mungo's arm as if they were just now leaving the floor of the ballroom, and glided up to the headquarters and to her friends.

'Let's go inside,' said Charlotte.

'Now,' the little corporal screamed, 'it's important to keep the bloody coffin on a level. The bloody sawhorse is the bloody coffin. Remember that, eh? Can't go around dipping it. You've gotta keep it on the same level. Now, put it down.'

They stopped under one arc light.

'Right. Bend together. Not like that, you, you're not having sexual intercourse with one of yer mates. Knees bent like so. Pick it up. There'll be steps down from the church, there bloody well always are. Now, carry it back into the hut. Up the steps.'

They disappeared with strangely mechanical strides.

The corporal sat for a moment on one of the beds and lit the stub of a cigarette.

'Now listen. The rest of the bloody trainees are going out with you tonight. Only difference is, you'll be riding with the coffin. You've got to load it right. The Colonel will be there, and the fucker's *inside*. You've got to load it right. Flag over it, and you've got to do the church part right. And the rest of you, the grave part, the firing party part. Ya getting extra pay but you'll have to keep your uniforms on a couple of days more. Get me?'

They nodded.

'Now, it's important to honour the dead. I mean, there's a special way of doing it. His father wants it. So God Fuck the Queen. Get me?'

They nodded.

'Come on, on your feet.' He ground the cigarette out on the

floor. 'It's a challenge, see. You've got to get arms drill perfect, the rest of ya,' he turned to the other small squad, 'you'll have to get your arms drill perfect. *Perfect*.

'Now, you lot on the coffin. The Padre has finished saying what a fine lad he was, even if he's never set eyes on him before. Not even for a quick feel in the confessional. So he's finished.

'He says he died for Queen and Country. You lot take your position either side of the coffin. All his family will be there, his bloody mother weeping buckets, poor old chook.

'Now get this into your heads. A body is a dead weight. Brace yourselves. Come on, straighten your shoulders a bit. You're soldiers.'

They moved down.

'Keep it slow, you're not galloping off to the pub yet.'

Perfectly in time, they reached the third step.

'Good!' the corporal slapped his leg in imitation of his commanding officer.

The procession continued across the parade ground to the white line the corporal had designated as either the hearse or the open grave.

'Now, look straight ahead. There's no time for looking to the side.'

Colonel Leinon felt for the master switch as they reached the top steps. The lights faded off, and after a moment's incomprehension, the moon was there again, and in the shelter of the rubble, the Stationkeeper, sitting with the cat on his knees.

'That'll do,' called out Colonel Hans von Leinon from the verandah headquarters.

Mungo and Charlotte had been given permission to leave at once, and Lotta had promised them whatever they wanted out of her house, for their first home.

The Colonel busied himself with pouring out champagne to toast the young couple, and their friendship, and the camp.

Charlotte wore her emerald engagement ring since all was now formal, and tomorrow it would be in the papers, with the date for the wedding, a month later.

The men shook hands.

Charlotte gave the Colonel her cheek to be kissed.

Mungo stared at the darkness, fumbling with words to say. The Colonel read them on his face, and was not unhappy when the other found he could not find the right expression to make their adieux.

They drove away, their lights full on as the street lamps had now been turned out. But next week they would be back to pick up this and that. And of course, Lotta and Hans would stay with Natalia while finalizing plans for Vienna.

The express arrived on time.

Its light swept down the station platform with a white rush over the coffin, the flag over it, the eight trainee soldiers, and the firing party somewhat apart.

The Stationkeeper, high up in the signal box, looked down as the soldiers lifted the coffin. Behind them stood the Colonel and Lotta.

Lotta had insisted. 'It is only right, Hans, that since there is no mother I should be here to mourn. It is the done thing.'

She was a trifle tipsy, wore a black coat and hat with a whisp of black veil.

The smoke from the engine curled along the station and around her white legs as the bugler stepped forward.

Colonel Leinon stiffened into a salute as the coffin slid into the goods wagon. It lay among the clutter of three chained-up dogs and some crates of hens.

The bugler finished.

With a womanly gesture, Lotta moved forward and placed on the flag a small spray of flowers she and George had found after a diligent search. She moved back beside the Colonel as the guard pushed the door shut. The last trainees filed quietly onto the train that was taking them home.

Hans didn't notice the curious but respectful faces of the travellers. Lotta, of course, did. Tonight was her apotheosis. How
often had she stood beneath the sign marking the camp. How
rarely had somebody seen her well enough and in time, to wave
back?

Now she was tempted to raise her hand, and knew they would
all, every face she could see, acknowledge her. But protocol
forbade it.

Ahead of the train, the twin embankments. Beyond and on,
the rails stretched to the horizon. But always the headlamp
could thrust aside the dark and give enough light, at least for
the driver.

The Stationkeeper switched the signals to green. Slowly the
engine held its steam. The wheels moved over, the carriages,
coupled one to the next, began to roll forwards into the plain.

Lotta stood very straight. She was, after all, beside her Colonel,
and there was nowhere else to be. She allowed herself a small
glance backward as she left the station and walked away with
Hans down the dust road. For a moment, passing the ditch, she
realized something had changed. A noise?

'It's the water,' he said. 'It's been turned off.'

'I see.'

She shivered and glanced around her with bright interest, as
if it were the first time she had noticed the camp approaches.
And she realized that he still had said nothing about tomorrow
or the day after.

Control yourself, she thought. Think of something. What will
we do with the furniture she wondered in a panic. Of course I'll
take my portrait, the silver and things like that. But the piano,
the chairs, the refrigerator? Shall we leave them here to rot if
Charlotte doesn't want them?

The house was dark as they walked up the front path, and
they hadn't really eaten dinner.

Lotta stumbled through the passage, avoiding, in panic, the
mirrors.

It was twelve-thirty: after midnight.

She applied rouge to her face and glanced at the portrait of

Hans she kept on her dresser. He was now, technically, out of the Army — by half an hour on his pension.

'Plans must be made,' she said while the cat purred and washed. 'I must freight you to Vienna, pussy cat. Won't that be exciting?'

On the bed was the black lace dress she planned to wear, but she changed her mind and chose instead one long blue silk creation. She took some jewellery from the back of the drawer. 'I will wear the diamond brooch and earrings he gave me, he won't forget them. They belonged to his mother.'

She dabbed some perfume behind her ears.

She was thirsty. In the fridge was some fruit juice and she went for it, poured, drank, knocked over a bowl of podded peas. What did it matter?

And she heard him coming down the hall.

She lifted up her skirt to get first to the drawing room. Without knowing how, she found herself standing in front of the piano. She sat down and tried to play.

He watched.

She knew it was tonight. Everything would be decided. She closed the piano.

'Hans?'

He poured himself a whisky and put in ice.

There could be no pretence.

'Hans.' She stood close to him, but far enough away so that he could reply in truth. Truth was suddenly important.

She smoothed at her skirt. 'The Camp has closed. We haven't begun to pack all our things . . . I must know how you intend to dispose of me.'

Colonel Leinon could see the Stationkeeper out on the lawn. He had watched on many evenings the shadowplay of his other personas. They were all one finally, at some perhaps not-too-distant point.

'We are beginning a new part of our lives,' she was saying. 'We are both young enough to start off again somewhere. In Vienna? I have . . . I have bought tickets for Vienna. I saved from the housekeeping money — for five years. No, seven. We could go into antiques, or flowers.'

She groped in the air, searching for a shape to present to him, so he would understand. Finally there were no shapes.

'You want us to be together – for always?'

'Yes. It is not too much.'

She raised her hands in despair. It seemed they would stretch out in supplication to the sky, blocked by the pineapple-and-pear plaster ceiling.

'Hans, Hans!' She was falling onto her knees and sobbing. He went quickly to the windows and pulled down the blinds.

'Please, darling Hans. Love me a little. Even if you can't love me very much. Let us be man and wife.'

She felt herself being raised, and his hand smoothing down her hair and his handkerchief wiping away her tears.

'Yes, of course, Lotta. We'll get married. When we leave here.'

'Oh, Hans.'

'We will return to Vienna — whenever you like.'

He smiled at her. 'Of course I love you, Lotta. We have done so much together. I will look after you — if it is allowed. Don't be frightened.'

'Now.' She clapped her hands together. 'I will have to pick up the peas. How foolish of me to forget.'

She tripped out of the room, body erect. A mission to accomplish. The packing to start properly. What should be thrown out?

Colonel Leinon felt a clearing of perspective.

Lotta sang in the kitchen. She clattered a few pans to show that the battle had been fought and won. She crowed and sang, breaking open the quiet. The magpies were awakened and cawed and cackled in benign agreement with her pleasure.

Hans opened the front door and observed the lay of the land.

'I'm going to walk a little,' he called out.

'I'll come,' she said.

They strolled together.

The elm still put out some suckers of a delicate green which he could touch, or even more absurd, kiss.

They went back inside and he sat in one of the easy chairs. Lotta played the piano. It was a Chopin nocturne. Her fingers had regained their old competence.

There was so little she was attached to, Lotta realized. The windows were wide open to the night, but she did not mind how many moths came in and took up residence: and she had on all her important rings. She blew thoughtfully on a large sapphire as she remembered the Stationkeeper and saw him again at the window.

'I would like to have a swim. We could have a swim, together.'

She smiled to her Colonel and left the room. As she expected, the Stationkeeper was on the other side of the front door. She checked herself in the mirror and composed a gracious smile for him.

'Dear Kaufman,' she whispered from the porch, 'I cannot talk now. We are going for a swim. While the Colonel changes we can . . . say our farewells?'

She returned to the house, humming to herself, and went to put on her bathing suit. She hoped the Colonel had the key for the front gate; it was so annoying to arrive and not be able to get in.

'Have you the key, Hans?' she called down the hall.

He was already carrying his towel and bathing suit.

She led the way across the plain. Tomorrow she would take a lot of snaps so that people at home could see the Colonel's last command.

And there was dear Kaufman following her.

She sighed as they came up to the gate which was swinging wide open. Silly of her, really, to think it would be shut when there was no one to shut it against.

Hans Leinon took off his clothes, and knew, as he hit the water, the privilege of this place. He saw the high diving board glowing white under the moon. He thought to climb it, but he knew this was for younger men, or for himself at a moment later than this.

Lotta was at the gate in her floral and frilled bathing gown.

'Dear Kaufman, you must be quick.' She patted the keeper on the cheek. 'I will miss you very much.' She made bird noises at the Captain's budgie which George must have just collected.

The Colonel turned and saw them. He swam to the edge and pulled himself out.

Lotta walked towards him, the Stationkeeper following her.

'I am telling Mr Kaufman, Hans dear, that we will be gone
tomorrow. I know,' she told the Stationkeeper, 'that you'll be
happy in whatever job you get later.' She took his withered hand
and kicked, by mistake, the cage. 'And remember you have played
an essential part in the Colonel's last intake of trainees – doing
the garden, polishing the brass.'

They were all, for a moment, in shadow.

'And I have managed to help you a little.'

The Colonel was fidgeting.

Lotta leaned towards Kaufman. 'Had the world been different,'
she whispered, 'we might have been happy.'

The moon came out from behind its cloud and Lotta saw with
amazement that Kaufman carried the Colonel's old Luger.

It should have been rusting in Charlotte's garden.

The Stationkeeper was clear eyed.

And then Lotta realized what he intended to do.

'Oh? Christ forgive me!' she screamed. She leapt at him as the
gun spoke. The bullet ploughed through the embroidered corn-
flower on her robe.

The Stationkeeper howled as Colonel Leinon ran to her.

Lotta's face, fat and wrinkling and red, burst with light when
she saw Hans von Leinon.

'I saved you, Hans?' She was incredulous at her good fortune.

Colonel Leinon held her to him. Blood dribbed from her lips
but she found the strength to reach up, and with her fingers to
trace the contours of his face. Then she gasped and shook.

He took the towel from around his waist and laid it over her.

He looked around him at the water and the sky.

He felt the concrete under his feet, and with her gone, he too
was ready.

He noticed, as he had not before, that the Stationkeeper was
carrying the Captain's budgie. It was upset, and batted its eyes
suspiciously.

Hans Leinon knew what the other was about to do, and he
hoped Kaufman wouldn't be tempted to explain his act. This
was granted. The Stationkeeper stepped forward and pulled the
trigger.

The Colonel put his hand down to his chest and drew it up again to his eyes. It was bright arterial red. He caught sight of the blue wings as the budgie began another determined fluttering in the cage.

The Stationkeeper might hang, and when, like a small child, he came to stare at the other's face, the Colonel gently took the revolver from him, wiped it as best as he could, and held it himself so that they would find his fingerprints.

He, after all, was leaving for good, and would never be this way again.

He fell backwards into the water. The impetus floated him towards the centre like a calm boat, and the blood, welling out of him in a more gentle flow, stained the water and drifted to the edge of the ripples.

The stars were still shining, and although his eyes would soon only reflect back their light, he knew his way.

The Stationkeeper had left?

Of course! The signal had to be changed!

A glimmer of moonlight gave clarity to the diving board while the mountains became only shadows, floating with the wind currents that blew down to Burnham Camp.

The heat was still here, as was life, stored in the grains of dust and the cellophane fibres of the grasses that had grown too tall with the late winter rains, and now paid the penalty for too much life by being nothing again. They rustled to themselves and bent slowly towards the earth and back to the sky.

Where were the stars? He could no longer see them although he felt them closer than before . . .

And realized that he had taken on himself the burden of his existence; and fought to understand; and that he had lived and was living; widening; his heart flooding with this moment.

And as he knew himself he was beyond the pool which was already still, all ripples from his passage absorbed.

MORE ABOUT PENGUINS AND PELICANS

For further information about books available from Penguin please write to Dept EP, Penguin Books Ltd, Harmondsworth, Middlesex UB7 ODA.

In Australia: For a complete list of books available from Penguin in Australia write to the Marketing Department, Penguin Books Australia Ltd, P.O. Box 257, Ringwood, Victoria 3134.

In New Zealand: For a complete list of books available from Penguin in New Zealand write to the Marketing Department, Penguin Books (N.Z.) Ltd, Private Bag, Takapuna, Auckland 9.

In the U.S.A.: For a complete list of books available from Penguin in the United States write to Dept DG, Penguin Books, 299 Murray Hill Parkway, East Rutherford, New Jersey 07073.

In Canada: For a complete list of books available from Penguin in Canada write to Penguin Books Canada Ltd, 2801 John Street, Markham, Ontario L3R 1B4.

LANDSCAPE WITH LANDSCAPE

Gerald Murnane

A man resolves to tell the truth about himself to an audience of women, but the more he struggles the more he becomes trapped behind the layers of his own dreams.

Another man searches in the hills around Melbourne for twenty years for a landscape and a woman that no artist can paint.

These stories and four others make up *Landscape with Landscape*. Read together they make up an elaborate and unforgettable pattern of dreams and reality.

'*Landscape with Landscape* is a work of extraordinary power and vision, one which will surely be an outstanding novel of the decade.'

Helen Daniel, *Age*

STORIES FROM THE WARM ZONE
AND SYDNEY STORIES

Jessica Anderson

Jessica Anderson's evocative stories recreate, through the eyes of a child, the atmosphere of Australia between the wars. A stammer becomes a blessing in disguise; the prospect of a middle name converts a reluctant child to baptism. These autobiographical stories of a Brisbane childhood glow with the warmth of memory.

The formless sprawl of Sydney in the 1980s is a very different world. Here the lives of other characters are changed by the uncertainties of divorce, chance meetings and the disintegration and generation of relationships.

'Jessica Anderson has a penetrating exact eye . . . and a fine sense of verbal nuance.' *Weekend Australian*
'The pleasure is not in what happens but in how it happens — how we reveal ourselves in every word, every gesture and every opinion.' *Belles Lettres*

FLY AWAY PETER

David Malouf

For three very different people brought together by their
love of birds, life on the Queensland coast in 1914 is the
timeless and idyllic world of sandpipers, ibises and
kingfishers.

In another hemisphere civilization rushes headlong into
brutal conflict.

Inevitably the two young men are drawn into the mud and
horror of the trenches of Armentieres, and their friend
Imogen, alone on the beach, must acknowledge that the
past cannot be held.